REMEMBRANCE OF THINGS PAST

"When to the sessions of sweet silent thought
I summon up remembrance of things past . . ."

VOLUME XII
TIME REGAINED

"Oui, si le souvenir grâce à l'oubli, n'a pu
contracter aucun lien, jeter aucun chaînon
entre lui et la minute présente, s'il est resté
à sa place, à sa date, s'il a gardé ses distances,
son isolement dans le creux d'une vallée, où à
la pointe d'un sommet, il nous fait tout à
coup respirer un air nouveau, précisément
parce que c'est un air qu'on a respiré autre-
fois, cet air plus pur que les poètes ont
vainement essayé de faire régner dans le
Paradis et qui ne pourrait donner cette
sensation profonde de renouvellement que s'il
avait été respiré déjà, car les vrais paradis
sont les paradis qu'on a perdus."

Marcel Proust's continuous novel *À la Recherche du Temps Perdu* (REMEMBRANCE OF THINGS PAST) was originally published in eight parts, the titles and dates of which were: I. *Du Côté de Chez Swann* (1913); II. *À l'Ombre des Jeunes Filles en Fleurs* (1918), awarded the Prix Goncourt in 1919; III. *Le Côté de Guermantes* I (1920); IV. *Le Côté de Guermantes* II, *Sodome et Gomorrhe* I (1921); V. *Sodome et Gomorrhe* II (1922); VI. *La Prisonnière* (1923); VII. *Albertine Disparue* (1925); VIII. *Le Temps Retrouvé* (1927).

Du Côté de Chez Swann has been published in English as SWANN'S WAY: *À l'Ombre des Jeunes Filles en Fleurs* as WITHIN A BUDDING GROVE: *Le Côté de Guermantes* as THE GUERMANTES WAY: *Sodome et Gomorrhe* as CITIES OF THE PLAIN: *La Prisonnière* as THE CAPTIVE: *Albertine Disparue* as THE SWEET CHEAT GONE: and *Le Temps Retrouvé* as TIME REGAINED. The first seven parts were translated by C. K. Scott Moncrieff; the eighth was first translated by Stephen Hudson but is now re-issued in a new translation by Andreas Mayor.

In the present uniform edition the volumes are as follows:—

VOL.
1. SWANN'S WAY.   PART I
2. SWANN'S WAY.   PART II
3. WITHIN A BUDDING GROVE.   PART I
4. WITHIN A BUDDING GROVE.   PART II
5. THE GUERMANTES WAY.   PART I
6. THE GUERMANTES WAY.   PART II
7. CITIES OF THE PLAIN.   PART I
8. CITIES OF THE PLAIN.   PART II
9. THE CAPTIVE.   PART I
10. THE CAPTIVE.   PART II
11. THE SWEET CHEAT GONE
12. TIME REGAINED

BERMA

MARCEL PROUST

TIME REGAINED

Translated by
Andreas Mayor

1970
CHATTO & WINDUS
LONDON

Published by
Chatto & Windus Ltd
40 William IV Street
London WC2

*

Clarke, Irwin & Co. Ltd
Toronto

ISBN 0 7011 1680 3

First published in English (cr. 8vo) 1931
First issued in the Uniform Edition
(12 vols.) 1941; re-set and reprinted 1944
Reprinted 1949 and 1951
Illustrated Edition 1957
This translation first published (large cr. 8vo) 1970
First issued in the Uniform Edition 1970

This translation © Chatto & Windus Ltd 1970

Printed in Great Britain by
Butler & Tanner Ltd, Frome and London

TIME REGAINED
A Vision and a Vocation

Les vrais paradis sont les paradis qu'on a perdus.

Ce que l'être par trois fois et quatre fois ressuscité en moi venait de goûter, c'était peut-être bien des fragments d'existence sous-traits au temps, mais cette contemplation, quoique d'éternité, était fugitive. Et pourtant je sentais que le plaisir qu'elle m'avait, à de rares intervalles, donné dans ma vie, était le seul qui fût fécond et véritable.

L'art est ce qu'il y a de plus réel, la plus austère école de la vie, et le vrai Jugement dernier.

Ce livre essentiel, le seul livre vrai, un grand écrivain n'a pas, dans le sens courant, à l'inventer, puisqu'il existe déjà en chacun de nous.

Je compris que tous ces matériaux de l'œuvre littéraire c'était ma vie passée... toute ma vie jusqu'à ce jour aurait pu être résumée sous ce titre: Une vocation.

Du moins ne manquerais-je pas de décrire les hommes comme occupant une place dans le Temps.

Le Temps Retrouvé is the last part of a long novel, not a treatise on the nature of art. Nevertheless, before Proust wrote even one line of *A la Recherche* he had certain very definite views on the significance of literature in general and of the novel which he himself proposed to write. These views he states more explicitly in *Le Temps Retrouvé* than anywhere else, above all in the long passage in which the narrator, as he waits to be shown into the Princesse de Guermantes's party, struggles to arrive at a deeper understanding of the phenomenon of involuntary memory and the happiness which it brings. The passages quoted above (torn from their contexts and shorn of qualifications) may help the reader to follow him in his labyrinthine search. They will be found on pp. 228, 234, 241, 255, 267 and 473 of the present translation.

TRANSLATOR'S NOTE

When Proust died in November, 1922, three of the seven sections of *A la Recherche* were still unpublished. *La Prisonnière* (published in 1923) had been typed and revised but was not yet in proof. *Albertine Disparue* (published in 1925), on which he was working at the time of his death, and *Le Temps Retrouvé* (published in 1927) were still in manuscript, in those patched and corrected notebooks which Françoise calls the narrator's *paperoles*. Of the whole novel *Le Temps Retrouvé* is, in the words of the 1954 Pléiade editors, the section "qui se présenté dans l'état le plus inachevé". A first version was probably already in existence in 1912. Additions and revisions made at various times during the following ten years—particularly at the end of and after the war—had transformed the text without altering the general design. How much more Proust would have written if he had lived it is difficult to say, if only because for a writer with his extraordinary fertility of invention revision was always essentially amplification. He cut and he tidied and he re-arranged but above all he added. So that if *Le Temps Retrouvé* seems to us substantially complete as it stands, we can be sure that before handing it over to the printers Proust would have made here and there some extensive interpolations. He would also have removed the countless minor blemishes caused by haste or carelessness in the original composition or the successive revisions, and he would have reconciled contradictions, smoothed away awkwardnesses of transition and in a few cases almost certainly altered the order of paragraphs or longer passages.

A superficial revision of this kind was attempted—quite

legitimately, as the Pléiade editors point out (i, xxx)—by the
Nouvelle Revue Française editors of 1927. From Proust's
notebooks, with the help of a posthumous typescript made
when these were more legible than they are now, they produced a more or less coherent text, in which, however, mis-
readings and ill-advised emendations unfortunately abound.
A few examples will indicate its unreliability:

> *cérébrale* for *centrale* (Pléiade, iii, 890)
> *point royaliste* for *port-royaliste* (iii, 894)
> *péripétie* for *prophétie* (iii, 908)
> *un peu de vie* for *un peu dévié* (iii, 956).

These are errors caused by the difficulty of deciphering
Proust's manuscript; others, such as the omission of *le roi
des Belges* from a list of "Germans who had embraced the
French cause" (iii, 913), are apparently deliberate. Moreover, there are numerous sentences of which the meaning
has been altered or even destroyed by faulty punctuation or
by minor emendations producing sense of a kind but not the
perhaps more elusive sense which Proust wished to convey.
This 1927 text was all that was available to Proust's friend
Sydney Schiff, when he added *Time Regained* to the great
translation of *A la Recherche* which Scott Moncrieff died
too soon to complete. Schiff—who as novelist and translator
used the name Stephen Hudson—was aware of the defects
of the French text but his only means of improving it was
conjectural emendation.

An opportunity for a new translation which would bring
the English reader of *Le Temps Retrouvé* nearer to the
original text arose with the publication of Librairie Galli-
mard's Pléiade edition of *A la Recherche* in 1954. The
Pléiade editors, M. Pierre Clarac and M. André Ferré, were
charged by Proust's heirs with the task of "establishing a text

of his novel which should be as faithful as possible to his intentions". This meant examining with the utmost care all the available relevant material: notebooks, typescripts and proof-sheets, revised and unrevised, as well as the original edition, and the result was a revised edition of almost flawless scholarship, which as it proceeds towards the end of the long novel departs more and more often from what had hitherto been the only known text. In *Le Temps Retrouvé* there is scarcely a single page without at least one discrepancy between the two texts, and although many of these are no more than differences of punctuation many others have a substantial effect upon the meaning. Moreover the Pléiade editors restore to the text two passages of considerable length (iii, 743–46, 779–81, both concerned with homosexuality) and a great many of a few lines or less which for one reason or another the original editors thought fit to omit. At the foot of the page they print thirty-six passages (some of twenty lines or more) which are afterthoughts not worked into the main sequence of the text—most of these are also in the original edition, but often in a modified form and in a different position—and in their elaborate critical notes they print all the significant variants found in the notebooks and a number of unfinished sentences which Proust would probably have used as the germ of lengthy developments.

This revised French text urgently called for a revised English translation. A reworking of Stephen Hudson's *Time Regained* was considered, but it was apparent that alterations of one kind or another would have to be made in almost every sentence and that it would be simpler as well as more satisfactory to prepare an entirely new translation. In translating I have allowed myself rather more freedom in departing from the authority of Proust's manuscript than the Pléiade editors. French readers want to know exactly what

Proust wrote; they can guess for themselves what he might have written had he had time to revise. But English readers do not want a critical edition of a French text left in an unfinished state by its author, they want to read it with enjoyment and to understand it (since it is sometimes difficult) without too much difficulty. To help them to do this I have taken certain liberties: I have at many points altered the order of sentences or paragraphs and the division into paragraphs, I have sometimes eased the transition from one passage to another, and I have occasionally dared to add a few explanatory words—in fact I have done something of what the 1927 editors tried to do. I have, however, had the advantage of an accurate transcription of the notebooks, I have scrupulously respected Proust's words whenever I have thought that they could represent his considered intention and I have included in my translation almost all that the 1927 editors omitted, including much of the material relegated to the critical notes by the Pléiade editors and leaving out only what is obviously repetitive or else too unformed to give any clear idea of Proust's meaning.

I have followed the 1927 editors and Stephen Hudson in dividing the volume into three chapters of unequal length. The frailty of the ordinary reader requires that some such division should be made, but this was not Proust's intention, for *A la Recherche* is *une œuvre de longue haleine*. Proust would have liked his ideal reader to take a deep breath, begin at the beginning and continue reading until, after a million and a quarter words, he reached the end. He had no use for chapters and only the exigencies of publication induced him to allow the work to be broken up into comparatively short volumes. For what was to be the final volume the title *Le Temps Retrouvé* was used by him as early as 1913, but it is not clear where Proust meant *La Prisonnière* to end and this last volume to begin. The break might as conveniently come at the beginning of the Tansonville episode (Pléiade, iii, 677) or at the point chosen by the Pléiade editors (iii, 691) as at the one preferred by the 1925 editors of *Albertine Disparue* (iii, 697). This last was naturally the point at which Scott Moncrieff ended *The Sweet Cheat Gone* and is therefore the one adopted by Stephen Hudson and by the present translation.

My warmest thanks are due to Miss Sylvia Townsend Warner and Mr. George Painter for generously given advice and criticism of my work at various stages.

TRANSLATOR'S NOTE

... within the text. The ... is occasionally used ... the names of the characters. ... of their names ... the final ... or of ... point the final syllable of the manuscript is ... through pointed by the last editions ... Rashid Dawood ... this has been naturally ... the point at which many ... translation ... the [Arabic] ... Coran is printed in the ... made up ... by ... and ... the ...

My warmest thanks are due to Miss ... for reading the ... Vaughan and Mrs George Rainier for ... criticism and tuition of my work on this version.

CONTENTS

*

xiii

ILLUSTRATIONS

✳

CHAPTER I

TANSONVILLE

ALL day long, in that slightly too countrified house which seemed no more than a place for a rest between walks or during a storm, one of those houses in which all the sitting-rooms look like arbours and, on the wall-papers of the bedrooms, here the roses from the garden, there the birds from the trees outside join you and keep you company, isolated from the world—for they were old wall-papers on which every rose was so distinct that, had it been alive, you could have picked it, every bird you could have put in a cage and tamed, quite different from those grandiose bedroom decorations of today where, on a silver background, all the apple-trees of Normandy display their outlines in the Japanese style to hallucinate the hours you spend in bed—all day long I remained in my room which looked over the fine greenery of the park and the lilacs near its entrance, over the green leaves of the great trees by the edge of the lake, sparkling in the sun, and the forest of Méséglise. Yet I looked at all this with pleasure only because I said to myself: "How nice to be able to see so much greenery from my bedroom window", until the moment when, in the vast verdant picture, I recognised, painted in a contrasting dark blue simply because it was further away, the steeple of Combray church. Not a representation of the steeple, but the steeple itself, which, putting in visible form a distance of miles and of years, had come, intruding its discordant tone into the midst of the luminous verdure—a tone so colourless that it seemed little more than a preliminary sketch—and engraved itself upon my window-pane. And if I left my room for a moment, I saw at the end of the corridor, in a little sitting-room which faced in another direction, what seemed to be a band of scarlet—for this room was hung with a plain silk, but a red one, ready to burst into flames if a ray of sun fell upon it.

The love of Albertine had disappeared from my memory. But it seems that there exists too an involuntary memory of the limbs, a pale and sterile imitation of the other but longer-lived, just as there are animals or vegetables without intelligence which are longer-lived than man. Our legs and our arms are full of torpid memories. And once, when I had said goodnight to Gilberte rather early, I woke up in the middle of the night in my room at Tansonville and, still half-asleep called out: "Albertine!" It was not that I had thought of her or dreamt of her, nor that I was confusing her with Gilberte, but a memory in my arm, opening like a flower, had made me fumble behind my back for the bell, as though I had been in my bedroom in Paris. And not finding it, I had called out: "Albertine!", thinking that my dead mistress was lying by my side, as she had often done in the evening, and that we were both dropping off to sleep, and reckoning, as I woke up, that, because of the time it would take Françoise to reach my room, Albertine might without imprudence pull the bell which I could not find.

During our walks Gilberte intimated to me that Robert was turning away from her, but only in order to run after other women. And it is true that many women encumbered his life, yet always these associations, like certain masculine friendships in the lives of men who love women, had that quality of ineffectual resistance, of purposelessly filling an empty space that often in a house may be seen in objects which are not there to be used.

He came several times to Tansonville while I was there and I found him very different from the man I had known. His life had not coarsened him or slowed him down, as had happened with M. de Charlus; on the contrary, working in him an inverse change, it had given him, in a degree in which he had never had it before—and this although he had resigned his commission on his marriage—the grace and ease of a cavalry officer. Gradually, just as M. de Charlus had grown heavier, Robert (it is true that he was very much younger, but one felt that with age he would only get nearer and nearer to this ideal), had, like those women who resolutely sacrifice their faces to their figures and after a certain moment never stir from Marienbad (they realise that they cannot preserve more than one kind of youth and think that a youthful figure will serve best to represent youth in general), become slimmer and taken to moving more rapidly, a contrary effect of an identical vice. This swiftness of movement had, moreover, various psychological causes, the fear of being seen, the wish to conceal that fear, the feverishness which is generated by self-dissatisfaction and boredom. He was in the habit of visiting certain low haunts into which, as he did not wish to be seen going in or coming out, he would hurl himself in such a way as to present the smallest possible target to the un-friendly glances of possible passers-by, like a soldier going into an attack. And this manner of moving like a gust of wind had become a habit. Perhaps also it symbolised the superficial intrepidity of a man who wants to show that he is not afraid and does not want to give himself time to think. We must mention too, if our account is to be complete, a desire, the older he grew, to appear young, and also the impatience char-acteristic of those perpetually bored and perpetually cynical men that people inevitably turn into when they are too intelli-gent for the relatively idle lives they lead, in which their faculties do not have full play. No doubt idleness, in these men as in others, may express itself in inertia. But in these days especially, when physical exercise is so much in favour, there exists also, even outside the actual hours of sport, an athletic form of idleness which finds expression not in inertia but in a feverish vivacity that hopes to leave boredom neither time nor space to develop in.

Becoming—at any rate during this tiresome phase—much harder in his manner, towards his friends, towards for example myself, he now scarcely exhibited any trace of tenderness. Towards Gilberte on the other hand he behaved with an affectation of sentiment carried to the point of theatricality, which was most disagreeable. Not that he was in fact indifferent to her. No, he loved her. But he lied to her all the time and his untruthfulness, if not the actual purpose of his lies, was invariably detected; and then he thought that the only way to extricate himself was to exaggerate to a ridiculous degree the genuine distress which he felt at having hurt her. He would arrive at Tansonville, obliged, he said, to leave again the next morning because of some business with a certain neighbouring landowner who was supposed to be waiting for him in Paris; but the neighbour, when they happened to meet him near Combray the same evening, would unintentionally expose the lie, of which Robert had neglected to inform him, by saying that he had come to the country for a month's rest and would not be going back to Paris during his stay. Robert would blush, would observe Gilberte's melancholy and understanding smile, get rid of the blundering friend with a few sharp words, go home before his wife, send her a desperate note saying that he had told this lie in order not to hurt her, so that she should not think, when she saw him go off for a reason which he could not avow to her, that he did not love her (and all this, though Robert thought that he was lying when he wrote it, was in substance true), and then would ask permission to come to her room and there—part genuine distress, part the nervous

4

strain of the life he led, part a pretence which became every day more brazen—would sob, plunge his head into cold water, talk about his imminent death, sometimes throw himself on the floor as though he had been taken ill. Gilberte did not know how far she should believe him, supposed that in each particular case he was lying but that in a general way he loved her, and was worried by this presentiment of an imminent death, thinking that he perhaps had some illness she did not know of, so that for that reason she did not dare to thwart him or ask him to give up his travels. All this, however, did not help me to understand why Robert insisted on Morel's being accepted as the son of the house—as much a part of it as Bergotte—wherever he and his wife were, in Paris or at Tansonville.

Françoise, who had seen all that M. de Charlus had done for Jupien and saw now all that Robert de Saint-Loup was doing for Morel, did not conclude that this was a characteristic which reappeared from generation to generation in the Guermantes family. She, who was so moral and so full of prejudices, had come rather to believe—as Legrandin too was so kind to Théodore—that this was a custom rendered respectable by its universality. She would say of a young man, whether it were Morel or Théodore: "He has found a gentleman who takes an interest in him and has done a great deal to help him." And as in such cases it is the protectors who love and suffer and forgive, Françoise, faced with a choice between the "gentlemen" and the youths whom they seduced, did not hesitate to award her sympathy to the seducers, to decide that it was they who "really had hearts". She blamed Théodore for all the tricks he played on Legrandin—and yet it seemed scarcely possible that she could have any doubt about the nature of their relations, for she would add: "Then the boy realised that it was his turn to make a move and said:

5

'Take me with you, I will love you, I will do my best to please you', and upon my word the gentleman has such a heart that I'm sure Théodore is sure to do well with him. Perhaps much better than he deserves, for he's a proper madcap, but the gentleman is so good that I've often said to Jeannette (Théodore's fiancée): 'My girl, if ever you're in trouble, go to the gentleman. He'd give you his bed rather than let you sleep on the floor. He's been too fond of that lad (Théodore) to turn him out. You can be sure he'll never desert him.'" Out of politeness I enquired what was the surname of Théodore, who was now living somewhere in the south of France, and she told me that it was Sanilon. "Then that's who it was," I exclaimed, "who wrote to me about my article in *Le Figaro*."

In the same way Françoise had a higher esteem for Saint-Loup than for Morel and gave it as her opinion that, in spite of all the tricks the lad (Morel) had played, the Marquis would always come to his rescue if he were in trouble, for he was a man with a real heart—or if he didn't, it would only be because he himself had suffered some great disaster.

Saint-Loup insisted that I should stay on at Tansonville and once, although he never now visibly sought to give me pleasure, let slip the remark that my coming had been so great a joy to his wife that it had caused her, as she had told him, a transport of happiness which lasted a whole evening, an evening when she had been feeling so miserable that my unexpected arrival had miraculously saved her from despair, "Perhaps from something worse," he added. He asked me to try to persuade her that he loved her and told me that, though he loved another woman, he loved her less than his wife and would soon break with her. "And yet," he continued, with such self-satisfaction and such an evident need to confide that there were moments when I thought the name of Charlie

6

would, for all Robert's efforts, "come up" like a number in a
lottery, "I had something to be proud of. This woman who
has given me so many proofs of her affection and whom I am
about to sacrifice to Gilberte, had never looked at a man
before, she even thought herself incapable of falling in love.
I am the first man in her life. I knew that she had refused
offers right and left, so that when I received the marvellous
letter in which she told me that there could be no happiness
for her except with me, I just could not get over it. Obviously,
there would be something here for me to lose my head about,
were it not that the thought of seeing poor Gilberte in tears
is intolerable to me. Don't you see something of Rachel in
her?" he went on. And indeed I had been struck by a vague
resemblance which one could, if one tried, now find between
them. Perhaps it was due to a real similarity of certain features
(owing possibly to the Hebrew origin of both, though of this
there was little evidence in Gilberte) which had caused
Robert, when his family had insisted that he should marry,
to feel himself more attracted to Gilberte than to any other
girl who was equally rich. But it was due also to the fact that
Gilberte, having come across some hidden photographs of
Rachel, whose name even had been unknown to her, tried to
please Robert by imitating certain habits dear to the actress,
such as always wearing a red ribbon in her hair and a black
velvet ribbon on her arm, and by dyeing her hair in order to
look dark. Then, feeling that her unhappiness was spoiling her
looks, she tried to do something about it. Sometimes she went
a great deal too far. One day, when Robert was coming to
Tansonville for a single night, I was astounded to see her
take her place at table looking so strangely different, not
merely from what she had been in the past, but from her
present self of every day, that I sat dumbfounded as if I had
before my eyes an actress, a sort of Theodora. I felt that in

7

spite of myself I was staring at her, so curious was I to know what it was that was changed. My curiosity was soon satisfied when she blew her nose—in spite of all the precautions with which she did this. For from the many colours which were left on her handkerchief, turning it into a sumptuous palette, I saw that she was heavily made up. This it was that gave her that bleeding mouth which she tried hard to contort into laughter in the belief that it was becoming to her, while the thought that the time of her husband's train was approaching and still she did not know whether he would really come or whether he would send one of those telegrams of which M. de Guermantes had wittily fixed the formula: "Cannot come, lie follows," turned her cheeks pale beneath the violet sweat of her grease-paint and drew dark rings round her eyes.

"Ah! Don't you see?" he would say to me—in an artificially affectionate manner which contrasted painfully with his spontaneous affection of the old days, with the voice of an alcoholic and an actor's intonations—"Gilberte happy, there is nothing I would not give to see that. She has done so much for me. You can't possibly know." And the most disagreeable part of all this was once again his vanity, for he was flattered at being loved by Gilberte and, without daring to say that it was Charlie whom he loved, gave, nevertheless, of the love which the violinist was supposed to feel for him, details which he, the Saint-Loup from whom Charlie every day demanded more and more money, knew to be wildly exaggerated if not invented from start to finish. And so, entrusting Gilberte to my care, he would go off to Paris again. In Paris (to anticipate a little, for I am still at Tansonville) I once had an opportunity of observing him at a party and from a distance and on this occasion, though the way in which he spoke was still alive and charming and enabled me to rediscover the past, I was struck by the great changes taking place in him. More and more he resembled his mother: the haughtily elegant manner which he had inherited from her and which she, by means of the most elaborate training, had perfected in him was now freezing into exaggeration; the penetrating glance proper to him as a Guermantes gave him the air of inspecting every place in which he happened to be, but of doing this in an almost unconscious fashion, as though from habit, in obedience to a sort of animal characteristic. Even when he was at rest the colouring which he possessed in a greater degree than any other Guermantes—that air of being merely the solidified sunniness of a golden day—gave him as it seemed a plumage so strange, made of him a species so rare and so precious, that one would have liked to acquire him for an ornithological collection; but when, in addition, this ray of light metamorphosed into a bird started into movement, into action, when for instance I saw Robert de Saint-Loup enter this evening party at which I was present, the way in which he tossed back his head, so silkily and proudly crested with the golden tuft of his slightly moulting hair, and moved his neck from side to side, was so much more supple, so much more aloof and yet more delicate than anything to be expected of a human being that, fired by the sight with curiosity and wonder, half social and half zoological, one asked oneself whether one was really in the Faubourg Saint-Germain and not rather in the Jardin des Plantes, whether one was watching the passage of a great nobleman through a drawing-room or a bird pacing its cage. And if one was prepared to exercise a little imagination, the twittering lent itself just as well to this second interpretation as the plumage. For he was beginning to use phrases which he thought redolent of the age of Louis XIV, and though in this he was simply imitating the manners of the Guermantes, in him some indefinable nuance was turning them into the manners of

M. de Charlus. "I must leave you for a moment," he said to me for instance, at this party, at which Mme de Marsantes was standing a little way away from us. "I have to present my humble respects to my mother."

To return to this "love", of which he could not stop talking to me, it was not only love for Charlie, although this was the only love that counted for him. Whatever be the nature of a man's loves, one always makes mistakes as to the number of people with whom he has affairs, partly from wrongly interpreting friendships as love affairs, an error which exaggerates the total, but also through believing that one proved love affair excludes another, which is an error of a contrary kind. Two people may say: "X's mistress, yes, I know her," they may pronounce two different names and neither of them may be mistaken. A woman whom we love seldom satisfies all our needs and we deceive her with a woman whom we do not love. As to the species of loves that Saint-Loup had inherited from M. de Charlus, a husband who is that way inclined usually makes his wife happy. This is a general rule to which the Guermantes contrived to be an exception, because those of them who had this taste wanted it to be believed that on the contrary they were fond of women. So they made themselves conspicuous with one woman or another and drove their own wives to despair. The Courvoisiers were more sensible. The young Vicomte de Courvoisier thought he was the only man alive, perhaps the only man since the beginning of the world, to be tempted by someone of his own sex. Supposing this inclination to come to him from the devil, he struggled against it, married an extremely pretty wife and had children by her. Then one of his cousins taught him that the tendency is fairly wide-spread and was even so kind as to take him to places where he could indulge it. M. de Courvoisier became fonder than ever of his wife and redoubled his philoprogenitive zeal, and he and she were quoted as the happiest couple in Paris. That could not possibly be said of the Saint-Loups, because Robert, instead of being content with inversion, made his wife ill with jealousy by keeping mistresses without pleasure to himself.

It is possible that Morel, being excessively dark, was necessary to Saint-Loup in the way that shadow is necessary to the sunbeam. Can one not imagine some golden-haired aristocrat sprung from an ancient family such as his, intelligent and endowed with every kind of prestige, concealing within him, unbeknown to all his friends, a secret taste for negroes?

Robert never allowed the conversation to touch upon his own species of loves. If I said a word about it, "Oh! I don't know," he would reply, with a detachment so profound that it caused him to drop his monocle, "I am utterly ignorant about those things. If you want information about them, my dear boy, I advise you to go elsewhere. I am a soldier, that's all I can say for myself. The things you speak of leave me cold. What I *am* interested in, passionately, is the course of the Balkan war. That sort of thing interested you too once, the 'etymology' of battles. I told you in those days that we should see again, even in greatly changed circumstances, battles conforming to certain types, for example the great exercise in lateral envelopment, the battle of Ulm. Well! However special these Balkan wars may be, Lüleburgaz is Ulm all over again: lateral envelopment. These are the subjects you can talk to me about. As for the sort of thing you allude to, it means about as much to me as Sanskrit."

While Robert thus expressed his disdain for the subject, Gilberte on the contrary, after he had left, was very willing to raise it in the conversations which I had with her. Not with reference to her husband certainly, for she knew, or pretended to know, nothing. But she liked to discuss it at length in so

11

far as other men were concerned, whether because she saw in this a sort of indirect excuse for Robert or because he, divided like his uncle between an austere silence with regard to the subject and a need to let himself go and talk slander, had opened her eyes in many directions. M. de Charlus was one of those who were not spared, doubtless because Robert, without mentioning Charlie to Gilberte, could not help, when he was with her, repeating in one form or another what the violinist had told him; and the latter pursued his former benefactor with unrelenting hate. These conversations, and Gilberte's evident liking for them, gave me a chance to ask her whether, in a parallel category, Albertine, whose name I had first heard from Gilberte herself when they were attending the same classes, had comparable tastes. Gilberte could not give me any information on this point. And in any case it had long ceased to be of interest to me. But I continued to make enquiries mechanically, as an old man with a failing memory from time to time asks for news of the son he has lost.

What is odd, though I cannot here enlarge upon the topic, is the degree to which at the time I am writing about all the people whom Albertine loved, all those who might have been able to persuade her to do what they wanted, asked, entreated, I will even say begged to be allowed to have, if not my friendship, at least some sort of acquaintance with me. No longer should I have had to offer money to Mme Bontemps as an inducement to send Albertine back to me. But this turn of fortune's wheel, taking place when it was no longer of the slightest use, merely saddened me profoundly, not because of Albertine, whom I would have received without pleasure had she been brought back not from Touraine but from the other world, but because of a young woman with whom I was in love and whom I could not contrive to meet. I told myself that, if she died, or if I no longer loved her, all those who might have brought us together would suddenly be at my feet. Meanwhile, I tried in vain to work upon them, not having been cured by experience, which ought to have taught me—if ever it taught anybody anything—that loving is like an evil spell in a fairy-story against which one is powerless until the enchantment has passed.

"As a matter of fact the book I'm reading at the moment talks about that sort of thing," Gilberte said to me. "It is an old Balzac which I am swotting up so as to be as well-informed as my uncles, *La Fille aux Yeux d'Or*. But it is absurd, improbable, nightmarish. For one thing, I suppose a woman might be kept under surveillance in that way by another woman, but surely not by a man." "You are wrong, I once knew a woman who was loved by a man who in the end literally imprisoned her; she was never allowed to see anybody, she could only go out with trusted servants." "Well, you who are so kind must be horrified at the idea. By the way, we were saying, Robert and I, that you ought to get married. Your wife would improve your health and you would make her happy." "No, I have too bad a character." "How absurd!" "I mean it. Besides, I was engaged once. But I couldn't quite make up my mind to marry the girl—and anyhow she thought better of it herself, because of my undecided and cantankerous character." This was, in fact, the excessively simple light in which I regarded my adventure with Albertine, now that I saw it only from outside.

Back in my bedroom again, I thought sadly that I had not once been back to revisit Combray church, which seemed to be waiting for me amidst green foliage in a violet-tinted window. "Never mind," I said to myself, "that can wait for another year, if I don't die in the meanwhile," seeing no other possible obstacle but my own death and not envisaging that of the church which must, as I supposed, endure for centuries after my death as it had for centuries before my birth.

One day I spoke to Gilberte about Albertine, and asked her whether Albertine loved women. "Not in the least!" "But you used to say that you didn't approve of her." "I said that? No, I'm sure you're mistaken. In any case, if I said it— but you're wrong about that—what I was referring to was flirtations with young men. And anyhow, at her age, it probably didn't go very far." Did Gilberte say this in order to conceal from me that she herself—or so Albertine had told me—loved women and had made advances to Albertine? Or did she (for other people are often better informed about our life than we think) know that I had loved and been jealous of Albertine, and did she (since, though others may know more of the truth about us than we think, they may also stretch it too far and fall into the error of supposing too much, whereas we had hoped that they made the mistake of supposing nothing at all) imagine that this was still the case, was she, out of kindness, placing over my eyes that bandage with which we are always ready to blindfold the jealous? In any case, Gilberte's remarks, from the "disapproval" of the old days to the present certificate of respectability, were pursuing an opposite course to the statements of Albertine, who in the end had almost admitted some sort of an affair with Gilberte. In this Albertine had astonished me, just as I had been astonished by what Andrée had told me, for with all the girls in the little band, if I had at first believed, before knowing them, in their perversity, I had come round to the view that my suspicions were false, as must often happen when one finds a virtuous girl, almost ignorant of the facts of love, in surroundings which one had wrongly supposed to be extremely depraved. Then later I had travelled the same road in the opposite direction, back to a belief in the truth of my original suspicions. But perhaps Albertine had told me this because she wanted to appear more experienced than she was and to dazzle me in Paris with the prestige of her depravity, as on the earlier occasion at Balbec with that of her virtue; or quite simply, when I had talked about women who loved women, had not wanted to appear not to know what I meant, just as, if Fourier or Tobolsk is mentioned in a conversation, one tries to look as if one understood even if one has no idea what they are. She had perhaps lived, though in proximity to Mlle Vinteuil's friend and to Andrée, yet separated from them by a watertight partition, so that they thought that she was "not one", and had perhaps only got to know about the subject later—in the spirit of a woman who marries a man of letters and tries to improve her mind—in order to please me by making herself capable of answering my questions, until the day when she realised that the questions were inspired by jealousy, when she had hastily gone into reverse. Unless it was Gilberte who was lying to me. It even occurred to me that it was because he had learnt from Gilberte, while flirting with her with an eye all the while on his real interests, that she did not altogether dislike women, that Robert had married her, hoping for pleasures which, since he now went elsewhere for them, he must have failed to obtain from her. None of these hypotheses was absurd, for with women like Odette's daughter or the girls of the little band there is such a diversity, such an accumulation of alternating if not actually simultaneous tastes, that they pass easily from an affair with a woman to a great love for a man, so that to define the real and dominating taste must always be difficult.

I did not want to borrow Gilberte's copy of *La Fille aux Yeux d'Or* as she was reading it herself. But she lent me to read in bed, on that last evening of my stay with her, a book which produced on me a strong but mixed impression, which did not, however, prove to be lasting. It was a volume of the unpublished Journal of the Goncourts. And when, before putting out my candle, I read the passage which I am about to transcribe, my lack of talent for literature, of which I had had a presentiment long ago on the Guermantes way and which had been confirmed during the stay of which this was the last evening—one of those evenings before a departure when we emerge from the torpor of habits about to be broken and attempt to judge ourselves—struck me as something less to be regretted, since literature, if I was to trust the evidence of this book, had not any very profound truths to reveal; and at the same time it seemed to me sad that literature was not what I had thought it to be. On the other hand, the state of ill-health which was soon to shut me up in a sanatorium seemed to me also less to be regretted, if the beautiful things of which books speak were not more beautiful than what I had seen myself. And yet, by an odd contradiction, now that they were being spoken of in this book I had a desire to see them. Here are the pages that I read before fatigue closed my eyes . . .

"The day before yesterday there drops in here to carry me off to dine with him Verdurin, former critic of the *Revue*, author of that book on Whistler in which the workmanship, the painterly colouration of the American eccentric is interpreted sometimes with great delicacy by the lover of all the refinements, all the *prettinesses* of the painted canvas that Verdurin is. And while I am getting dressed to accompany him, he treats me to a long narrative, almost at moments a timidly stammered confession, about his renunciation of writing immediately after his marriage to Fromentin's

'Madeleine', a renunciation brought about, he says, by his addiction to morphia and which had the result, according to Verdurin, that most of the frequenters of his wife's drawing-room did not even know that her husband had ever been a writer and spoke to him of Charles Blanc, of Saint-Victor, of Sainte-Beuve, of Burty, as individuals to whom they considered him, Verdurin, altogether inferior. 'Now, you Goncourts, you know—and Gautier knew too—that my *Salons* were on a different plane to those pitiful *Maîtres d'Autrefois* which are deemed a masterpiece in my wife's family.' Then, through a dusk in which, as we pass the towers of the Trocadéro, the last glimmer of a gleam of daylight makes them positively resemble those towers of red-currant jelly that pastry-cooks used to make, the conversation continues in the carriage on its way to the Quai Conti, where is their mansion, which its owner claims was once the mansion of the Venetian Ambassadors and in which there is a room used as a smoking-room which Verdurin tells me was transported lock, stock and barrel, as in a tale of the *Thousand and One Nights*, from a celebrated *palazzo* whose name I forget, a *palazzo* boasting a well-head decorated with a Coronation of the Virgin which Verdurin maintains is positively one of Sansovino's finest things and which now, he says, their guests find useful as a receptacle for cigar-ash. And upon my word, when we arrive, in the watery shimmer of a moonlight really just like that in which the painting of the great age enwraps Venice, against which the silhouetted dome of the Institut makes one think of the Salute in Guardi's pictures, I have almost the illusion of looking out over the Grand Canal. And the illusion is preserved by the way in which the house is built so that from the first floor one cannot see the quay, and by the evocative remark of its owner, who affirms that the name of the Rue du Bac—the devil if ever I'd thought of it—comes from the ferry which once upon a time used to take an order of nuns, the Miramiones, across to hear divine office in Notre Dame. A whole quarter which my childhood used idly to explore when my aunt de Courmont lived there, and which I am inspired to *re-love* by re-discovering, almost next door to the Verdurin mansion, the sign of 'Little Dunkirk', one of the rare shops surviving elsewhere than in the crayon and wash vignettes of Gabriel de Saint-Aubin, to which the eighteenth-century connoisseur would come to pass a few leisure moments in cheapening trinkets French and foreign and 'all the newest products of the arts', as an invoice of this Little Dunkirk puts it, an invoice of which we two, Verdurin and myself, are, I believe, alone in possessing copies, one of those flimsy master-pieces of engraved paper upon which the reign of Louis XV made out its accounts, with a headpiece representing a billowy sea laden with vessels, a sea of billows which might be an illustration in the Fermiers Généraux La Fontaine, to 'The Oyster and the Litigants'. The mistress of the house, who has placed me next to her at dinner, graciously tells me before we go in that she has flowered her table with nothing but Japanese chrysanthemums—but chrysanthemums dis-played in vases which are the rarest masterpieces, one in par-ticular of bronze on which petals of red-gold copper seem to have been shed by the living flower. Cottard, the doctor, is there, his wife, the Polish sculptor Viradobetski, Swann the collector, and an aristocratic Russian lady, a princess with a name ending in -off which I fail to catch (Cottard whispers in my ear that she is the woman who is supposed to have fired point-blank at the Archduke Rudolf), accord-ing to whom in Galicia and the whole of the north of Poland my reputation stands extraordinarily high, no young girl ever giving her consent to an offer of marriage without first ascertaining whether her fiancé is an admirer of *La Faustin*.

'You cannot understand that, you western Europeans,'—
this is thrown in as a sort of coda by the Princess, who, upon
my word, strikes me as a person of a really superior intelligence—'that penetration by a writer of a woman's most
intimate feelings'. A man with a close-shaven chin and lip
and the side-whiskers of a butler, rolling out in a condescending
tone the witticisms of a fifth-form schoolmaster unbending
among his prize pupils on St. Charlemagne's holiday—this is
Brichot, of the university. I am introduced to him by Verdurin but he utters not a word of reference to our books, and
I am filled with a mixture of discouragement and anger at
this conspiracy organised against us by the Sorbonne, which
brings even into this pleasant dwelling where I am received as
an honoured guest the contradiction, the hostility, of deliberate silence. We go in to dinner, and there follows an extraordinary cavalcade of plates which are nothing less than
masterpieces of the porcelainist's art, that artist whose chatter,
during an exquisite meal, is heard with more pleasure than
any fellow-guest's by the titillated attention of the connoisseur—Yung Cheng plates with nasturtium-coloured borders
and purple-blue irises, leafless and tumid, and those supremely
decorative flights of kingfishers and cranes trailing across a
dawn sky, a dawn that has just the early-morning tones
glimpsed daily from Boulevard Montmorency by my awak-
ening eyes—Dresden plates daintier and of more graceful
workmanship, with drowsy, bloodless roses fading into violet,
with ragged-edged tulips the colour of wine-lees, with the
rococo elegance of a pink or a forget-me-not—Sèvres plates
meshed with the close guilloche of their white fluting, whorled
in gold, or knotted with a golden ribbon that stands in gallant
relief upon the creamy smoothness of the paste—finally a
whole service of silver plate arabesqued with those myrtles
of Luciennes that were not unknown to the Dubarry. And

what is perhaps equally rare is the truly quite remarkable quality of the things served upon these plates, a meal most subtly concocted, a real spread such as Parisians, one cannot say it too emphatically, never have at their really grand dinner-parties and which reminds me of certain prize dishes of Jean d'Heurs. Even the foie gras bears no resemblance to the insipid mousse customarily served under that name; and I do not know many places in which a simple potato salad is made as it is here with potatoes firm as Japanese ivory buttons and patina'd like those little ivory spoons with which Chinese women sprinkle water over their new-caught fish. Into the Venetian glass which I have before me is poured, like a rich cascade of red jewels, an extraordinary Léoville bought at M. Montalivet's sale, and it is a delight to the imagination of the eye and also, I am not afraid to say it, of what used to be called the gullet, to see a brill placed before us which has nothing in common with those anything but fresh brills that are served at the most luxurious tables, which in the slow course of their journey from the sea have had the pattern of their bones imprinted upon their backs; a brill that is served not with the sticky paste prepared under the name of white sauce by so many chefs in great houses, but with a genuine white sauce, made with butter that costs five francs a pound; to see this brill brought in on a wonderful Ching Hon dish streaked with the purple rays of a sun setting above a sea upon which ludicrously sails a flotilla of large lobsters, their spiky stippling rendered with such extraordinary skill that they seem to have been moulded from living shells, with a border too depicting a little Chinaman who plays with rod and line a fish whose silver and azure belly makes it a marvel of iridescent colour. When I remark to Verdurin what an exquisite pleasure it must be for him to eat this rare and subtle food off a collection such as no prince today possesses in his show cases: 'It is easy to see that you don't know him,' gloomily interjects the mistress of the house. And she speaks to me of her husband as of an eccentric maniac, indifferent to all these pretty things, 'a maniac,' she repeats, 'yes, that is the only word for it, a maniac who would get more enjoyment from a bottle of cider drunk in the proletarian coolness of a Normandy farm'. And this charming woman, whose speech betrays her positive adoration of local colouring, talks with overflowing enthusiasm of the Normandy in which they once lived, a Normandy, so she says, like an immense English park, with the fragrance of tall woodlands that Lawrence might have painted, with the cryptomeria-coloured velvet of natural lawns bordered with the porcelain of pink hydrangeas, with crumpled sulphur-roses which, as they cascade over a cottage-door, above which the incrustation of two entwined pear-trees has the effect of a purely decorative sign over a shop, make one think of the free arabesque of a flowery branch of bronze in a candle-bracket by Gouthière, a Normandy absolutely unsuspected by the Parisian holiday-makers, protected by the iron gates of each of its little properties, gates which the Verdurins confessed to me that they did not scruple to open one and all. At the end of the day, in the drowsy extinguishment of all colours, when the only light was from an almost curdled sea, blue-white like whey ('No, not in the least like the sea you know,' frantically protests my neighbour, when I start to tell her that Flaubert once took us, my brother and me, to Trouville, 'not the slightest bit, you must come with me, otherwise you will never find out'), they would go home, through the forests—absolute forests abloom with pink tulle—of the great rhododendrons, quite drunk with the smell of the sardine fisheries which gave her husband terrible attacks of asthma —'Yes,' she insists, 'I mean it, real attacks of asthma.' Thereupon, the following summer, they returned, lodging a whole colony of artists in an old cloister which they rented for next to nothing, and which made an admirable mediaeval abode. And upon my word, as I listen to this woman who, in passing through so many social circles of real distinction, has nevertheless preserved in her speech a little of the freshness and freedom of language of a woman of the people, a language which shows you things with the colour which your imagination sees in them, my mouth waters at the life which she avows to me they lived down there, each one working in his cell and the whole party assembling before luncheon, in a drawing-room so vast that it had two fireplaces, for really intelligent conversation interspersed with parlour games, a life which makes me think of the one we read of in that masterpiece of Diderot, the *Lettres à Mademoiselle Volland*. Then, after luncheon, they would all go out, even on the days when the weather was unsettled, in a brief burst of sunshine or the diffused radiance of a shower, a shower whose filtered light sharpened the knotted outlines of a magnificent avenue of century-old beeches which began just behind the house and brought almost up to the iron grill that vegetable embodiment of 'the beautiful' so dear to eighteenth-century taste, and of the ornamental trees which held suspended in their branches not buds about to flower but drops of rain. They would stop to listen to the delicate splish-splash of a bull-finch, enamoured of coolness, bathing itself in the tiny dainty Nymphenburg bath made for it by the corolla of a white rose. And when I mention to Mme Verdurin Elstir's delicate pastel sketches of the landscapes and the flowers of that coast: 'But it is through me that he discovered all those things', she bursts out, with an angry toss of the head, 'all of them, yes, all, make no mistake about it, the interesting spots, every one of his subjects—I threw it in his teeth when he left us, didn't I, Auguste?—every one of the subjects he has painted.

Things he has always known about, there one must be fair, one must admit that. But as for flowers, he had never seen any, he couldn't tell a mallow from a hollyhock. It is I who taught him—you won't believe this—to recognise *jasmin*.' And one must admit that it is a curious thought that the artist who is cited by connoisseurs today as our leading flower-painter, superior even to Fantin-Latour, would perhaps never, without the help of the woman sitting beside me, have known how to paint jasmin. 'Yes, honestly, jasmin. And all the roses he has done have been painted in my house, or else it was I who took them to him. Among us he was always known simply as Monsieur Tiche; ask Cottard, ask Brichot, ask anybody here, whether we treated him as a great man. He would have laughed at the idea himself. I taught him to arrange his flowers; at first he couldn't manage it at all. He never learnt how to make a bouquet. He had no natural taste in selecting, I had to say to him: "No, don't paint that, that's no good, paint this." Ah! if he had listened to us about the arrangement of his life as he did about the arrangement of his flowers, and hadn't made that vile marriage!' And of a sudden, her eyes feverish from her absorption in thoughts of the past, plucking nervously at the silk sleeves of her bodice as she frenziedly tenses her fingers, she presents, in the distortion of her grief-stricken pose, an admirable picture which has, I think, never been painted, a picture in which one would see portrayed all the restrained revolt, all the passionate susceptibilities of a female friend outraged in the delicate feelings, the modesty of a woman. Thereupon she talks about the admirable portrait which Elstir did for her, the portrait of the Cottard family, which she gave to the Luxembourg at the time of her quarrel with the painter, confessing that it was she who gave him the idea of painting the man in dress clothes in order to get all that splendid ebullition of fine linen, and she who chose the woman's velvet gown which forms a solid mass amid all the glitter of the bright tones of the carpets, the flowers, the fruit, the little girls' muslin dresses that look like dancers' tutus. It is she too, she tells me, who gave him the idea of the woman brushing her hair, an idea for which the artist was subsequently much praised and which consisted simply in painting her not as if she were on show but surprised in the intimacy of her everyday life. '"In a woman doing her hair," I used to say to him, "or wiping her face, or warming her feet, when she thinks she is not observed, there is a multitude of interesting movements, movements of a grace and charm that are positively Leonardesque!"' But at a sign from Verdurin indicating that the revival of these old indignations is dangerous for the health of his wife, who is really a mass of nerves, Swann points out to me the wonderful necklace of black pearls which the mistress of the house is wearing, which she bought, as a necklace of white pearls, at the sale of a descendant of Mme de La Fayette, to whom they were given by Henrietta of England, and which became black as the result of a fire which destroyed part of a house which the Verdurins had in a street whose name I do not remember, after which fire the casket containing these pearls was found, with the pearls completely black inside it. 'And I know the portrait of these pearls, on the shoulders of Mme de La Fayette herself, yes, positively their portrait,' insists Swann, checking the exclamations of the slightly astonished guests, 'their authentic portrait, in the collection of the Duc de Guermantes.' A collection which has not its equal in the world, proclaims Swann, and which I ought to go and see, a collection inherited by the celebrated Duke, who was her favourite nephew, from his aunt Mme de Beausergent, who afterwards became Mme d'Hazfeld and was the sister of the Marquise de Villeparisis and of the Princess of Hanover, in whose house years ago my brother and I became so fond of him under the guise of the charming infant known as Basin, which is indeed the Duke's first name. Thereupon Doctor Cottard, with that keen intelligence which shows him to be a man of real distinction, harks back to the story of the pearls and informs us that catastrophes of this kind can produce changes in people's brains which are just like those that may be observed in inanimate matter, and, discoursing in a philosophical vein well beyond the powers of most doctors, quotes as an example Mme Verdurin's own valet, who from the terrible shock of this fire in which he very nearly lost his life became a changed man, with a handwriting so altered that when his master and mistress, then in Normandy, first received a letter from him with the news of the fire, they thought that someone was playing a practical joke upon them. And not only an altered handwriting, according to Cottard, who maintains that this man, hitherto always sober, became such an abominable sot that Mme Verdurin was obliged to get rid of him. And the doctor's stimulating dissertation passes, upon a gracious sign from the mistress of the house, from the dining-room to the Venetian smoking-room, where he tells us that he has witnessed cases of what can only be called dual personality, citing as an instance one of his patients, whom he is so kind as to offer to bring to my house, whose temples he only has to touch, so he says, to awaken him to a second life, a life during which he remembers nothing of his first life and so different that, while he behaves most respectably in the first, he has more than once been arrested for thefts committed in the second, in which he is nothing more nor less than an abominable scoundrel. Whereupon Mme Verdurin acutely observes that medical science could provide the theatre with truer themes than those now in favour, themes in which the comicality of the plot would be based upon misunderstandings of a pathological kind, and this, by a natural transition, leads Mme Cottard to say that a very similar subject has been employed by a story-teller who is her children's favourite at bedtime, the Scotsman Stevenson, a name which brings from Swann the peremptory statement: 'But he is a really great writer, Stevenson, I assure you, M. de Goncourt, a very great writer, equal to the greatest.' Next, after I have admired the ceiling of the room where we are smoking, with its escutcheoned coffers from the old Barberini palace, when I intimate my regret at the progressive blackening of a certain stone basin by the ash of our 'Havanas' and Swann remarks that similar stains on books from the library of Napoleon which are now, despite his anti-Bonapartist opinions, in the possession of the Duc de Guermantes, bear witness to the fact that the Emperor chewed tobacco, Cottard, who evinces a truly penetrating curiosity in all things, declares that the stains do not come from that at all—'No, no, no, not at all,' he insists with authority—but from the habit the Emperor had of always, even on the field of battle, clutching in his hand the liquorice tablets which he took to relieve the pain in his liver. 'For he had a disease of the liver and that is what he died of,' concludes the doctor."

There I stopped, for I was leaving the next morning; and besides it was the hour at which I was habitually summoned by that other master in whose service we spend, every day, a part of our time. The task which he assigns to us we accomplish with our eyes closed. Every morning he hands us back to the master who shares us with him, knowing that, unless he did so, we should be remiss in his own service. Curious, when our intelligence reopens its eyes, to know what we can have done under this master who first makes his slaves lie down and then puts them to work at full speed, the most artful among us try, the moment their task is finished, to take a covert glance. But sleep is racing against them to obliterate the traces of what they would like to see. And after all these centuries we still know very little about the matter.

I closed the Journal of the Goncourts. Prestige of literature! I wished I could have seen the Cottards again, asked them all sorts of details about Elstir, gone to look at the shop called Little Dunkirk, if it still existed, asked permission to visit the Verdurin mansion where I had once dined. But I felt vaguely depressed. Certainly, I had never concealed from myself that I knew neither how to listen nor, once I was not alone, how to look. My eyes were blind to the sort of necklace an old woman might be wearing, and the things I might be told about her pearls never entered my ears. All the same, I had known these people in daily life, I had dined with them often, they were simply the Verdurins and the Duc de Guermantes and the Cottards, and each one of them I had found just as commonplace as my grandmother had found that Basin of whom she had no suspicion that he was the darling nephew, the enchanting young hero, of Mme de Beausergent, each one of them had seemed to me insipid; I could remember the vulgarities without number of which each of them was composed. . . .

Et que tout cela fasse un astre dans la nuit!

But provisionally I decided to ignore the objections against literature raised in my mind by the pages of Goncourt which I had read on the evening before I left Tansonville. Even without taking into account the manifest naivety of this particular diarist, I could in any case reassure myself on various counts. First, in so far as my own character was concerned, my incapacity for looking and listening, which the passage from the Journal had so painfully illustrated to me, was nevertheless not total. There was in me a personage who knew more or less how to look, but it was an intermittent personage, coming to life only in the presence of some general essence common to a number of things, these essences being its nourishment and its joy. Then the personage looked and listened, but at a certain depth only, without my powers of superficial observation being enhanced. Just as a geometer, stripping things of their sensible qualities, sees only the linear substratum beneath them, so the stories that people told escaped me, for what interested me was not what they were trying to say but the manner in which they said it and the way in which this manner revealed their character or their foibles; or rather I was interested in what had always, because it gave me specific pleasure, been more particularly the goal of my investigations: the point that was common to one being and another. As soon as I perceived this my intelligence— until that moment slumbering, even if sometimes the apparent animation of my talk might disguise from others a profound intellectual torpor—at once set off joyously in pursuit, but its quarry then, for instance the identity of the Verdurin drawing-room in various places and at various times, was situated in the middle distance, behind actual appearances, in a plane that was rather more withdrawn. So the apparent, copiable charm of things and people escaped me, because I had not the ability to stop short there—I was like a surgeon who beneath the smooth surface of a woman's belly sees the internal disease which is devouring it. If I went to a dinner-party I did not see the guests: when I thought I was looking at them, I was in fact examining them with X-rays. And the result was that, when all the observations I had succeeded in making about the guests during the party were linked together, the pattern of the lines I had traced took the form of a collection of psychological laws in which the actual purport of the remarks of each guest occupied but a very small space. But did this take away all merit from my portraits, which in fact I did not intend as such? If, in the realm of painting, one portrait makes manifest certain truths concerning volume, light, movement, does that mean that it is necessarily inferior to another completely different portrait of the same person, in which a thousand details omitted in the first are minutely transcribed, from which second portrait one would conclude that the model was ravishingly beautiful while from the first one would have thought him or her ugly, a fact which may be of documentary, even of historical importance, but is not necessarily an artistic truth? Furthermore my frivolity, the moment I was not alone, made me eager to please, more eager to amuse by chattering than to acquire knowledge by listening, unless it happened that I had gone out into society in search of information about some particular artistic question or some jealous suspicion which my mind had previously been revolving. Always I was incapable of seeing anything for which a desire had not already been roused in me by something I had read, anything of which I had not myself traced in advance a sketch which I wanted now to confront with reality. How often— and I was well aware of this even without being apprised of it by these pages of Goncourt—have I remained incapable of bestowing my attention upon things or people that later, once their image has been presented to me in solitude by an artist, I would have travelled many miles, risked death to find again! Then and then only has my imagination been set in motion, has it begun to paint. And of something which a year before had made me yawn I have said to myself with anguish, longingly contemplating it in advance: "Shall I really be unable to see this thing? I would give anything for a sight of it!" When one reads articles about people, perhaps mere fashionable people, who are described as "the last representatives of a society of which no eye-witness now exists", one may of course exclaim: "Fancy using such extravagant language about so insignificant a creature! This is what I should have lamented never having known if I had only read the newspapers and the monthly reviews and had not met the man!" But I was tempted rather, when I read such pages in the newspapers, to think: "How unfortunate that in those days when I was solely preoccupied with meeting Gilberte or Albertine again I did not pay more attention to this gentleman! I took him for a society bore, a mere dummy. On the contrary he was a Distinguished Figure!" The pages of Goncourt which I had read made me regret this tendency of mine. For though I might have inferred from them that life teaches us to cheapen the value of a book, and shows us that what a writer extols was in fact worth very little, it was equally possible for me to come to the contrary conclusion, that reading teaches us to take a more exalted view of the value of life, a value which at the time we did not know how to appreciate and of whose magnitude we have only become aware through the book. We may, without too much difficulty, console ourselves for having taken little pleasure in the society of a Vinteuil, a Bergotte. But the prudish respectability of the one, the intolerable defects of the other, even the pretentious vulgarity of an Elstir in his early days—for I had discovered from the Goncourt Journal that he was none other than the "Monsieur Tiche" whose twaddle had once exasperated Swann in the Verdurins' drawing-room—prove nothing against them: their genius is manifested in their works. What man of genius has not in his conversation adopted the irritating mannerisms of the artists of his set, before attaining (as Elstir had eventually done, though this does not always happen) to a good taste that rises above them? Are not Balzac's letters, for instance, strewn with vulgar expressions which Swann would have suffered a thousand deaths rather than employ? Yet can one doubt that Swann, finely intelligent as he was, purged of all odious absurdities, would have been incapable of writing *La Cousine Bette* or *Le Curé de Tours*? As for the Vinteuils, the Bergottes, the Elstirs, the question whether it is we or the writers of memoirs who are at fault when they represent the society of these men as charming whereas we found it disagreeable, is a question of slight importance, since even if our estimate were the correct one, this would be no argument against the value of life if life can produce such geniuses.

Right at the other pole of experience, when I saw that the most piquant anecdotes, which form the inexhaustible material of the Goncourt Journal and provide the reader with entertainment for many solitary evenings, had been related to the writer by these people whom he had met at dinner and who, though on the evidence of his pages we should certainly have wanted to meet them, had in my mind left no trace of any interesting recollection, that too was not altogether difficult to explain. In spite of the naivety of Goncourt, who inferred from the interest of these anecdotes the probable distinction of the man who related them, it might well be that commonplace men had seen during their lives, or heard related, remarkable things which they in their turn had described. Goncourt knew how to listen, just as he knew how to see; I did not. Besides, all these facts needed to be considered and judged separately. Certainly M. de Guermantes had not given me the impression of that adorable model of the youthful graces which my grandmother so wished she had known and which she set before me, in the Memoirs of Mme de Beausergent, as an inimitable example. But one must remember that Basin was then seven years old, that the writer was his aunt, and that even a husband who within a few months will be suing for divorce will praise his wife to the skies. In one of his most delightful poems Sainte-Beuve describes an apparition beside a fountain—a little girl crowned with every gift and every grace, young Mlle de Champlâtreux, whose age at the time cannot have been ten. And in spite of all the affectionate respect which the poet of genius who is the Comtesse de Noailles bore for her husband's mother, the Duchesse de Noailles *née* Champlâtreux, one wonders whether, had she had occasion to portray her, the result might not have contrasted rather sharply with the portrait drawn by Sainte-Beuve fifty years earlier.

More puzzling perhaps were the people in between the two extremes, those in whom what the writer says of them implies more than a memory which has succeeded in retaining a piquant anecdote, with whom, nevertheless, one has not, as with the Vinteuils, the Bergottes, the resource of judging them on their work, for they have created none: they have only—to the great astonishment of us who found them so commonplace—inspired the work of others. I could, it is true, understand how the drawing-room which, seen on the walls of a museum, will give a greater impression of elegance than anything since the great paintings of the Renaissance, might be that of the ridiculous middle-class woman whom, had I not known her, I would have longed, as I stood before the picture, to be able to approach in reality, hoping to learn from her the most precious secrets of the painter's art which his canvas did not reveal to me, and how her lace and her stately train of velvet might have become a piece of painting as lovely as anything in Titian. For I had already realised long ago that it is not the man with the liveliest mind, the most wel!-informed, the best supplied with friends and acquaintances, but the one who knows how to become a mirror and in this way can reflect his life, commonplace though it may be, who becomes a Bergotte (even if his contemporaries once thought him less witty than Swann, less erudite than Bréauté), and could one not say as much, and with better reason, of a painter's models? The artist may paint anything in the world that he chooses, but when beauty is awakened within him the model for that elegance in which he will find themes of beauty will be provided for him by people a little richer than he is himself, in whose house he will find what he does not see every day around him in his studio of an unrecognised man of genius selling his canvases for fifty francs: a drawing-room with chairs and sofas covered in old brocades, an abundance of lamps, beautiful flowers, beautiful fruit, beautiful dresses—people in a relatively modest position, or who would seem to be so to people of real social brilliance (who are not even aware of their existence), but who, for that reason, are more within reach of the obscure artist's acquaintance, more likely to appreciate him, to invite him, to buy his pictures, than men and women of the aristocracy who, like the Pope and heads of states, get themselves painted by academicians. Will not posterity, when it looks at our time, find the poetry of an elegant home and beautifully dressed women in the drawing-room of the publisher Charpentier as painted by Renoir, rather than in the portraits of the Princesse de Sagan or the Comtesse de La Rochefoucauld by Cotte or Chaplin? The artists who have given us the most splendid visions of elegance have gathered the materials for them from among people who were rarely the leaders of fashion in their age, for the leaders of fashion rarely commission pictures from the unknown bearer of a new type of beauty which they are unable to distinguish in his canvases, concealed as it is by the interposition of that formula of hackneyed charm which floats in the eye of the public like the subjective visions which a sick man supposes really to exist before his eyes. This, I say, I could understand; but that these commonplace models whom I had known should in addition have inspired and advised certain arrangements which had enchanted me, that the presence of one or another of them in a painting should be not merely that of a model but of a friend whom an artist wants to put into his pictures, this made me ask myself whether all the people whom we regret not having known because Balzac depicted them in his novels or dedicated books to them in homage and admiration, the people about whom Sainte-Beuve or Baudelaire wrote their loveliest poems, still more whether all the Récamiers, all the Pompadours, would not have seemed to me insignificant creatures, either owing to an infirmity of my nature, which, if it were so, made me furious at being ill and therefore unable to go back and see again all the people whom I had misjudged, or because they owed their prestige only to an illusory magic of literature, in which case I had been barking up the wrong tree and need not repine at being obliged almost any day now by the steady deterioration of my health to break with society, renounce travel and museums, and go to a sanatorium for treatment.

CHAPTER II

These ideas, tending on the one hand to diminish, and on the other to increase, my regret that I had no gift for literature, were entirely absent from my mind during the long years—in which I had in any case completely renounced the project of writing—which I spent far from Paris receiving treatment in a sanatorium, until there came a time, at the beginning of 1916, when it could no longer get medical staff. I then returned to a Paris very different from the city to which, as we shall see presently, I had come back once before in August 1914 for a medical consultation, after which I had withdrawn again to my sanatorium.

On one of the first evenings of my second return, in 1916, wanting to hear people talk about the only thing that interested me at the time, the war, I went out after dinner to call on Mme Verdurin, who was, with Mme Bontemps, one of the queens of this war-time Paris which made one think of the Directory. As if by the germination of a tiny quantity of yeast, apparently of spontaneous generation, young women now went about all day with tall cylindrical turbans on their heads, as a contemporary of Mme Tallien's might have done, and from a sense of patriotic duty wore Egyptian tunics, straight and dark and very "war", over very short skirts; they wore shoes with ankle-straps recalling the buskin as worn by Talma, or else long gaiters recalling those of our dear boys at the front; it was, so they said, because they did not forget that it was their duty to rejoice the eyes of these "boys at the front", that they still decked themselves of an evening not only in flowing dresses, but in jewellery which suggested the army by its choice of decorative themes, when indeed the actual material from which it was made did not come from, had not been wrought in the army; for instead of Egyptian ornaments recalling the campaign in Egypt, the fashion now was for rings or bracelets made out of fragments of exploded shells or copper bands from 75 millimetre ammunition, and for cigarette-lighters constructed out of two English pennies to which a soldier, in his dug-out, had succeeded in giving a patina so beautiful that the profile of Queen Victoria looked as if it had been drawn by the hand of Pisanello; and it was also because they never stopped thinking of the dear boys, so they said, that when one of their own kin fell they scarcely wore mourning for him, on the pretext that "their grief was mingled with pride", which permitted them to wear a bonnet of white English crêpe (a bonnet with the most charming effect, "authorising every hope" and "inspired by an invincible assurance of final victory") and to replace the cashmere of former days by satin and chiffon, and even to keep their pearls, "while observing the tact and propriety of which there is no need to remind Frenchwomen".

The Louvre and all the other museums were closed, and when one saw at the head of an article in a newspaper the words: "A sensational exhibition", one could be sure that the exhibition in question was not one of paintings but of dresses, of dresses moreover which aimed at reviving "those refined joys of art of which the women of Paris have for too long been deprived". So it was that fashion and pleasure had returned, fashion, in the absence of the arts, apologising for its survival as the arts had done in 1793, in which year the artists exhibiting in the revolutionary Salon proclaimed that, though "stern Republicans might find it strange that we should occupy ourselves with the arts when Europe united in coalition is besieging the soil of liberty", they would be wrong. The same sort of thing was said in 1916 by the dressmakers, who, with

the self-conscious pride of artists, affirmed that "to create
something new, to get away from banality, to assert an individual character, to prepare for victory, to evolve for the
post-war generations a new formula of beauty, such was the
ambition that tormented them, the chimaera that they pursued, as would be apparent to anyone who cared to visit their
salons, delightfully installed in the Rue de la . . ., where to
efface by a note of luminous gaiety the heavy sadness of the
hour seems to be the watchword, with the discretion, naturally, that circumstances impose. The sadness of the hour"—
it was true—"might prove too strong for feminine energies,
were it not that we had so many lofty examples of courage
and endurance to contemplate. So, as we think of our warriors
dreaming in their trenches of more comfort and more pretty
things for the girl they have left behind them, we shall not
pause in our ever more strenuous efforts to create dresses that
answer to the needs of the moment. The vogue"—and
what could be more natural?—"is for the fashion-houses of
our English allies, and the rage this year is the barrel-dress,
which, with its charming informality, gives us all an amusing
little *cachet* of rare distinction. We may even say that one of
the happiest consequences of this sad war will be," added the
delightful chronicler (and one expected: "the return of our
lost provinces" or "the reawakening of national sentiment")
—"one of the happiest consequences of this sad war will be
that we have achieved some charming results in the realm of
fashion, without ill-considered and unseemly luxury, with
the simplest materials, that we have created prettiness out of
mere nothings. To the dresses of the great designers, reproduced in a number of copies, women prefer just now dresses
made at home, which affirm the intelligence, the taste and the
personal preferences of the individual."

As for charity, the thought of all the miseries that had

37

sprung from the invasion, of all the wounded and disabled, meant naturally that it was obliged to develop forms "more ingenious than ever before", and this meant that the ladies in tall turbans were obliged to spend the latter part of the afternoon at "teas" round a bridge table, discussing the news from the "front", while their cars waited at the door with a handsome soldier in the driver's seat who chatted to the footman. It was, moreover, not only the headdresses with their strange cylinders towering above the ladies' faces that were new. The faces were new themselves. These ladies in new-fangled hats were young women who had come one did not quite know from where and had been the flower of fashion, some for six months, others for two years, others for four. And these differences were of as much importance for them as had been, at the time when I took my first steps in society, for two families like the Guermantes and the La Rochefoucaulds a difference of three or four centuries of proven antiquity. The lady who had known the Guermantes since 1914 looked upon the lady who had been introduced to them in 1916 as an upstart, greeted her with the air of a dowager, quizzed her with her lorgnette, and admitted with a little grimace that no one even knew for certain whether or no she was married. "It is all rather nauseating", concluded the lady of 1914, who would have liked the cycle of new admissions to have come to a halt after herself. These new ladies, whom the young men found pretty ancient and whom, also, certain elderly men who had not moved exclusively in the best circles thought that they recognised as being not so new as all that, did not merely recommend themselves to society by offering it its favourite amusements of political conversation and music in intimate surroundings; part of their appeal was that it was *they* who offered these amenities, for in order that things should appear new even if they are old—and indeed even if they are new—

there must in art, as in medicine and in fashion, be new names. (New names indeed there were in certain spheres. For instance, Mme Verdurin had visited Venice during the war, but —like those people who cannot bear sad talk or display of personal feelings—when she said that "it" was "marvellous" she was referring not to Venice, or St. Mark's, or the palaces, all that I had so loved and she thought so unimportant, but to the effect of the searchlights in the sky, of which searchlights she could give you a detailed account supported by statistics. So from age to age is reborn a certain realism which reacts against what the previous age has admired.)

The Sainte-Euverte salon was a faded banner now, and the presence beneath it of the greatest artists, the most influential ministers, would have attracted nobody. But people would run to listen to the secretary of one of these same artists or a subordinate official of one of the ministers holding forth in the houses of the new turbaned ladies whose winged and chattering invasion filled Paris. The ladies of the first Directory had a queen who was young and beautiful and was called Mme Tallien. Those of the second had two, who were old and ugly and were called Mme Verdurin and Mme Bontemps. Who now could look down on Mme Bontemps because in the Dreyfus affair her husband had played a role which the *Echo de Paris* had sharply criticised? The whole Chamber having at a certain moment become revisionist, it was inevitably from among former revisionists—and also from among former socialists—that the party of social order, of religious tolerance, of military preparedness, had been obliged to enlist its recruits. Time was when M. Bontemps would have been abominated, because then the antipatriots bore the name of Dreyfusards. But presently this name had been forgotten and replaced by that of "opponent of the law of three years' military service". M. Bontemps, far from being its opponent, was one of the sponsors of this law; consequently he was a patriot. In society (and this social phenomenon is merely a particular case of a much more general psychological law) novelties, whether blameworthy or not, excite horror only so long as they have not been assimilated and enveloped by reassuring elements. It was the same with Dreyfusism as with that marriage between Saint-Loup and the daughter of Odette which had at first produced such an outcry. Now that "everybody one knew" was seen at the parties given by the Saint-Loups, Gilberte might have had the morals of Odette herself but people would have "gone there" just the same and would have thought it quite right that she should disapprove like a dowager of any moral novelties that had not been assimilated. Dreyfusism was now integrated in a scheme of respectable and familiar things. As for asking oneself whether intrinsically it was good or bad, the idea no more entered anybody's head, now when it was accepted, than in the past when it was condemned. It was no longer "shocking" and that was all that mattered. People hardly remembered that it had once been thought so, just as, when a certain time has elapsed, they no longer know whether a girl's father was a thief or not. One can always say, if the subject crops up: "No, it's the brother-in-law, or someone else with the same name, that you're thinking of. There has never been a breath of scandal about her father." In the same way, there had undeniably been Dreyfusism and Dreyfusism, and a man who was received by the Duchesse de Montmorency and was helping to pass the three years law could not be bad. And then, as the saying goes, there's a pardon for every sin. If Dreyfusism was accorded an amnesty, so, *a fortiori*, were Dreyfusards. In fact, there no longer were Dreyfusards in politics, since at one moment every politician had been one if he wanted to belong to the government, even those who represented the contrary of what at the time of its shocking novelty—the time when Saint-Loup had been getting into bad ways—Dreyfusism had incarnated: anti-patriotism, irreligion, anarchy, etc. So the Dreyfusism of M. Bontemps, invisible and constitutional like that of every other politician, was no more apparent than the bones beneath the skin. No one troubled to remember that he had been a Dreyfusard, for people in society are scatter-brained and forgetful and, besides, all *that* had been a very long time ago, a "time" which these people affected to think longer than it was, for one of the ideas most in vogue was that the pre-war days were separated from the war by something as profound, something of apparently as long a duration, as a geological period, and Brichot himself, that great nationalist, when he alluded to the Dreyfus case now talked of "those pre-historic days". (The truth is that this profound change wrought by the war was in inverse proportion to the quality of the minds which it affected, at least above a certain level. At the very bottom of the scale the really stupid people, who lived only for pleasure, did not bother about the fact that there was a war. But, at the other end of the scale too, people who have made for themselves a circumambient interior life usually pay small regard to the importance of events. What profoundly modifies their system of thought is much more likely to be something that in itself seems to have no importance, something that reverses the order of time for them by making them contemporaneous with another epoch in their lives. And that this is so we may see in practice from the beauty of the writing which is inspired in this particular way: the song of a bird in the park at Montboissier, or a breeze laden with the scent of mignonette, are obviously phenomena of less consequence than the great events of the Revolution and the Empire; but they inspired Chateaubriand to write pages of infinitely greater value in his *Mémoires d'Outre-tombe*.) The words Dreyfusard and anti-Dreyfusard no longer had any meaning then. But the very people who said this would have been dumbfounded and horrified if one had told them that probably in a few centuries, or perhaps even sooner, the word Boche would have only the curiosity value of such words as *sans-culotte, chouan* and *bleu*.

Things had altered so little that people still found it quite natural to use the old catchwords "right-minded" and "not right-minded". And yet change of a kind there was, for, just as former partisans of the Commune had at a later date been anti-revisionists, so now the most extreme Dreyfusards of the old days wanted to shoot people right and left, and the generals supported them in this policy just as they had supported Galliffet's opponents at the time of the Case.

M. Bontemps did not want there to be any question of peace until Germany had been broken up into tiny states as it had been in the Middle Ages, the fall of the House of Hohenzollern pronounced, and William stood up against a wall and shot. In a word he was what Brichot called a *jusquauboutiste*, and this was the highest certificate of patriotism that could be conferred upon him. Doubtless for the first three days Mme Bontemps had been a little bewildered in the midst of the people who had asked Mme Verdurin to introduce them to her, and it was in a tone of some slight asperity that Mme Verdurin had replied: "No, my dear, the Comte", when Mme Bontemps said to her "That was the Duc d'Haussonville you introduced to me just now, wasn't it?", either out of total ignorance and failure to associate the name Haussonville with any title whatsoever or, on the contrary, from excess of information and an association of ideas with the "Party of the Dukes", to which she had been told that in the Academy M. d'Haussonville belonged. But by the fourth day she had begun to be firmly installed in the Faubourg Saint-Germain. Sometimes there could still be seen around her the nameless fragments of a world that one did not know, which, in those who knew the egg from which Mme Bontemps had emerged, evoked no more surprise than the débris of shell around a chick. But after a fortnight she had shaken them off, and before the end of the first month, when she said: "I am going to the Lévis'", everybody understood, without her having to explain herself, that it was the Lévis-Mirepoix she meant, and not a duchess would have gone to bed without having enquired of Mme Bontemps or Mme Verdurin, at least by telephone, what there had been in the evening communiqué, what had been deliberately left out, how the Greek situation was developing, what offensive was being prepared, in a word all the news that the public would know only on the following day or later but of which the two ladies staged the equivalent of a dressmaker's private view. In conversation, when she was announcing news, Mme Verdurin would say "we" when she meant France. "Now listen: we demand of the King of Greece that he should withdraw from the Peloponnese, etc.; we send him, etc." And in all her stories there was constant mention of G.H.Q. ("I telephoned to G.H.Q."), an abbreviation which gave her, as it fell from her lips, the pleasure that in former days women who did not know the Prince d'Agrigente had got from asking with a smile, when his name was mentioned, so as to show that they were not out of their depth: "Grigri?", a pleasure which in untroubled times is confined to the fashionable world but in great crises comes within the reach of the lower classes. Our butler, for instance, if the King of Greece was mentioned, was able, thanks to the newspapers, to say like the Emperor William: "Tino?", whereas hitherto his familiarity with kings had been of his own invention and of a more plebeian kind, as when at one time he had been in the habit of referring to the King of Spain as "Fonfonse." Another noticeable change was that, as more and

more smart people made advances to Mme Verdurin, inversely the number of those whom she dubbed "bores" diminished.
By a sort of magical transformation, every bore who had come
to call on her and asked to be invited to her parties immediately
became a charming and intelligent person. In short, at the end
of a year, the number of bores had dwindled to such an extent
that "the fear and awfulness of being bored", which had filled
so large a place in the conversation and played so great a role
in the life of Mme Verdurin, had almost entirely disappeared.
In her latter days, it seemed, this awfulness of being bored
(which anyhow, as she had formerly assured people, she had
not known in her early youth) afflicted her less, just as certain
kinds of migraine, certain nervous asthmatic conditions lose
their force as one grows older. And the terror of being bored
would doubtless, for want of bores, have entirely abandoned
Mme Verdurin had she not, in some slight degree, replaced
the vanishing bores by others recruited from the ranks of the
former faithful.

Be that as it may, to conclude the subject of the duchesses
who now frequented Mme Verdurin's house, they came,
though they did not realise this, in search of exactly the same
thing as the Dreyfusards had sought there in the old days, that
is to say a social pleasure so compounded that their enjoyment
of it at the same time assuaged their political curiosities and
satisfied their need to discuss with others like themselves the
incidents about which they had read in the newspapers. Mme
Verdurin said: "Come at 5 o'clock to talk about the war"
as she would have said in the past: "Come and talk about
the Case", or at an intermediate period: "Come to hear Morel".

Morel, incidentally, ought not to have been there, for the
reason that he had not, as was supposed, been discharged from
the army. He had simply failed to rejoin his regiment and was
a deserter, but nobody knew this.

One of the stars of the drawing-room was Andrée's husband, once known to me as "I am in the soup", who in spite of his sportive tastes had got himself discharged and whom I now thought of mainly as the author of an admirable work which was constantly in my thoughts. To such an extent had he assumed for me this new character that it was only by chance, when from time to time I established a transverse current linking two series of memories, that it crossed my mind that he was also the person who had brought about the departure of Albertine from my house. And even this transverse current ended, as far as these vestigial memories of Albertine were concerned, in a channel which petered out completely at a distance of several years from the present. For I never thought of her now. That was a channel of memories, a route, which I had quite ceased to take. Whereas the works of "I am in the soup" were recent and this route of memory was one perpetually visited and used by my mind.

I ought to say that the acquaintance of Andrée's husband was neither very easy nor very agreeable to make, and that any attempt to make friends with him was destined to numerous disappointments. He was, in fact, at this time already seriously ill and spared himself all fatigues except those which he thought likely to give him pleasure. Now in this category he included only meetings with people whom he did not yet know, whom his ardent imagination represented to him doubtless as being possibly different from others. When it came to people he was already acquainted with, he knew too well what they were like and what they would be like again and they no longer seemed to him worth the trouble of a fatigue that would be dangerous and might even be fatal to him. In short, he was a very poor friend. And perhaps in his taste for new people there was still something to be found of the frenzied daring which he had shown in the old days at Balbec, in sport, in gambling, in excesses of eating and drinking.

Whenever Andrée and I were there together Mme Verdurin tried to introduce me to her, being unable to accept the fact that we were already acquainted. Andrée did not often come with her husband, but she at least was an admirable and sincere friend to me. Faithful to the aesthetic ideas of her husband, who had reacted against the Russian Ballet, she was always saying of the Marquis de Polignac: "He's had his house decorated by Bakst. How can one sleep with all that round one? I would rather have Dubuffe." The Verdurins, too, swept along by the fatal progress of aestheticism which ends by eating its own tail, said now that they could not endure *art nouveau* (besides, it came from Munich) or white rooms; they cared only for old French furniture in a sombre colour-scheme.

I saw a lot of Andrée at this time. We did not know what to say to each other, and once there came into my mind that name, Juliette, which had risen from the depths of Albertine's memory like a mysterious flower. Mysterious then, but now it no longer stirred any feeling in me: many subjects that were indifferent to me I discussed but on this subject I was silent, not that it meant less to me than others, but a sort of supersaturation takes place when one has thought about a thing too much. Perhaps the epoch in my life when I saw so many mysteries in that name was the true one. But as these epochs will not last for ever, it is a mistake for a man to sacrifice his health and his fortune to the elucidation of mysteries which one day will no longer interest him.

Now that Mme Verdurin could get anyone she wanted to come to her house, people were very surprised to see her make indirect advances to someone she had completely lost sight of, Odette, the general opinion being that Odette could add nothing to the brilliant set that the little group had become. But a prolonged separation, which has the effect of appeasing resentments, in some cases also reawakens feelings of friendship. And then too the phenomenon of the dying man who pronounces none but familiar names from the past, or the old man who finds pleasure in his childhood memories, has its social equivalent. To succeed in the project of making Odette return to her, Mme Verdurin employed, naturally, not the "ultras" but the less faithful members of the group who had kept a foot in each of the two drawing-rooms. "I can't think why we no longer see her here," she said to them. "She may have fallen out with me, I haven't with her. After all, what harm have I done her? It was in my house that she met both her husbands. If she wants to come back, let her know that the door is open." These words, which would have involved a sacrifice of pride for the Mistress if they had not been dictated to her by her imagination, were passed on, but without success. Mme Verdurin waited in vain for Odette, until events which will come to our notice later brought about, for entirely different reasons, what the embassy of the "deserters", for all their zeal, had been unable to achieve. So rarely do we meet either with easy success or with irreversible defeat.

To these parties Mme Verdurin used to invite a few ladies of rather recent origin, known for their good works, who at first came magnificently dressed, with great pearl necklaces that Odette, who had a necklace just as beautiful the display of which she had herself formerly overdone, regarded, now that she was "dressed for war" in imitation of the ladies of the Faubourg, with some severity. But women know how to adapt themselves. After three or four appearances they realised that the clothes which they had thought smart were precisely the ones proscribed by people who were smart; they laid aside their gold dresses and resigned themselves to simplicity.

"It is too bad," Mme Verdurin would say. "I must telephone to Bontemps to get things put right for to-morrow, they have *blue-pencilled* the whole of the end of Norpois' article and just because he hinted that Percin had been *bowler-hatted*." For the idiocy of the times caused people to pride themselves on using the expressions of the times; in this way they hoped to show that they were in the fashion, like the middle-class woman who says, when M. de Bréauté or d'Agrigente or de Charlus is mentioned: "You mean Babal de Bréauté?, Grigri? Mémé de Charlus?" As a matter of fact duchesses do this too, and duchesses felt the same pleasure in saying "bowler-hatted", for it is in their names that these ladies—for the commoner with a poetical imagination—are exceptional; in their language and their ideas they conform to the intellectual category to which they belong and to which also belong a vast number of middle-class people. The classes of the intellect take no account of birth.

All this telephoning that Mme Verdurin did was not, however, without its disadvantages. Although we have forgotten to mention the fact, the Verdurin "salon", if it continued to exist in spirit and in all essentials, had been temporarily transferred to one of the largest hotels in Paris, the lack of coal and light making it too difficult for the Verdurins to entertain in the former mansion of the Venetian Ambassadors, which was extremely damp. But the new drawing-room was not altogether disagreeable. Just as, in Venice, the restrictions that water imposes upon a site dictate the shape of a palace, and in Paris a scrap of garden is more ravishing than a whole park in the country, so the narrow dining-room that Mme Verdurin had in the hotel made, with the dazzling white walls of its irregular quadrilateral, a sort of screen upon which figured every Wednesday, indeed almost every day of the week, all the most interesting men of every kind, all the smartest women in Paris, only too delighted to avail themselves of the luxury of the Verdurins, which went on increasing, with their wealth, at a time when other very rich people were economising, because part of their income was frozen. In their altered form the receptions had not ceased to enchant Brichot, who, as the circle of the Verdurins' acquaintance grew wider and wider, found in their parties ever new pleasures, packed tight together in a tiny space like surprises in a Christmas stocking. On some days the guests were so numerous that the dining-room of the private suite was too small and the dinner was given in the huge dining-room downstairs, where the faithful, if they feigned a hypocritical regret for the intimacy of up-stairs, were at heart delighted—while keeping themselves to themselves, as in the old days on the little train—to be a spectacle and an object of envy for neighbouring tables. Doubtless, under normal peace-time conditions, a "society" note surreptitiously sent to *Le Figaro* or *Le Gaulois* would have informed a larger public than could be contained in the dining-room of the Majestic that Brichot had dined with the Duchesse de Duras. But since the war, the social reporters having suppressed this type of news (they made up for it, however, in funerals, "mentions in despatches" and Franco-American banquets), publicity could only be attained through a more embryonic, a more restricted medium, worthy of primitive ages and anterior to the discovery of Gutenberg: one had actually to be seen at Mme Verdurin's table. After dinner the guests went upstairs to the Mistress's reception rooms, and then the telephoning began. But many large hotels were at this period peopled with spies, who duly noted the news announced over the telephone by Bontemps with an indiscretion which might have had serious consequences but for a fortunate lack of accuracy in his reports, which invariably were contradicted by events.

Before the hour at which the afternoon tea-parties came to an end, at the close of the day, in the still light sky one saw, far off, little brown dots which one might have taken, in the blue evening, for midges or birds. In the same way, when one sees a mountain at a great distance one can imagine it to be a cloud. But because one knows that this "cloud" is huge, solid and resistant one's emotions are stirred. And I too was moved by the thought that the brown dot in the summer sky was neither midge nor bird but an aeroplane with a crew of men keeping guard over Paris. (The memory of the aeroplanes which I had seen with Albertine on our last drive, near Versailles, played no part in this emotion, for the memory of that drive had become indifferent to me.)

When the time came for dinner, the restaurants were full; and if, passing in the street, I saw a wretched soldier on leave, escaped for six days from the constant danger of death and about to return to the trenches, halt his gaze for a moment upon the illuminated windows, I suffered as I had in the hotel at Balbec when fishermen used to watch us at dinner, but I suffered more now because I knew that the misery of the soldier is greater than that of the poor, since it combines in itself all miseries, and more touching still because more resigned, more noble, and because it was with a philosophical shake of the head, without hatred, that on the eve of setting out again for the war the soldier would say to himself, as he saw the shirkers jostling one another in their efforts to secure a table: "You'ld never know there was a war on here." Then at half past nine, before anyone had had time to finish dinner, the lights were all suddenly turned out because of the police regulations, so that at nine thirty-five the second jostling of shirkers snatching their overcoats from the page-boys of the restaurant where I had dined with Saint-Loup one evening when he was on leave took place in a mysterious half-darkness which might have been that of a room in which slides are being shown on a magic lantern, or of the auditorium, during the exhibition of a film, of one of those cinemas towards which the men and women who had been dining would presently rush.

But at any later hour for those who, like myself on the evening which I am going to describe, had had dinner at home and were going out to see friends, Paris, at least in certain quarters, was even blacker than had been the Combray of my childhood; the visits that people paid one another were like the visits of country neighbours. Ah! if Albertine had been alive, how delightful it would have been, on the evenings when I had dined out, to arrange to meet her out of doors, under the arcades! At first I should have seen nothing, I should have had the pang of thinking that she had failed to turn up, when suddenly I should have seen one of her dear grey dresses emerge from the black wall, then her smiling eyes which had already seen me, and we could have walked along with our arms round each other without any fear of being recognised or disturbed, and then at length gone home. But alas, I was alone and I felt as if I was setting out to pay a neighbourly visit in the country, like those that Swann used to pay us after dinner, without meeting more people on his way through the darkness of Tansonville, along the little tow-path and as far as the Rue du Saint-Esprit, than I now met in the streets, transformed into winding rustic lanes, between Sainte Clotilde and the Rue Bonaparte. Or again—since the effect of those fragments of landscape which travel in obedience to the moods of the weather was no longer nullified by surroundings which had become invisible—on evenings when the wind was chasing an icy shower of rain I had, now, much more strongly the impression of being on the shore of that raging sea of which I had once so longingly dreamed than I had had when I was actually at Balbec; and other natural features also, which had not existed in Paris hitherto, helped to create the illusion that one had just got out of the train and arrived to spend a holiday in the depth of the country: for example the contrast of light and shadow on the ground that one had all round one on evenings when the moon was shining. There were effects of moonlight normally unknown in towns, sometimes in the middle of winter even, when the rays of the moon lay out-poured upon the snow on Boulevard Haussmann, untouched now by the broom of any sweeper, as they would have lain upon a glacier in the Alps. Against this snow of bluish gold the silhouettes of the trees were outlined clear and pure, with the delicacy that they have in certain Japanese paintings or in certain backgrounds of Raphael; and on the ground at the foot of the tree itself there was stretched out its shadow as often one sees trees' shadows in the country at sunset, when the light inundates and polishes to the smoothness of a mirror some meadow in which they are planted at regular intervals. But by a refinement of exquisite delicacy the meadow upon which were displayed these shadows of trees, light as souls, was a meadow of paradise, not green but of a whiteness so dazzling because of the moonlight shining upon the jade-like snow that it might have been a meadow woven entirely from petals of flowering pear-trees. And in the squares the divinities of the public fountains, holding a jet of ice in their hand, looked like statues wrought in two different materials by a sculptor who had decided to marry pure bronze to pure crystal. On these exceptional days all the houses were black. But in the spring, on the contrary, here and there, defying the regulations of the police, a private house, or simply one floor of a house, or even simply one room of one floor, had failed to close its shutters and appeared, mysteriously supported by dark impalpable shadows, to be no more than a projection of light, an apparition without substance. And the woman whom, if one raised one's eyes high above the street, one could distinguish in this golden penumbra, assumed, in this night in which one was oneself lost and in which she too seemed to be hidden away, the mysterious and veiled charm of an oriental vision. Then one passed on and nothing more interrupted the rustic tramp, wholesome and monotonous, of one's feet through the darkness.

I reflected that it was a long time since I had seen any of the personages who have been mentioned in this work. In 1914, it was true, during the two months that I had spent in Paris, I had caught a glimpse of M. de Charlus and seen something of Bloch and Saint-Loup, the latter only twice. The second occasion was certainly that on which he had been most himself; he had quite effaced that disagreeable impression of insincerity which he had made on me during the stay at Tansonville that I have described, and I had once more recognised in him all the fine qualities of his earlier days. On the earlier occasion, which was less than a week after the declaration of war, while Bloch made a display of the most chauvinistic sentiments, Saint-Loup, once Bloch had left us, was unashamedly cynical about the fact that he himself had not joined his regiment, and I had been almost shocked at the violence of his tone. (Saint-Loup had just come back from Balbec. I learnt later, indirectly, that he had made unsuccessful advances to the manager of the restaurant. The latter owed his position to the money he had inherited from M. Nissim Bernard. He was, in fact, none other than the young waiter whom in the past Bloch's uncle had "protected".

But wealth in his case had brought with it virtue and it was in vain that Saint-Loup had attempted to seduce him. Thus, by a process of compensation, while virtuous young men abandon themselves in their later years to the passions of which they have at length become conscious, promiscuous youths turn into men of principle from whom any Charlus who turns up too late on the strength of old stories will get an unpleasant rebuff. It is all a question of chronology.) "No," he exclaimed, gaily and with force, "if a man doesn't fight, whatever reason he may give, it is because he doesn't want to be killed, because he is *afraid*." And with the same affirming gesture, even more energetic than that which he had used to underline the fear of others, he added: "And that goes for me too. If I haven't rejoined my regiment, it is quite simply from *fear*—so there!" I had already observed in more than one person that the affectation of praiseworthy sentiments is not the only method of covering up bad ones; another, less obvious method is to make a display of these bad sentiments, so that at least one does not appear to be unaware of them. Moreover, in Saint-Loup this tendency was strengthened by his habit, when he had committed an indiscretion or made a blunder for which he expected to be blamed, of proclaiming it aloud and saying that it had been done on purpose. A habit which, I believe, must have come to him from some instructor at the Ecole de Guerre whom he had known well and greatly admired. I had, therefore, no hesitation in interpreting this outburst as the verbal confirmation of a sentiment which, since it had dictated the conduct of Saint-Loup and his non-participation in the war now beginning, he preferred to proclaim aloud. "Have you heard the rumour," he asked, as he left me, "that my aunt Oriane is going to get a divorce? Personally I know nothing about it whatsoever. There have been rumours of the kind from time to time, and I have so often heard that it's imminent that I shall wait until it happens before I believe it. I must admit, it would be very understandable. My uncle is a charming man, not only socially but as a friend and in the family. He even, in a way, has much more heart than my aunt, who is a saint but makes him terribly aware of it. Only he is a dreadful husband, who has never ceased to be unfaithful to his wife, to insult her, to bully her, to keep her short of money. It would be so natural for her to leave him that that is a reason for the story to be true, but also a reason why it may not be true—the idea occurs to people and inevitably they talk about it. And then she has put up with him for so long! Of course I know quite well that there are lots of things which are reported falsely, and then denied, but later do become true." This put it into my head to ask him whether there had ever been any question of his marrying Mlle de Guermantes. He seemed amazed and assured me that there had not, that it was merely one of those rumours of the fashionable world which arise from time to time one does not know why and vanish in the same way, without their falsity causing those who believed them to be any more cautious when a new rumour arises, of an engagement or a divorce, or a political rumour, in giving credence to it and spreading it.

Forty-eight hours had not elapsed before certain facts which I learnt proved to me that I had been absolutely wrong in my interpretation of Robert's words: "If a man is not at the front, it is because he is afraid." Saint-Loup had said this in order to shine in conversation, to appear in the role of an original psychologist, so long as he was not sure that his own enlistment would be accepted. But meanwhile he was moving heaven and earth to bring this about and showing himself in this less "original", in the meaning that he thought it necessary to give to the word, but more profoundly a Frenchman of Saint-André-des-Champs, more in conformity with all that at this moment was best in the Frenchmen of Saint-André-des-Champs, lords, citizens and serfs—feudally respectful serfs and serfs in revolt, those two divisions, both equally French, of the same family, the Françoise branch and the Morel branch, from which two arrows were now converging upon a common target, the frontier. Bloch had been enchanted to hear a confession of cowardice from a nationalist (who was, as a matter of fact, so little of a nationalist) and when Saint-Loup had asked him whether he himself would soon be off, had assumed a high-priestly air and replied: "Myopic." But Bloch had completely changed his mind about the war a few days later, when he came to see me in a state of frenzy. Although "myopic", he had been passed fit for service. I was accompanying him home when we met Saint-Loup, who was on his way to an interview at the Ministry of War with a colonel to whom he was to be introduced by a retired officer—"M. de Cambremer", he said to me, and added: "Oh! but of course, he is an old acquaintance of yours. You know Cancan as well as I do." I replied that I did indeed know him and his wife too, and that I didn't have a particularly high opinion of them. But I was so much in the habit, ever since I had first met them, of considering the wife as in her way a remarkable woman, who knew her Schopenhauer and at least had access to an intellectual sphere which was closed to her boorish husband, that I was at first astonished to hear Saint-Loup reply: "His wife is idiotic, I won't try to defend her. But *he* is an excellent man—he was talented once and is still a very pleasant person." By the "idiocy" of the wife, Saint-Loup meant no doubt her desperate desire to move in grand society, which is the thing that grand society judges most severely; by the good qualities of the husband, he meant perhaps something of the qualities that were recognised in him by his niece when she declared that he was the best of the family. He, at least, did not worry about duchesses, though this it must be admitted is a form of "intelligence" which differs as much from the intelligence that characterises thinkers as the "intelligence" admired by the public in this or that rich man who has "been clever enough to make a fortune". However Saint-Loup's words did not displease me, because they reminded me that pretentiousness is near akin to stupidity and that simplicity has a flavour which though it lies beneath the surface is agreeable. I had, it is true, had no opportunity to savour that of M. de Cambremer. But this was merely an instance of the law that a person is many different persons according to who is judging him, quite apart from the different standards by which different people judge. In the case of M. de Cambremer, I had known only the rind. His flavour, therefore, though avouched to me by others, was to me personally unknown.

Bloch left us outside his house, overflowing with bitterness against Saint-Loup and saying to his face that men of his sort, privileged dandies who strutted about at headquarters, ran no risks and that he, as a plain private soldier, had no wish to "get a hole in his skin just because of William". "It seems that the Emperor William is seriously ill," replied Saint-Loup. Bloch, like everybody connected with the Stock Exchange, was more than usually credulous of sensational reports. "Yes," he said, "there is even a strong rumour that he is dead." In Stock Exchange circles every monarch who is ill, whether it be Edward VII or William II, is dead, every town which is about to be besieged has already been captured. "It is only being kept secret", added Bloch, "in order not to damage the morale of the Boches. But he died the night before last. My father has it from an absolutely first-class source." Absolutely first-class sources were the only ones to which M. Bloch senior paid any attention, and it was always with such a source that thanks to his "important connections" he was fortunate enough to be in touch, when he heard before anyone else that Foreign Bonds were going to go up or that De Beers were going to fall. However, if just at that moment De Beers had a rise or Foreign Bonds "came on offer", if the market in the former was "firm and active" and that in the latter "hesitant and weak, with a note of caution", the first-class source did not, for that reason, cease to be a first-class source. So Bloch informed us of the death of the Kaiser with an air of mystery and importance, but also of fury. He was exasperated beyond measure at hearing Robert say: "the Emperor William". I believe that under the blade of the guillotine Saint-Loup and M. de Guermantes could have said nothing else. Two men from "society", surviving alone on a desert island where they would have nobody to impress by a display of good manners, would recognise each other by these little signs of breeding, just as two Latinists in the same circumstances would continue to quote Virgil correctly. Saint-Loup, even under torture at the hands of the Germans, could never have used any other expression than "the Emperor William". And this good breeding, whatever else one may think of it, is a symptom of formidable mental shackles. The man who cannot throw them off can never be more than a man of the world. However, his elegant mediocrity—particularly when it is allied, as is often the case, with hidden generosity and unexpressed heroism—is a delightful quality in comparison with the vulgarity of Bloch, at once coward and braggart, who started now to scream at Saint-Loup: "Can't you simply say William? The trouble is you've got the wind up. Even in Paris you crawl on your belly before him! Pooh! we're going to have some fine soldiers at the frontier, they'll lick the boots of the Boches. You and your friends in fancy uniforms, you're fit to parade in a tournament and that's about all."

"Poor Bloch is absolutely determined that I am to do nothing but strut about on parade," said Saint-Loup to me with a smile, when we had left our friend. And I sensed that this was not at all what Robert wished to do, although at the time I did not realise what his intentions were as clearly as I did later when, as the cavalry remained inactive, he got leave to serve as an officer in the infantry and then in the light infantry, or when, later still, there came the sequel which the reader will learn in due course. But Robert's patriotism was something that Bloch was unaware of simply because Robert chose not to display it. If Bloch had treated us to a viciously anti-militarist profession of faith once he had been passed as "fit", he had previously made the most chauvinistic statements when he thought that he would be discharged on the grounds of short sight. But Saint-Loup would have been incapable of making these statements; in the first place from that sort of moral delicacy which prevents people from expressing sentiments that lie too deep within them and that seem to them quite natural. My mother, in the past, would not only not have hesitated for a second to die for my grandmother, but would have suffered horribly if anyone had prevented her from doing so. Nevertheless, I cannot retrospectively imagine on her lips any such phrase as "I would give my life for my mother." And the same reticence, in his love of France, was displayed by Robert, who at this moment seemed to me much more Saint-Loup (in so far as I could form a picture of his father) than Guermantes. And then Robert would also have been saved from expressing the chauvinistic sentiments of Bloch by the fact that his intelligence was in itself to some extent a moral quality. Among intelligent and genuinely serious workers there is a certain aversion for those who make literature out of the subject they are engaged on, those who use it for self-display. Robert and I had not been at the Lycée

or at the Sorbonne together, but we had attended, independently, certain courses of lectures by the same teachers,
and I remember the smile he had for the ones who—as
happens sometimes when a man is giving a remarkable series
of lectures—tried to pass themselves off as geniuses by giving
their theories an ambitious name. We only had to mention
them for Robert to burst out laughing. Our personal and
instinctive preference was, naturally, not for the Cottards or
the Brichots, but we had nevertheless a certain respect for
any man with a really thorough knowledge of Greek or
medicine who did not for that reason think himself entitled
to behave as a charlatan. I have said that, if in the past all
Mama's actions had as their basis the sentiment that she would
have given her life for her mother, she had yet never formu-
lated this sentiment to herself, and that in any case it would
have seemed to her not merely unnecessary and ridiculous but
shocking and shameful to express it to others; in the same way
it was impossible for me to imagine on the lips of Saint-Loup—
talking to me about his equipment, the things he had to do in
Paris, our chances of victory, the weakness of the Russian
army, how England would act—it is impossible for me to imagine on his lips even the most eloquent phrase that even the
most deservedly popular minister might have addressed to a
wildly cheering Chamber of Deputies. I cannot, however, say
that in this negativeness which checked him from expressing
the noble sentiments that he felt he was not to some extent
influenced by the "Guermantes spirit", of which we have seen
so many similar instances in Swann. For, if I found him more
Saint-Loup than anything else, he was, nevertheless, also Guermantes, and consequently, among the numerous motives which
animated his courage, there were some which did not exist
for his friends of Doncières, those young men enamoured
of their profession with whom I had dined night after

night and of whom so many went to their death at the battle of the Marne or elsewhere, leading their men into action.

As for the young socialists who were at Doncières when I was there but whom I did not get to know because they did not belong to the same set as Saint-Loup, they could see now for themselves that the officers of that set were by no means "nobs", with the implications of haughty pride and base self-indulgence which the "plebs", the ex-ranker officers, the free-masons attached to that word. And conversely, this same patriotism was found by the officers of aristocratic birth to exist in full measure among the socialists whom I had heard them accuse, while I was at Doncières at the height of the Dreyfus case, of being "men without a country". The patriotism of the military caste, as sincere and profound as any other, had assumed a fixed form which the members of that caste regarded as sacrosanct and which they were infuriated to see sullied by "disgrace", but the radical-socialists, who were independent and to some extent unconscious patriots without any fixed patriotic religion, had failed to perceive the profound and living reality that lay behind what they thought were empty and malignant formulas.

No doubt, like his friends, Saint-Loup had formed the habit of inwardly cultivating, as the truest part of himself, the search for and the elaboration of the best possible manœuvres which would lead to the greatest strategic and tactical successes, so that, for him as for them, the life of the body was something relatively unimportant which could easily be sacrificed to this inner part of the self, the real vital core within them, around which their personal existence was of value only as a protective outer skin. But in Saint-Loup's courage there were also more individual elements, and amongst these it would have been easy to recognise the generosity which in its early days had

constituted the charm of our friendship, and also the hereditary vice which had later awoken from dormancy in him
and which, at the particular intellectual level which he had not
been able to transcend, caused him not only to admire courage
but to exaggerate his horror of effeminacy into a sort of intoxication at any contact with virility. He derived, chastely no
doubt, from spending days and nights in the open with
Senegalese soldiers who might at any moment be called upon
to sacrifice their lives, a cerebral gratification of desire into
which there entered a vigorous contempt for "little scented
gentlemen" and which, however contrary it might seem, was
not so very different from that which he had obtained from the
cocaine in which he had indulged excessively at Tansonville
and of which heroism—one drug taking the place of another
—was now curing him. And another essential part of his courage was that double habit of courtesy which, on the one hand,
caused him to bestow praise on others but where he himself
was concerned made him content to do what had to be done
and say nothing about it—the opposite of a Bloch, who had
said to him just now "You—of course you'd funk" and yet
was doing nothing himself—and on the other hand impelled
him to hold as of no value the things that he himself possessed,
his fortune, his rank, and even his life, so that he was ready to
give them away: in a word, the true nobility of his nature.

"Are we in for a long war?" I said to Saint-Loup. "No, I
believe it will be very short," he replied. But here, as always,
his arguments were bookish. "Bearing in mind the prophecies
of Moltke, re-read," he said to me, as if I had already read
it, "the decree of the 28th October, 1913, about the command
of large formations; you will see that the replacement of peace-
time reserves has not been organised or even foreseen, a thing
which the authorities could not have failed to do if the war
were likely to be a long one." It seemed to me that the decree

in question could be interpreted not as a proof that the war would be short, but as a failure on the part of its authors to foresee that it would be long, and what kind of war it would be, the truth being that they suspected neither the appalling wastage of material of every kind that would take place in a war of stable fronts nor the interdependence of different theatres of operations.

Outside the limits of homosexuality, among the men who are most opposed by nature to homosexuality, there exists a certain conventional idea of virility, which the homosexual finding at his disposal proceeds, unless he is a man of unusual intelligence, to distort. This ideal—to be seen in certain professional soldiers, certain diplomats—can be singularly exasperating. In its crudest form it is simply the gruffness of the man with the heart of gold who is determined not to show his emotions, the man who at the moment of parting from a friend who may very possibly be killed has a secret desire to weep, which no one suspects because he conceals it beneath a mounting anger which culminates, at the actual moment of farewell, in a sort of explosion: "Well, now, damn it! Shake hands with me, you old ruffian, and take this purse, it's no use to me, don't be an idiot." The diplomat, the officer, the man who believes that nothing counts except a great task in the service of the nation but who was fond nevertheless of the "poor boy" in his legation or his battalion who has died from a fever or a bullet exhibits the same taste for virility in a form that is less clumsy, and more sophisticated, but at bottom just as odious. He does not want to mourn for the "poor boy", he knows that soon he and everybody else will forget him, just as a kind-hearted surgeon soon forgets though for a whole evening after some little girl has died in an epidemic he feels a grief which he does not express. Should the diplomat be a writer and describe this death, he will not say that he felt grief. No—

first from "masculine decency," secondly from that skilled artistry which arouses emotion by dissembling it. With one of his colleagues he will watch by the side of the dying man. Not for one second will they say that they feel grief. They will talk of the affairs of the legation or the battalion and their remarks may be even more terse than usual:

"B. said to me: 'Don't forget we have the general's inspection tomorrow. See to it that your men are well turned out.' Habitually so gentle, he spoke in a sharper tone than usual. I noticed that he avoided looking at me, I too felt myself to be overwrought." And the reader understands that this "sharp tone" is simply grief showing itself in men who do not want to appear to feel grief, an attitude which might be ridiculous and nothing more but is in fact also sinister and ugly, because it is the manner of feeling grief of those who think that grief does not matter, that there are more serious things in life than being parted from one's friends, etc., so that when someone dies they give the same impression of falsehood, of nothingness, as on New Year's Day the gentleman who hands you a present of *marrons glacés* and just manages to say with a titter: "I wish you a very happy New Year."

To conclude the narrative of the officer or the diplomat watching at the deathbed, his head covered because the wounded or sick man has been carried out of doors, the moment comes when all is over. " 'I must go back and get my kit cleaned,' I thought. But I do not know why, at the moment when the doctor let go the pulse, simultaneously B. and I, without any sign passing between us—the sun was beating vertically down, perhaps we were hot standing beside the bed—removed our caps." And the reader knows that it was not because of the heat of the sun but from emotion in the presence of the majesty of death that the two virile men, on whose lips the words grief and affection were almost unknown, now bared their heads.

In homosexuals like Saint-Loup the ideal of virility is not the same, but it is just as conventional and just as false. The falsehood consists for them in the fact that they do not want to admit to themselves that physical desire lies at the root of the sentiments to which they ascribe another origin. M. de Charlus had detested effeminacy. Saint-Loup admired the courage of young men, the intoxication of cavalry charges, the intellectual and moral nobility of friendships between man and man, entirely pure friendships, in which each is prepared to sacrifice his life for the other. War, which turns capital cities, where only women remain, into an abomination for homosexuals, is at the same time a story of passionate adventure for homosexuals if they are intelligent enough to concoct dream figures, and not intelligent enough to see through them, to recognise their origin, to pass judgment on themselves. So that while some young men were enlisting simply in order to join in the latest sport—in the spirit in which one year everybody plays diabolo—for Saint-Loup, on the other hand, war was the very ideal which he imagined himself to be pursuing in his desires (which were in fact much more concrete but were clouded by ideology), an ideal which he could serve in common with those whom he preferred to all others, in a purely masculine order of chivalry, far from women, where he would be able to risk his life to save his orderly and die inspiring a fanatical love in his men. And thus, though there were many elements in his courage, the fact that he was a great nobleman was one of them, and another, in an unrecognisable and idealised form, was M. de Charlus's dogma that it was of the essence of a man to have nothing effeminate about him. But just as in philosophy and in art ideas acquire their value only from the manner in which they are developed, and two analogous ones may differ greatly according to whether they have been expounded by Xenophon or by Plato, so, while I recognise how much, in his behaviour, the one has in common with the other, I admire Saint-Loup, for asking to be sent |to the point of greatest danger, infinitely more than I do M. de Charlus for refusing to wear brightly coloured cravats.

I spoke to Saint-Loup about my friend the manager of the Grand Hotel at Balbec, who, it seems, had alleged that at the beginning of the war there had been in certain French regiments defections, which he called "defectuosities", and had accused what he called the "Prussian militariat" of having provoked the war; he had even, at one moment, believed in a simultaneous landing by the Japanese, the Germans and the Cossacks at Rivebelle as a threat to Balbec, and had said that the only thing to do was to "decramp". He also thought that the departure of the government and the ministries for Bordeaux was a little precipitous and declared that they were wrong to "decramp" so soon. This German-hater would say with a laugh of his brother: "He is in the trenches, twenty-five yards away from the Boches," until the authorities, having discovered that he was a "Boche" himself, put him in a concentration camp. "Talking of Balbec, do you remember the lift-boy who used to be in the hotel?" said Saint-Loup as he left me, in a tone suggesting that he did not quite know who the lift-boy was and was counting on me for enlightenment. "He is joining up and has written to ask me to get him into the flying corps." No doubt the young man was tired of going up in the captive cage of the lift, and the heights of the staircase of the Grand Hotel no longer sufficed him. He was going to "get his stripes" otherwise than by becoming a hall-porter, for our destiny is not always what we had supposed. "I shall certainly support his application," said Saint-Loup. "I was saying to Gilberte only this morning, we shall never have enough

66

aeroplanes. It is aeroplanes that will enable us to see what the enemy is preparing, and aeroplanes that will rob him of the greatest advantage of attack, which is surprise. The best army will be, perhaps, the army with the best eyes. And tell me about poor Françoise, has she succeeded in getting her nephew discharged?" But Françoise, who for a long time had been making every effort to achieve this, and who, when she had been offered through the Guermantes a recommendation to Général de Saint-Joseph, had replied in a tone of despair: "Oh no, that would be quite useless, there's nothing to be got from that old fogy, he's as bad as could be, he's patriotic," Françoise, as soon as there had been any question of war, however much she suffered at the thought of it, was of the opinion that it would be wrong to abandon the "poor Russians" since we were "allianced" to them. The butler, who in any case was convinced that the war would only last ten days and would end in a brilliant victory for France, would not have dared, for fear of being contradicted by events—and would not even have had enough imagination—to predict a long and indecisive war. But from this complete and immediate victory he tried at least to extract in advance the maximum of suffering for Françoise. "Things may well take an ugly turn, because it seems there are lots who refuse to march, boys of sixteen in floods of tears." And this trick of telling her disagreeable things in order to "vex" her was what he called "throwing the pip, chucking an apostrophe, aiming a pun at her". "Sixteen, Holy Mother!" said Françoise, and then suspicious for a moment: "But they said they only took them at twenty, at sixteen they're still children." "Naturally the papers have been told to say nothing about it. Anyhow, the young men, one and all, will be off to the front and there won't be many to come back. In one way it'll do some good. A good blood-letting, you know, is useful now and again. And then it will help trade. And I promise you, if there are any lads who are a bit soft and think twice about it, they'll be for the firing-squad, bang, bang, bang! I suppose it has to be done. And then, the officers, what does it matter to them? They get paid their screw, that's all they ask." Françoise turned so pale whenever one of these conversations took place that we were afraid the butler might cause her death from a heart attack.

But this did not mean that she had lost her old faults. Whenever I had a visit from a girl, however much the old servant's legs might be hurting her, if I happened to leave my room for a moment there she was at the top of a ladder in the dressing-room, searching, so she said, for some overcoat of mine to see if the moths had got into it, but really in order to eavesdrop. And she still, in spite of all my complaints, had her insidious manner of asking questions in an indirect way, the phrase she now used for this purpose being "because of course". Not daring to say to me: "Has this lady her own house?" she would say, her eyes timidly raised like the eyes of a good dog: "Because of course this lady has her own house . . .", avoiding a blatant interrogative not so much in order to be polite as in order not to seem too curious. Then again, as the servants whom we love most—and this is particularly true when they have almost ceased to give us either the service or the respect proper to their employment—remain, unfortunately, servants and only make more clear the limitations of their caste, which we ourselves would like to do away with, when they imagine that they are penetrating most successfully into ours, Françoise often addressed me ("to get under my skin", as the butler would have said) with odd remarks which someone of my own class could not have made: for instance, with a joy carefully dissembled but as profound as if she had detected a serious illness, she would say to me if I was hot and there were beads of sweat which I had not noticed on my forehead: "But you're

absolutely dripping," looking astonished as though this were
some strange phenomenon and at the same time with that little
smile of contempt with which we greet an impropriety ("Are
you going out? You know you've forgotten to put your tie
on") and also with the anxious voice which we assume when
we want to alarm someone about the state of his health. One
would have thought that no one in the world had ever been
"dripping" before. Finally, she no longer spoke good French
as she had in the past. For in her humility, in her affectionate
admiration for people infinitely inferior to herself, she had
come to adopt their ugly habits of speech. Her daughter having
complained to me about her and having used the words (I do
not know where she had heard them): "She's always finding
fault with me because I don't shut the doors properly and
patati patali and *patata patala*," Françoise clearly thought
that only her imperfect education had deprived her until now
of this beautiful idiom. And from those lips which I had once
seen bloom with the purest French I heard several times a day:
"And *patati patali* and *patata patala*." It is indeed curious
how little not only the expressions but also the ideas of an individual vary. The butler, having got into the habit of declaring
that M. Poincaré was a wicked man, not because he was after
money but because he had been absolutely determined to have
a war, repeated this seven or eight times a day to an audience
which was always the same and always just as interested. Not
a word was altered, not a gesture or an intonation. The performance only lasted two minutes, but it was unvarying, like
that of an actor. And his faulty French was quite as much to
blame as that of her daughter for corrupting the language of
Françoise. He thought that what M. de Rambuteau had been
so annoyed one day to hear the Duc de Guermantes call
"Rambuteau shelters" were called "rinals". No doubt in his
childhood he had failed to hear the "u" and had never realised

his mistake, so every time he used the word—and he used it frequently—he mispronounced it. Françoise, embarrassed at first, ended by using it too, and liked to complain that the same sort of thing did not exist for women as well as for men. But as a result of her humility and her admiration for the butler she never said "urinals" but—with a slight concession to common usage—"arinals".

She no longer slept, no longer ate. Every day she insisted on the bulletins, of which she understood nothing, being read to her by the butler who understood hardly more of them than she did, and in whom the desire to torment François was frequently dominated by a patriotic cheerfulness: he would say, with a sympathetic laugh, referring to the Germans: "Things are hotting up for them, it won't be long before old Joffre puts salt on the tail of the comet." Françoise had no idea what comet he was alluding to, but this strengthened her conviction that the phrase was one of those amiable and original extravagances to which a well-bred person is required by the laws of courtesy to respond good-humouredly, so gaily shrugging her shoulders as if to say: "He's always the same", she tempered her tears with a smile. At least she was happy that her new butcher's boy, who in spite of his trade was anything but courageous (his first job nevertheless had been in the slaughter-houses), was not old enough to be called up. Otherwise she would have been quite capable of going to see the Minister of War to get him exempted.

The butler had not enough imagination to realise that the bulletins were not excellent and that we were not advancing towards Berlin, since he kept reading: "We have repulsed with heavy enemy losses, etc.," actions which he celebrated as a succession of victories. I, however, was alarmed at the speed with which the scene of these victories was approaching Paris, and was astonished that even the butler, having seen in one bulletin that an engagement had taken place near Lens, was not disturbed to read in the newspaper next day that it had been followed by satisfactory operations in the neighbour-hood of Jouy-le-Vicomte, of which the approaches were firmly in our hands. Now the butler knew Jouy-le-Vicomte well by name, for it was not so very far from Combray. But we read the newspapers as we love, blindfold. We do not try to understand the facts. We listen to the soothing words of the editor as we listen to the words of our mistress. We are "beaten and happy" because we believe that we are not beaten but victorious.

I had, in any case, not remained long in Paris but had returned very soon to my sanatorium. Although in principle the doctor's treatment consisted in isolation, I had been allowed to receive, at different times, a letter from Gilberte and a letter from Robert. Gilberte wrote (this was in about September 1914) that, however much she would have liked to stay in Paris in order to get news of Robert more easily, the constant Taube raids on the city had caused her such alarm, particularly for her little girl, that she had fled by the last train to leave for Combray, that the train had not even got as far as Combray, and that it was only thanks to a peasant's cart, on which she had had an appalling journey of ten hours, that she had succeeded in reaching Tansonville! "And there, imagine what awaited your old friend," she concluded her letter. "I had left Paris to escape from the German aeroplanes, supposing that at Tansonville I should be perfectly safe. Before I had been there two days you will never imagine what turned up: the Germans, who having defeated our troops near La Fère were overrunning the district. A German head-quarters staff, with a regiment just behind it, presented itself at the gates of Tansonville and I was obliged to take them in, and not a hope of getting away, no more trains, nothing."

Whether the German staff had really behaved well, or whether it was right to detect in Gilberte's letter the influence, by contagion, of the spirit of those Guermantes who were of Bavarian stock and related to the highest aristocracy of Germany, she was lavish in her praise of the perfect breeding of the staff-officers, and even of the soldiers who had only asked her for "permission to pick a few of the forget-me-nots growing near the pond", a good breeding which she contrasted with the disorderly violence of the fleeing French troops, who had pillaged everything as they crossed the property before the arrival of the German generals. In any case, if Gilberte's letter was in some ways impregnated with the spirit of the Guermantes—others would say the spirit of Jewish internationalism, which would probably have been unfair to her, as we shall see—the letter which I received several months later from Robert was, on the other hand, much more Saint-Loup than Guermantes and reflected in addition all the liberal culture which he had acquired. Altogether, it was a delightful letter. Unfortunately, he did not talk about strategy as he had in our conversations at Doncières, nor did he tell me to what extent he considered that the war confirmed or invalidated the principles which he had then expounded to me. All he said was that since 1914 there had in reality been a series of wars, the lessons of each one influencing the conduct of the one that followed. For example, the theory of the "break-through" had been supplemented by a new idea: that it was necessary, before breaking through, for the ground held by the enemy to be completely devastated by the artillery. But then it had been found that on the contrary this devastation made it impossible for the infantry and the artillery to advance over ground in which thousands of shell-holes created as many obstacles. "War," he wrote, "does not escape the laws of our old friend Hegel. It is in a state of perpetual becoming." This was meagre in comparison with what I should have liked to know. But what was still more annoying was that he was forbidden to mention the names of generals. And anyhow, according to the little that the newspapers told me, the generals as to whom at Doncières I had been so eager to know which among them would prove most effective and courageous in a war, were not the ones who were now in command. Geslin de Bourgogne, Galliffet, Négrier were dead. Pau had retired from active service almost at the beginning of the war. Of Joffre, of Foch, of Castelnau, of Pétain, Robert and I had never spoken. "My dear boy," he wrote, "I recognise that expressions like *passeront pas* and *on les aura* are not agreeable; they have always set my teeth on edge as much as *poilu* and the rest, and of course it is tiresome to be composing an epic with words and phrases which are—worse than an error of grammar or of taste—an appalling contradiction in terms, a vulgar affectation and pretension of the kind that you and I abominate, as bad as when people think it clever to say 'coco' instead of 'cocaine'. But if you could see everybody here, particularly the men of the humbler classes, working men and small shopkeepers, who did not suspect what heroism they concealed within them and might have died in their beds without suspecting it—if you could see them running under fire to help a comrade or carry off a wounded officer and then, when they have been hit themselves, smiling a few moments before they die because the medical officer has told them that the trench has been recaptured from the Germans, I assure you, my dear boy, it gives you a magnificent idea of the French people, makes you begin to understand those great periods in history which seemed to us a little extraordinary when we learned about them as students. The epic is so magnificent that you would find, as I do, that words no longer matter. Cannot Rodin or Maillol create a masterpiece from

73

some hideous raw material which he transforms out of all recognition? At the touch of such greatness, the word *poilu* has for me become something of which I no more feel that it may originally have contained an allusion or a joke than one does, for instance, when one reads about the *chouans*. But I do know that *poilu* is already waiting for great poets, like other words, 'deluge', or 'Christ', or 'barbarians', which were already instinct with greatness before Hugo, Vigny and the rest made use of them. As I say, the people, the working men, are the best of all, but everybody is splendid. Poor young Vaugoubert, the ambassador's son, was wounded seven times before he was killed, and each time he came back from a raid without having 'copped it' he seemed to want to apologise and to say that it was not his fault. He was a charming creature. We had become close friends. His parents were given permission to come to the funeral, on condition that they did not wear mourning and only stayed five minutes because of the shelling. The mother, a great horse of a woman whom I dare say you know, was no doubt deeply moved but showed no sign of it. But the poor father was in such a state that I assure you that I, who am now totally unfeeling because I have got used to seeing the head of the comrade who is talking to me suddenly ripped open by a mine or even severed from its trunk, I could not contain myself when I saw the collapse of poor Vaugoubert, who was an utter wreck. The general tried to tell him that it was for France, that his son had behaved like a hero, but it was no use, this only redoubled the sobs of the poor man, who could not tear himself away from his son's body. The fact is, and that is why we must learn to put up with *passeront pas*, it is men like these, like my poor valet, like Vaugoubert, who have prevented the Germans from 'passing'. You may think we are not advancing much, but logic is beside the point, there is a secret inner feeling which tells an army that it is victorious—or a dying man that he is finished. We know that victory will be ours and we are determined that it shall be, so that we can dictate a just peace, I don't mean 'just' simply for ourselves, but truly just, just to the French and just to the Germans."

I do not wish to imply that the "calamity" had raised Saint-Loup's intelligence to a new level. But just as soldier heroes with commonplace and trivial minds, if they happened to write poems during their convalescence placed themselves, in order to describe the war, at the level not of events, which in themselves are nothing, but of the commonplace aesthetic whose rules they had obeyed in the past, and talked, as they would have ten years earlier, of the "blood-stained dawn", "victory's tremulous wings", and so on, so Saint-Loup, by nature much more intelligent and much more of an artist, remained intelligent and an artist and it was with the greatest good taste that he now recorded for my benefit the observations of landscape which he made if he had to halt at the edge of a marshy forest, very much as he would have done if he had been out duck-shooting. To help me to understand certain contrasts of light and shade which had been "the enchantment of his morning", he alluded in his letter to certain paintings which we both loved and was not afraid to cite a passage of Romain Rolland, or even of Nietzsche, with the independent spirit of the man at the front, who had not the civilian's terror of pronouncing a German name, and also— in thus quoting an enemy—with a touch of coquetry, like Colonel du Paty de Clam who, waiting among the witnesses at Zola's trial and chancing to pass Pierre Quillard, the violently Dreyfusard poet, whom he did not even know, recited some lines from his symbolist play, *La Fille aux Mains Coupées.* In the same way if Saint-Loup had occasion in a letter to mention a song by Schumann, he never gave any but the German title, nor did he use any periphrasis to tell me that, when at dawn on the edge of the forest he had heard the first twittering of a bird, his rapture had been as great as though he had been addressed by the bird in that "sublime *Siegfried*" which he so looked forward to hearing after the war.

And now, on my second return to Paris, I had received, the day after I arrived, another letter from Gilberte, who had doubtless forgotten, or at least forgotten what she had said in, the letter I have described, for in this new letter her departure from Paris at the end of 1914 was presented retrospectively in a very different light. "Perhaps you do not know, my dear friend," she wrote, "that I have now been at Tansonville for nearly two years. I arrived here at the same time as the Germans. Everybody had tried to prevent me from leaving. I was regarded as mad. 'What,' my friends said, 'here you are safe in Paris and you want to go off to enemy-occupied territory just when everybody is trying to escape from it.' I was quite aware of the strength of this argument. But I can't help it; if I have one good quality, it is that I am not a coward, or perhaps I should say, I am loyal, and when I knew that my beloved Tansonville was threatened, I simply could not leave our old bailiff to defend it alone. I felt that my place was by his side. And it was, in fact, thanks to this decision that I succeeded in more or less saving the house when all the other big houses in the neighbourhood, abandoned by their panic-stricken owners, were almost without exception reduced to ruins—and in saving not only the house but the valuable collections too, which dear Papa was so fond of." In a word, Gilberte was now persuaded that she had gone to Tansonville not, as she had written to me in 1914, in order to escape from the Germans and be in a safe place, but on the contrary in order to face them and defend her house against them.

They had, as a matter of fact, not stayed long at Tansonville, but since then the house had witnessed a constant coming and going of soldiers, far more intensive than that marching up and down the streets of Combray which had once drawn tears to the eyes of Françoise, and Gilberte had not ceased, as she said, this time quite truly, to live the life of the front. So that the newspapers spoke with the highest praise of her wonderful conduct and there was some question of giving her a decoration. The end of the letter was absolutely truthful. "You have no idea what this war is like, my dear friend, or of the importance that a road, a bridge, a height can assume. How often have I thought of you, of those walks of ours together which you made so delightful, through all this now ravaged countryside, where vast battles are fought to gain possession of some path, some slope which you once loved and which we so often explored together! Probably, like me, you did not imagine that obscure Roussainville and boring Méséglise, where our letters used to be brought from and where the doctor was once fetched when you were ill, would ever be famous places. Well, my dear friend, they have become for ever a part of history, with the same claim to glory as Austerlitz or Valmy. The battle of Méséglise lasted for more than eight months; the Germans lost in it more than six hundred thousand men, they destroyed Méséglise, but they did not capture it. As for the short cut up the hill which you were so fond of and which we used to call the hawthorn path, where you claim that as a small child you fell in love with me (whereas I assure you in all truthfulness it was I who was in love with you), I cannot tell you how important it has become. The huge field of corn upon which it emerges is the famous Hill 307, which you must have seen mentioned again and again in the bulletins. The French blew up the little bridge over the Vivonne which you said did not remind you of your childhood as much as you would have wished, and the Germans have thrown other bridges across the river. For a year and a half they held one half of Combray and the French the other."

The day after I received this letter, that is to say two days before the evening on which, as I have described, I made my way through the dark streets with the sound of my footsteps in my ears and all these memories revolving in my mind, Saint-Loup, arrived from the front and very shortly to return to it, had come to see me for a few moments only, and the mere announcement of his visit had violently moved me. Françoise had been tempted to fling herself upon him, in the hope that he could obtain an exemption for the timid butcher's boy whose class was to be called up the following year. But she had been checked, without my saying anything to her, by the thought of the futility of this endeavour, for the timid slaughterer of animals had moved to another butcher's some time previously. And whether our butcher's wife was afraid of losing our custom, or whether she was telling the truth, she declared to Françoise that she did not know where the boy— who, in any case, would never make a good butcher—was working. Françoise had searched everywhere. But Paris is large and butcher's shops are numerous, and although she had visited a great many she had never succeeded in finding the timid and blood-stained young man.

When Saint-Loup came into my room I had gone up to him with that feeling of timidity, that impression of something supernatural which was in fact induced by all soldiers on leave and which one feels when one enters the presence of a man suffering from a fatal disease, who still, nevertheless, leaves his bed, gets dressed, goes for walks. It seemed (above all it had seemed at first, for upon those who had not lived, as I had, at a distance from Paris, there had descended Habit, which cuts off from things which we have witnessed a number of times the root of profound impression and of thought which gives them their real meaning), it seemed almost that there was something cruel in these leaves granted to the men at the front. When they first came on leave, one said to oneself: "They will refuse to go back, they will desert." And indeed they came not merely from places which seemed to us unreal, because we had only heard them spoken of in the newspapers and could not conceive how a man was able to take part in these titanic battles and emerge with nothing worse than a bruise on his shoulder; it was from the shores of death, whither they would soon return, that they came to spend a few moments in our midst, incomprehensible to us, filling us with tenderness and terror and a feeling of mystery, like phantoms whom we summon from the dead, who appear to us for a second, whom we dare not question, and who could, in any case, only reply: "You cannot possibly imagine." For it is extraordinary how, in the survivors of battle, which is what soldiers on leave are, or in living men hypnotised or dead men summoned by a medium, the only effect of contact with mystery is to increase, if that be possible, the insignificance of the things people say. Such were my feelings when I greeted Robert, who still had a scar on his forehead, more august and more mysterious in my eyes than the imprint left upon the earth by a giant's foot. And I had not dared to put a single question to him and he had made only the simplest remarks to me. Remarks that even differed very little from the ones he might have made before the war, as though people, in spite of the war, continued to be what they were; the tone of conversation was the same, only the subject-matter differed—and even that not so very much!

I guessed from what he told me that in the army he had found opportunities which had gradually made him forget that

Morel had behaved as badly towards him as towards his uncle. However, he still felt a great affection for him and was seized by sudden cravings to see him again, though he always postponed doing this. I thought it kinder to Gilberte not to inform Robert that to find Morel he had only to pay a call on Mme Verdurin.

I remarked apologetically to Robert how little one felt the war·in Paris. He replied that even in Paris it was sometimes "pretty extraordinary". This was an allusion to a Zeppelin raid which had taken place the previous night and he went on to ask me if I had had a good view, very much as in the old days he might have questioned me about some spectacle of great aesthetic beauty. At the front, I could see, there might be a sort of bravado in saying: "Isn't it marvellous? What a pink! And that pale green!" when at any moment you might be killed, but here in Paris there could be no question of any such pose in Saint-Loup's way of speaking about an insignificant raid, which had in fact looked marvellously beautiful from our balcony when the silence of the night was broken by a display which was more than a display because it was real, with fireworks that were purposeful and protective and bugle-calls that did more than summon on parade. I spoke of the beauty of the aeroplanes climbing up into the night. "And perhaps they are even more beautiful when they come down," he said. "I grant that it is a magnificent moment when they climb, when they fly off in *constellation*, in obedience to laws as precise as those that govern the constellations of the stars— for what seems to you a mere spectacle is the rallying of the squadrons, then the orders they receive, their departure in pursuit, etc. But don't you prefer the moment when, just as you have got used to thinking of them as stars, they break away to pursue an enemy or to return to the ground after the all-clear, the moment of *apocalypse*, when even the stars are hurled from their courses? And then the sirens, could they

have been more Wagnerian, and what could be more appropriate as a salute to the arrival of the Germans?—it might
have been the national anthem, with the Crown Prince and
the Princesses in the imperial box, the *Wacht am Rhein*; one
had to ask oneself whether they were indeed pilots and not
Walkyries who were sailing upwards." He seemed to be
delighted with this comparison of the pilots to Walkyries, and
went on to explain it on purely musical grounds: "That's it,
the music of the sirens was a 'Ride of the Walkyries'! There's
no doubt about it, the Germans have to arrive before you can
hear Wagner in Paris." In some ways the simile was not misleading. The town from being a black shapeless mass seemed
suddenly to rise out of the abyss and the night into the luminous sky, where one after another the pilots soared upwards in
answer to the heart-rending appeal of the sirens, while with a
movement slower but more insidious, more alarming—for
their gaze made one think of the object, still invisible but
perhaps already very near, which it sought—the searchlights
strayed ceaselessly to and fro, scenting the enemy, encircling
him with their beams until the moment when the aeroplanes
should be unleashed to bound after him in pursuit and seize
him. And squadron after squadron, each pilot, as he soared
thus above the town, itself now transported into the sky,
resembled indeed a Walkyrie. Meanwhile on ground-level, at
the height of the houses, there were also scraps of illumination,
and I told Saint-Loup that, if he had been at home the previous evening, he might, while contemplating the apocalypse in
the sky, at the same time have watched on the ground (as in El
Greco's *Burial of Count Orgaz*, in which the two planes are
distinct and parallel) a first-rate farce acted by characters in
night attire, whose famous names merited a report to some
successor of that Ferrari whose society paragraphs had so often
provided amusement to the two of us, Saint-Loup and myself.

that we used also to amuse ourselves by inventing imaginary ones. And that is what we did once more on the day I am describing, just as though we were not in the middle of a war, although our theme, the fear of the Zeppelins, was very much a "war" one: "Seen about town: the Duchesse de Guermantes magnificent in a night-dress, the Duc de Guermantes indescribable in pink pyjamas and a bath-robe, etc." "I am sure," he said, "that in all the large hotels you would have seen American Jewesses in their night-dresses, hugging to their ravaged bosoms the pearl necklaces which will enable them to marry a ruined duke. The Ritz, on these evenings when the Zeppelins are overhead, must look like Feydeau's *Hôtel du libre échange.*")

"Do you remember," I said to him, "our conversations at Doncières?" "Ah! those were the days! What a gulf separates us from them! Will those times ever re-emerge

> *du gouffre interdit à nos sondes,*
> *Comme montent au ciel les soleils rajeunis*
> *Après s'être lavés au fond des mers profondes?*"

"But don't let's think about those conversations simply in order to remind ourselves how delightful they were," I said. "I was attempting in them to arrive at a certain kind of truth. What do you think, does the present war, which has thrown everything into confusion—and most of all, so you say, the idea of war—does it render null and void what you used to tell me then about the types of battle, the battles of Napoleon, for instance, which would be imitated in the wars of the future?" "Not in the least," he said; "the Napoleonic battle still exists, particularly in this war, since Hindenburg is imbued with the Napoleonic spirit. His rapid movements of troops, his feints— the device, for instance, of leaving only a small covering force opposite one of his enemies while he falls with his united strength upon the other (Napoleon in 1814) or the other stratagem of pressing home a diversion so strongly that the enemy is compelled to keep up his strength on a front which is not the really important one (for example, Hindenburg's feint before Warsaw, which tricked the Russians into concentrating their resistance there and brought about their defeat at the Masurian Lakes)—his tactical withdrawals, analogous to those with which Austerlitz, Arcola, Eckmühl began, everything in Hindenburg is Napoleonic, and we haven't seen the end of him. I must add that if, when we are no longer together, you try, as the war proceeds, to interpret its events, you should not rely too exclusively on this particular aspect of Hindenburg to reveal to you the meaning of what he is doing and the key to what he is about to do. A general is like a writer who sets out to write a certain play, a certain book, and then the book itself, with the unexpected potentialities which it reveals here, the impassable obstacles which it presents there, makes him deviate to an enormous degree from his preconceived plan. You know, for instance, that a diversion should only be made against a position which is itself of considerable importance; well, suppose the diversion succeeds beyond all expectation, while the principal operation results in a deadlock: the diversion may then become the principal operation. But there is one type of Napoleonic battle which I am waiting to see Hindenburg attempt, and that is the one which consists in driving a wedge between two allies, in this case the English and ourselves."

I have said that the war had not altered the stature of Saint-Loup's intelligence, but I ought to add that this intelligence, developing in accordance with laws in which heredity counted for much, had acquired a brilliancy which I had never seen in him before. What a difference between the fair-haired boy who had once been run after by smart women or women who were hoping to become smart, and the voluble talker, the theorist who never stopped juggling with words! In another generation, grafted upon another stock, like an actor re-interpreting a part played years ago by Bressant or Delaunay, he was like a successor—pink, fair and golden, whereas the other had been half and half very dark and quite white—of M. de Charlus. It was true that he did not agree with his uncle about the war, since he had ranged himself with that section of the aristocracy which put France above everything else in the world while M. de Charlus was at heart defeatist, but nevertheless he could demonstrate to anyone who had not seen the "creator of the part" what a success could be made in the role of verbal acrobat. "It seems that Hindenburg is a revelation," I said to him. "An old revelation," he retorted instantly, "or a future revolution. Instead of being soft with the enemy, we should have supported Mangin in his offensive, then we might have smashed Austria and Germany and europeanised Turkey instead of balkanising France." "But soon we shall have the help of the United States," I said. "Meanwhile, I see here only the spectacle of the disunited states. Why refuse to make more generous concessions to Italy for fear of dechristianising France?" "How shocked your uncle Charlus would be to hear you!" I said. "The fact is that you would be only too pleased to give the Pope another slap in the face, while your uncle is in despair at the thought of the damage that may be done to the throne of Franz Josef. And in this he says that he is in the tradition of Talleyrand and the Congress of Vienna." "The age of the Congress of Vienna is dead and gone," he replied; "the old secret diplomacy must be replaced by concrete diplomacy. My uncle is at heart an impenitent monarchist, who can be made to swallow carps like Mme Molé and scamps like Arthur Meyer provided that both carps and scamps are *à la*

Chambord. He so hates the tricolour flag that I believe he would rather serve under the duster of the Red Bonnet, which he would take in good faith for the white flag of the Monarchists." Admittedly, this was mere play on words and Saint-Loup was far from possessing the sometimes profound originality of his uncle. But he was as affable and agreeable in character as the other was jealous and suspicious. And he had remained charming and pink as he had been at Balbec beneath his shock of golden hair. And one family characteristic he possessed in at least as high a degree as his uncle, that attitude of mind of the Faubourg Saint-Germain which remains deeply implanted in the men of that world who fancy that they have most completely detached themselves from it, the attitude which combines respect for clever men who are not of good family (a respect which flourishes, in fact, only among the aristocracy, which is why revolutions are sometimes so unjust) with a fatuous satisfaction with themselves. Through this mixture of humility and pride, of acquired intellectual curiosity and innate authority, M. de Charlus and Saint-Loup, by different paths, and with opposite opinions, had become, with the gap of a generation between them, intellectuals whom every new idea interested and talkers whom no interruption could silence. So that a not very intelligent person might, according to the humour in which he happened to be, have found both the one and the other either dazzling or insufferably tedious.

I had gone on walking as I turned over in my mind this recent meeting with Saint-Loup and had come a long way out of my way; I was almost at the Pont des Invalides. The lamps (there were very few of them, on account of the Gothas) had already been lit, a little too early because "the clocks had been put forward" a little too early, when the night still came rather quickly, the time having been "changed" once and for all for the whole of the summer just as a central heating system is turned on or off once and for all on a fixed date; and above the city with its nocturnal illumination, in one whole quarter of the sky—the sky that knew nothing of summer time and winter time and did not deign to recognise that half past eight had become half past nine—in one whole quarter of the sky from which the blue had not vanished there was still a little daylight. Over that whole portion of the city which is dominated by the towers of the Trocadéro the sky looked like a vast sea the colour of turquoise, from which gradually there emerged, as it ebbed, a whole line of little black rocks, which might even have been nothing more than a row of fishermen's nets and which were in fact small clouds— a sea at that moment the colour of turquoise, sweeping along with it, without their noticing, the whole human race in the wake of the vast revolution of the earth, that earth upon which they are mad enough to continue their own revolutions, their futile wars, like the war which at this very moment was staining France crimson with blood. But if one looked for long at the sky, this lazy, too beautiful sky which did not condescend to change its time-table and above the city, where the lamps had been lit, indolently prolonged its lingering day in these bluish tones, one was seized with giddiness: it was no longer a flat expanse of sea but a vertically stepped series of blue glaciers. And the towers of the Trocadéro which seemed so near to the turquoise steps must, one realised, be infinitely remote from them, like the twin towers of certain towns in Switzerland which at a distance one would suppose to be near neighbours of the upper mountain slopes.

I retraced my steps, but once I had left the Pont des Invalides there was no longer any trace of day in the sky and there was practically no light in the town, so that stumbling here and there against dust-bins and mistaking one direction for another, I found to my surprise that, by mechanically following a labyrinth of dark streets, I had arrived on the boulevards. There, the impression of an oriental vision which I had had earlier in the evening came to me again, and I thought too of the Paris of an earlier age, not now so much of the Paris of the Directory as of the Paris of 1815. As in 1815 there was a march past of allied troops in the most variegated uniforms; and among them, the Africans in their red divided skirts, the Indians in their white turbans were enough to transform for me this Paris through which I was walking into a whole imaginary exotic city, an oriental scene which was at once meticulously accurate with respect to the costumes and the colours of the faces and arbitrarily fanciful when it came to the background, just as out of the town in which he lived Carpaccio made a Jerusalem or a Constantinople by assembling in its streets a crowd whose marvellous motley was not more rich in colour than that of the crowd around me. Walking close behind two zouaves who seemed hardly to be aware of him, I noticed a tall, stout man in a soft felt hat and a long heavy overcoat, to whose purplish face I hesitated whether I should give the name of an actor or a painter, both equally notorious for innumerable sodomist scandals. I was certain in any case that I was not acquainted with him; so I was not a little surprised, when his glance met mine, to see that he appeared to be embarrassed and deliberately stopped and came towards me like a man who wants to prove that you have not surprised him in an occupation which he would prefer to remain secret. For a second I asked myself who it was that was greeting me: it was M. de Charlus. One may say that for him the evolution of his malady or the revolution of his vice had reached the extreme point at which the tiny original personality of the individual, the specific qualities he has inherited from his ancestors, are entirely eclipsed by the transit across them of some generic defect or malady which is their satellite. M. de Charlus had travelled as far as was possible from himself, or rather he was himself but so perfectly masked by what he had become, by what belonged not to him alone but to many other inverts, that for a moment I had taken him for some other invert, as he walked behind these zouaves down the wide pavement of the boulevard, for some other invert who was not M. de Charlus, who was not a great nobleman or a man of imagination and intelligence, and whose only point of resemblance to the Baron was the look that was common to them all, which in him now, at least until one had taken the trouble to observe him carefully, concealed every other quality from view.

Thus it was that, having intended to call on Mme Verdurin, I had met M. de Charlus. And certainly I should not now as in the past have found him in her drawing-room; their quarrel had grown steadily more bitter and Mme Verdurin even took advantage of present events to discredit him further. Having said for years that she found him stale, finished, more out of date in his professed audacities than the dullest philistine, she now summed up this condemnation in such a way as to make him an object of general aversion, by saying that he was "pre-war". The war had set between him and the present, so the little clan declared, an abyss which left him stranded in the deadest of dead pasts. Besides—and this was addressed particularly to the political world, which was less well informed—she made him out to be just as "bogus", just as much an "outsider" from the point of view of social position as from that of intellectual merit. "He sees nobody, nobody invites him," she said to M. Bontemps, whom she easily convinced. Anyhow, there was an element of truth in these

words. The position of M. de Charlus had changed. Caring
less and less about society, having quarrelled, because of his
cantankerous character and having disdained, because of his
high opinion of his own social importance, to reconcile himself with most of the men and women who were the flower of
society, he lived in a relative isolation which was not caused,
like that in which Mme de Villeparisis had died, by the fact
that the aristocracy had ostracised him, but which nevertheless in the eyes of the public for two reasons appeared to be
worse. The bad reputation which M. de Charlus was now
known to enjoy made ill-informed people think that it was for
this reason that his company was not sought by people whom
in fact he himself made a point of refusing to see. So that what
was really the result of his own spleen seemed to be due to the
contempt of the people upon whom he vented it. Secondly,
Mme de Villeparisis had had one great bulwark: the family.
But between his family and himself M. de Charlus had multi-
plied quarrels. His family in any case—particularly the "old
Faubourg" side of it, the Courvoisier side—had always seemed
to him uninteresting. And he was far from suspecting, he who,
from a spirit of opposition to the Courvoisiers, had made such
audacious advances in the direction of art, that the feature in
him which would most have interested, for example, a Bergotte, was precisely his kinship with the whole of this old
Faubourg which he despised, and the descriptions he could
have given of the almost provincial life led by his female
cousins, in that district bounded by the Rue de la Chaise and
the Place du Palais Bourbon in one direction and the Rue
Garancière in the other.

And then, considering the question from another point of
view, less transcendent and more practical, Mme Verdurin
affected to believe that he was not French. "What is his
nationality exactly, is he an Austrian?" M. Verdurin would

ask innocently. "No, certainly not," Comtesse Molé would reply, her first reaction being one rather of common sense than of resentment. "No, he is Prussian," the Mistress would say. "Yes, I know what I am talking about, he has told us countless times that he is a hereditary member of the Prussian Chamber of Peers and a Durchlaucht." "Still, the Queen of Naples told me . . ." "You know she is a dreadful spy," screamed Mme Verdurin, who had not forgotten how the fallen sovereign had behaved in her house one evening. "I know—there is absolutely no question about it—that that is what she has been living on. If we had a more energetic government, she and her kind ought all to be in a concentration camp. I mean it! In any case, you will be wise not to receive visits from that charming set, because I know that the Minister of the Interior has his eye on them, your house would be watched. I have not the slightest doubt that for two years Charlus did nothing but spy on us all." And thinking probably that there might be some doubt as to the interest that the German government would show in even the most circumstantial reports on the organisation of the little clan, Mme Verdurin went on, with a mild and perspicacious air, like someone who knows that the value of what she is saying will only seem greater if she does not raise her voice: "Let me tell you, I said to my husband the very first day: 'I don't like the way that man wormed his way into my house. There's something shady here.' We had a property which stood on very high ground, looking down over a bay. Quite obviously he had been sent by the Germans to prepare a base for their submarines. There were many things which surprised me at the time, but which I understand now. For instance, at first, he would not come by the train with my other regular guests. I was so kind as to offer to put him up in the house. But no, he preferred to stay at Doncières, which was swarming with soldiers. All this stank to high heaven of espionage."

About the first of the charges brought against the Baron de Charlus, that of being out of date, fashionable people were only too ready to agree with Mme Verdurin. In this they were ungrateful, for M. de Charlus was to some extent their poet, the man who had been able to extract from the world of fashion a sort of essential poetry, which had in it elements of history, of beauty, of the picturesque, of the comic, of frivolous elegance. But people in society, incapable of understanding this poetry, did not see that it existed in their own lives; they sought for it rather elsewhere, and on an infinitely higher peak than M. de Charlus placed men who were much stupider than him but who professed to despise "society" and liked instead to hold forth about sociology and political economy, M. de Charlus, for instance, took a delight in repeating unconsciously characteristic remarks of the Duchesse de Montmorency and in describing the studied charm of her clothes, and spoke of her as if she were something sublime, but this merely gave him the reputation of an utter idiot in the eyes of the sort of society women who thought that the Duchesse de Montmorency was an uninteresting fool, and that dresses are made to be worn but without the wearer appearing to give them a moment's attention, and who meanwhile gave proof of their own superior intelligence by running to hear lectures at the Sorbonne or Deschanel speak in the Chamber.

In short, people in society had become disillusioned about M. de Charlus, not from having penetrated too far, but without having penetrated at all, his rare intellectual merit. The reason why he was found to be "pre-war", old fashioned, was that the people who are least capable of judging the worth of individuals are also the most inclined to adopt fashion as a principle by which to classify them; they have not exhausted,

or even grazed the surface of, the talented men of one generation, when suddenly they are obliged to condemn them all
en bloc, for here is a new generation with a new label which
will be no better understood than its predecessor.

As for the second accusation, that of being pro-German,
fashionable people because of their dislike of extreme views
tended to reject it, but the charge had an unwearying and
particularly cruel advocate in Morel, who, having managed
to retain in the newspapers and even in society the position
which M. de Charlus had first achieved for him and then
tried equally hard, but without success, to undermine, pursued
the Baron with a hatred that was all the more infamous since,
whatever the precise relations between them had been, Morel
had seen and known the side of him that he concealed from
so many people: his profound kindness. M. de Charlus had
shown such generosity, such delicacy towards the violinist,
had been so scrupulous about fulfilling his promises to him
that, when Charlie left him, the image of the Baron that remained in his mind was not at all that of a vicious man (at
most he regarded the Baron's vice as a disease) but of a man
with loftier ideas than any other he had ever known, a
man with extraordinary capacity for feeling, a kind of saint.
So little disposed was he to deny this that even after the
quarrel he would say in all sincerity to a young man's parents:
"You can trust your son to him, he can only have the most
excellent influence on him." And so when by his articles in
the papers he tried to make him suffer, it was in his imagination not vice but virtue incarnate that he was scourging. Not
long before the war there had begun to appear short "pieces",
transparent to the so-called initiated, in which M. de Charlus
was most monstrously libelled. Of one, entitled *The Misfortunes of a Dowager ending in -us or the Latter Days of the
Baroness*, Mme Verdurin had bought fifty copies in order to

be able to lend it to her acquaintances and M. Verdurin declaring that Voltaire himself did not write better, took to reading it aloud. Since the war the tone of these pieces had changed. Not only was the Baron's inversion denounced, but also his alleged Germanic nationality: "Frau Bosch", "Frau van den Bosch" were the names habitually used to designate M. de Charlus. A little composition of a poetic nature appeared with the title—borrowed from some of Beethoven's dances—*Une Allemande.* Finally two short stories, *The Uncle from America and the Aunt from Frankfurt* and *The Jolly Sailor*, read in proof in the little clan, had delighted even Brichot himself, who exclaimed: "So long as the most high and puissant Lady Censorship does not blue-pencil us!" The articles themselves were cleverer than their ridiculous titles. Their style derived from Bergotte but in a way which, for the reason that follows, perhaps no one but myself perceived. Bergotte's *writings* had had not the slightest influence on Morel. The fertilisation had been effected in a most unusual way, which I record here only because of its rarity. I have described earlier the very special manner which Bergotte had, when he spoke, of choosing and pronouncing his words. Morel, who for a long time had been in the habit of meeting him at the Saint-Loups, had at that period done "imitations" of him, in which he exactly mimicked his voice, using just the words that Bergotte would have chosen. And now that he had taken to writing, Morel used to transcribe passages of "spoken Bergotte", but without first transposing them in the way which would have turned them into "written Bergotte". Not many people having known Bergotte as a talker, the tone of his voice was not recognised, since it differed from the style of his pen. This oral fertilisation is so rare that I have thought it worth mentioning here. The flowers that it produces are, however, always sterile.

Morel, who was in the Press Office, found after a while, his French blood boiling in his veins like the juice of the grapes of Combray, that there was not much to be said for being in an office during the war, and he ended by joining up, although Mme Verdurin did everything she could to persuade him to stay in Paris. Admittedly she was indignant that M. de Cambremer, at his age, should be on the general staff, and of every man who did not come to her parties she would say: "I can't think where the wretch has managed to hide himself all this time," and if someone assured her that the wretch had been in the front line since the first day, would reply, without any scruple about telling a lie or perhaps just because she was so used to getting things wrong: "Not at all, he has not budged from Paris, he's doing something about as dangerous as taking a Minister for walks, I know what I am talking about, you can take my word for it, I was told by someone who has seen him at it"; but where the faithful were concerned it was not the same thing, she did not want to let them go off to the war, and looked upon it as a great "bore" who caused them to desert. And so she pulled every possible string to keep them in Paris, which would give her the double pleasure of having them at her dinner-parties and at the same time, before they arrived or after they left, making scathing remarks about their inactivity. However, the faithful in each case had to be made to agree to the soft job she had found for him and she was bitterly distressed to find Morel recalcitrant; in vain had she said to him over and over again: "But don't you see, you are *serving* in your office, and serving more than you would be at the front. The important thing is to be useful, to be really part of the war, to be in it. There are those who are in it, and there are the shirkers. Now you, you're in it, you have nothing to worry about, everybody knows this, nobody's going to throw stones at you." In the same way, in different circumstances, although men were at that time not so scarce and she had not been, as she was now, obliged to have a preponderance of women, if a man had lost his mother she had not hesitated to try and convince him that there was no objection to his continuing to come to her parties. "Grief is worn in the heart. If you wanted to go to a dance" (she never gave one) "I should be the first to advise you not to do it, but here, at my little Wednesdays, or in a box, nobody will be in the least surprised. We all know you have had a great grief. . . ." Men were scarcer now and mourning more frequent though no longer needed to prevent men from going to parties, the war itself having put a stop to that. Mme Verdurin hung on to the survivors. She tried to persuade them that they were more useful to France if they stayed in Paris, just as in the past she would have assured them that the deceased would have been happy to see them enjoying themselves. In spite of all her efforts she did not have many men; perhaps sometimes she regretted that between herself and M. de Charlus she had brought about a rupture which left no hope of a return to their former relations.

But, if M. de Charlus and Mme Verdurin no longer saw one another, they continued nevertheless, Mme Verdurin to entertain, M. de Charlus to pursue his pleasures, very much as if nothing had changed. A few little differences there were, but of no great importance: Cottard, for instance, was now to be seen at Mme Verdurin's parties in a colonel's uniform which might have come out of Loti's *Ile du Rêve* (it bore a striking resemblance to that of a Haitian admiral and at the same time, with its broad sky-blue ribbon, recalled that of the "Children of Mary"); and M. de Charlus, finding himself in a town from which the mature men for whom he had hitherto had a taste had vanished, followed the example of those Frenchmen who, after being womanisers in France, go to live in the colonies: from necessity he had acquired first the habit of and then the taste for little boys.

But the first of these newly acquired characteristics was not in evidence for long: Cottard soon died "facing the enemy", so the newspapers said, though he had never left Paris—but it was true that he had exerted himself too much for his age —and he was soon followed by M. Verdurin, whose death caused grief to one person only and that, strangely enough, was Elstir. For whereas I had been able to study Elstir's work from a point of view which was to some extent objective, the painter himself, particularly as he grew older, linked it superstitiously to the society which had provided him with models and which had also, after thus transforming itself within him through the alchemy of impressions into a work of art, given him his public, his spectators. More and more he was inclined to believe materialistically that a not inconsiderable part of beauty is inherent in objects, and just as, at the beginning, he had adored in Mme Elstir the archetype of that rather heavy beauty which he had pursued and caressed in his paintings and in tapestries, so now in the death of M. Verdurin he saw the disappearance of one of the last relics of the social frame-work, the perishable frame-work—as swift to crumble away as the very fashions in clothes which form part of it—which supports an art and certifies its authenticity, and he was as saddened and distressed by this event as a painter of *fêtes galantes* might have been by the Revolution which destroyed the elegances of the eighteenth century, or Renoir by the disappearance of Montmartre and the Moulin de la Galette; but more than this, with M. Verdurin he saw disappear the eyes, the brain, which had had the truest vision of his painting, in which, in the form of a cherished memory, his painting was to some extent inherent. No doubt young men had come along who also loved painting, but painting of another kind; they had not, like Swann, like M. Verdurin, received lessons in taste from Whistler, lessons in truth from Monet, lessons which alone would have qualified them to judge Elstir with justice. So the death of M. Verdurin left Elstir feeling lonelier, although they had not been on speaking terms for a great many years: it was for him as though a little of the beauty of his own work had been eclipsed, since there had perished a little of the universe's sum total of awareness of its special beauty.

As for the change which had overtaken the pleasures of M. de Charlus, this was no more than intermittent: by maintaining a correspondence with numerous soldiers at the front, who sometimes came on leave, he did not altogether lack the company of mature men.

At the time when I believed what people said I should have been tempted, hearing Germany, or later Bulgaria or Greece, declare their intentions to be pacific, to give credence to these statements. But since life with Albertine and with Françoise had accustomed me to suspect in them thoughts and projects which they did not disclose, I now allowed no pronouncement, however specious, of William II or Ferdinand of Bulgaria or Constantine of Greece, to deceive my instinct and prevent it from divining what each one of them was plotting. Of course my quarrels with Françoise or with Albertine had been merely private quarrels, of interest only to the life of that little cell, endowed with mind, that a human being is. But just as there are animal bodies and human bodies, each one of which is an assemblage of cells as large in relation to a single cell as Mont Blanc, so there exist huge organised accumulations of individuals which are called nations: their life does no more than repeat on a larger scale the lives of their constituent cells, and anybody who is incapable of comprehending the mystery, the reactions, the laws of these smaller lives, will only make futile pronouncements when he talks about struggles between nations. But if he is master of the psychology of individuals, then these colossal masses of conglomerated individuals will assume in his eyes, as they confront one another, a beauty more potent than that of the struggle which arises from a mere conflict between two characters; and they will seem to him as huge as the body of a tall man would seem to the infusoria of which more than ten thousand would be required to fill the space of a cubic millimetre. So it had been now for some time past: the huge irregular geometric figure France, filled to its perimeter with millions of little polygons of various shapes, and another figure filled with an even greater number of polygons, Germany, had been engaged in one of these quarrels. And considered from this point of view, the body Germany and the body France, and the allied and enemy bodies, were behaving to some extent like individuals, and the blows which they were exchanging were governed by the innumerable rules of that art of boxing which Saint-Loup had expounded to me; but as, even if one chose to consider them as individuals, they were at the same time giant assemblages of individuals, the quarrel took on immense and magnificent forms, like the surge of a million-waved ocean which tries to shatter an age-old line of cliffs, or like gigantic glaciers which with their slow destructive oscillations attempt to break down the frame of mountains which surrounds them. But in spite of this, life continued almost unchanged for many of those who have played a part in this story, and not least for M. de Charlus and the Verdurins, just as if the Germans had not been as near them as they were, since the threat of a danger momentarily checked but permanently alive leaves us absolutely indifferent if we do not picture it to ourselves. People, as they go about their pleasures, do not normally stop to think that, if certain moderating and weakening influences should happen to be suspended, the proliferation of infusoria would attain its maximum theoretical rate and after a very few days the organisms that might have been contained in a cubic milli-metre would take a leap of many millions of miles and become a mass a million times greater than the sun, having in the pro-cess destroyed all our oxygen and all the substances on which we live, so that there would exist neither humanity nor animals nor earth, nor do they reflect that an irremediable and by no means improbable catastrophe may one day be generated in the ether by the incessant and frenzied activity which lies behind the apparent immutability of the sun; they busy them-selves with their own affairs without thinking about these two worlds, the one too small, the other too large for us to be aware of the cosmic menaces with which they envelop us.

So it was that the Verdurins gave dinner-parties (then, after a time, Mme Verdurin gave them alone, for M. Verdurin died) and M. de Charlus went about his pleasures and hardly ever stopped to reflect that the Germans—immobilised, it is true, by a bleeding barrier perpetually renewed—were only an hour by car from Paris. The Verdurins, one would imagine, did think about this fact, since they had a political drawing-room in which every evening they and their friends discussed the situation not only of the armies but of the fleets. They thought certainly of these hecatombs of regiments annihilated and passengers swallowed by the waves; but there is a law of inverse proportion which multiplies to such an extent anything that concerns our own welfare and divides by such a formidable figure anything that does not concern it, that the death of un-known millions is felt by us as the most insignificant of sensa-tions, hardly even as disagreeable as a draught. Mme Verdurin, who suffered even more from her headaches now that she could no longer get croissants to dip in her breakfast coffee, had eventually obtained a prescription from Cottard permit-ting her to have them specially made in a certain restaurant of which we have spoken. This had been almost as difficult to wangle with the authorities as the appointment of a general. The first of these special croissants arrived on the morning on which the newspapers reported the sinking of the *Lusitania*. As she dipped it in her coffee and gave a series of little flicks to her newspaper with one hand so as to make it stay open without her having to remove her other hand from the cup, "How horrible!" she said. "This is something more horrible than the most terrible stage tragedy." But the death of all these drowned people must have been reduced a thousand million times before it impinged upon her, for even as, with her mouth full, she made these distressful observations, the expression which spread over her face, brought there (one must suppose) by the savour of that so precious remedy against headaches, the croissant, was in fact one of satisfaction and pleasure.

As for M. de Charlus, his case was a little different, but worse even, for he went beyond not passionately desiring the victory of France: he desired rather, without admitting it to himself, that Germany should, if not triumph, at least not be crushed as everybody hoped she would be. And for this attitude of his the reason was, again, that the great collections of individuals called nations themselves behave to some extent like individuals. The logic that governs them is an inner logic, wrought and perpetually re-wrought by passions, like that of men and women at grips with one another in an amorous or domestic quarrel, the quarrel of a son with his father, or of a cook with her mistress, or a wife with her husband. The party who is in the wrong believes nevertheless that he is in the right—this was so in the case of Germany—and the party who is in the right sometimes supports his excellent cause with arguments which appear to him to be irrefutable only because they answer to his own passionate feelings. In these quarrels of individuals, the surest way of being convinced of the excellence of the cause of one party or the other is actually to be that party: a spectator will never to the same extent give his unqualified approval. Now within a nation the individual, if he is truly part of the nation, is simply a cell of the nation-individual. It is ridiculous to talk about the power of propaganda. Had the French been told that they were going to be beaten, no single Frenchman would have given way to despair any more than he would if he had been told that he was going to be killed by the Berthas. The real propaganda is what—if we are genuinely a living member of a nation—we tell ourselves because we have hope, hope being a symbol of a nation's instinct of self-preservation. To remain blind to the unjustness of the cause of the individual "Germany", to recognise at every moment the justness of the cause of the individual "France", the surest way was not for a German to be without judgment, or for a Frenchman to possess it, it was, both for the one and for the other, to be possessed of patriotism. M. de Charlus, who had rare moral qualities, who was susceptible to pity, generous, capable of affection and devotion, on the other hand for various reasons—among which the fact that his mother had been a Duchess of Bavaria may have played a part—did not have patriotism. He belonged, in consequence, no more to the body France than to the body Germany. Even I myself, had I been devoid of patriotism, had I not felt myself to be one of the cells of the body France, could not, it seems to me, have judged the quarrel in the manner in which I might have judged it in the past. In my adolescence, when I believed word for word what I was told, I should no doubt, hearing the German government protest its good faith, have been tempted to believe that this good faith existed; but I had learned long ago that our thoughts do not always accord with our words; not only had I one day, from the window on the staircase, discovered a Charlus whose existence I did not suspect, more important, in Françoise, and then, alas, in Albertine, I had seen the formation of opinions and projects so contrary to their words that now, even in the role of mere spectator, I should not have allowed any of the pronouncements of the Emperor or the King of Bulgaria to deceive my instinct. But after all I can only conjecture what I might have done if I had not been an actor in the drama, if I had not been a part of the actor France in the same way as, in my quarrels with Albertine, my sad gaze and the choking feeling in my throat had been parts of the individual "me" who was passionately interested in my cause; I could not arrive at detachment. That of M. de Charlus was complete. And given that he was nothing more than a spectator, and that, without being genuinely French, he was living in France, there was every reason why he was likely to be pro-German. In the first place, he was very intelligent and in every country fools form the bulk of the population; no doubt, had he lived in Germany, the German fools defending foolishly and with passion an unjust cause would have irritated him; but living as he did in France, the French fools defending foolishly and with passion a just cause irritated him quite as much. The logic of passion, even if it happens to be in the service of the best possible cause, is never irrefutable for the man who is not himself passionate. Inevitably M. de Charlus with his critical intelligence seized on every weak point in the reasoning of the patriots. And then the complacency that an imbecile derives from the excellence of his cause, and the certainty of victory, are particularly irritating phenomena. Inevitably M. de Charlus was irritated by the triumphant optimism of people who did not know Germany and Germany's strength as he did, who believed every month in a crushing victory for the following month, and at the end of the year were as confident in making fresh predictions as though they had never, with equal confidence, made false ones—which they had, however, forgotten, saying, if they were reminded of them, that it "was not the same thing". (Yet M. de Charlus, profound as his intelligence was in some directions, would perhaps have failed to see that this same reasoning applies also to new developments in art and that when a conservative critic of Manet replies to the argument "But people said the same thing about Delacroix" by saying "This is not the same thing", it is the critic who is wrong.)

Then again, M. de Charlus was merciful, the idea of a vanquished opponent caused him pain, he was always on the side of the underdog, he refrained from reading the law reports in the newspapers in order not to have to suffer in his own flesh from the anguish of the condemned man and from the impossibility of assassinating the judge, the executioner and the crowd that stood gloating to see "justice done". He was certain in any case that France could not be defeated now, and he knew on the other hand that the Germans were suffering from famine and would be obliged sooner or later to sue for mercy. And this idea too he more particularly disliked owing to the fact that he was living in France. His memories of Germany, after all, were distant, while the French who spoke of the crushing defeat of Germany with a joy which disgusted him, were people whose defects were known to him, their personalities unsympathetic. In such circumstances we pity more readily those whom we do not know, whom we merely imagine, than those who are near us in the vulgarity of daily life, unless—once again—we ourselves altogether are the latter and form but one flesh with them, since patriotism accomplishes the miracle that we are "for" our country as in a quarrel between lovers we are "for" ourself. So the war for M. de Charlus was an extraordinarily fertile breeding-ground of those hatreds he was prone to which sprang up in him in a moment and had only a very brief existence, during which, however, he would have abandoned himself to any violent impulse. When he read the newspapers, the air of triumph with which day after day the journalists portrayed Germany as beaten—"the Beast at bay, reduced to impotence"—while the contrary was only too true, their cheerful and savage stupidity, intoxicated him with rage. The newspapers at this moment were written partly by well-known men who found this a means of "serving their country again", men such as Brichot, Norpois, Morel even, and Legrandin. M. de Charlus longed to meet them, to heap the most bitter sarcasms on their heads. Always particularly well-informed about sexual irregularities, he knew of some in individuals who, believing their own to be unknown, complacently denounced such things in the sovereigns of the "Empires of Prey", in Wagner, etc. He had a furious desire to find himself face to face with these men, to rub their noses in their own vice before the eyes of the world and leave them, these insulters of a vanquished opponent, dishonoured and gasping for breath.

Finally, M. de Charlus had also more particular reasons for being the pro-German that he was. One was that, himself a man of the world, he had lived much among men of the world, honourable men and men of honour, men who will not shake hands with a scoundrel; he was acquainted with their scruples and also with their hardness, he knew them to be insensible to the tears of a man whom they expel from a club or with whom they refuse to fight a duel, even if this act of "moral hygiene" should bring about the death of the black sheep's mother. And so in spite of himself, whatever admiration he might feel for England and for the admirable fashion in which she entered the war, nevertheless this impeccable England—incapable of falsehood but forbidding the entry of wheat and milk into Germany—was in his eyes a little too much the man of honour among nations, the professional second in duels, the arbiter of affairs of honour, whereas his experience told him that men of a different type, men with a blot upon their reputation, scoundrels like some of Dostoievsky's characters, may in fact be better—though I have never been able to understand why he identified the Germans with such men, since falsehood and deceit are in themselves no evidence of a kind heart, which is something the Germans do not seem to have displayed.

One last trait must be mentioned to complete this account of the pro-Germanism of M. de Charlus: he owed it, and through a most bizarre reaction, to his "charlism". He found the Germans very ugly, perhaps because they were rather too near to his own blood—it was the Moroccans he was mad about and even more the Anglo-Saxons, in whom he saw living statues by Pheidias. Now in him pleasure was not unaccompanied by a certain idea of cruelty of which I had not at that time learned the full force: the man whom he loved appeared to him in the guise of a delightful torturer. In taking sides against the Germans he would have seemed to himself to be acting as he did only in his hours of physical pleasure, to be acting, that is, in a manner contrary to his merciful nature, fired with passion for seductive evil and helping to crush virtuous ugliness. This too was his reaction at the time of the murder of Rasputin, an event which, happening as it did at a supper-party *à la* Dostoievsky, caused a general surprise because people found in it so strong a Russian flavour (this impression would have been stronger still had the public not been unaware of aspects of the case that were perfectly well known to M. de Charlus), because life disappoints us so often that in the end we come to believe that literature bears no relation to it and we are therefore astounded when we see the precious ideas that literature has revealed to us display themselves, without fear of getting spoiled, gratuitously, naturally, in the midst of daily life, when we see, for instance, that a supper-party and a murder taking place in Russia actually have something Russian about them.

The war dragged on indefinitely and those who, already several years earlier, had reported on good authority that negotiations for peace had been begun, even specifiying the clauses of the treaty, were at no pains now, when they talked to you, to make excuses for their previous false rumours. They had forgotten them and were ready in all sincerity to propagate others which they would forget just as quickly. It was the period when there were constant Gotha raids; the air was perpetually buzzing with the vibration, vigilant and sonorous, of French aeroplanes. But at intervals the siren rang out like the heart-rending scream of a Walkyrie—the only German music to have been heard since the war—until the moment when the fire-engines announced that the alert was over, while beside them, like an invisible street-urchin, the all-clear at regular intervals commented on the good news and hurled its cry of joy into the air.

M. de Charlus was astonished to see that even men like Brichot who before the war had been militarists and had never ceased to reproach France for her lack of military preparedness, were not content now with reproaching Germany for the excesses of her militarism, but criticised even her admiration of the army. No doubt they expressed quite different opinions the moment there was any danger of slowing down the war against Germany and continued, for the best reasons, to denounce the pacifists of their own country. But Brichot, for example, having consented, in spite of his bad eyesight, to discuss in some lectures certain works which had appeared in neutral countries, gave high praise to a novel by a Swiss author which has a satirical passage about two children—militarists in embryo—who are struck dumb with symbolic admiration at

the sight of a guardsman. There were other reasons why this
satire was likely to displease M. de Charlus, who deemed that
a guardsman may be a very beautiful thing. But above all he
did not understand Brichot's admiration, if not for the book,
which the Baron had not read, at least for its spirit, so different
from that which had animated Brichot himself before the
war. At that time everything that a military man did was
right, even the irregularities of General de Boisdeffre, the
disguises and strategies of Colonel du Paty de Clam, the
forgery of Colonel Henry. By what extraordinary *volte-face*
(it was in reality merely another aspect of the same very noble
passion, the passion of patriotism, which, from being militarist
when it was struggling against Dreyfusism, a phenomenon of
anti-militarist tendencies, had been obliged itself to become
almost anti-militarist now that the struggle was against the
hyper-militaristic Germany) had Brichot come to exclaim:
"O marvellous and mighty spectacle, fit lure for the youth of
an age that is all brutality and knows only the cult of force: a
guardsman! Well may one judge what the base soldiery will
be of a generation reared in the cult of these manifestations
of brutal force". He approved too of another Swiss novelist
Spitteler, who "wanting something to oppose to the hideous
conception of the sword supreme, symbolically exiled to the
depths of the forests the dreamy figure, mocked, calumniated
and solitary, whom he calls the Mad Student, his delightful
incarnation of the sweetness—unfashionable, alas, and perhaps soon to be forgotten if the grim rule of the ancient god of
the militarists is not destroyed—the adorable sweetness of the
times of peace".

"Now tell me," M. de Charlus said to me, "you know
Cottard and you know Cambremer. Every time I see them,
they talk to me about Germany's extraordinary lack of
psychology. But between ourselves, do you think that hitherto

they have cared much about psychology, or that even now they are capable of giving proof of any skill in it? You may be sure that I am not exaggerating. Even if he is talking about the very greatest of Germans, about Nietzsche or Goethe himself, you will hear Cottard say: 'with the habitual lack of psychology which characterises the Teutonic race'. Naturally there are things in the war which cause me greater distress, but you must admit that this is exasperating. Norpois is more intelligent, I grant you, although since the beginning of the war he has on every occasion been wrong. But what can one say of these articles of Brichot's which are arousing universal enthusiasm? You know as well as I do, my dear Sir, the merit of the man, whom I like very much, even after the schism which has cut me off from his little church, which causes me to see much less of him than I used to. But still I have a certain regard for this usher with the gift of the gab and a vast amount of learning, and I confess that it is very touching that at his age—and with his strength failing as it clearly has been failing for some years past—he should, as he says, have taken it upon himself to 'serve again'. But after all, good intentions are one thing, talent is another, and talent Brichot has never had. I admit that I share his admiration for certain elements of greatness in the present war. I do, however, find it strange that a blind partisan of antiquity like Brichot, who could not be sarcastic enough about Zola for discovering more poetry in a working-class home or a coal-mine than in the famous palaces of history, or about Goncourt for elevating Diderot above Homer and Watteau above Raphael, should incessantly drum into our ears that Thermopylae and even Austerlitz were nothing compared with Vauquois. And this time, to make things worse, the public, after resisting the modernists of literature and art, is falling into line with the modernists of war, because it is an accepted fashion to think like this and also because little minds are crushed, not by the beauty, but by the hugeness of the action. It is true that *kolossal* is now spelt only with a *k*, but fundamentally, what people are bowing the knee to is simply the colossal. By the way, talking of Brichot, have you seen Morel? I am told that he wants to see me again. He has only to take the first step. I am the older man, it is not for me to make a move."

Unfortunately only the next day, to anticipate a little, M. de Charlus found himself face to face with Morel in the street; Morel, to inflame his jealousy, took him by the arm and told him various tales which were more or less true and which agitated M. de Charlus and made him feel that he needed Morel's presence beside him that evening, that he must not be allowed to go anywhere else. But the young man, catching sight of a friend of his own age, quickly said good-bye to M. de Charlus, whereupon the Baron, hoping that this threat —which naturally he would never carry out—would make Morel stay, said to him: "Take care, I shall have my revenge." Morel, however, went off with a laugh, giving his astonished young friend a pat on the neck and putting his arm round his waist.

No doubt the remark which M. de Charlus had just made to me about Morel's wishing to see him was proof of the extent to which love—and that of the Baron must have been extremely persistent—while it makes a man more imaginative and quicker to take offence, at the same time makes him more credulous and less proud. But when M. de Charlus went on: "He is a boy who is mad about women and thinks of nothing else," his words were truer than he thought. He said this out of vanity and out of love, so that people might suppose that Morel's attachment for him had not been followed by others of the same nature. I certainly did not believe a word of it, I who had seen, what M. de Charlus still did not know, that for fifty francs Morel had once given himself to the Prince de Guermantes for a night. And if, when he saw M. de Charlus pass in the street, Morel (except on the days when, from a need to confess, he would bump into him so as to have the opportunity to say gloomily: "Oh! I am so sorry, I quite see that I have behaved disgustingly towards you"), seated at a café on the pavement with his friends, would join them in noisily pointing at the Baron and making those little clucking noises with which people make fun of an old invert, I was persuaded that this was in order to conceal his own activities; and that likewise, taken aside by the Baron, each one of these public accusers would have done everything that the latter asked of him. I was wrong. If a strange development had brought to inversion—and in every social class—men like Saint-Loup who were furthest removed from it, a movement in the contrary direction had detached from these practices those in whom they were most habitual. In some the change had been wrought by tardy religious scruples, by the emotion they had felt when certain scandals had blazed into publicity, or by the fear of non-existent diseases in which they had been made to believe either, in all sincerity, by a relative who was often a concierge or a valet, or, disingenuously, by a jealous lover who had thought that in this way he would keep for himself alone a young man whom he had, on the contrary, succeeded in detaching from himself as well as from others. Thus it was that the former lift-boy at Balbec would now not have accepted for silver or gold propositions which he had come to regard as no less criminal than treasonable proposals from the enemy. In the case of Morel, however, his refusal of all offers without exception, as to which M. de Charlus had unwittingly spoken a truth which at one and the same time justified his illusions and destroyed his hopes, came from the fact that, two years after having left M. de Charlus, he had fallen in love with a woman whom he now lived with and that she, having the stronger will of the two, had managed to impose upon him an absolute fidelity. So that Morel, who at the time when M. de Charlus was showering so much money upon him had given a night to the Prince de Guermantes for fifty francs, would not now have accepted from the latter or from any other man whatever an offer even of fifty thousand. In default of honour and disinterestedness, his mistress had inculcated in him a certain respect for public opinion, which was not averse even to demonstrating, with a show of bravado, that all the money in the world meant nothing to him when it was offered on certain conditions. Thus, in the flowering of the human species, the interplay of different psychological laws operates always in such a way as to compensate any process that might otherwise, in one direction or the other, through plethora or through rarefaction, bring about the annihilation of the race. And thus, too, among flowers, a similar wisdom, which Darwin was the first to bring to light, governs their different modes of fertilisation, opposing them successively one to another.

"It is a strange thing." M. de Charlus went on, in the shrill little voice with which he sometimes spoke, "I hear people who appear to be perfectly happy all day long and enjoy their cocktails, declare that they will never last until the end of the war, that their hearts won't stand it, that they can think of nothing else, that they will quite suddenly die. And what is really extraordinary is that this does in fact happen! How curious it is! Is it a question of nourishment, because the food they eat is all so badly prepared now, or is it because, to prove their zeal, they harness themselves to tasks which are useless but destroy the mode of life which kept them alive? Anyhow, I have noted an astonishing number of these strange premature deaths, premature at least from the point of view of the deceased. I forget what I was saying to you just now, about Norpois and his admiration for the war. But what a singular manner he has of writing about it! First, have you noticed the pullulation in his articles of new expressions which, when they have eventually worn themselves out by dint of being employed day after day—for really Norpois is indefatigable, I think the death of my aunt Villeparisis must have given him a second youth—are immediately replaced by yet other commonplaces? In the old days I remember you used to amuse yourself by recording the fashionable phrases which appeared and had their vogue and then disappeared: 'he who sows the wind reaps the whirlwind'; 'the dogs bark, the caravan passes'; 'give me sound politics and I will give you sound finances as Baron Louis said'; 'these are symptoms which it would be exaggerated to take tragically but wise to take seriously'; 'to work for the King of Prussia' (this last, inevitably, has come to life again). Well, since then, alas, how many of the species have I seen born and die! We have had 'the scrap of paper', 'the Empires of Prey', 'the famous *Kultur* which consists in massacring defenceless women and children', 'victory belongs, as the Japanese say, to the side which can hold out for a quarter of an hour longer than the other', 'the Germano-Turanians', 'scientific barbarism', 'if we want to win the war, as Mr. Lloyd George has forcibly said' (but that's out of date now), and 'the fighting spirit of the troops' or 'the pluck of the troops'. Even the syntax of the excellent Norpois has undergone in consequence of the war as profound a change as the baking of bread or the speed of transport. Have you observed that the excellent man, wanting to proclaim his own desires as a truth on the verge of being realised, does not dare nevertheless to employ the future pure and simple, since this would run the risk of being contradicted by events, but has adopted as a sign of future tense the verb 'to know'?" I

confessed to M. de Charlus that I did not quite understand
what he meant.

(I ought to mention here that the Duc de Guermantes by
no means shared his brother's pessimism. Furthermore, he was
an anglophile as M. de Charlus was anglophobe. And he regarded M. Caillaux as a traitor who deserved a thousand times
over to be shot. When his brother asked him for proofs of the
man's treason, M. de Guermantes replied that, if we were only
to convict people who signed a statement saying "I am a
traitor", the crime of treason would never be punished. But
in case I should not have occasion to return to the subject, I
will mention also that a few years later, when Caillaux was
on trial, the Duc de Guermantes, animated as he was by
the purest anti-Caillautism, met an English military attaché
and his wife, an exceptionally cultivated couple with whom
he made friends, as he had done at the time of the Dreyfus
case with the three charming ladies; that on the first day of the
acquaintance he was astounded, talking of Caillaux, whom he
regarded as obviously guilty and certain to be convicted, to
hear the cultivated and charming couple say: "But he will
probably be acquitted, there is absolutely no evidence against
him." M. de Guermantes tried to argue that M. de Norpois,
in the witness box, had fixed the unhappy Caillaux with his
gaze and said to him: "You are the Giolitti of France, yes,
Monsieur Caillaux, you are the Giolitti of France." But the
cultivated and charming couple had smiled, made fun of
M. de Norpois, cited proofs of his senility and concluded that,
though *Le Figaro* might have said that he had addressed these
words to "the unhappy M. Caillaux", he had probably in fact
addressed them to a highly amused M. Caillaux. The Duc de
Guermantes lost no time in changing his opinions. That this
change could be brought about by the influence of an English-
woman is not so extraordinary as one might have supposed had

it been foretold even as late as 1919, when the English still spoke of the Germans only as "the Huns" and demanded savage penalties for the guilty. For their opinions too had changed and now—less than a year later—they approved every decision which was likely to distress France and be of help to Germany.)

To return to M. de Charlus: "Yes," he said, in reply to my confession that I did not quite understand. "I mean exactly what I say: 'to know', in the articles of Norpois, indicates the future, it indicates that is to say, the desires of Norpois, and indeed the desires of us all," he added, perhaps without complete sincerity. "I am sure you will agree with me. If 'to know' had not become simply a sign of the future tense, one might just find it intelligible for the subject of this verb to be a country. For instance, every time Norpois says: 'America would not know how to remain indifferent to these repeated violations of international law', 'the bicephalous monarchy would not know how to fail to come to its senses', it is clear that such phrases express the desires of Norpois (they are also mine, and yours)—but here nevertheless the verb can still just retain its original meaning, for a country can 'know', America can 'know', the 'bicephalous' monarchy itself can 'know' (in spite of its eternal 'lack of psychology'). But when Norpois writes: 'These systematic devastations would not know how to persuade the neutrals', 'the region of the Lakes would not know how to fail to fall speedily into the hands of the Allies', 'the results of these neutralist elections would not know how to reflect the opinion of the vast majority of the country', there is no longer any possibility of doubt. For it is certain that these devastations, these regions, these electoral results are inanimate things which cannot 'know'. And in using this formula Norpois is simply addressing to the neutrals an injunction (which, I regret to say, they do not appear to be obeying) to abandon their neutrality, or to the region of the Lakes an injunction no longer to belong to the 'Boches' " (M. de Charlus gave the impression of having to pluck up courage to pronounce the word "Boche", very much as in the past, in the "tram" at Balbec, he had when he had talked about men whose taste is not for women). "And then, have you noticed the wily fashion in which, ever since 1914, Norpois has begun his articles to the neutrals? He starts by declaring that of course it is not for France to interfere in the politics of Italy (or of Rumania or Bulgaria or whatever country it may be). These powers alone must decide, in full independence and with only their own national interests in view, whether or no it is their duty to abandon neutrality. But if these opening statements of the article (what would once have been called the exordium) are disinterested, the sequel is generally much less so. 'Nevertheless,'—this is the gist of what Norpois goes on to say—'it is quite clear that only those nations will derive a material benefit from the struggle which have ranged themselves on the side of Law and Justice. It cannot be expected that the Allies should reward, by bestowing upon them the territories which for centuries have resounded with the groans of their oppressed brethren, those peoples who, following a policy of the least possible effort, have not drawn their sword in the service of the Allies.' Once he has taken this first step towards a counsel of intervention, there is no holding Norpois, it is not only the principle but the moment of intervention as to which, with less and less attempt at disguise, he delivers advice. 'Certainly,' he says, sailing, as he himself would say, under false colours, 'it is for Italy, for Rumania alone to decide when the hour has come to strike and what form their intervention shall take. They cannot, however, be unaware that, if they protract their tergiversations, they run the risk of losing their opportunity. Already the hoofs of the Russian cavalry are sending a shiver of unspeakable panic through the trapped millions of Germany. It must be evident that the peoples who will have done nothing more than fly to the help of that victory of which already we see the resplendent dawn, will have no right or title to the reward that they may still, if they hasten, etc.' It is like the notices you see at the theatre: 'Book now. The last remaining seats will soon be sold.' And what makes this reasoning all the stupider is that Norpois has to revise it every six months, saying to Rumania at regular intervals: 'The hour has come for Rumania to determine whether or no she wishes to realise her national aspirations. Any further delay and it may be too late.' But though he has been saying this for three years, not only has the 'too late' not yet come, the offers that are made to Rumania are constantly being improved. In the same way he invites France, etc., to intervene in Greece by virtue of her status as a protective power because the treaty that bound Greece to Serbia has not been observed. But, candidly, if France were not at war and did not desire the assistance or the benevolent neutrality of Greece, would she take it into her head to intervene as a protective power? Those moral sentiments which make France raise her voice in horror because Greece has not kept her engagements towards Serbia, are they not silent the moment it is a question of the equally flagrant violation of treaties by Rumania or Italy, which countries— rightly I think, and the same is true of Greece—have failed to carry out their obligations (though these are less imperative and less far-reaching than they are said to be) as Allies of Germany? The truth is that people see everything through the medium of their newspaper, and what else could they do seeing that they are not personally acquainted with the men or the events under discussion? At the time of the Case in which you took so passionate and so bizarre an interest, in that epoch from which it is now the convention to say that we are

separated by centuries—for the philosophers of the war have
spread the doctrine that all links with the past are broken—I
was shocked to see men and women of my family express high
esteem for anti-clericals with a Communard past whom their
newspaper represented to them as anti-Dreyfusards, and at the
same time severe disapproval of a Catholic general of good
family who happened to be a revisionist. I am no less shocked
now to see all Frenchmen execrate that same Emperor Franz
Josef whom once they venerated—and rightly, I may say, I
who have known him well and whom he is gracious enough to
treat as his cousin. Ah! I haven't written to him since the war,"
he added, as if he were boldly confessing a fault for which he
knew quite well he could not be blamed. "No, the first year
I did write, but once only. But what would you have me do?
My respect for him is unaltered, but I have many young relatives here fighting in our lines who would, I know, be most
displeased were I to carry on a regular correspondence with
the head of a nation that is at war with us. What else could I
do? Criticise me he who will," he continued, and again he
seemed bravely to invite my reproaches, "but in these times I
have not wanted a letter signed Charlus to arrive in Vienna.
There is only one point in the conduct of the old monarch
that I would wish to criticise at all severely, and that is that a
nobleman of his rank, head of one of the most ancient and
illustrious houses of Europe, should have allowed himself to
be led astray by a petty land-owner—a very intelligent man, of
course, but still a complete upstart—like William of Hohenzollern. It is one of the more shocking anomalies of this war."
And as, the moment he returned to considerations of geneal-
ogy and precedence, which for him fundamentally dominated
all others, M. de Charlus became capable of extraordinary
childishness, he said to me, in the tone that he might have used
in speaking of the Marne or Verdun, that there were

important and extremely curious things which ought not to be omitted by anyone who came to write the history of this war. "For instance," he said, "everybody is so ignorant that no one has bothered to point out this very striking fact: the Grand Master of the Order of Malta, who is a pure Boche, continues none the less to live in Rome where, as Grand Master of our order, he enjoys the privilege of extraterritoriality. Most interesting," he added significantly, as if to say: "You see that you have not wasted your evening by meeting me." I thanked him, and he assumed the modest air of one who asks no reward for services rendered.

M. de Charlus still retained all his respect and all his affection for certain great ladies who were accused of defeatism, just as he had in the past for others who had been accused of Dreyfusism. He regretted only that by stooping to meddle in politics they had given a handle to the "polemics of the journalists". In his own attitude to them nothing had changed. So systematic was his frivolity that for him birth, combined with beauty and with other sources of prestige, was the durable thing and the war, like the Dreyfus case, merely a vulgar and fugitive fashion. Had the Duchesse de Guermantes been shot for trying to make a separate peace with Austria, he would still have considered her no less noble than before, no more dishonoured by this mischance than is Marie Antoinette in our eyes from having been condemned to the guillotine. He was speaking seriously now and for a brief instant, with the noble air of a Saint-Vallier or a Saint-Mégrin, erect and stiff and solemn, he was free of all those mannerisms by which men of his sort betray themselves. And yet, why is it that not one of these men can ever have a voice which hits absolutely the right note? Even at this moment, when M. de Charlus's voice was so very near to solemnity, its pitch was still false, it still needed the tuning-fork to correct it. "Now, what was I saying to you?" he went on. "Ah! yes, that people hate Franz Josef now, because they take their cue from their newspaper. As for King Constantine of Greece and the Tsar of Bulgaria, the public has oscillated more than once between aversion and sympathy, according as it has been said turn and turn about that they would join the side of the Entente or of what Brichot calls the Central Empires. Brichot, by the way, is telling us at every moment that 'the hour of Venizelos will strike'. Now I do not doubt that M. Venizelos is a statesman of great capabilities, but who says that the Greeks are so particularly eager to have him? We are told that he wanted Greece to keep her engagements towards Serbia. Even so, it would be as well to know what these engagements were and whether they were more far-reaching than those which Italy and Rumania did not scruple to violate. We display for the manner in which Greece implements her treaties and respects her constitution an anxiety which we certainly would not display were it not in our interest to do so. Had there been no war, do you think the 'guarantor' powers would even have noticed the dissolution of the Chambers? What I see is simply that one by one the supports of the King of Greece are being withdrawn from him, so that when the day arrives when he no longer has an army to defend him he can be thrown out of the country or put into prison. I was saying just now that the public judges the King of Greece and the King of the Bulgars only as it is told to judge them by the newspapers. But here again, what opinion of these monarchs could people have except that of their newspapers, seeing that they are not acquainted with them? I personally have seen a great deal of them both, I knew Constantine of Greece very well indeed when he was Diadoch, he is a really splendid man. I have always thought that the Emperor Nicholas had a great affection for him. Of course I mean to imply nothing dishonourable. Princess Christian used to talk openly about it, but she is a terrible scandal-monger. As for the Tsar of the Bulgars, he is an out-and-out nancy and a monstrous liar, but very intelligent, a remarkable man. He likes me very much."

M. de Charlus, who could be so delightful, became horrid when he touched on these subjects. He brought to them that same sort of complacency which we find so exasperating in the invalid who keeps drawing attention to his good health. I have often thought that in the "Twister" of Balbec the faithful who so longed to hear the admission which he was too secretive to make, would in fact have been unable to endure any real display of his mania; ill at ease, breathing with difficulty as one does in a sick-room or in the presence of a morphia addict who takes out his syringe in public, they would themselves have put a stop to the confidences which they imagined they desired. It was, indeed, exasperating to hear the whole world accused, and often without any semblance of proof, by someone who omitted himself from the special category to which one knew perfectly well that he belonged and in which he so readily included others. In spite of all his intelligence, he had in this context fabricated for himself a narrow little philosophy (at the bottom of which there was perhaps just a spark of that interest in the curiousness of life which Swann had felt) which explained everything by reference to these special causes and in which, as always happens when a man stoops to the level of his own vice, he was not only unworthy of himself but exceptionally satisfied with himself. Thus it was that this dignified and noble man put on the most imbecile smile to complete the following little speech: "As there are strong presumptions of the same kind as for Ferdinand of Coburg in the case of the Emperor William, this may well be the reason why Tsar Ferdinand has joined the side of the 'Empires of Prey'.

After all, it is very understandable, one is indulgent to a *sister*, one refuses her nothing. To my mind that would be a very pretty explanation of Bulgaria's alliance with Germany." And at this stupid explanation M. de Charlus pealed with laughter as though he really found it most ingenious—an explanation which, even had it been based upon true facts, was in the same puerile category as the observations which M. de Charlus made about the war when he judged it from the point of view of a feudal lord or a Knight of St. John of Jerusalem. He ended with a more sensible remark: "What is astonishing," he said, "is that this public which judges the men and events of the war solely from the newspapers, is persuaded that it forms its own opinions."

In this M. de Charlus was right. I have been told that it was fascinating to see the moments of silence and hesitation, so exactly like those that are necessary not merely to the pronouncement but to the formation of a personal opinion, which Mme de Forcheville used to have before declaring, as though it were a heart-felt sentiment: "No, I do not think they will take Warsaw"; "I have the impression that it cannot last another winter"; "the worst thing that could happen is a patched-up peace"; "what alarms me, if you want to know, is the Chamber"; "yes, I believe all the same, that we shall succeed in breaking through". And to make these statements Odette assumed a simpering air which became even more exaggerated when she said: "I don't say the German armies do not fight well, but they lack what is called pluck." In pronouncing the word "pluck" (and it was the same when she merely said "fighting spirit") she executed with her hand the sculptural gesture, and with her eyes the wink, of an art student employing a technical term of the studios. Her language now, however, even more than in the past bore witness to her admiration for the English, whom she was no longer obliged to call, as formerly, merely "our neighbours across the Channel", or at most "our friends the English": they were "our loyal allies". Needless to say she never failed, relevant or not, to quote the expression "fair play" (and to point out that in the eyes of the English the Germans were unfair players) and also: "the important thing is to win the war, as our brave allies say." She even had an unfortunate habit of associating the name of her son-in-law with the subject of English soldiers and of referring to the pleasure which he derived from living shoulder to shoulder with Australians and Scotsmen, New Zealanders and Canadians. "My son-in-law Saint-Loup has learned the slang of all the brave 'tommies', he can make himself understood by the ones from the most distant 'dominions'—and I don't mean just the general in command of the base, he fraternises with the humblest 'private'."

May this parenthesis on Mme de Forcheville serve as my excuse, while I am strolling along the boulevards side by side with M. de Charlus, for embarking upon another, of greater length but useful as an illustration of this era, on the relations of Mme Verdurin with Brichot. The truth is that if, as we have seen, poor Brichot was judged without indulgence by M. de Charlus (because the latter was both extremely intelligent and more or less unconsciously pro-German), he was treated still worse by the Verdurins. They no doubt were chauvinistic, and this ought to have made them appreciate Brichot's articles, which were in any case quite as good as many pieces of writing which delighted Mme Verdurin. But first, the reader may remember that already at La Raspelière Brichot had become for the Verdurins, instead of the great man that he had once been in their eyes, if not actually a scapegoat like Saniette at any rate a target for their scarcely disguised ridicule. Still, at that period he remained a faithful of

the faithful and thus was entitled to a share in the advantages
tacitly conferred by the statutes upon all the founding or associate members of the little group. But while, under cover of
the war perhaps, or through the rapid crystallisation of a long-
delayed social prestige, of which in fact all the necessary elements had for a long time existed in it, invisible and in a state
of saturation, the drawing-room of the Verdurins had been
opening itself to a new world and the faithful, at first the baits
to attract this new world, had ended by being invited less and
less themselves, at the same time a parallel phenomenon had
been taking place in the life of Brichot. In spite of the Sorbonne, in spite of the Institut, before the war he had been a
celebrity only inside the Verdurin drawing-room. But when
he began to write, almost every day, articles adorned with that
second-rate brilliance which we have so often seen him scatter
open-handed in the presence of the faithful, yet enriched too
with a perfectly genuine learning which, like a true man of
the Sorbonne, he made no attempt to conceal however he
might clothe it in agreeable forms, the "great world" was
literally dazzled. And for once it had bestowed its favour
upon someone who was far from being a nonentity, upon a
man who could hold the attention of an audience by the
fertility of his intelligence and the resources of his memory.
So that now, while three duchesses spent the evening with
Mme Verdurin, three other duchesses contested the honour
of having the great man at their dinner table, and one of these
invitations the great man usually accepted, feeling all the freer
to do this since Mme Verdurin, exasperated by the success of
his articles with the Faubourg Saint-Germain, was careful
never to ask him to her house when some smart woman was
to be there whom he did not yet know and who would lose
no time in luring him away. Thus journalism (into which he
was really doing no more than pour belatedly, with applause

and in return for a magnificent financial reward, what all his
life he had squandered incognito and for nothing in the Verdurin drawing-room—for his articles, since he had so much
knowledge and wrote with such ease, cost him no more trouble
than his conversation) might have led, indeed at one moment
seemed to be leading Brichot to an indefeasible glory, had
it not been for Mme Verdurin. Admittedly, these articles
were far from being as remarkable as fashionable people supposed. The vulgarity of the man was apparent in every line
beneath the pedantry of the scholar. And side by side with
images which had absolutely no meaning ("the Germans will
no longer be able to look Beethoven's statue in the face;
Schiller must have shuddered in his tomb; the ink which had
guaranteed the neutrality of Belgium was scarcely dry; Lenin
speaks, but his words are scattered on the winds of the steppe")
there were trivialities such as: "twenty thousand prisoners,
that is indeed a figure; our command will know how to keep
a weather eye open; we mean to win, that sums it up in a
nutshell." Yet mixed with all this, how much knowledge,
how much intelligence, what just reasoning! Mme Verdurin,
however, never began an article by Brichot without first dwelling upon the enjoyable thought that she was going to find
ridiculous things in it, and she read it with the most sustained
attention in order to be certain of not letting them escape her.
And unfortunately it could not be denied that ridiculous things
there were. But the faithful did not even wait until they had
found them. The most felicitous quotation from an author
who was really very little known, at least in the work to which
Brichot referred, was seized upon as proof of the most in-
sufferable pedantry, and Mme Verdurin could hardly wait for
the hour of dinner when she would unloose the torrential
laughter of her guests. "Well, what do you say to to-night's
Brichot? I thought of you when I read the quotation from

Cuvier. I honestly think the man is going mad." "I haven't read it yet," Cottard would say. "What, you haven't read it yet? But you don't know what delights you are missing. I promise you you will die of laughter." And pleased at heart that someone had not yet read the latest Brichot, since this meant that she herself could call attention to the ludicrous things in it, Mme Verdurin would tell the butler to bring *Le Temps* and would herself read the article aloud, lingering with emphasis on the most simple phrases. After dinner, for the whole of the evening, the anti-Brichot campaign would continue, but with hypocritical reservations. "I won't say it too loud because I am afraid that over there", she would say, indicating Comtesse Molé, "there is a good deal of admiration for this stuff. Fashionable people are more foolish than is generally supposed." In saying this she did her best, by speaking just loud enough, to let Mme Molé hear that she was being talked about, and at the same time to convey to her, by occasionally lowering her voice, that she did not want her to hear what she was saying. Mme Molé was cowardly enough to disown Brichot, whom in fact she thought the equal of Michelet. She said that of course Mme Verdurin was right, and so as to end by nevertheless saying something which seemed to her incontestably true, added: "What one must allow him, is that it is well written." "You call that well written?" said Mme Verdurin. "Personally, I consider that it might have been written by a pig"—an audacity which always made her fashionable guests laugh, particularly as Mme Verdurin, as though she herself were frightened by the word "pig", uttered it in a whisper, holding her hand to her lips. Her rage against Brichot was still further increased by the naive fashion in which he displayed his pleasure at his success, in spite of the fits of ill humour provoked in him by the censorship every time that it—as he expressed it, for he liked to employ new words in order to show that he was not too donnish—"blue-pencilled" part of his article. In his presence, however, Mme Verdurin did not reveal too clearly, save by a certain grumpiness which might have been a warning to a more perspicacious man, the poor opinion which she had of the writings of "Chochotte". Only once did she criticise him, for using the word "I" too often. And it was true that he was in the habit of using it continually, firstly because, with his professorial habits, he was constantly employing phrases like "I grant that" and even (in the sense of "I am willing to admit that") "I am willing that", as for instance: "I am willing that the vast development of the fronts should necessitate, etc.", but principally because, as a militant anti-Dreyfusard of the old days who had had suspicions of German preparations long before the war, he had frequently had occasion to write: "Since 1897 I have been denouncing": "I pointed out in 1901"; "In my little pamphlet, of the greatest rarity today *(habent sua fata libelli)* I drew attention", and the habit, once formed, had remained with him. He turned crimson at Mme Verdurin's remark, which had been made with acerbity. "You are right, Madame. A man who was no friend of the Jesuits—I am referring to M. Combes—although he never had the honour of a preface from our sweet master of delicious scepticism, Anatole France, who was, if I am not mistaken, my adversary . . . before the Flood, has observed that the first person singular is always odious." From that moment Brichot replaced "I" by "one", but *one* did not prevent the reader from seeing that the author was speaking of himself, indeed it permitted him to speak of himself more frequently than ever, to comment on the most insignificant of his own phrases, to build a whole article round a single negative statement, always behind the protective screen of *one*. If for example Brichot had said, in another article perhaps, that the German armies had lost some of their strength, he would begin thus: "One does not camouflage the truth here. One has said that the German armies have lost some of their strength. One has not said that they do not still possess great strength. Still less will one write that they no longer have any strength at all. Nor will one say that the ground gained, if it is not, etc." In short, simply by enunciating all that he would not say and by recalling all that he had said some years ago and all that Clausewitz, Jomini, Ovid, Apollonius of Tyana and others had said in the more recent or more remote past, Brichot could easily have put together the material for a solid volume. It is to be regretted that he did not publish one, for these erudite articles are now difficult to come by. The Faubourg Saint-Germain, admonished by Mme Verdurin, began by laughing at Brichot in her drawing-room, but continued, after departing from the little clan, to admire him. Then after a while it became the fashion to scoff at him as it had previously been to admire him, and even those ladies who continued to find him interesting in secret while they were actually reading his articles, checked themselves and mocked as soon as they were no longer alone, so as not to appear less clever than their friends. Never was Brichot so much discussed in the little clan as at this period, but in a spirit of derision. The criterion for judging the intelligence of a newcomer was simply his opinion of Brichot's articles, and if the first time he gave the wrong reply no pains were spared to instruct him how it was that you were recognised to be foolish or clever.

"Well, my poor friend," M. de Charlus went on, "all this is very dreadful, and tedious articles are not the only things we have to deplore. We hear talk of vandalism, of the destruction of statues. But the destruction of so many marvellous young men, who while they lived were incomparable polychrome statues, is that not also vandalism? Will not a town which has lost all its beautiful men be like a town of which all the sculpture has been smashed to pieces? What pleasure can I get from dining in a restaurant where I am served by moth-eaten old buffoons who look like Father Didon, if not by hags in mob-caps who make me think I have strayed into one of Duval's soup-kitchens? Yes, it's as bad as that, my boy, and I think I have the right to say these things, because Beauty is still Beauty when it exists in a living material. How delightful to be served by rachitic creatures with spectacles on their noses and the reason for their exemption from military service written all over their faces! In these changed times, if you wish to rest your eyes on someone nice-looking in a res-taurant, you must look not among the waiters who are serving you but among the customers who are eating and drinking. And then in the old days one could always see a waiter a second time, although they frequently changed, but with some English lieutenant who has perhaps never been to the restaur-ant before and may well be killed tomorrow what hope is there of finding out who he is and when he will return? When Augustus of Poland, as we are told by the charming Morand, the delightful author of *Clarisse*, exchanged one of his regi-ments for a collection of Chinese porcelain, it is my opinion that he made a bad bargain. To think that all those huge foot-men six foot tall and more, who used to adorn the monumental staircases of the lovely hostesses whose houses we visited, have one and all been killed, and that most of them joined up be-cause it was dinned into them that the war would last two months! Ah! they did not know as I do the strength of Ger-many, the courage of the Prussian race," he said, forgetting himself. And then, realising that he had revealed too much of his point of view, he went on: "It is not so much Germany that I fear for France as the war itself. People away from the front imagine that the war is no more than a gigantic boxing match, of which, thanks to the newspapers, they are spectators at a comfortable distance. But it is nothing of the sort. It is an illness which, when it seems to have been defeated at one point, returns at another. Today Noyon will be recovered from the enemy, tomorrow there will be no bread or chocolate, the next day the man who thought he was safe and was prepared, if necessary, to face death on the battlefield because he had not imagined it, will be panic-stricken to read in the newspapers that his class has been called up. As for monuments, it is not so much the quality as the quantity of the destruction that appals me, I am less horrified at the disappearance of a unique monument like Rheims than at that of all the living wholes which once made the smallest village in France instructive and charming."

My mind turned immediately to Combray, but in the past I had thought that I would lower myself in the eyes of Mme de Guermantes by confessing to the humble position which my family occupied there. I asked myself now whether the facts had not been revealed to the Guermantes and to M. de Charlus, either by Legrandin or by Swann or Saint-Loup or Morel, and I said nothing, even this silence being less painful to me than a retrospective explanation. I only hoped that M. de Charlus would not mention Combray.

"I do not wish to speak ill of the Americans, Monsieur," he went on, "it seems that they are inexhaustibly generous, and as there has been nobody to conduct the orchestra in this war, as each performer has joined in a long time after the one before and the Americans only began when we had almost finished, they may possibly have an ardour which in us four years of war have succeeded in damping. Even before the war they were fond of our country and our art, they paid high prices for our masterpieces. They have taken many home with them. But this uprooted art, as M. Barrès would call it, is precisely the opposite of what once formed the delicious charm of France. The *château* explained the church, which itself, because it had been a place of pilgrimage, explained the *chanson de geste*. I need not dwell upon the illustriousness of my family and my connections, which in any case is not the subject that concerns us. But recently I had occasion, to settle a matter of business, and in spite of a certain coolness that exists between the young couple and myself, to visit my niece Saint-Loup who lives at Combray. Combray was simply a small town like hundreds of others. But the ancestors of my family were portrayed as donors in some of the windows in the church, and in others our armorial bearings were depicted. We had our chapel there, and our tombs. And now this church has been destroyed by the French and the English because it served as an observation-post to the Germans. All that mixture of art and still-living history that was France is being destroyed, and we have not seen the end of the process yet. Of course I am not so absurd as to compare, for family reasons, the destruction of the church of Combray with that of the cathedral of Rheims, that miracle of a Gothic cathedral which seemed, somehow naturally, to have re-discovered the purity of antique sculpture, or of the cathedral of Amiens. I do not know whether the raised arm of St. Firmin is still intact today or whether it has been broken. If so, the loftiest affirmation of faith and energy ever made has disappeared from this world." "You mean its symbol, Monsieur," I interrupted. "And I adore certain symbols no less than you do. But it would be absurd to sacrifice to the symbol the reality that it symbolises. Cathedrals are to be adored until the day when, to preserve them, it would be necessary to deny the truths which they teach. The raised arm of St. Firmin said, with an almost military gesture of command: 'Let us be broken, if honour requires.' Do not sacrifice men to stones whose beauty comes precisely from their having for a moment given fixed form to human truths." "I understand what you mean," M. de Charlus replied, "and M. Barrès, who has sent us, alas, on too many pilgrimages to the statue of Strasbourg and the tomb of M. Déroulède, was both moving and graceful when he wrote that the cathedral of Rheims itself was less dear to us than the lives of our infantrymen. An assertion which makes nonsense of the wrath of our newspapers against the German general in command there who said that the cathedral of Rheims was less precious to him than the life of one German soldier. Indeed, the exasperating and depressing thing is that each country says the same. The reasons for which the industrialists of Germany declare the possession of Belfort indispensable for safeguarding their nation against our ideas of revenge, are the very same reasons as those which Barrès gives for demanding Mainz as a protection against the recurrent urge to invade which possesses the Boches. Why is it that the recovery of Alsace-Lorraine seemed to France an insufficient motive for embarking on a war, yet a sufficient motive for continuing one, for redeclaring it afresh year after year? You appear to believe that nothing can rob France of victory now and with all my heart I hope that you are right, you may be quite sure of that. But is it not a fact that since, rightly or wrongly, the Allies have come to believe that they are sure to win (for my part naturally I should be enchanted by this solution, but what I see is mostly a profusion of victories on paper, Pyrrhic victories whose cost is not revealed to us) and the Boches no longer believe that they are sure to win, we see Germany striving to make peace quickly and France to prolong the war, France which is a just nation and does right to pronounce words of justice but is also sweet, gentle France and ought to pronounce words of mercy, were it only in order to spare her own children and to allow the flowers which bloom with each

new spring to shed their lustre on other things than tombs?
Be honest, my friend, you yourself once propounded a theory
to me about things existing only in virtue of a creation which
is perpetually renewed. The creation of the world did not take
place once and for all, you said, it is, of necessity, taking place
every day. Well, if you are sincere, you cannot except war
from this theory. Never mind if the excellent Norpois has
written (trotting out one of those oratorical phrases which are
as dear to him as 'the dawn of victory' and 'General Winter'):
'Now that Germany has determined on war, the die is cast',
the truth is that every morning war is declared afresh. And
the men who wish to continue it are as guilty as the men who
began it, more guilty perhaps, for the latter perhaps did not
foresee all its horrors. Besides, can we be sure that a war thus
prolonged, even if it must eventually end in victory, is without
danger? It is difficult to speak of things which have no pre-
cedent and of the repercussions upon an organism of an operation which is being attempted for the first time. Generally, it
is true, novelties which people find alarming pass off very
well. The most prudent republicans thought that it was mad
to separate the church from the state. It was as easy as sending
a letter through the post. Dreyfus was rehabilitated, Picquart
was made Minister of War, and nobody uttered a murmur.
Yet what may we not fear from the stress and strain of a war
which has continued without pause for several years? What
will men do when they return from it? Will fatigue have
broken them or will it have driven them mad? All this could
have grave results, if not for France, at least for the government, perhaps even for the present form of government. You
once made me read Maurras' excellent novel *Aimée de Coigny*.
The original Aimée, you remember, was waiting for the
collapse of the Empire to ensue from the war that it was
waging in 1812, and I should be surprised if she has not her

counterpart today. If a present-day Aimée de Coigny exists, will her hopes with regard to the Republic be fulfilled? I should be sorry to see that happen. But to return to the war itself, can we say that the man who first began it was the Emperor William? I am very doubtful about that. And if it was, what has he done that Napoleon, for instance, did not do —something that I certainly find abominable, but that I am astonished to see also inspiring such horror in those who burn incense before Napoleon, those who on the day that war was declared exclaimed like General Pau: 'I have been waiting forty years for this day. It is the most glorious day of my life.' Heaven knows whether anyone protested with greater energy than myself at the time when a deference out of all proportion was paid by society to the nationalists and the military men, when every friend of the arts was accused of occupying himself with things of baleful import to France and all civilisation of an unwarlike nature was thought to be pernicious! In those days an authentic member of the best society hardly counted compared with a general. Some madwoman came within an inch of presenting *me* to M. Syveton, as if *I* were *his* inferior. You will tell me that the rules I was striving to maintain were merely social ones. But for all their apparent frivolity they might have prevented many excesses. I have always honoured the defenders of grammar or logic. We realise fifty years later that they have averted serious dangers. Today our nationalists are the most anti-German of men, the most determined to persevere to the bitter end. But in the last fifteen years their philosophy has completely changed. It is true that they are pressing for the continuation of the war. But they are doing this only in order to exterminate a warlike race, they are doing it from love of peace. The idea of a martial civilisation, which fifteen years ago they thought so beautiful, now fills them with horror; not only do they reproach the Prussians for having allowed the military element to predominate in their state, they claim that throughout the ages military civilisations have been destructive of all that they now hold precious, not only of the arts but also of chivalry towards women. And if any critic of their views is converted to nationalism he at the same moment becomes a friend of peace. He is persuaded that in all martial civilisations women have been humiliated and crushed. One dare not reply that the 'lady' of a knight in the Middle Ages or the Beatrice of Dante was perhaps placed upon a throne as elevated as the heroines of M. Becque. Any day now I expect to see myself placed at table beneath a Russian revolutionary or simply beneath one of these generals of ours who wage war out of horror of war and in order to punish a people for cultivating an ideal which fifteen years ago they themselves regarded as the only one that could invigorate a nation. It is not many months since the unhappy Tsar was honoured for his part in assembling the conference at The Hague. But now that people hail the advent of a free Russia they forget his claim to glory. So turns the wheel of the world. Meanwhile Germany uses expressions so similar to those of France that one can hardly believe she is not quoting her, she never tires of saying that she is 'struggling for existence'. When I read: 'We shall struggle against an implacable and cruel enemy until we have obtained a peace which will give us guarantees for the future against all aggression and ensure that the blood of our brave soldiers shall not have flowed in vain', or: 'he who is not for us is against us,' I do not know whether the words are the Emperor William's or M. Poincaré's, for they have both of them, with a few trifling differences, pronounced such phrases twenty times, although to be truthful I must admit that in this instance it is the Emperor who has copied the President of the Republic. France would perhaps have been less eager to prolong the war if she had remained weak, and Germany certainly would have been in less of a hurry to end it if she had not ceased to be strong. I should say, to be as strong as she was; for strong, as you will see, she still is."

He had got into the habit of talking at the top of his voice, from nervousness, from the need to find an outlet for impressions which, never having cultivated any art, he was obliged to discharge—as an airman, if necessary, discharges his bombs in open country—even where his words could impinge upon nobody, particularly in society, where they fell completely at random and where people listened to him out of snobbishness, uncritically and (to such an extent did he tyrannise his audience) one may say under compulsion and even from fear. On the boulevards this loud harangue of his was also a mark of contempt for the passers-by, for whom he no more lowered his voice than he would have stepped aside to avoid them. But it struck a discordant note there and caused astonishment and, worse than that, rendered audible to the people who turned round to look at us remarks which might well have made them take us for defeatists. I pointed this out to M. de Charlus but succeeded only in arousing his mirth. "You must admit that that would be most amusing," he said. "After all," he went on, "one never knows, every evening each one of us runs the risk of being part of the next day's news. Is there really any reason why I should not be shot in a ditch at Vincennes? That is what happened to my great-uncle the Duc d'Enghien. The thirst for noble blood maddens a certain rabble—and here they show a greater fastidiousness than lions, for those beasts, as you know, would throw themselves even upon Mme Verdurin if she had so much as a scratch upon her nose. Upon what in my youth we would have called her boko!" And he began to roar with laughter as if we had been alone in a room.

At moments, seeing suspicious-looking individuals drawn out of the shadows by the passage of M. de Charlus conglomerate at a little distance from him, I asked myself whether it would be more agreeable to him if I left him alone or remained with him. In the same way, if you meet an old man who is subject to frequent epileptic fits and see from the incoherence of his gait that an attack is probably imminent, you may ask yourself whether your company is more desired by him as a support or dreaded as that of a witness from whom he would prefer to conceal the attack and whose mere presence may perhaps suffice to bring it on, whereas absolute calm might succeed in averting it. But in the case of the sick man the possibility of the event upon which you are uncertain whether or no you ought to turn your back is revealed by his walking in circles as if he were drunk; while in that of M. de Charlus the divagations—sign of a possible incident as to which I did not know whether he desired or feared that my presence should prevent its occurrence—were transferred, as in an ingenious stage production, from the Baron himself, who was walking straight ahead, to a whole circle of supernumerary actors. All the same, it is my belief that he preferred to avoid the encounter, for he dragged me down a side-street, darker than the boulevard but into which nevertheless the latter was incessantly discharging—or else like a tributary stream they were flowing towards it—soldiers of every arm and of every nation, a rising youthful tide, compensatory and consoling for M. de Charlus, the reverse of that ebb-tide of all men towards the frontier which in the first days of mobilisation had made a vacuum in the capital. At every moment M. de Charlus expressed his admiration for the brilliant uniforms which passed before us, which made of Paris a town as cosmopolitan as a port, as unreal as a stage setting designed by a painter who has simply put up a few scraps of architecture as an excuse for assembling the most variegated and glittering costumes. Literally he did not know which way to turn his head; often he raised it, regretting that he did not have a pair of field-glasses (which would in fact have been of very little use to him), since because of the Zeppelin raid of two days earlier, which had caused the authorities to redouble their precautions, there were soldiers in greater numbers than usual even in the sky. The aeroplanes which a few hours earlier I had seen, like insects, as brown dots upon the surface of the blue evening, now passed like luminous fire-ships through the darkness of the night, which was made darker still by the partial extinction of the street lamps. And perhaps the greatest impression of beauty that these human shooting stars made us feel came simply from their forcing us to look at the sky, towards which normally we so seldom raise our eyes. In this Paris, whose beauty in 1914 I had seen awaiting almost defenceless the threat of the approaching enemy, there was certainly, as there had been then, the ancient unalterable splendour of a moon cruelly and mysteriously serene, which poured down its useless beauty upon the still untouched buildings of the capital; but as in 1914, and more now than in 1914, there was also something else, there were lights from a different source, intermittent beams which, whether they came from the aeroplanes or from the searchlights of the Eiffel Tower, one knew to be directed by an intelligent will, by a friendly vigilance which gave one the same kind of emotion, inspired the same sort of gratitude and calm that I had felt in Saint-Loup's room at Doncières, in the cell of that military cloister where so many fervent and disciplined hearts were exercising themselves in readiness for the day when, without hesitation, in the midst of their youth, they would consummate their sacrifice.

After the raid of two days earlier, when it had been more full of movement than the earth, the sky had become calm again as the sea becomes calm after a storm. But like the sea after a storm, it had not yet recovered absolute tranquillity. Aeroplanes were still mounting like rockets to the level of the stars, and searchlights, as they quartered the sky, wafted slowly across it what looked like a pale dust of stars, of errant milky ways. Meanwhile the aeroplanes took their places among the constellations and seeing these "new stars" one might well have supposed oneself to be in another hemisphere. M. de Charlus spoke to me of his admiration for these airmen of ours, and went on, since he was no more capable of checking the flow of his pro-German feelings than of his other inclinations, even though at the same time he denied both the one and the other tendency: "I must add of course that I have just as much admiration for the Germans who go up in the Gothas. And when it comes to the Zeppelins, think of the courage that is needed! They are heroes, there is no other word for it. What difference can it make that they are attacking civilians, if guns are firing at them? Are you afraid of the Gothas and the bombardment?" I admitted that I was not, but perhaps I was wrong. No doubt, my idleness having given me the habit, when it was a question of my work, of putting it off from one day to another, I imagined that death too might be postponed in the same fashion. How should one be afraid of a bombardment when one is convinced that one will not be hit today? Anyhow, formed in isolation, the idea of bombs being dropped, the idea of the possibility of death, had added nothing tragic to the image which I had in my mind of the German airships, until from one of them, storm-tossed and partly hidden from my sight by the thick billowing mists of an agitated sky, from a flying object which, though I knew it to be murderous, I imagined only as stellar and celestial, I had one evening seen the gesture of a bomb dropped upon us. For the novel reality of a danger is perceived only through the medium of that new thing, not assimilable to anything that we already know, to which we give the name "an impression" and which is often, as in the present case, epitomised in a line, a line which defines an intention and possesses the latent potentiality of the action which has given it its particular form, like the invisible line described by this falling bomb or those other lines which I had seen at the same time from the Pont de la Concorde, on all sides of the threatening, hunted aeroplane, as though they had been reflections in the clouds of the fountains of the Champs Elysées and the Place de la Concorde and the Tuileries: the beams of the searchlights travelling through the sky like luminous jets of water, which also were lines full of intention, full of the provident and protective intentions of men of power and wisdom to whom, as on that night in the barracks at Doncières, I felt grateful for condescending to employ their strength, with this so beautiful precision, in watching over our safety.

The night was as beautiful as in 1914, and the threat to Paris was as great. The moonlight was like a soft and steady magnesium flare, by the light of which some camera might, for the last time, have been recording nocturnal images of those lovely groups of buildings like the Place Vendôme and the Place de la Concorde, to which my fear of the shells that were perhaps about to destroy them imparted by contrast, as they stood in their still intact beauty, a sort of plenitude, as if they were bending forward and freely offering their defenceless architecture to the blows that might fall. "You are not afraid?" M. de Charlus repeated. "The people of Paris don't realise the situation. I am told that Mme Verdurin gives parties every day. I know it only from hearsay, personally I know absolutely nothing about them, I have completely broken off relations," he added, lowering not only his eyes as if a telegraph boy had passed, but also his head and his shoulders and raising his arm with the gesture that signifies, if not "I wash my hands of them" at any rate "I can tell you nothing about them" (not that I had asked him anything). "I know that Morel still goes there a lot," he went on (it was the first time that he had mentioned him again). "It is rumoured that he much regrets the past and would like to make it up with me," he continued, exhibiting at one and the same time the credulity of a man of the Faubourg who says: "People say that there are more talks than ever going on between France and Germany, and even that negotiations have been started", and that of the lover whom the most cruel rebuffs are unable to convince. "In any case, if he wants it, he only has to say so. I am older than he, it is not for me to take the first step." And certainly there was no need to say this, so evident was it. But it was not even sincere, and this made one very embarrassed for M. de Charlus, for one felt that, by saying that it was not for him to take the first step, he was in fact making one and was waiting for me to offer to undertake a reconciliation.

Naturally I was familiar with the credulity, naive or pretended, of people who love someone, or simply are not invited to someone's house, and attribute to that someone a desire of which, in fact, in spite of wearisome solicitations, he has given no hint. But from the sudden tremor of the voice with which M. de Charlus pronounced these words, from the anxious look which flickered in the depths of his eyes, I got the impression that there was something more here than an ordinary attempt at bluff. I was not mistaken, and I will relate straight away the two facts which proved subsequently that I was right. (I take a leap of many years for the second of these incidents, which was posterior to the death of M. de Charlus, who was not to die until a much later period and whom we shall have occasion to see again a number of times, greatly changed from what we have known him to be, particularly the last time of all, when he had come to forget Morel completely.) The first of these incidents took place only two or three years after the evening on which, as I am describing, I walked down the boulevards with M. de Charlus. About two years after this evening then, I met Morel. I thought immediately of M. de Charlus, of the pleasure it would give him to see the violinist again, and I urged Morel to go and see him, even if it were only once. "He has been good to you," I said, "he is an old man now, he may die, you should settle old scores and obliterate all trace of your quarrel." Morel appeared to be entirely of my opinion as to the desirability of making peace, but he none the less refused categorically to visit M. de Charlus even once. "You are wrong," I said. "Is it from obstinacy, from indolence, from spite, from misplaced vanity, from concern for your virtue (you may be sure that it will not be attacked), from coquettishness?" At this point the violinist, twisting his features as he forced himself to make an admission which no doubt was extremely painful, replied with a shudder: "No, it is from none of all those things. As for virtue, I don't give a damn for it. Spite? On the contrary, I am beginning to pity him. It is not from coquettishness, which could serve no purpose. It is not from having too much to do, for there are whole days when I stay at home and twiddle my thumbs. No, it is not for any of these reasons. It is—but never say this to anybody, I am mad to tell you—it is, it is . . . from fear!" He began to tremble in every limb. I confessed that I did not understand him. "No, don't ask me, don't let's talk about it, you do not know him as I do, I may say that you do not know him at all." "But what harm can he do you? In any case, he won't want to harm you if you put an end to the bitterness that exists between you. And then, you know that at heart he is very kind." "Good heavens, yes! I know he is kind. And wonderfully considerate, and honest. But let me alone, don't let's talk about it, I beseech you—it's a shameful admission, but I am afraid!"

The second incident dates from after the death of M. de Charlus. I was brought one or two things which he had left me as mementoes, and also a letter enclosed in three envelopes, which he had written at least ten years before his death. He had been seriously ill at the time and had put all his affairs in order, but then had recovered, only to fall later into the condition in which we shall see him on the day of an afternoon party given by the Princesse de Guermantes—and the letter, put aside in a strong-box with the objects which he was bequeathing to a few friends, had remained there for seven years, seven years during which he had completely forgotten Morel. It was written in a firm and delicate hand-writing and was couched in the following terms:

"My dear friend, the ways of Providence are inscrutable. Sometimes a fault in a very ordinary man is made to serve its purposes by helping one of the just not to slip from his lofty eminence. You know Morel, you know the humbleness of his origin and the height (my own level, no less) to which I wished to raise him. You are aware that he preferred to return not to the dust and ashes from which every man—for man surely is the true phoenix—may be born again, but to the slime in which the viper crawls. He fell, and in so doing he saved me from falling from where I belong. You know that my arms contain the device of Our Lord himself: *Inculcabis super leonem et aspidem*, with the crest of a man having beneath the soles of his feet, as heraldic supporters, a lion and a serpent. Well, if I have succeeded as I have in crushing the lion proper that I am, it is thanks to the serpent and his prudence, which just now I was thoughtless enough to call a fault, for the profound wisdom of the Gospel makes a virtue of it, a virtue at least for other people. Our serpent, of the once harmonious and well modulated hisses, was, when he had a charmer—a charmer charmed, moreover—not merely musical and reptilian, he had, to the point of cowardice, that virtue, Prudence, which I now hold to be divine. This divine prudence it was that made him resist the appeals to come back and see me which I conveyed to him, and I shall have no peace in this world or hope of forgiveness in the next if I do not confess the truth to you. He was, in resisting my appeals, the instrument of divine Wisdom, for I was resolved, had he come, that he should not leave my house alive. One of us two had to disappear. I had decided to kill him. God counselled him prudence to preserve me from crime. I do not doubt that the intercession of the Archangel Michael, my patron saint, played a great part in this and I beseech him to pardon me for having so neglected him over many years and for having so ill responded to the innumerable favours which he has conferred upon me, especially in my struggle against evil. I owe it to this Servant of God—I say the words in the plenitude of my faith and my understanding—that the heavenly Father inspired Morel not to come. And so it is I who am now about to die.

> Your faithfully devoted, *Semper idem*,
> P. G. Charlus."

Reading these words I understood Morel's fear. Certainly there was in the letter more than a small element of pride and of literature. But the confession was true. And Morel had known better than I that the "practically mad side" of her brother-in-law's character which Mme de Guermantes used to hint at was not confined, as until this revelation I had supposed, to his momentary exhibitions of superficial and ineffective rage.

But I must return to my narrative. I am walking down the boulevards by the side of M. de Charlus, who has just made a vague attempt to use me as an intermediary for overtures of peace between himself and Morel. Seeing that I made no reply, "Anyhow", he went on, "I do not know why it is that he no longer gives concerts. There is no music now on the pretext that there is a war on, but people dance and go out to dinner and women invent something called Ambrine for their skin. Social amusements fill what may prove, if the Germans continue to advance, to be the last days of our Pompeii. And if the city is indeed doomed, that in itself will save it from frivolity. The lava of some German Vesuvius—and their naval guns are no less terrible than a volcano—has only to surprise these good people at their toilet and to eternise their gestures by interrupting them, and in days to come it will be part of a child's education to look at pictures in his school-books of Mme Molé about to put on a last layer of powder before going out to dine with a sister-in-law, or Sosthène de Guermantes adding the final touches to his false eyebrows; these things will be the subject of lectures by the Brichots of the future, for the frivolity of an age, when ten centuries have passed over it, is matter for the gravest erudition, particularly if it has been embalmed by a volcanic eruption or by the substances akin to lava which a bombardment projects. What documents for the future historian if asphyxiating gases, like the fumes of Vesuvius, and the collapse of a whole city, like the catastrophe which buried Pompeii, should preserve intact all the imprudent dowagers who have not yet sent off their paintings and their statues to safety in Bayonne! And indeed, for the last year, have we not already seen fragments of Pompeii every evening: people burying themselves in their cellars, not in order to emerge with some old bottle of Mouton Rothschild or Saint Emilion, but to conceal along with themselves

their most treasured belongings, like the priests of Herculaneum whom death surprised in the act of carrying away the
sacred vessels? Attachment to an object always brings death to
its possessor. True, Paris was not, like Herculaneum, founded
by Hercules. But how many points of resemblance leap to the
eye! And this lucid vision that is given to us is not unique to
ourselves, it has been granted to every age. If I reflect that tomorrow we may suffer the fate of the cities of Vesuvius, these
in their turn sensed that they were threatened with the doom
of the accursed cities of the Bible. On the wall of a house in
Pompeii has been found the revealing inscription: *Sodoma,
Gomora*." Perhaps it was this name of Sodom and the ideas
that it evoked in him, or possibly the idea of the bombardment, that made M. de Charlus for an instant raise his eyes
to heaven, but soon he brought them back to earth. "I
admire all the heroes of this war," he said. "Why, my
dear boy, those English soldiers whom at the beginning I
rather thoughtlessly dismissed as mere players of football pre-
sumptuous enough to measure themselves against professionals
—and what professionals!—well, purely from the aesthetic
point of view they are quite simply Greek athletes, you understand me, my boy, Greek athletes, they are the young men of
Plato, or rather they are Spartiates. I have a friend who has
been to Rouen where their base is, he has seen marvels,
marvels almost unimaginable. It is not Rouen any longer, it
is another town. Of course the old Rouen still exists, with the
emaciated saints of the cathedral. And naturally, that is
beautiful too, but it is something quite different. And our
poilus! I cannot tell you how deliciously full of character I
find our *poilus*, the young Parisian boys, like that one there,
for instance, who is passing us, with his knowing expression,
his alert and humorous face. I often stop them for one
reason or another and we chat for a moment or two, and what

subtlety, what good sense! And the boys from the provinces, how amusing and nice they are, with the way they roll their r's and their regional dialects! I have always lived a lot in the country, I have slept in farms, I know how to talk to them. Still, our admiration for the French must not make us depreciate our enemies, that would only be to disparage ourselves. And you don't know what a soldier the German soldier is; you haven't seen him, as I have, march past on parade, doing the goose-step, *unter den Linden.*" And returning to that ideal of virility which he had outlined to me at Balbec and which, with time, had assumed a more philosophical form in his mind, but using also absurd arguments which at moments, even just after he had said something remarkably clever, gave his hearer a glimpse of the flimsiness of mental fabric of someone who is no more than a man of the world, albeit an intelligent man of the world: "You see," he said to me, "that splendid sturdy fellow the Boche soldier is strong and healthy and thinks only of the greatness of his country, *Deutschland über alles*, which is not so stupid as you might think, whereas we, while they were preparing themselves in a virile fashion, were hopelessly sunk in dilettantism." This word probably signified for M. de Charlus something analogous to literature, for immediately, remembering no doubt that I was fond of literature and had at one time intended to devote myself to it, he tapped me on the shoulder (taking the opportunity to lean so heavily upon me that the blow hurt as much as, in the days when I was doing my military service, the recoil of a "76" against my shoulder-blade) and said, as if to soften the reproach: "Yes, we were sunk in dilettantism, all of us, you too, you may remember. Like me you may say your *mea culpa*. We have been too dilettante." From astonishment at this reproach, from lack of readiness in repartee, from deference towards my interlocutor, and also because I was touched by his friendly kindness, I replied as though I too, as he suggested, had cause to beat my breast—an idiotic reaction, for I had not the shadow of dilettantism to reproach myself with. "Well," he said to me, "I must leave you here" (the group which had escorted him at a distance had finally abandoned us), "I am going off to bed like a very old gentleman, particularly as, so it seems, the war has changed all our habits—isn't that one of the imbecile aphorisms which Norpois is so fond of?" I knew, as a matter of fact, that when he went home at night M. de Charlus did not cease to be surrounded by soldiers, for he had turned his house into a military hospital and had done this, I believe, in obedience to the dictates much less of his imagination than of his kind heart.

It was a transparent and breathless night; I imagined that the Seine, flowing between the twin semi-circles of the span and the reflection of its bridges, must look like the Bosporus. And—symbol perhaps of the invasion foretold by the defeatism of M. de Charlus, or else of the co-operation of our Mussulman brothers with the armies of France—the moon, narrow and curved like a sequin, seemed to have placed the sky of Paris beneath the oriental sign of the crescent.

M. de Charlus lingered a few moments more, while he said good-bye to me with a shake of my hand powerful enough to crush it to pieces—a Germanic peculiarity to be found in those who think like the Baron. For several seconds he continued, as Cottard would have said, to "knead" my hand, as if he had wished to restore to my joints a suppleness which they had never lost. In certain blind men the sense of touch makes good to a certain extent the lack of sight. I do not exactly know what sense it was taking the place of here. Perhaps he thought that he was merely shaking my hand, as no doubt he thought that he was merely seeing a Senegalese soldier who passed in the darkness without deigning to notice that he was being admired. But in each case the Baron was mistaken, the intensity of contact and of gaze was greater than propriety permitted. "Don't you see all the Orient of Decamps and Fromentin and Ingres and Delacroix in this scene?" he asked me, still immobilised by the passage of the Senegalese. "As you know, I for my part am interested in things and in people only as a painter, a philosopher. Besides, I am too old. But how unfortunate that to complete the picture one of us two is not an odalisque!"

It was not the Orient of Decamps or even of Delacroix that began to haunt my imagination when the Baron had left me, but the old Orient of those *Thousand and One Nights* which I had been so fond of; losing myself gradually in the network of these dark streets, I thought of the Caliph Harun al-Rashid going in search of adventures in the hidden quarters of Bagdad. The weather was warm and my walk had made me hot and thirsty, but the bars had all closed long ago and, because of the scarcity of petrol, the rare taxis which I met, driven by Levantines or negroes, did not even take the trouble to reply to my signs. The only place where I might have been able to get something to drink and rest until I felt strong enough to walk home would have been a hotel. But in the street rather remote from the centre of the town to which I had penetrated, every hotel, since the Gothas had begun to drop their bombs on Paris, had closed. The same was true of almost all the shops, the shop-keepers, either owing to lack of staff or because they had taken fright themselves, having fled to the country and left on their door a hand-written notice announcing in some conventional phrase that they would re-open at a distant date (though even that seemed problematical). The few establishments which had managed to survive announced in the same fashion that they were open only twice a week. One felt that poverty, dereliction, fear inhabited the whole quarter. I was all the more surprised, therefore, to see that among these abandoned houses there was one in which life seemed, on the contrary, to have been victorious and terror and bankruptcy to have yielded to activity and wealth. Behind the closed shutters of each window the lights, dimmed on account of police regulations, revealed nevertheless a complete disregard for economy. And at every moment the door opened to allow some fresh visitor to enter or leave. It was a hotel which, because of the money its proprietors must be making, could not fail to have aroused the envy of all the neighbouring tradespeople; and I too became curious when, at a distance of fifteen yards, that is to say too far off for me to be able to make him out clearly in the profound darkness, I saw an officer come out and walk rapidly away.

Something, however, struck me: not his face, which I did not see, nor his uniform, which was disguised by a heavy greatcoat, but the extraordinary disproportion between the number of different points which his body successively occupied and the very small number of seconds within which he made good this departure which had almost the air of a sortie from a besieged town. So that my mind turned, if I did not explicitly recognise him——I will not say even to the build, nor to the slimness or the carriage or the swift movements of Saint-Loup——but to the sort of ubiquity which was so special to him. This military man with the ability to occupy so many different positions in space in such a short time disappeared down a side-street without seeing me, and I was left wondering whether it would be wise to enter a hotel whose modest appearance made me think that it could hardly have been Saint-Loup who had emerged. And yet I recalled involuntarily that he had—unjustly—been involved in a case of espionage because his name had been found in some letters captured on a German officer. He had, of course, been completely exonerated by the military authorities. But in spite of myself I associated this recollection with what I now saw. Was this hotel being used as a meeting-place of spies?

The officer had only just disappeared when I saw some ordinary soldiers of various arms go in, which further strengthened my suspicions. I was now, however, extremely thirsty. I should probably be able to get something to drink inside and at the same time I might attempt, although I felt nervous at the prospect, to assuage my curiosity. And so, but not, I think, primarily from curiosity about the officer I had seen, I hesitated no longer but climbed the little staircase at the top of which the door of a sort of hall stood open, no doubt on account of the heat. I thought at first that I might fail to discover very much, for from the staircase, where I remained in shadow, I saw several people come and ask for a room and receive the answer that there were absolutely none left. The objection to these people, I guessed, was simply that they did not belong to the nest of espionage, for a moment later a common sailor presented himself and was promptly given room No. 28. From where I stood in the darkness I could, without being seen, observe a few soldiers and two men of the working classes who were chatting tranquilly in a stiflingly hot little room, gaudily decorated with coloured pictures of women cut from illustrated magazines and reviews.

These men, as they chatted quietly together, were expounding patriotic ideas: "What do you expect, you've got to do what the other blokes do," said one. "Pooh, you can be jolly sure *I* don't mean to get killed," was the reply of another, who evidently was going off the next day to a dangerous post, to some expression of good wishes which I had not heard.

"Really, at twenty-two, after only doing six months, it would be a bit much," he exclaimed in a voice in which could be heard, even more plainly than the desire to go on living, the assurance that his reasoning was correct, as though the fact that he was only twenty-two could not fail to give him a better chance of survival, as though it were out of the question that he should be killed. "It's amazing in Paris," said another; "you'ld never know there's a war on. How about you, Julot, d'you still mean to join up?" "Of course I do, I can't wait to take a pot shot or two at these filthy Boches." "This Joffre, you know, he's just a man who sleeps with the politicians' wives, he's never done a thing himself." "That's a dreadful way to talk," said a slightly older man, an airman, and then, turning to the workman who had just made the statement: "I should advise you not to talk like that in the front line, the *poilus* would soon do you in." The banality of these scraps of conversation did not inspire me with any great wish to hear more, and I was about to make my entrance or go back down the stairs when I was jolted out of my indifference by hearing a series of remarks which made me shudder: "I'm amazed the *patron* isn't back yet, damn it, at this hour of the night I don't know where he's going to find any chains." "Anyhow, the chap's already tied up." "Tied up? Well, he is and he isn't. Tie me up like that and I'ld soon untie myself." "But the padlock's closed." "Of course it's closed, but it's not so impossible to open it. The trouble is the chains aren't long enough. Don't you try and tell me, I was beating the stuffing out of him all last night until my hands were covered with blood." "Are you going to beat to-night?" "No. It's not me, it's Maurice. But it'll be me on Sunday, the *patron* promised me." I understood now why the strong arm of the sailor had been needed. If peaceable citizens had been turned away, it was not because the hotel was a nest of spies. An appalling crime was about to be committed, unless someone arrived in time to discover it and have the criminals arrested. And yet the whole scene, in the midst of this peaceful and threatened night, was like a dream or a fairy-tale, so that it was at once with the pride of an emissary of justice and the rapture of a poet that I at length, my mind made up, entered the hotel.

I touched my hat lightly and the people in the room, without rising to their feet, replied more or less civilly to the greeting. "Can you tell me who is in charge here? I should like a room and something to drink sent up to it." "Will you wait a minute, the *patron* has gone out." "There's the boss, he's upstairs," suggested one of the men who had taken part in the conversation. "But you know he can't be disturbed." "Do you think they will give me a room?" "Expect so." "43 must be free," said the young man who was sure he would not be killed because he was twenty-two years old. And he moved a little way along the sofa to make room for me. "Suppose we open the window a bit, you can cut the smoke with a knife in here!" said the airman; and indeed they all had their pipe or their cigarette. "Yes, but in that case close the shutters first, you know it's forbidden to show any light because of the Zeppelins." "We've finished with the Zeppelins. There's even been something in the papers about their having all been shot down." "We've finished with this, we've finished with that, what d'you know about it? When you've done fifteen months at the front, as I have, and shot down your fifth Boche aeroplane, you'll be able to talk. What d'you want to believe the papers for? They were over Compiègne yesterday, they killed a mother and two children." "A mother and two children!" said the young man who hoped not to be killed, with blazing eyes and a look of profound compassion upon his energetic and open countenance, which I found very likeable. "There's been no news of big Julot lately. His 'god-mother' hasn't had a letter from him for eight days, and it's the first time he's been so long without writing." "Who is she, his 'god-mother'?" "The woman who looks after the toilets just beyond the Olympia." "Do they sleep together?" "What an idea! She's a married woman, she couldn't be more respectable. She sends him money every week out of pure kindness of heart. She's a real good sort." "Do you know him then, big Julot?" "Do I know him!" retorted scornfully the young man of twenty-two. "He's a close friend of mine and one of the best. There's not many I think as highly of as I do of him: a real pal, always ready to do you a good turn. Yes, it would be a catastrophe all right if anything had happened to him." Someone proposed a game of dice and, from the feverish haste with which the young man of twenty-two shook them and cried out the results, with his eyes starting out of his head, it was easy to see that he had the gambler's temperament. I did not quite catch the next remark that someone made to him, but he exclaimed with a note of profound pity in his voice: "Julot a ponce! You mean he *says* he's a ponce. But he's no more a ponce than I am. I've seen him with my own eyes paying his woman, yes, paying her. That's to say, I don't say Jeanne l'Algérienne didn't give him a little something now and then, but it was never more than five francs, and what's that from a woman in a brothel earning more than fifty francs a day? A present of five francs! Some men are just too stupid to live. And now she's at the front, well, her life may be hard, I grant you, but she can earn as much as she wants—and she sends him nothing. Bah, that chap a ponce? There's plenty who could call themselves a ponce at that rate. Not only is he not a ponce, in my opinion he's an imbecile." The oldest of the group, whom the *patron* had no doubt for that reason put in charge of the others, with instructions to make them behave with a certain restraint, had been to the lavatory for a moment and heard only the end of this conversation. But he could not help looking in my direction and seemed visibly upset at the impression such talk must have made on me. Without addressing himself specially to the young man of twenty-two, though it was he who had been expounding this theory of venal love, he said, in a general manner: "You're talking too much and too loud, the window is open, there are people asleep at this hour. You know quite well that if the *patron* came back and heard you talking like that, he wouldn't be at all pleased."

At that very moment the door was heard to open and everyone was silent, thinking it was the *patron*, but it was only a foreign chauffeur who was welcomed as an old friend by everybody in the room. But seeing a magnificent watch-chain displayed upon the chauffeur's jacket, the young man of twenty-two threw him a questioning and amused glance, followed by a frown and a severe wink in my direction. I understood that the first look meant: "What's that, did you steal it? My congratulations." And the second: "Don't say anything, because of this character whom we don't know." Suddenly the *patron* came in, carrying several yards of heavy iron chains—sufficient to secure quite a number of convicts—and sweating. "What a weight!" he said. "If you weren't all so idle, I shouldn't be obliged to fetch them myself." I told him that I wanted a room. "Just for a few hours. I can't find a cab and I am rather unwell. But I should like something to drink sent up." "Pierrot, go and fetch some *cassis* from the cellar and tell them to get No. 43 ready. There's 7 ringing again. They say they're ill. Ill my foot, I wouldn't be surprised if they'd been doping themselves, they look half cracked, it's time they were shown the door. Has anybody put a pair of sheets in 22? Good! There goes 7 again, run and see what it is. Well, Maurice, what are you standing there for? You know someone's waiting for you, go up to 14b. And get a move on." And Maurice hurried out after the *patron*, who seemed a little annoyed that I had seen his chains and disappeared carrying them with him. "How is it you're so late?" the young man of twenty-two asked the chauffeur. "What do you mean, late? I'm an hour early. But it's too hot in the streets. My appointment's not till midnight." "Who have you come for then?" "Pretty Pamela," said the dark-skinned chauffeur, whose laugh uncovered a set of fine white teeth. "Ah!" said the young man of twenty-two.

Presently I was taken up to Room 43, but it was so unpleasantly stuffy and my curiosity was so great that, having drunk my *cassis*, I started to go downstairs again, then, changing my mind, turned round and went up past the floor of Room 43 to the top of the building. Suddenly, from a room situated by itself at the end of a corridor, I thought I heard stifled groans. I walked rapidly towards the sounds and put my ear to the door. "I beseech you, mercy, have pity, untie me, don't beat me so hard," said a voice. "I kiss your feet, I abase myself, I promise not to offend again. Have pity on me." "No, you filthy brute," replied another voice, "and if you yell and drag yourself about on your knees like that, you'll be tied to the bed, no mercy for you," and I heard the noise of the crack of a whip, which I guessed to be reinforced with nails, for it was followed by cries of pain. At this moment I noticed that there was a small oval window opening from the room onto the corridor and that the curtain had not been drawn across it; stealthily in the darkness I crept as far as this window and there in the room, chained to a bed like Prometheus to his rock, receiving the blows that Maurice rained upon him with a whip which was in fact studded with nails, I saw, with blood already flowing from him and

covered with blotches which proved that the chastisement was
not taking place for the first time—I saw before me M. de
Charlus.

Suddenly the door opened and a man came in who fortunately did not see me. It was Jupien. He went up to the
Baron with an air of respect and a smile of understanding:
"Well, you don't need me, do you?" The Baron asked
Jupien to send Maurice out of the room for a moment.
Jupien did so with perfect unconcern. "We can't be heard,
can we?" said the Baron to Jupien, who assured him that this
was the case. The Baron knew that Jupien, with an intelligence worthy of a man of letters, was yet quite lacking in
practical sense and constantly talked about people in their
presence with innuendoes which deceived nobody and nick-
names which everybody understood.

"One second," interrupted Jupien, who had heard a bell
ring in Room No. 3. It was a deputy of the Liberal Action
party, who was about to leave. Jupien did not need to look
at the bell-board, for he recognised the man's ring. Indeed
the deputy came every day after luncheon, but today he had
been obliged to re-arrange his time-table, for at twelve o'clock
he had given away his daughter in marriage at the church of
Saint Pierre de Chaillot. So he had come in the evening but
was anxious to leave early on account of his wife, who very
easily became nervous if he was late in getting home, particularly in these days of bombardment. Jupien always liked to
accompany him downstairs in order to show his deference for
the status of "honourable", and in this he was quite disinterested. For although this deputy (who repudiated the exagger-
ations of *L'Action Française* and would in any case have been
incapable of understanding a line of Charles Maurras or
Léon Daudet) stood well with the Ministers, whom he
flattered by inviting them to his shooting-parties, Jupien

JUPIEN IN HIS HOTEL

would not have dared to ask him for the slightest support in his difficulties with the police. He knew that, had he ventured to mention that subject to the affluent and apprehensive legislator, he would not have saved himself even the most harmless "raid" but would immediately have lost the most generous of his clients. After having escorted the deputy as far as the door, from which he set off with his hat pulled down over his eyes and his collar turned up and with a rapid gliding movement not unlike the style of his electoral manifestos, by which devices he hoped to render his face invisible, Jupien went upstairs again to M. de Charlus. "It was Monsieur Eugène," he said to him. In Jupien's establishment, as in a sanatorium, people were referred to only by their Christian names, though their real names, either to satisfy the curiosity of the visitor or to enhance the prestige of the house, were invariably added in a whisper. Sometimes, however, Jupien was unaware of the real personality of a client and imagined and said that he was some well-known financier or nobleman or artist—fleeting errors not without charm for the man to whom the wrong name was attached—and in the end had to resign himself to the idea that he still did not know who Monsieur Victor was. Sometimes too, to please the Baron, he was in the habit of inverting the procedure that is customary on certain social occasions ("Let me introduce you to M. Lebrun", then a whisper: "He wants to be called M. Lebrun but he is really Grand Duke X— of Russia"). Jupien on the other hand felt that it was not quite sufficient to introduce M. de Charlus to a young milkman. He would murmur to him with a wink: "He's a milkman but he's also one of the most dangerous thugs in Belleville" (and it was with a superbly salacious note in his voice that Jupien uttered the word "thug"). And as if this recommendation were not sufficient, he would try to add one or two further "mentions in despatches". "He has had several convictions for theft and burglary, he was in Fresnes for assaulting" (the same salacious note in his voice) "and practically murdering people in the street, and he's been in a punishment battalion in Africa. He killed his sergeant."

The Baron was slightly cross with Jupien for his lack of prudence, for he knew that in this house which he had instructed his factotum to purchase for him and to manage through a subordinate, everybody, thanks to the blunders of Mlle d'Oloron's uncle, was more or less aware of his personality and his name (many, however, thought that it was not a title but a nickname and mispronounced and distorted it, so that their own stupidity and not the discretion of Jupien had served to protect the Baron). But he found it simpler to let himself be reassured by Jupien's assurances, and now, relieved to know that they could not be heard, he said to him: "I did not want to speak in front of that boy, who is very nice and does his best. But I don't find him sufficiently brutal. He has a charming face, but when he calls me a filthy brute he might be just repeating a lesson." "I assure you, nobody has said a word to him," replied Jupien, without perceiving how improbable this statement was. "And then, you know he was involved in the murder of that woman who was a concierge in La Villette." "Ah! that is extremely interesting," said the Baron with a smile. "But I'll tell you whom I have here: the killer of oxen, the man of the slaughter-houses, who is so like this boy; he happened to be passing. Would you care to try him?" "Yes, certainly I should." I saw the man of the slaughter-houses enter the room; he was indeed a little like Maurice, but—and this was odder—they both had in them something of a type which I had never myself consciously observed in Morel's face but which I now clearly saw to exist there, they bore a resemblance, if not to Morel as I had seen him, at least to a certain countenance which eyes seeing

Morel otherwise than I did might have constructed out of his features. No sooner had I, out of features borrowed from my recollections of Morel, privately made for myself this rough model of what he might represent to somebody else, than I realised that the two young men, one of whom was a jeweller's assistant while the other worked in a hotel, were in a vague way substitutes for Morel. Was I to conclude that M. de Charlus, at least in a certain aspect of his loves, was always faithful to a particular type and that the desire which had made him select these two young men one after the other was the identical desire which had made him accost Morel on the platform at Doncières station; that all three resembled a little the ephebe whose form, engraved in the sapphire-like eyes of M. de Charlus, gave to his glance that strange quality which had alarmed me the first day at Balbec? Or that, his love for Morel having modified the type which he pursued, to console himself for Morel's absence he sought men who resembled him? A third hypothesis which occurred to me was that perhaps, in spite of appearances, there had never existed between him and Morel anything more than relations of friendship, and that M. de Charlus caused young men who resembled Morel to come to Jupien's establishment so that he might have the illusion, while he was with them, of enjoying pleasure with Morel himself. It is true that, if one thought of everything that M. de Charlus had done for Morel, this hypothesis was bound to seem most unlikely, did one not know that love drives us not only to the greatest sacrifices on behalf of the person whom we love, but sometimes even to the sacrifice of our desire itself, a desire which in any case we find all the harder to gratify if the loved person is aware of the strength of our love. And something else that made this hypothesis less improbable than at first sight it appears to be (though I have little doubt that it was not in fact the true one) was the influence of the nervous temperament, the profoundly passionate character of M. de Charlus—in this not unlike Saint-Loup—which in the early days of his relations with Morel might have had the same negative effect of making him behave with greater propriety that a similar cause had had on his nephew in the early days of his relations with Rachel. A man's relations with a woman whom he loves (and the same may be true of love for a young man) may remain platonic for a reason which is neither the woman's virtue nor a lack of sensuality in the love which she inspires. The reason may be that the lover, too impatient from the very excess of his love, does not know how to wait with a sufficient show of in-difference for the moment when he will obtain what he desires. Over and over again he returns to the charge, he writes incessantly to the woman, he tries constantly to see her, she refuses, he is in despair. Henceforth she understands that if she accords him her company, her friendship, this happiness in itself will seem so considerable to the man who thought he had lost it, that she may spare herself the trouble of giving him anything more and may take advantage of a moment when he can no longer endure not to see her, when he is determined at any price to end the war, to impose upon him a peace of which the first condition will be the platonic nature of their relations. In any case, during the period which preceded this treaty, the lover, always anxious, hoping all the time for a letter, a glance, has given up thinking of physical pos-session, which at first had been the object of the desire which had tormented him; that desire has withered away with waiting and its place has been taken by needs of another order, needs which can, however, if they remain unsatisfied, cause him yet greater pain. So that the pleasure which at the beginning he had hoped to obtain from caresses, he receives later not in its natural form but instead from friendly words, from mere promises of the loved woman's presence, which after the effects of uncertainty—sometimes after a single look, black with a heavy cloud of disdain, which has withdrawn her to such a distance that he thinks he will never see her again—bring with them a delicious relief from tension. A woman divines these things and knows that she can afford the luxury of never giving herself to a man who, because he has been too nervous to conceal it during the first few days, has allowed her to become aware of his incurable desire for her. She is only too pleased to receive, without giving anything in return, much more than she is accustomed to be given when she gives herself. Men with a nervous temperament believe therefore in the virtue of their idol. And the halo which they place round her is a product, but as we have seen an indirect one, of their excessive love. The woman then finds herself very much in the position—though she of course is conscious, while they are not—of those unwittingly crafty drugs like sleeping-draughts and morphia. It is not to the people to whom they bring the pleasure of sleep or a genuine wellbeing that these drugs are an absolute necessity; it is not by such people as these that they would be bought for the price of their weight in gold, bartered against all the sick man's possessions, but by that other class of sick men (who may perhaps be the same individuals but become different with the passage of a few years), those whom the medicine does not send to sleep, to whom it gives no thrill of pleasure, but who, so long as they are without it, are prey to an agitation which at any price, even the price of their own death, they need desperately to end.

In the case of M. de Charlus, which on the whole, with slight discrepancies due to the identity of sex, accords very well with the general laws of love, it might well be that he belonged to a family more ancient than the Capets, that he was rich and vainly sought after by fashionable society while Morel was nobody, nevertheless, he would have got nowhere by saying to Morel, as he had once said to me: "I am a prince, I want to help you,"—it was still Morel who had the upper hand so long as he refused to surrender. And for him to persist in this refusal, it was perhaps enough that he should feel himself to be loved. The horror that grand people have for the snobs who move heaven and earth to make their acquaintance is felt also by the virile man for the invert, by a woman for every man who is too much in love with her. M. de Charlus possessed, and would have offered Morel a share in, immense advantages. But it is possible that all this might have hurled itself in vain against a determined will. And in that case, M. de Charlus would have suffered the same fate as the Germans—in whose ranks in fact his ancestry placed him —who in the war at that moment taking its course were indeed, as the Baron was a little too fond of repeating, victorious on every front. But of what use were their victories, since after every one they found the Allies yet more firmly resolved to refuse them the one thing that they, the Germans, wanted: peace and reconciliation? Napoleon too, as he advanced into Russia, had again and again magnanimously invited the authorities to meet him. But nobody came.

I made my way downstairs and went back into the little ante-room where Maurice, uncertain whether he would be sent for again (he had been told by Jupien to wait just in case), was engaged in a game of cards with one of his friends. There was a lot of excitement about a *croix de guerre* which had been found lying on the ground—nobody knew who had lost it and to whom it ought to be returned so that the owner should not be punished. Then there was talk of the generosity of an officer who had been killed trying to save his orderly. "All the same, there are some good blokes among the rich.

I'd gladly get myself killed for a chap like that," said Maurice, who evidently performed his terrible fustigations of the Baron simply from mechanical habit, as a result of a neglected education, from need of money and from a certain preference for making it in a manner which was supposed to be less trouble, and was perhaps really more trouble, than ordinary work. But as M. de Charlus had feared, he was perhaps really very kind-hearted and certainly, so it seemed, a young man of exemplary courage. He almost had tears in his eyes as he spoke of the death of this officer, and the young man of twenty-two was no less moved. "Yes, indeed, they're fine blokes. For poor chaps like us there's not much to lose, but when it's a toff who has a whole troop of flunkeys and can go to posh bars every night of his life, that's really hot stuff! You can scoff as much as you like, but when you see blokes like that dying, it really does something to you. Rich people like that, God shouldn't let them die—for one thing they're too useful to the working man. A death like that makes you want to kill every Boche to the last man. And then look what they did at Louvain, and that cutting off the hands of little children! No, I don't know, I'm no better than the next man, but I'd rather face the music and be shot to bits than give in to barbarians like that; for they're not men, they're real barbarians, don't you try and tell me anything else." All these young men were patriots at heart. One only, who had been slightly wounded in the arm but was soon going to have to return to the front, did not rise to the level of the others. "Really," he said; "that was a poor sort of wound" (not the kind that gets you discharged), very much as in the past Mme Swann would have said: "Somehow or other I've caught this most tiresome influenza."

The door opened to re-admit the chauffeur, who had been taking the air for a moment. "What, finished already? You weren't long," he said, catching sight of Maurice, whom he supposed to be still engaged in beating the individual whom, in allusion to a newspaper which was appearing at that time, they had nicknamed "the Man in Chains". "It may not have seemed long to you out in the fresh air," replied Maurice, vexed that the others should see that he had failed to give satisfaction upstairs. "But if you'd been obliged to wallop away with all your might in this heat, like me! If it weren't for the fifty francs he gives . . ." "And then, he's a man who talks well; you can see he's educated. Does he say it will soon be over?" "He says we'll never beat them, it will end without either side really winning." "Well, blood is thicker than water, if he says that he must be a Boche. . . ." "I've already told you you're talking too loud," said the oldest of the group to the others, seeing that I had returned, and then to me: "Have you finished with your room?" "Shut your trap, you're not the boss here." "Yes, I've finished, and I've come to pay." "It would be better if you paid the *patron*. Maurice, go and fetch him." "But I don't want to bother you." "It's no trouble." Maurice went upstairs, and came back saying: "The *patron* will be down in a second." I gave him two francs for his pains. He blushed with pleasure. "Oh! thank you very much. I'll send it to my brother who's a prisoner. No, he doesn't have a bad time. It depends a lot on the camp you're in."

Meanwhile, two very smart clients, in white tie and tails and wearing overcoats—two Russians, as I guessed from the very slight accent with which they spoke—were standing in the door-way and deliberating whether they should enter. It was visibly the first time that they had been to the place, to which no doubt they had come on somebody's recommendation, and they appeared torn between desire, temptation and extreme fright. One of the two—a good-looking young

man—kept repeating every ten seconds to the other, with a
smile that was half a question and half an attempt at persuasion:
"Well! After all, what do we care?" But though no doubt he
meant by this that after all they did not care about the consequences, it is probable that he cared rather more than he
implied, for the remark was not followed by any movement
to cross the threshold but by a further glance at his companion, followed by the same smile and the same "After all,
what do we care?" And in this "After all, what do we care?",
I saw a perfect example of that portentous language, so unlike
the language we habitually speak, in which emotion deflects
what we had intended to say and causes to emerge in its place
an entirely different phrase, issued from an unknown lake
wherein dwell these expressions alien to our thoughts which
by virtue of that very fact reveal them. I remember an
occasion when Françoise, whose approach we had not heard,
was about to come into the room while Albertine was completely naked in my arms, and Albertine, wanting to warn me,
blurted out: "Good heavens, here's beautiful Françoise!"
Françoise, whose sight was no longer very good and who was
merely going to cross the room at some distance from us,
would no doubt have noticed nothing. But the unprecedented
phrase "beautiful Françoise", which Albertine had never
uttered before in her life, was in itself enough to betray its
origin; Françoise sensed that the words had been snatched at
random by emotion and had no need to look to understand
what was happening; she went out muttering in her dialect
the word *poutana*. On another occasion, many years later,
after Bloch had become the father of a family and had
married off one of his daughters to a Catholic, an ill-mannered
gentleman said to the young woman that he thought he had
heard that her father was a Jew and asked what his name was.
Whereupon she, who had been Mlle Bloch (with a *k* sound)

from the day she was born, replied instead "Bloch", with the Teutonic *ch* which the Duc de Guermantes would have used.

The *patron*, to return to the scene in the hotel (into which the two Russians had decided to penetrate—"After all, what do we care?") had still not arrived when Jupien came in to say that they were talking too loud and that the neighbours would complain. But seeing me he was rooted to the spot in amazement. "Go out on to the landing all of you." They were all rising to their feet, when I said to him: "It would be simpler if these young men stayed where they are and you and I went outside for a moment." He followed me, very agitated. I explained to him why I had come. Clients could be heard enquiring of the *patron* whether he could not introduce them to a footman, a choir-boy, a negro chauffeur. Every profession interested these old lunatics, every branch of the armed forces, every one of the allied nations. Some asked particularly for Canadians, influenced perhaps unconsciously by the charm of an accent so slight that one does not know whether it comes from the France of the past or from England. The Scots too, because of their kilts and because dreams of a landscape with lakes are often associated with these desires, were at a premium. And as every form of madness is, if not in every case aggravated by circumstances, at least imprinted by them with particular characteristics, an old man in whom curiosity of every kind had no doubt been satisfied was asking insistently to be introduced to a disabled soldier. Slow footsteps were heard on the stairs. With the indiscretion that was natural to him, Jupien could not refrain from telling me that it was the Baron who was coming down, and at all costs he must not see me, but that if I liked to go into the bedroom adjoining the ante-room where the young men were, he would open the ventilator, a device which he had fixed up so that the Baron could see and hear without being seen, and which he said he would use in my favour against him. "Only don't make a move." And pushing me into the dark, he left me. In any case he had no other room to give me, his hotel, in spite of the war, being full. The one which I had just left had been taken by the Vicomte de Courvoisier who, having got away from the Red Cross at X— for two days, had come to Paris for an hour's entertainment before going on to the Château de Courvoisier to be reunited with his wife, to whom he would explain that he had not been able to catch the fast train. He had no suspicion that M. de Charlus was a few yards away from him, and the latter would have been equally surprised to know that his cousin was there, never having met him in the establishment of Jupien, who was himself ignorant of the Vicomte's carefully concealed identity.

The Baron soon entered the ante-room, walking with difficulty on account of his injuries, though doubtless he must have been used to them. Although his pleasure was at an end and he had only come in to give Maurice the money which he owed him, he directed at the young men a tender and curious glance which travelled round the whole circle, promising himself with each of them the pleasure of a moment's chat, platonic but amorously prolonged. And in the sprightly frivolity which he exhibited before this harem which appeared almost to intimidate him, I recognised those jerky movements of the body and the head, those languishing glances which had struck me on the evening of his first visit to La Raspelière, graces inherited from some grandmother whom I had not known, which in ordinary life were disguised by more virile expressions on his face but which from time to time were made to blossom there coquettishly, when circumstances made him anxious to please an inferior audience, by the desire to appear a great lady.

Jupien had recommended the young men to the Baron's favour by swearing that they were all pimps from Belleville and would sell you their own sisters for a few francs. And in this he was at the same time lying and telling the truth. Better, more soft-hearted than he made them out to be, they did not belong to a race of savages. But the clients who believed them to be thugs spoke to them nevertheless with complete truthfulness, a truthfulness which they imagined these terrible beings to share. For a man given to sadistic pleasures may believe that he is talking to a murderer but this will not alter his own purity of heart, he will still be astounded by the mendacity of his companion, who is not a murderer at all but wants to earn a little easy money and whose father or mother or sister alternately die, come to life, and die again as he contradicts himself in his conversation with the client whom he is attempting to please. The client, in his naïvety, is astounded, for with his arbitrary conception of the gigolo, while he gets a thrill of delight from the numerous murders of which he believes him to be guilty, he is horrified by any simple contradiction or lie which he detects in his words.

Everybody in the room seemed to know him, and M. de Charlus stopped for a long time before each one, talking to them in what he thought was their language, both from a pretentious affectation of local colour and because he got a sadistic pleasure from contact with a life of depravity. "You're disgusting, you are, I saw you outside the Olympia with two tickets in your hand. After a bit of brass, no doubt. Just shows how faithful you are to me." Luckily for the man to whom these remarks were addressed, he did not have time to declare that he would never have accepted "brass" from a woman, a claim which would have damped the Baron's ardour, but reserved his protest for the final phrase, which he answered by saying: "But of course I'm faithful to you." This remark gave M. de Charlus a lively pleasure, and as, in spite of himself, the kind of intelligence that was natural to him showed through the character which he affected, he turned to Jupien: "How nice of him to say that! And how well he says it! One would really think it was true. And after all, what does it matter whether it is true or not since he manages to make me believe it? What charming little eyes he has! There, I'm going to give you two big kisses for your trouble, my dear boy. You will think of me in the trenches. Things are not too bad there?" "Whew, there are some days, when a grenade just misses you. . . ." And the young man proceeded to imitate the noise of the grenade, the aeroplanes, etc. "But one's got to do what the others do, and you can be absolutely sure that we will go on to the end." "To the end! If one only knew to what end!" said the Baron in a melancholy manner, giving rein to his "pessimism". "You haven't seen what Sarah Bernhardt said in the papers: 'France will go on to the end. If necessary, the French will let themselves be killed to the last man.'" "I do not doubt for a single moment that the French would bravely let themselves be killed to the last man," said M. de Charlus, as if this were the simplest thing in the world and although he himself had no intention of doing anything whatsoever, hoping by this remark to correct the impression of pacifism which he gave when he forgot himself. "That I do not doubt, but I ask myself to what extent *Madame* Sarah Bernhardt is qualified to speak in the name of France. . . . But I don't think I have made the acquaintance of this charming, this delightful young man," he added, spying another whom he did not recognise or perhaps had not seen before. He greeted him as he would have greeted a prince at Versailles, and making the most of this opportunity to have a supplementary pleasure for nothing—just as, when I was little and my mother had finished giving an order at Boissier's or Gouache's, I would accept the offer of a sweet which one of the ladies behind the counter would invite me to select from those glass bowls over which she and her colleagues held sway—he took the hand of the charming young man and gave it a long squeeze, in the Prussian manner, smilingly fixing him with his eyes for the interminable time which photographers used to take to pose you when the light was bad. "Sir, I am charmed, I am enchanted to make your acquaintance." "What pretty hair he has!" he said, turning to Jupien. Next he went up to Maurice to give him his fifty francs, but first, putting his arm round his waist: "You never told me that you had knifed an old hag of a concierge in Belleville." And M. de Charlus went off into ecstatic laughter and brought his face close to that of Maurice. "Oh! Monsieur le Baron," said the gigolo, who had not been warned, "how can you believe such a thing?" Whether the report was in fact false, or whether it was true and the perpetrator of the deed nevertheless thought it abominable and one of those things that it is better to deny, he went on: "Me touch a fellow-creature? A Boche, yes, because that's war, but a woman, and an old woman at that!" This declaration of virtuous principles had the effect of a douche of cold water upon the Baron, who brusquely moved away from Maurice, having first handed him his money, but with the disgusted air of someone who has been cheated, who pays because he does not want to make a fuss but is far from pleased. The bad impression made upon the Baron was accentuated by the manner in which the recipient thanked him, with the words: "I shall send this to the old folks and keep a bit for my brother at the front as well." By these touching sentiments M. de Charlus was almost as gravely disappointed as he was irritated by the rather conventional peasant's language in which they were expressed. Occasionally Jupien warned the young men that they would have to be more perverse. Then one of them, as if he were confessing to something diabolical, would hazard: "Do you know, Baron, you won't believe me, but when I was a kid I used to watch my parents making love through the key-hole. Pretty vicious, wasn't it? You look as if you think that's a cock and bull story, but I swear it's the truth." And M. de Charlus was driven at once to despair and to exasperation by this factitious attempt at perversity, the result of which was only to reveal such depths both of stupidity and of innocence. Yet even the most determined thief or murderer would not have satisfied him, for that sort of man does not talk about his crimes; and besides there exists in the sadist—however kind he may be, in fact all the more the kinder he is—a thirst for evil which wicked men, doing what they do, not because it is wicked but from other motives, are unable to assuage.

The young man realised his mistake and tried to repair it by saying that he loathed the sight of a copper and by insolently asking the Baron to "fork out a date" (meaning a rendezvous), but it was too late, the charm was dispelled. His remarks were obviously unauthentic, like the books of authors who force themselves to write slang. It was in vain that the young man described in detail all the "filthy things" that he did with his wife; M. de Charlus merely reflected that these "filthy things" amounted to very little. And in this he was not simply being insincere. Nothing is more limited than pleasure and vice. In that sense one may say truly, altering slightly the meaning of the phrase, that we revolve always in the same vicious circle.

If M. de Charlus was believed to be not a baron but a prince, there was, conversely, general regret in the establishment for the death of someone of whom the gigolos said: "I don't know his name, but it seems that he is a baron", and who was none other than the Prince de Foix (the father of Saint-Loup's friend). Supposed by his wife to spend a lot of time at his club, in reality he would sit for hours at Jupien's, retailing fashionable gossip to an audience from the underworld. Like his son he was tall and good-looking. M. de Charlus, no doubt because he had always known him in society, remained strangely ignorant that the Prince shared his own tastes, to such a degree that he was even said to have had designs at one time upon his own son, Saint-Loup's friend, then still at school. This was probably untrue: on the contrary, excellently informed about activities whose existence many do not suspect, he watched with care over the company kept by his son. One day a man—and a man not of exalted origin—followed the young Prince de Foix as far as his father's house, where he threw a note in at the window, which the father picked up. But the follower, though genealogically this was not the case, from another point of view belonged to the same world as M. de Foix the father. He therefore had no difficulty in finding among those who shared their common secrets an intermediary who silenced M. de Foix by proving to him that it was his son who had himself provoked this rash act of an elderly man. And this was quite possible. For the Prince de Foix had succeeded in preserving his son from the external influence of bad company but not from heredity. The young Prince de Foix, however, remained, like his father, in this respect unknown to his social equals, although in a different world his behaviour was wild in the extreme.

"How simple he is! You would never say he was a baron," said some of the frequenters of the establishment when M. de Charlus had left, after being escorted to the street door by Jupien, to whom he did not fail to complain of the young man's virtuousness. From the air of annoyance of Jupien, whose duty it was to have trained the young man in advance, it was clear that the fictitious murderer would presently get a terrific dressing-down. "The truth is exactly the opposite of what you told me," added the Baron, so that Jupien might profit by the lesson for another time. "He seems most good-natured, he expresses sentiments of respect for his family." "Still, he's on bad terms with his father," Jupien objected. "It's true they live together, but they work in different bars." Obviously this was not much of a crime compared with murder, but Jupien had been caught unprepared with an answer. The Baron said no more, for, if he wanted others to prepare his pleasures for him, he wanted to give himself the illusion that they were unprepared. "He is a real crook, he said all that to mislead you, you are too gullible," Jupien went on, in an attempt to exculpate himself which succeeded only in wounding the vanity of M. de Charlus.

"It seems that he has a million francs a day to spend," said the young man of twenty-two, who saw no improbability in this statement. The car which had come to fetch M. de Charlus was now heard to drive away. At the same moment there entered the room with a slow step, by the side of a soldier who had evidently emerged with her from a neighbouring bedroom, what appeared to me to be an elderly lady in a black skirt. I soon realised my mistake: it was a priest—that thing so rare, and in France altogether exceptional, a bad priest. Evidently the soldier was teasing his companion about the discrepancy between his conduct and his habit, for the other with a serious air, raising a finger towards his hideous face with the gesture of a doctor of theology, said sententiously: "What do you expect? I am not" (I expected him to say "a saint") "a good girl." He was, however, ready to depart and he said good-bye to Jupien, who had just come upstairs again after seeing the Baron to the door. But absent-mindedly the bad priest had forgotten to pay for his room.

Jupien, who had always a ready wit, shook the collecting box in which he placed the contribution of each client and said, as he made it clink: "For the expenses of the church, Monsieur l'Abbé!" The horrid creature apologised, put in his coin and disappeared.

Jupien came to fetch me from the cave of darkness in which I had been standing without daring to move. "Come into the hall for a moment where my young men are sitting, while I go upstairs and lock up the bedroom; since you have taken a room, it's quite natural." The *patron* was there, so I paid him. At that moment a young man in a dinner-jacket came in and asked the *patron* with an air of authority: "Will I be able to have Léon at a quarter to eleven instead of eleven tomorrow morning, as I have a luncheon engagement?" "That will depend," replied the *patron*, "on how long the Abbé keeps him." This reply appeared not to satisfy the young man in a dinner-jacket, who seemed to be on the point of launching into abuse of the Abbé, but his fury was diverted when he caught sight of me. Going straight up to the *patron*: "Who is this? What does this mean?" he murmured in a quiet but angry voice. The *patron*, very put out, explained that my presence was quite harmless, that I had taken a room. The young man in a dinner-jacket appeared to be not in the slightest degree pacified by this explanation. He kept repeating: "This is extremely unpleasant, things of this sort ought not to happen, you know I detest them, if you are not careful I will never set foot here again." The execution of this threat did not, however, appear to be imminent, for he went off in a rage, but not without asking that Léon should try to be free at a quarter to eleven, or better still half past ten. Jupien came back to fetch me and we went downstairs together and out into the street.

"I do not want you to misjudge me," he said to me. "This

house does not bring me in as much profit as you might think. I am obliged to let rooms to respectable people, though of course if they were my only customers I should simply be throwing money down the drain. Here, contrary to the doctrine of the Carmelites, it is thanks to vice that virtue is able to live. No, if I took this house, or rather if I got the manager whom you have seen to take it, it was purely and simply in order to render a service to the Baron and amuse his old age." Jupien was here referring not merely to scenes of sadism like those which I had witnessed and to the actual vicious practices of the Baron. The latter, even for conversation, for company, for a game of cards, now only enjoyed the society of lower-class people who exploited him. No doubt the snobbery of the gutter may be understood as easily as snobbery of the other kind. The two had in fact long been united, alternating one with the other, in M. de Charlus, who thought no one was smart enough to be numbered among his social acquaintances, no one sufficiently a ruffian to be worth knowing in other ways. "I detest the intermediate style," he would say. "Bourgeois comedy is stiff and affected. Let me have either the princesses of classical tragedy or broad farce. No half-way houses—either *Phèdre* or *Les Saltimbanques*." But in the end the balance between the two forms of snobbery had been broken. Perhaps because he was an old man and tired, perhaps because sensuality had come to enter into even his trivial relationships, the Baron now lived only among his "inferiors", thus unintentionally taking his place as the successor of more than one among his great ancestors, the Duc de La Rochefoucauld, the Prince d'Harcourt, the Duc de Berry, whom we see in the pages of Saint-Simon passing their lives in the midst of their lackeys, who extracted enormous sums from them, and sharing their amusements, to such an extent that people who had to visit them were embarrassed, for their sakes, to find these great noblemen familiarly engaged in a game of cards or a drinking-bout with their domestic servants. "And above all," Jupien went on, "it is to keep him out of trouble, because the Baron, you know, is a big baby. Even now that he has here everything that he can desire, he still wanders about in search of sordid adventures. And with his generosity, that sort of thing could have disagreeable consequences in these days. Only the other day there was a page-boy from a hotel who was absolutely terrified because of all the money the Baron offered him if he would go to his house! (To his house, what imprudence!) The boy, who in fact only cares about women, was reassured when he understood what was wanted of him. Hearing all these promises of money, he had taken the Baron for a spy. And he was greatly relieved when he realised that he was being asked to sell not his country but his body, which is possibly not a more moral thing to do, but less dangerous and in any case easier." And listening to Jupien, I said to myself: "How unfortunate it is that M. de Charlus is not a novelist or a poet! Not merely so that he could describe what he sees, but because the position in which a Charlus finds himself with regard to desire by causing scandals to spring up round him compels him to take life seriously, to load pleasure with a weight of emotion. He cannot get stuck in an ironical and superficial view of things because a current of pain is perpetually re-awakened within him. Almost every time he makes a declaration of love he is violently snubbed, if he does not run the risk of being sent to prison." A slap in the face or a box on the ear helps to educate not only children but poets. If M. de Charlus had been a novelist, the house which Jupien had set up for him, by reducing so greatly the risks—at least (for a raid by the police was always a possibility) the risk emanating from an individual casually encountered in the street, of whose inclinations the Baron could not have felt certain—would have been a misfortune for him. But in the sphere of art M. de Charlus was no more than a dilettante, who never thought of writing and had no gift for it.

"Besides, I may as well admit to you," Jupien continued, "that I have very few scruples about making money in this way. The actual thing that is done here is—I can no longer conceal the fact from you—something that I like, it is what I have a taste for myself. Well, is it forbidden to receive payment for things that one does not regard as wickedness? You are better educated than I am, and you will tell me no doubt that Socrates was of the opinion that he could not accept money for his lessons. But in our age professors of philosophy do not hold that view, nor do doctors or painters or playwrights or theatrical producers. Do not imagine that this trade of mine brings me into contact only with the dregs of society. No doubt the director of an establishment of this kind, like a great courtesan, receives only men, but he receives men who are conspicuous in every walk of life and who are generally, on their own level, among the most intelligent, the most sensitive, the most agreeable of their profession. In no time at all, I assure you, this house could be transformed into an information bureau or a school of wit." Nevertheless, I was still under the impression of the blows which I had seen inflicted upon M. de Charlus.

And the truth is that, when one knew M. de Charlus well —his pride, his satiety with social pleasures, his fancies which changed easily into passions for men of the lowest class and the worst character—one could very easily understand that the possession of a huge fortune, the charm of which, had he been an upstart, would have been that it enabled him to marry his daughter to a duke and invite Highnesses to his shooting-parties, pleased him simply because it allowed him to have at his disposal in this way one or perhaps several establishments with a permanent supply of young men whose company he enjoyed. And perhaps this might have come to pass even without his special vice, heir as he was to so many great noblemen, dukes or princes of the blood, of whom Saint-Simon tells us that they never associated with anybody "who could boast a name".

"Meanwhile", I said to Jupien, "this house is anything but what you say it might become. It is worse than a madhouse, since the mad fancies of the lunatics who inhabit it are played out as actual, visible drama—it is a veritable pandemonium. I thought that I had arrived, like the Caliph in the *Thousand and One Nights*, in the nick of time to rescue a man who was being beaten, and in fact it was a different tale from the *Thousand and One Nights* which I saw enacted before me, the one in which a woman who has been turned into a dog willingly submits to being beaten in order to recover her former shape." Jupien appeared to be very upset by my words, for he realised that I had seen the Baron being beaten. He was silent for a moment, while I stopped a cab which was passing; then suddenly, with that pretty wit which had so often struck me in this self-educated man when in the courtyard of our house he had greeted me or Françoise with some graceful phrase: "You have mentioned one or two of the tales in the *Thousand and One Nights*," he said. "But there is another I know of, not unrelated to the title of a book which I think I have seen at the Baron's" (he was alluding to a translation of Ruskin's *Sesame and Lilies* which I had sent M. de Charlus). "If ever you are curious, one evening, to see, I will not say forty but a dozen thieves, you have only to come here; to know whether I am in the house you have only to look up at that window; if I leave my little window open with a light visible it means that I am in the house and you may come in;

it is my private Sesame. I say only Sesame. As for Lilies, if they are what you seek I advise you to go elsewhere." And with a somewhat offhand gesture of farewell—for an aristocratic clientèle and the habit of ruling like a pirate chief over a gang of young men had imparted a certain lordliness to his manners—he was about to take his leave of me when the noise of an explosion—a bomb which had fallen before the sirens could give warning—made him advise me to stay with him for a moment. Soon the anti-aircraft barrage began, and with such violence that one could sense very near, just above our heads, the presence of the German aeroplane.

In an instant the streets became totally black. At moments only, an enemy aeroplane flying very low lit up the spot upon which it wished to drop a bomb. I set off, but very soon I was lost. I thought of that day when, on my way to La Raspelière, I had met an aeroplane and my horse had reared as at the apparition of a god. Now, I thought, it would be a different meeting—with the god of evil, who would kill me. I started to walk faster in order to escape, like a traveller pursued by the bore of a river; I groped my way round dark squares from which I could find no way out. At last the flames of a blazing building showed me where I was and I got back onto the right road, while all the time the shells burst noisily above my head. But my thoughts had turned to another subject. I was thinking of Jupien's house, perhaps by now reduced to ashes, for a bomb had fallen very near me just after I had left it— that house upon which M. de Charlus might prophetically have written *Sodoma*, as had done, with no less prescience or perhaps when the volcano had already started to erupt and the catastrophe had begun, the unknown inhabitants of Pompeii. But what mattered sirens and Gothas to the men who had come to seek their pleasure? The social setting or the natural scene which surrounds our love-making barely impinges upon our thoughts. The tempest may rage over the sea, the ship roll and plunge in every direction, the sky pour down avalanches convulsed by the wind, and at most we bestow the attention of a single second, forced from us by physical discomfort, upon this immense scenic background against which we ourselves are so insignificant, both we and the body which we long to approach. The siren with its warning of bombs troubled Jupien's visitors no more than an iceberg would have done. Indeed, the threat of physical danger delivered them from the fear which for long had morbidly harassed them. For it is wrong to suppose that the scale of our fears corresponds to that of the dangers by which they are inspired. A man may be afraid of not sleeping and not in the least afraid of a serious duel, afraid of a rat and not of a lion. For a few hours now the police would have their hands full looking after something as trivial as the lives of the city's inhabitants and their reputations were temporarily in no danger. But if some, their fears allayed, remained in Jupien's establishment, others were tempted not so much by the thought of recovering their moral liberty as by the darkness which had suddenly settled upon the streets. Some of these, like the Pompeians upon whom the fire from heaven was already raining, descended into the passages of the Métro, black as catacombs. They knew that they would not be alone there. And darkness, which envelops all things like a new element, has the effect, irresistibly tempting for certain people, of suppressing the first halt on the road to pleasure—it permits us to enter without impediment into a region of caresses to which normally we gain access only after a certain delay. Whether the coveted object be a woman or a man, supposing even that the first approach is easy and that there is no need of the gallant speeches which in a drawing-room might run on for ever (at any rate in daylight), on a normal evening, even in the most dimly lit street, there is at least a preamble in which the eyes alone feed on the repast which cannot yet be enjoyed and the fear of passers-by, the fear also of the man or woman before us, prevents us from doing more than look and speak. In the darkness this time-honoured ritual is instantly abolished—hands, lips, bodies may go into action at once. There is always the excuse of darkness, and of the mistakes that darkness engenders, if we are not well received. And if we are, this immediate response of a body which does not withdraw but approaches, gives us of the woman (or the man) whom we have selected the idea that she is without prejudices and full of vice, which adds an extra pleasure to the happiness of having bitten straight into the fruit without first coveting it with our eyes and without asking permission. Meanwhile the darkness persisted; plunged into the new element, imagining that they had travelled to a distant country and were witnessing a natural phenomenon like a tidal wave or an eclipse, that they were enjoying not an artificially prepared, sedentary pleasure but a chance encounter in the unknown, the men who had come away from Jupien's house celebrated, while the bombs mimicked the rumbling of a volcano, deep in the earth as in a Pompeian house of ill fame, their secret rites in the shadows of the catacombs.

The Pompeian paintings of Jupien's house were admirably suited, recalling as they did the later days of the Revolution, to the age so similar to the Directory which was about to begin. Already, without waiting for peace, concealing themselves in the darkness so as not too openly to infringe the regulations of the police, everywhere new-fangled dances were being evolved and frenziedly danced by their devotees throughout the night. And at the same time certain artistic opinions less anti-German in tone than those of the first years of the war were coming into vogue, allowing suffocated minds to breathe once more—but still before you dared to present these ideas you needed to produce a certificate of your patriotism. A professor might write a remarkable book on Schiller and it would be reviewed in the newspapers. But before discussing the author of the book they would record, as a sort of *imprimatur*, that he had been at the Marne or Verdun, that he had been mentioned in despatches five times or had two sons killed. Then and then only did they praise the lucidity, the depth of his work on Schiller, whom it was permissible to describe as "great" provided that he was called not "that great German" but "that great Boche". This was the pass-word, and having passed this test the article was allowed to proceed.

The clients who had not wished to leave had collected together in one room in Jupien's house. They were not acquainted with one another, but one could see that they all belonged nevertheless roughly to the same world, rich and aristocratic. The appearance of each one had in it something repugnant, a reflection, I presumed, of their failure to resist degrading pleasures. One, an enormous man, had a face covered with red blotches like a drunkard. I was told that formerly he had not drunk much himself but had merely enjoyed making young men drunk. But, terrified at the idea of being called up (although he seemed to be in his fifties) and being very stout, he had started to drink without stopping in order to get his weight above a hundred kilos, as nobody over this limit was accepted for the army. And now, this calculation having transformed itself into a passion, the moment that he was left alone, wherever it might be, he would disappear and be found again in a wine-shop. But as soon as he spoke I saw that, though his intelligence was commonplace, he was a man with a good deal of knowledge,

education and culture. Another man came in, very young and
of great physical distinction. This one, who clearly belonged
to the best society, had as yet it is true no external marks of
vice, but—and this was more disturbing—interior signs were
there. Very tall, with a charming face, his speech revealed
an intelligence of quite a different order from that of his
alcoholic neighbour, an intelligence that might without exaggeration be called really outstanding. But to everything that
he said there was added a facial expression which would have
suited a different phrase. As though, while possessing the
whole treasure-house of the expressions of the human countenance, he lived in some world of his own, he displayed these
expressions in the wrong order, appearing to scatter smiles
and glances at random without any connection with the
remarks that were being addressed to him. I hope for his
sake—if, as he certainly is, he is still alive—that he was the
victim not of a lasting malady but of a brief intoxication.
Probably, had one asked all these men for their visiting cards,
one would have been surprised to see that they belonged to an
exalted social class. But some vice or other, and that greatest
of all vices, the lack of will-power which prevents a man from
resisting any vice in particular, brought them together in this
place, in isolated rooms it is true, but evening after evening so
I was told, so that, though their names might be known to
fashionable hostesses, the latter had gradually lost sight of
their faces and no longer ever received their visits. Invitations
might still be sent to them, but habit brought them back to
their composite haunt of depravity. They made, moreover,
little attempt at concealment, unlike the page-boys, young
workmen, etc., who ministered to their pleasures. And this
fact, for which a number of reasons could be given, is best
explained by this one: for a man with a job, whether in
industry or in domestic service, to go to Jupien's was much

the same as for a woman supposed respectable to go to a house of assignation; some, while ready to admit that they had gone there, denied having gone more than once, and Jupien himself, lying to protect their reputations or to discourage competition, would declare: "Oh, no, he doesn't come to my establishment, he wouldn't go *there*." For men with a social position it was not so serious, particularly as other men with a social position who do not go *there* know nothing about the place and do not concern themselves with your life. But in an aeroplane factory, for instance, if one or two fitters have gone *there*, their comrades, who have spied on them, would not dream of following their example for fear of being found out.

As I made my way home, I reflected upon the speed with which conscience ceases to be a partner in our habits, which she allows to develop freely without bothering herself about them, and upon the astonishing picture which may consequently present itself to us if we observe simply from without, and in the belief that they engage the whole of the individual, the actions of men whose moral or intellectual virtues may at the same time be developing independently in an entirely different direction. Clearly it was a gross fault in their education, or a complete absence of education, combined with a propensity for making money in the way which, if not the least painful (for there were many forms of work which must in the long run be pleasanter—but then does not an invalid in the same way fabricate for himself, with fads, privations and remedies, an existence much more painful than the one imposed upon him by the often trivial disease against which he imagines himself to be fighting by these methods?) was at least less laborious than any other, which had led these ordinary young men to do, quite innocently one may almost say and for a very moderate reward, things which caused them no pleasure and which must in the beginning have inspired in

them a lively disgust. On this evidence one might have supposed them to be fundamentally bad, but not only were they
in the war splendid soldiers, men of incomparable courage,
in civil life too they had often been kind-hearted and sometimes wholly admirable people. They had long ceased to
speculate upon the morality or immorality of the life they
led, because it was the life that was led by everybody round
them. So it is that, when we study certain periods of ancient
history, we are astonished to see men and women individually
good participate without scruple in mass assassinations or
human sacrifices which probably seemed to them natural
things. And our own age no doubt, when its history is read
two thousand years hence, will seem to an equal degree
to have bathed men of pure and tender conscience in a
vital element which will strike the future reader as monstrously pernicious, but to which at the time these men
adapted themselves without difficulty. Similarly, I knew few
men, I may even say I knew none, who in point of intelligence and sensibility was as gifted as Jupien; for the store
of knowledge which gave such a delightful quality of wit to
his conversation came to him not from that instruction at
school or that liberal education at a university which might
have made him indeed a remarkable man, but from which
many fashionable youths derive no profit. It was simply his
innate good sense, his natural taste, which had enabled him,
from a few books read at random, without a guide, at odd
moments, to construct that correct and elegant manner of
speaking in which all the symmetries of language were revealed and their beauty displayed. Yet the trade that he followed might with good reason be regarded, though certainly
as one of the most lucrative, as the lowest of all. As for M. de
Charlus, whatever disdain his aristocratic pride may have
given him for the thought of what people would say, how

was it that some feeling of personal dignity and self-respect had not forced him to refuse his sensuality certain satisfactions for which the only imaginable excuse might seem to be complete insanity? But in him, as in Jupien, the practice of separating morality from a whole order of actions (and this is something that must also often happen to men who have public duties to perform, those of a judge for instance or a statesman and many others as well) must have been so long established that Habit, no longer asking Moral Sentiment for its opinion, had grown stronger from day to day until at last this consenting Prometheus had had himself nailed by Force to the rock of Pure Matter.

No doubt, as I saw clearly enough, a new stage had been reached in the malady of M. de Charlus, which since I had first observed it, had, to judge from the diverse phases which had presented themselves to my vision, pursued its development with ever-increasing speed. The poor Baron could not now be very far from the malady's final term, from death itself, though this possibly would be preceded, in accordance with the predictions and prayers of Mme Verdurin, by an imprisonment which at his age could only hasten its coming. Yet I have perhaps been inaccurate in speaking of the rock of Pure Matter. In this Pure Matter it is possible that a small quantum of Mind still survived. This madman knew, in spite of everything, that he was the victim of a form of madness and during his mad moments he nevertheless was playing a part, since he knew quite well that the young man who was beating him was not more wicked than the little boy who in a game of war is chosen by lot to be "the Prussians", upon whom all the others hurl themselves in a fury of genuine patriotism and pretended hate. The victim of a madness, yet a madness into which there entered nevertheless a little of the personality of M. de Charlus. Even in these aberrations (and this is true also of our loves or our travels), human nature still betrays its need for belief by its insistent demands for truth. Françoise, if I spoke to her about a church in Milan, a town which she would probably never visit, or about the cathedral of Rheims—or even merely that of Arras!—which she would not be able to see since they had been more or less destroyed, spoke enviously of the rich who can afford to visit such treasures or else exclaimed with nostalgic regret: "Ah! how lovely it must have been!" although, after all these years that she had lived in Paris, she had never had the curiosity to go and see Notre Dame. For Notre Dame is part of Paris and Paris was the town in which the daily life of Françoise took its course, the town, in consequence, in which it was difficult for our old servant—as it would have been for me had not the study of architecture corrected in me at certain points the instincts of Combray—to situate the objects of her dreams. In the people whom we love, there is, immanent, a certain dream which we cannot always clearly discern but which we pursue. It was my belief in Bergotte and in Swann which had made me love Gilberte, my belief in Gilbert the Bad which had made me love Mme de Guermantes. And what a vast expanse of sea had been hidden away in my love—the most full of suffering, the most jealous, seemingly the most individual of all my loves—for Albertine! In any case, just because we are furiously pursuing a dream in a succession of individuals, our loves for people cannot fail to be more or less of an aberration. (And are not even the maladies of the body, at least those that are at all closely connected with the nervous system, in the nature of special tastes or special fears acquired by our organs or our joints, which indicate in this manner that they have conceived for certain climates a horror as inexplicable and as obstinate as the fondness which certain men betray for, it might be, women with an eye-glass or women on horseback? Who can say to what long-lived and unconscious dream is linked the desire that never fails to re-awaken at the sight of a woman on horseback, an unconscious dream as mysterious as is, for example, for a man who has suffered all his life from asthma, the influence of a certain town, in appearance no different to any other town, in which for the first time he breathes freely?) And if there is something of aberration or perversion in all our loves, perversions in the narrower sense of the word are like loves in which the germ of disease has spread victoriously to every part. Even in the maddest of them love may still be recognised. If M. de Charlus insisted that his hands and feet should be bound with chains of proven strength, if he asked repeatedly for the "bar of justice" and, so Jupien told me, for other ferocious instruments which it was almost impossible to obtain even from sailors—for they served to inflict punishments which have been abolished even on board ship where discipline is more rigorous than anywhere else—at the bottom of all this there persisted in M. de Charlus his dream of virility, to be attested if need be by acts of brutality, and all that inner radiance, invisible to us but projecting in this manner a little reflected light, with which his mediaeval imagination adorned crosses of justice and feudal tortures. It was the same sentiment that made him, every time he arrived, say to Jupien: "I hope there will be no alert this evening, for already I see myself consumed by this fire from heaven like an inhabitant of Sodom." And he affected to be nervous of the Gothas, not that they caused him the slightest shadow of fear, but so as to have a pretext, as soon as the sirens sounded, to rush into the shelters in the Métro, where he hoped for pleasure from brief contact with unseen figures, accompanied by vague dreams of mediaeval dungeons and oubliettes. In short his desire to be bound in chains and beaten, with all its ugliness

betrayed a dream as poetical as, in other men, the longing to
go to Venice or to keep ballet-dancers. And M. de Charlus
was so determined that this dream should give him the illusion
of reality that Jupien was obliged to sell the wooden bed which
was in Room 43 and replace it by an iron bed which went
better with the chains.

The all-clear sounded at last as I was approaching my
house. A little boy in the street told me what a noise the
fire-engines had made. I met Françoise coming up from the
cellar with the butler. She thought that I had been killed.
She told me that Saint-Loup had looked in, with apologies, to
see whether he had not, in the course of the visit he had paid
me during the morning, dropped his *croix de guerre*. For he
had just noticed that he had lost it, and as he had to rejoin his
regiment the following morning he had wanted to make sure
that it was not in our flat. He had searched everywhere with
Françoise and had found nothing. Françoise thought that he
must have lost it before coming to see me, for, she said, she
was almost sure, in fact she could have sworn that he was not
wearing it when she saw him. In this she was mistaken. So
much for the value of evidence and memory! In any case it
was of no great importance. Saint-Loup was as much esteemed
by his officers as loved by his men, and the matter could
easily be arranged. However, I sensed immediately, from the
unenthusiastic manner in which they spoke of him, that
Saint-Loup had made a poor impression on Françoise and on
the butler. True, whereas the butler's son and Françoise's
nephew had made every effort to get themselves into safe jobs,
Saint-Loup had made efforts of the opposite kind, and with
success, to be sent to as dangerous a post as possible. But this,
because they judged from their own natures, was something
that Françoise and the butler were incapable of believing.
They were convinced that the rich are always put where there

is no danger. In any case, had they known the truth concerning the heroic courage of Robert, it would have left them unmoved. He did not say "Boches", he had praised the valour of the Germans, he did not attribute to treachery the fact that we had not been victorious from the first day. That is what they would have liked to hear, that is what would have seemed to them a sign of courage. So although they continued to search for the *croix de guerre*, I found them chilly on the subject of Robert. Having my suspicions as to where the cross had been forgotten, I advised Françoise and the butler to go to bed. (However, if Saint-Loup had amused himself that evening in the fashion which I suspected, it was only to pass the time of waiting, for he had been seized once more by the desire to see Morel and had made use of all his military connections to find out in what regiment he was serving, so that he could go and see him, but so far had only received hundreds of contradictory answers.) But the butler was never in a hurry to leave Françoise now that, thanks to the war, he had found a means of torturing her even more efficacious than the expulsion of the nuns or the Dreyfus case. That evening, and every time I went near them during the few more days that I spent in Paris before leaving to go to a new sanatorium, I heard the butler say to a terrified Françoise: "They're not in a hurry of course, they're biding their time, but when the pear is ripe they will take Paris, and on that day we shall see no mercy!" "Heavens above, Mother of God," cried Françoise, "aren't they satisfied to have conquered poor Belgium? She suffered enough, when they invaded her." "Belgium, Françoise? What they did in Belgium will be nothing compared to this!" And as the war had flooded the conversation of working-class people with a quantity of terms with which they had become acquainted through their eyes alone, by reading the newspapers, and which they consequently did not know how to pronounce, the butler went on to say: "I cannot understand how everybody can be so stupid. You will see, Françoise, they are preparing a new attack with a wider *scoop* than all the others." At this I rebelled, if not in the name of pity for Françoise and strategic common sense, at least in that of grammar, and declared that the word should be pronounced "scope", but succeeded only in causing the terrible phrase to be repeated to Françoise every time I entered the kitchen, for to the butler the pleasure of alarming his companion was scarcely greater than that of showing his master that, though he had once been a gardener at Combray and was nothing more than a butler, he was nevertheless a good Frenchman according to the rule of Saint-André-des-Champs and possessed, by virtue of the Declaration of the Rights of Man, the right to use the pronunciation "scoop" in full independence and not to let himself be dictated to on a point which formed no part of his service and upon which in consequence, since the Revolution had made us all equals, he need listen to nobody.

To my annoyance, therefore, I had to listen to him talking to Françoise about an operation of wide "scoop" with an emphasis which was intended to prove to me that this pronunciation was the result not of ignorance but of an act of will following upon ripe reflection. He confounded the government and the newspapers in a single "they" full of mistrust, saying: "They tell us about the losses of the Boches, they don't tell us about our own, it seems that they are ten times as big. They tell us that the enemy are at the end of their tether, that they have nothing to eat, personally I believe they are a hundred times better off than we are for food. It's no use stuffing us with lies. If the enemy had nothing to eat, they wouldn't fight as they did the other day when they killed a hundred thousand of our young men not twenty years old." Thus at every moment he exaggerated the triumphs of the Germans, as in the past he had those of the Radicals; and at the same time he recounted their atrocities in order that these triumphs might be yet more painful to Françoise, who never stopped saying: "Ah! Holy Mother of the Angels! Ah! Mary, Mother of God!", and sometimes, in order to be disagreeable to her in a different way, he said: "Anyhow, we are no better than they are, what we're doing in Greece is no prettier than what they have done in Belgium. You will see that we shall turn everybody against us, we shall find ourselves fighting every nation in the world," whereas the truth was exactly the opposite. On days when the news was good he destroyed its effect by assuring Françoise that the war would last thirty-five years, and if there was talk of the possibility of an armistice, he declared that peace would not last more than a few months and would be followed by battles which would make the present ones look like child's play, such battles that after them there would be nothing left of France.

The victory of the Allies seemed, if not near at hand, at least more or less certain, and it must unfortunately be admitted that the butler was greatly distressed at the prospect. For he had reduced the "world" war, like everything else, to the war which he was secretly waging against Françoise (of whom, nevertheless, he was fond, just as one may be fond of the person whom one enjoys infuriating every day by beating him at dominoes) and victory in his eyes took the shape of the first conversation in which he would have the pain of hearing Françoise say: "Well, it's over at last, and they'll have to give us more than we gave them in '70." He believed, nevertheless, that this fatal day of reckoning was perpetually about to arrive, for an unconscious patriotism made him suppose, like all Frenchmen, victims of the same mirage as myself since my illness, that victory—like my recovery—was just round

the corner. This event he anticipated by announcing to Françoise that victory might perhaps come, but that his heart bled
at the thought, for revolution would follow hard on its heels
and then invasion. "Ah! this fine old war, the Boches will be
the only ones to recover from it quickly, Françoise. They have
already made hundreds of thousands of millions out of it. But
as for their coughing up a *sou* to us, what nonsense! They will
print that in the newspapers perhaps," he added out of prudence and so as to be ready for any eventuality, "in order to
appease the people, just as for three years now they have been
saying that the war will be over tomorrow." Françoise was
only too easily disturbed by these words, because, having at
first believed the optimists rather than the butler, she saw now
that the war, which she had thought would end in a fortnight
in spite of "the innovation of poor Belgium", was indeed
still going on, that we were not advancing (the phenomenon
of fixed front warfare was beyond her comprehension) and
that, according to one of the innumerable "godsons" to whom
she gave everything that she earned with us, "they" were concealing various awkward facts. "It's the working man who
will have to pay," concluded the butler. "They will take your
field away from you, Françoise." "Ah! God in Heaven!"
But to these distant misfortunes he preferred nearer ones and
devoured the newspapers in the hope of being able to announce
a defeat to Françoise. He waited for pieces of bad news as
eagerly as if they had been Easter eggs, hoping that things
would go badly enough to terrify Françoise but not badly
enough to cause him any material suffering. Thus the prospect
of a Zeppelin raid enchanted him: he would have the spectacle
of Françoise hiding in the cellars, and at the same time he was
persuaded that in a town as large as Paris the bombs would
never happen to fall just on our house.

Françoise meanwhile was beginning at moments to return

to her Combray pacificism. She almost had doubts about the "German atrocities". "When the war started we were told that the Germans were murderers, brigands, real bandits, BBBoches. . . ." (If she gave several *b*'s to Boche, it was because the accusation that the Germans were murderers seemed to her quite plausible, but the idea that they were Boches, because of the enormity of the accusation, improbable in the extreme. Only it was not at all easy to understand what mysteriously terrifying sense Françoise gave to the word Boche, since the period she was talking about was the very beginning of the war, and also on account of the air of doubt with which she pronounced the word. For a doubt whether the Germans were criminals might be ill-founded in fact but did not contain in itself, from the point of view of logic, any contradiction. But how was it possible to doubt that they were Boches, since the word, in the popular language, means nothing more nor less than German? Perhaps she was simply repeating in an indirect fashion the violent remarks she had heard at the time, in which the word Boche was emphasised with particular energy.) "I believed all that," she went on, "but I am wondering now whether we are not every bit as scoundrelly as they are." This blasphemous thought had been slyly prepared in Françoise's mind by the butler, who, seeing that she had a certain fondness for King Constantine of Greece, had not ceased to represent him to her as literally starved by us until the day when he would yield. So the abdication of this monarch had aroused strong feelings in Françoise, who went so far as to declare: "We are no better than they are. If we were in Germany, we would do just the same."

I saw little of her, in any case, during these few days, for she spent much time at the house of those cousins of whom Mama had said to me one day: "But you know that they are richer than you are." These cousins had given an example of that beautiful conduct which was very frequent at this period throughout the country and which would bear witness, if there were a historian to perpetuate its memory, to the greatness of France, her greatness of soul, her greatness after the fashion of Saint-André-des-Champs, a kind of conduct displayed as much by thousands of civilians living in safety far from the front as by the soldiers who fell at the Marne. There had been killed at Berry-au-Bac a nephew of Françoise who was also a nephew of the millionaire cousins, former proprietors of a large café who had retired long since after making their fortune. The young man who was killed had been the owner of a very small café and quite poor; he had gone off, twenty-five years old, when the army was mobilised, leaving his young wife alone to look after the little bar to which he hoped to return in a few months. He had been killed. And then this is what happened. The millionaire cousins of Françoise, who were not related by blood to the young woman who was their nephew's widow, had left the home in the country to which they had retired ten years earlier and had set to work again as café proprietors, without putting a *sou* into their own pockets; every morning at six the millionairess, a real lady, was up and dressed together with Mademoiselle her daughter, ready to help their niece and cousin by marriage. And for nearly three years now they had been washing glasses and serving drinks from early morning until half-past nine at night, without a day's rest. In this book in which there is not a single incident which is not fictitious, not a single character who is a real person in disguise, in which everything has been invented by me in accordance with the requirements of my theme, I owe it to the credit of my country to say that only the millionaire cousins of Françoise who came out of retirement to help their niece when she was left without support, only they are real people who exist. And persuaded as I am that I shall not offend their modesty, for the reason that they will never read this book, it is both with childish pleasure and with a profound emotion that, being unable to record the names of so many others who undoubtedly acted in the same way, to all of whom France owes her survival, I transcribe here the real name of this family: they are called—and what name could be more French?—Larivière. If there were a few vile shirkers like the arrogant young man in a dinner-jacket whom I had seen in Jupien's establishment, whose only concern was to know whether he could have Léon at half past ten "as he had a luncheon engagement", they are redeemed by the innumerable throng of all the Frenchmen of Saint-André-des-Champs, by all the sublime soldiers and by those whom I rank as their equals, the Larivières.

The butler, to sharpen the fears of Françoise, showed her an old copy of *Lectures pour tous* which he had found, with a picture on its cover (it dated from before the war) of the "imperial family of Germany". "There's our lord and master to be," said the butler to Françoise, showing her "William". She goggled, then pointed to the feminine personage who stood by his side and said: "And there's the Williamess!"

My departure from Paris was delayed by a piece of news which distressed me so much that I was for some time rendered incapable of travelling. This was the death of Robert de Saint-Loup, killed two days after his return to the front while covering the retreat of his men. Never had any man felt less hatred for a nation than he (and as for the Emperor, for particular reasons, very possibly incorrect, he thought that William II had tried rather to prevent the war than to bring it about). Nor had he hated Germanism; the last words which I had heard on his lips, six days before he died, were the beginning of a song by Schumann, which he had started to hum in German on my staircase, until I had made him desist because of the neighbours. Accustomed by supreme good breeding to eliminate from his conduct all trace of apology or invective, all rhetoric, he had avoided in face of the enemy, as he had at the time of mobilisation, the actions which would have ensured his survival, through that tendency to efface himself before others of which all his behaviour was symbolic, down to his manner of coming out into the street bare-headed to close the door of my cab, every time I visited him. For several days I remained shut up in my room, thinking of him. I recalled his arrival the first time at Balbec, when, in an almost white suit, with his eyes greenish and mobile like the waves, he had crossed the hall adjoining the great dining-room whose windows gave onto the sea. I recalled the very special being that he had then seemed to me to be, the being for whose friendship I had so greatly wished. That wish had been realised beyond the limits of what I should ever have thought possible, without, however, at the time giving me more than a very slight pleasure; and then later I had come to understand the many great virtues and something else as well which lay concealed behind his elegant appearance. All this, the good as well as the bad, he had given without counting the cost, every day, as much on the last day when he advanced to attack a trench, out of generosity and because it was his habit to place at the service of others all that he possessed, as on that evening when he had run along the seats in the restaurant in order not to disturb me. And I the fact that had seen him really so little but against such varied backgrounds, in circumstances so diverse and separated by so many intervals —in that hall at Balbec, in the café at Rivebelle, in the cavalry barracks and at the military dinners in Doncières, at the theatre where he had slapped the face of the journalist, in the house of the Princesse de Guermantes—only had the effect

of giving me, of his life, pictures more striking and more
sharply defined and for his death a grief more lucid than we
are likely to have in the case of people whom we have loved
more, but with whom our association has been so nearly continuous that the image we retain of them is no more than a
sort of vague average between an infinity of imperceptibly
different images and our affection, satiated, has not, as with
those whom we have seen only for brief moments, during
meetings prematurely ended against their wish and ours, the
illusion that there was possible between us a still greater
affection of which circumstances alone have defrauded us.
A few days after the day on which I had seen him pursuing
his monocle and supposed him to be so haughty, in that hall
at Balbec, there was another living form which I had seen
for the first time on the beach at Balbec and which now, like
his, no longer existed save in the state of memory: Albertine,
making her progress along the sand that first evening, indifferent to everybody around her, a marine creature, like a
sea-gull. For her my love had come so swiftly that, in order to
be free to go out with her every day, I had never during my
stay at Balbec gone over to Doncières to see Saint-Loup. And
yet the history of my relations with him bore witness also to
the fact that at one period I had ceased to love Albertine, since
if later I had installed myself for a while near Robert at Doncières, the reason lay in my unhappiness at seeing that the
sentiment which I felt for Mme de Guermantes was not
returned. His life and Albertine's, so late made known to me,
both at Balbec, and so swiftly concluded, had scarcely crossed,
though it was he, I told myself, perceiving that the nimble
shuttles of the years weave links between those of our memories which seem at first most independent of each other, it
was he whom I had sent to see Mme Bontemps after Albertine had left me. And then it had turned out that their two

lives had each of them a parallel secret, which I had not suspected. Saint-Loup's secret caused me now more sadness perhaps than that of Albertine, whose life had become so alien to me. But I felt an inconsolable regret that her life as well as his had been so short. They had often said to me, both of them: "You who are ill . . .", they had looked after me. And yet it was they who were dead, while I, both of the one and of the other, could set side by side, separated by an interval which after all was really not very long, the final image—before the trench, in the river-bed—and the first image, which even in the case of Albertine I valued now only because it was associated in my mind with that of the sun setting over the sea.

Saint-Loup's death was received by Françoise with more compassion than that of Albertine. Immediately she assumed her role of hired mourner and descanted upon the memory of the dead man with frenzied threnodies and lamentations. She paraded her grief and only put on an unfeeling expression, at the same time averting her head, when in spite of myself I betrayed mine, which she wished to appear not to have seen. For like many emotional people, she was exasperated by the emotions of others, which bore no doubt too great a resemblance to her own. She loved now to draw attention to her slightest rheumatic twinge, to a fit of giddiness, to a bump. But if I referred to one of my symptoms, in an instant she was stoical and grave again and pretended not to have heard. "Poor Marquis," she said, although she continued to believe that he would have done anything in the world in order not to go the front and, once there, in order to run away from danger. "Poor lady," she said, thinking of Mme de Marsantes, "how she must have cried when she heard about her boy's death! If at least she had been able to see him again! But perhaps it's better that she didn't, because his nose was cut in two, he was completely disfaced." And the eyes of Françoise filled with tears, behind which, however, there was perceptible the cruel curiosity of the peasant woman. No doubt Françoise pitied the sorrow of Mme de Marsantes with all her heart, but she regretted not knowing the form which this sorrow had taken and not being able to enjoy the afflicting spectacle of it. And as she would dearly have loved to cry and to be seen by me to cry, she said, in order to work herself up: "This has really done something to me!" In me too she sought to detect the traces of grief, with an avidity which caused me to feign a certain indifference when I spoke of Robert. And, largely no doubt out of a spirit of imitation and because she had heard the phrase used—for there are clichés in the servants' hall as well as in social coteries—she kept repeating, not however without a poor man's satisfaction in her voice: "All his riches did not save him from dying like anybody else, and what use are they to him now?" The butler took advantage of the occasion to say to Françoise that of course it was sad, but that it hardly counted beside the millions of men who fell every day in spite of all the efforts which the government made to conceal the fact. But this time the butler did not succeed in augmenting the sorrow of Françoise as he had hoped. For she replied: "It is true that they also die for France, but they are nobodies; it is always more interesting when it is somebody whom one knows." And Françoise, who enjoyed crying, went on to add: "You must be sure to let me know if they talk about the death of the Marquis in the newspaper."

Robert had often said to me sadly, long before the war: "Oh! my life, don't let's talk about it, I am a condemned man from the start." Was he alluding to the vice which he had succeeded hitherto in concealing from the world, but of which he was himself aware and whose seriousness he perhaps exaggerated, just as children who make love for the first time, or merely before that age seek solitary pleasure, imagine themselves to be like a plant which cannot scatter its pollen without dying immediately afterwards? Perhaps this exaggeration, for Saint-Loup as for the children, came partly from the still unfamiliar idea of sin, partly from the fact that an entirely novel sensation has an almost terrible force which later will gradually diminish; or had he really, justifying it if need be by the death of his father at an early age, a presentiment of his own premature end? Such a presentiment would seem, no doubt, to be impossible. Yet death appears to be obedient to certain laws. Often for instance, one gets the impression that children of parents who have died very old or very young are almost compelled to disappear at the same age, the former protracting until their hundredth year their incurable miseries and ailments, the latter, in spite of a happy and healthy existence, swept away at the premature but inevitable date by an illness so opportune and so accidental (whatever deep roots it may have in the victim's temperament) that it appears to be merely the formality necessary for the realisation of death. And may it not be possible that accidental death too—like that of Saint-Loup, which was perhaps in any case linked to his character in more ways than I have thought it necessary to describe—is somehow recorded in advance, known only to the gods, invisible to men, but revealed by a peculiar sadness, half unconscious, half conscious (and even, insofar as it is conscious, proclaimed to others with that complete sincerity with which we foretell misfortunes which in our heart of hearts we believe we shall escape but which will nevertheless take place) to the man who bears and forever sees within himself, as though it were some heraldic device, a fatal date?

He must have been truly magnificent in those last hours. This man who throughout his life, even when sitting down, even when walking across a drawing-room, had seemed to be restraining an impulse to charge, while with a smile he dissembled the indomitable will which dwelt within his triangular head, at last had charged. Freed from the books which encumbered it, the feudal turret had become military once more. And this Guermantes had died more himself than ever before, or rather more a member of his race, into which slowly he dissolved until he became nothing more than a Guermantes, as was symbolically visible at his interment in the church of Saint-Hilaire at Combray, completely hung for the occasion with black draperies upon which stood out in red, beneath the closed circle of the coronet, without initials or Christian names or titles, the G of the Guermantes that he had again in death become.

Even before going to this interment, which did not take place immediately, I wrote to Gilberte. I ought perhaps to have written to the Duchesse de Guermantes, but I told myself that she would receive the death of Robert with the same indifference which I had seen her display towards the deaths of so many others who had seemed to be closely linked to her life, and that she would perhaps even, with her Guermantes wit, try to show that she did not share the superstition about ties of blood. And I was too unwell to write to everybody. In the past I had believed that she and Robert were fond of each other in the sense in which that phrase is used in society, that is to say that, when they were together, they said to each other tender things which at the moment they truly felt. But away from her, he did not hesitate to declare that she was an idiot, and if she sometimes derived an egotistical pleasure from seeing him, I had observed her on the other hand to be incapable of taking the slightest trouble, of making even the smallest use of her credit in order to render him a service or even to spare him an unpleasantness. Her spitefulness in refusing to give Robert a recommendation to General

de Saint-Joseph, at the time when he wanted to avoid returning to Morocco, proved surely that the devoted help which she
had given him on the occasion of his marriage was no more
than a sort of atonement which cost her almost nothing. So
I was very astonished to hear—she was unwell at the moment
when Robert was killed—that in order to spare her the shock
which the news would cause her her family had thought it
necessary to conceal from her for several days, under the most
fallacious pretexts, the newspapers which would have informed her of his death. And my surprise increased when I
heard that, after they had at last been obliged to tell her the
truth, the Duchess wept for a whole day, fell sick and for a
long time—more than a week, which was a long time for her
—was inconsolable. When I heard of her grief, I was touched.
It enabled society to say, and it enables me to vouch for the
truth of the statement, that a great friendship existed between
them. But then when I recall all the little malicious utter-
ances, all the ill-natured refusals to help each other which this
friendship had not excluded, I cannot help reflecting that in
society a great friendship does not amount to much.

However, a little later, in circumstances which, if they
touched my heart less, were historically more important,
Mme de Guermantes showed herself, to my mind, in a yet
more favourable light. This woman who as a girl, as the
reader may remember, had behaved with such audacious im-
pertinence towards the imperial family of Russia, and who
after her marriage had addressed them always with a freedom
which sometimes caused her to be charged with lack of tact,
was perhaps alone, after the Russian Revolution, in giving
proofs of a limitless devotion to the Grand Duchesses and the
Grand Dukes. Only the year before the war she had not a
little annoyed the Grand Duchess Vladimir by persistently
referring to Countess Hohenfelsen, the morganatic wife of the

Grand Duke Paul, as "the Grand Duchess Paul". Neverthe-less, no sooner had the Russian Revolution broken out than our ambassador in St. Petersburg, M. Paléologue ("Paléo" in diplomatic society, which like society at large has its sup-posedly witty abbreviations), was plagued with telegrams from the Duchesse de Guermantes asking for news of the Grand Duchess Maria Pavlovna. And for a long time the only marks of sympathy and respect which this Princess re-ceived came to her regularly and exclusively from Mme de Guermantes.

To various individuals Saint-Loup caused not so much by his death as by what he had done in the preceding weeks a distress greater than that which afflicted the Duchess. What happened was that, only the day after the evening on which I had seen him, and two days after the Baron had said to Morel "I will have my revenge," the enquiries which Saint-Loup had made about the whereabouts of Morel were successful; they succeeded, that is to say, in bringing to the notice of the general under whose command Morel should have been the fact that he was a deserter, whereupon the general had him searched for and arrested and, to apologise to Saint-Loup for the punishment which he was obliged to inflict upon someone in whom he took an interest, wrote to inform him how the matter stood. Morel did not doubt that his arrest had been brought about by the rancour of M. de Charlus. He remembered the words "I will have my revenge," thought that this was the threatened revenge, and asked to be allowed to make some disclosures. "It is quite true," he declared, "that I am a deserter. But if I have been led astray, is it altogether my fault?" He then told *à propos* of M. de Charlus and M. d'Argencourt, with whom also he had quarrelled, stories in which he had not in fact himself been directly in-volved, but which they, with the double expansiveness of

lovers and of inverts, had related to him, and the result was
the immediate arrest of both these gentlemen. But each of
them suffered less perhaps at being arrested than at learning—
what neither of them had known—that the other was his
rival, and the judicial examination revealed that they had an
enormous number of others, obscure, quotidian rivals, picked
up in the street. M. de Charlus and M. d'Argencourt were
soon released. So was Morel, because the general's letter
to Saint-Loup was returned to him with the information:
"Deceased, killed in action." Out of respect for the dead man
the general so arranged things that Morel was merely sent to
the front. He conducted himself bravely there, survived every
danger and returned, when the war was over, with the cross
which M. de Charlus had in the past vainly solicited for him
and which in this indirect fashion was procured for him by the
death of Saint-Loup.

I have often thought since then, remembering the *croix de
guerre* which went astray in Jupien's establishment, that if
Saint-Loup had lived, he could easily have got himself
elected a deputy in the elections which followed the armistice,
thanks to the scum of universal fatuousness which the war
left in its wake and the halo which still adhered to military
glory. For at that time, if the loss of a finger could abolish
centuries of prejudice and allow a man of humble birth to
make a brilliant marriage into an aristocratic family, the *croix
de guerre*, even one won by sitting in an office, sufficed for a
triumphal election to the Chamber of Deputies, if not to the
Académie Française. The election of Saint-Loup would have
caused M. Arthur Meyer to pour out floods of tears and ink
about the new deputy's "holy family". But perhaps he was too
sincerely fond of the people to be good at winning their votes,
though for the sake of the quarters on his escutcheon they
would probably have forgiven him his democratic ideas. These

he would no doubt have expounded with success before a
Chamber composed of aviators. Certainly these heroes would
have understood him, and a few other exceptionally intelligent
and high-minded men. But thanks to the platitudinous men-
tality of the National Bloc, the old lags of politics who are invariably re-elected had also turned up again, and such of them
as failed to enter a Chamber of aviators solicited, so that they
might at least get into the Académie Française, the suffrages
of the Marshals, of the President of the Republic, the President of the Chamber, etc. These men would have looked
with less favour upon Saint-Loup than they did upon another
of Jupien's habitués, the deputy of Liberal Action, who was
once more returned unopposed and who continued to wear
the uniform of a territorial officer long after the war had
been over. His election was hailed with joy by all the newspapers which had agreed to put his name forward, as well as
by the noble and wealthy ladies who now dressed only in rags
from feelings of propriety and from fear of taxes, while the
gentlemen of the Bourse never stopped buying diamonds, not
for their wives but because, having lost all confidence in the
credit of any nation, they were seeking refuge in this tangible
wealth and as a result sending up the price of De Beers by a
thousand francs. All this tomfoolery was not exactly popular,
but there was less disposition to blame the National Bloc
when suddenly there appeared on the scene the victims of
bolshevism, those Grand Duchesses in tatters whose husbands
had been assassinated in carts, while their sons after being left
to starve and then forced to work in the midst of abuse, had
finally been thrown into wells and buried beneath stones
because it was believed that they had the plague and might
pass it on. Those of them who succeeded in escaping suddenly
turned up in Paris.

CHAPTER III

AN AFTERNOON PARTY AT THE HOUSE OF THE
PRINCESSE DE GUERMANTES

The new sanatorium to which I withdrew was no more successful in curing me than the first one, and many years passed before I came away. During the train-journey which eventually took me back to Paris, the thought of my lack of talent for literature—a defect which I had first discovered, so I supposed, long ago on the Guermantes way, which I had again recognised, and been still more saddened by, in the course of the daily walks that I had taken with Gilberte before returning to dine very late at night at Tansonville, and which on the eve of my departure from that house I had come very near to identifying, after reading some pages of the Goncourt Journal, with the vanity, the falsehood of literature—this thought, less painful perhaps but more melancholy still if I referred it not to a private infirmity of my own but to the non-existence of the ideal in which I had believed, this thought, which for a very long time had not entered my mind, struck me afresh and with a force more lamentable than ever before. The train had stopped, I remember, in open country. The sun shone, flooding one half of each of their trunks with light, upon a line of trees which followed the course of the railway. "Trees," I thought, "you no longer have anything to say to me. My heart has grown cold and no longer hears you. I am in the midst of nature. Well, it is with indifference, with boredom that my eyes register the line which separates the luminous from the shadowy side of your trunks. If ever I thought of myself as a poet, I know now that I am not one. Perhaps in the new, the so desiccated part of my life which is about to begin, human

207

beings may yet inspire in me what nature can no longer say. But the years in which I might have been able to sing *her* praise will never return." But in thus consoling myself with the thought that the observation of humanity might possibly come to take the place of an unattainable inspiration, I knew that I was merely seeking to console myself, I knew that I knew myself to be worthless. If I really had the soul of an artist, surely I would be feeling pleasure at the sight of this curtain of trees lit by the setting sun, these little flowers on the bank which lifted themselves almost to the level of the steps of my compartment, flowers whose petals I was able to count but whose colour I would not, like many a worthy man of letters, attempt to describe, for can one hope to transmit to the reader a pleasure that one has not felt? A little later I had noticed with the same absence of emotion the glitter of gold and orange which the sun splashed upon the windows of a house; and finally, as the evening advanced, I had seen another house which appeared to be built out of a substance of a strange pink. But I had made these various observations with the same absolute indifference as if, walking in a garden with a lady, I had seen a pane of glass, and a little further on an object of an alabaster-like material, the unusual colour of which had failed to draw me out of the most languorous boredom, but as if, nevertheless, out of politeness towards the lady, in order to say something and also in order to show that I had noticed these colours, I had pointed in passing to the tinted glass and the fragment of stucco. In the same way, to satisfy my conscience, I indicated to myself now as to someone who was travelling with me and might be able to extract from them more pleasure than I, the flame-like reflections in the windows and the pink transparency of the house. But the companion whose attention I had drawn to these curious effects was evidently of a less enthusiastic nature than many more sympathetically disposed persons who are enraptured by such sights, for he had taken cognisance of the colours without any kind of joy.

My long absence from Paris had not prevented old friends from continuing, as my name remained on their lists, faithfully to send me invitations, and when on my return I found—together with one to a tea-party given by Berma for her daughter and her son-in-law—another to an afternoon party with music which was to take place the following day at the house of the Prince de Guermantes, the gloomy reflections which had passed through my mind in the train were not the least of the motives which urged me to accept. Really, I said to myself, what point is there in forgoing the pleasures of social life if, as seems to be the case, the famous "work" which for so long I have been hoping every day to start the next day, is something I am not, or am no longer, made for and perhaps does not even correspond to any reality. This reasoning was, it is true, completely negative and merely deprived of their force those other reasons which might have dissuaded me from going to this fashionable concert. The positive reason that made me decide to go was the name of Guermantes, absent long enough from my mind to be able, when I read it upon the invitation card, to re-awaken a ray of my attention, to draw up from the depths of my memory a sort of section of the past of the Guermantes, attended by all the images of seigniorial forest and tall flowers which at that earlier time of my life had accompanied it, and to resume for me the charm and the significance which I had found in it at Combray when, passing along the Rue de l'Oiseau on my way home, I used to see from outside, like some dark lacquer, the window of Gilbert the Bad, Lord of Guermantes. For a moment the Guermantes had once more seemed to me to be totally different from people in society, comparable neither with

H

them nor with any living being, even a reigning prince, creatures begotten of the union of the sharp and windy air of the dark town of Combray in which my childhood had been spent with the past which could be sensed there, in the little street, at the height of the stained-glass window. I had had a longing to go to the Guermantes party as if in going there I must have been brought nearer to my childhood and to the depths of my memory where my childhood dwelt. And I had continued to read and re-read the invitation until in the end, rising in revolt, the letters which composed this name at once so familiar and so mysterious, like that of Combray itself, resumed their independence and outlined before my tired eyes a name that I seemed never to have seen before. (Mama happened to be going to a little tea-party of Mme Sazerat's which she knew beforehand she would find extremely boring, so I had no scruples about going to the Princesse de Guermantes's.)

I took a cab to go to the Prince de Guermantes's house, which was no longer his former home but a magnificent mansion that he had recently built in the Avenue du Bois. One of the mistakes of people in society is not to realise that, if they want us to believe in them, it is first necessary that they should believe in themselves, or at least should respect the essential elements of our belief. At the time when I believed, even if I knew the contrary to be true, that the Guermantes lived in this or that grand house in virtue of a hereditary right, to penetrate into the palace of the sorcerer or the fairy, to compel to open before me the doors which yield only when one has pronounced the magic formula, seemed to me as difficult as to obtain an interview with the sorcerer or the fairy themselves. To persuade myself that the old man-servant engaged twenty-four hours earlier or supplied by Potel and Chabot was the son, the grandson, the scion of a whole line of menials who had been in the family's service since long before the Revolution was the easiest thing in the world, and I was only too happy to take for an ancestral portrait some painting which had been bought the previous month from Bernheim Jeune. But enchantment cannot be decanted from one vessel to another, memories are indivisible, and of the Prince de Guermantes, now that he had himself shattered the illusions of my belief by going to live in the Avenue du Bois, nothing much was left. The ceilings which I had once feared to see collapse upon the announcement of my name, those ceilings under which, for me, there would still have floated something of the enchantment and the fears of those early days, now looked down upon the parties of an American hostess in whom I took not the slightest interest. Intrinsically, material objects have in themselves no power, but, since it is our practice to bestow power upon them, doubtless at this moment some middle-class schoolboy was feeling, in front of the house in the Avenue du Bois, the same sentiments that I had once felt as I stood before the house where the Prince de Guermantes had lived in my youth. He, this schoolboy, was still at the age of beliefs, but I had passed beyond it, I had lost that privilege, just as after one's first years one loses the ability that a baby has to break up the milk which he ingests into digestible fragments, so that the prudent adult will drink milk only in small quantities whereas babies can continue to suck it in indefinitely without pausing for breath. But at least the Prince de Guermantes's change of residence had this advantage for me, that the cab which had come to fetch me and in which, as it took me to the party, I was making these reflections, was obliged to traverse the streets which lead to the Champs Elysées. They were very badly paved at this time, but the moment I found myself in them I was, none the less, detached from my thoughts by that sensation of extraordinary physical comfort which one has when suddenly a car in which one is travelling rolls more easily, more softly, without noise, because the gates of a park have been opened and one is gliding over alleys covered with fine sand or dead leaves; materially nothing of the sort had happened, but I felt suddenly that all external obstacles had been suppressed, simply because I no longer had to make that effort of adaptation or attention which we make, sometimes without being conscious of it, in the presence of new things: the streets through which I was passing at this moment were those, so long forgotten, which I used once upon a time to take with Françoise when we went to the Champs Elysées. The solid earth knew of its own accord where it had to go; its resistance was vanquished. And like an airman who hitherto has progressed laboriously along the ground, abruptly "taking off" I soared slowly towards the silent heights of memory. Among all the streets of Paris these streets will always stand out for me, as though they were made of a different substance from the others. When we reached the corner of the Rue Royale where once had stood the open-air vendor of the photographs beloved by Françoise, it seemed to me that the cab, feeling the pull of hundreds of former turns, could not do otherwise than turn of its own accord. I was not traversing the same streets as the people who were walking about the town that day, I was traversing a past, gliding, sad and sweet; a past which was moreover compounded of so many different pasts that it was difficult for me to recognise the cause of my melancholy, to know whether it was due to those walks in which the hope of meeting Gilberte had co-existed with the fear that she would not come, to the proximity of a certain house to which I had been told that Albertine had gone with Andrée, or to that vanity of all things which seems to be the significance of a route which one has followed a thousand times in a state of passion which has disappeared and which has borne no fruit, like the route which I used to take on those expeditions of feverish haste after luncheon to see, with the paste still damp upon them, the posters of *Phèdre* and *Le Domino Noir*.

The cab turned into the Champs Elysées and, as I did not particularly want to hear the whole of the concert which was being given at the Guermantes party, I stopped it and was preparing to get out in order to walk a few yards when I was struck by the spectacle presented by another cab which was also stopping. A man, his eyes fixed, his figure bent, was placed rather than seated in the back, and was making, to keep himself upright, the efforts that might have been made by a child who has been told to be good. But his straw hat failed to conceal an indomitable forest of hair which was entirely white, and a white beard, like those which snow forms on the statues of river-gods in public gardens, flowed from his chin. It was—with by his side Jupien, who was unremitting in his attentions to him—M. de Charlus, now convalescent after an attack of apoplexy of which I had had no knowledge (I had only been told that he had lost his sight, but in fact this trouble had been purely temporary and he could now see quite well again) and which had, unless the truth was that hitherto he had dyed his hair and that he had now been forbidden to continue so fatiguing a practice, had the effect, as in a sort of chemical precipitation, of rendering visible and brilliant all that saturation of metal which the locks of his hair and his beard, pure silver now, shot forth like so many geysers, so that upon the old fallen prince this latest illness had conferred the Shakespearian majesty of a King Lear. His eyes had not remained unaffected by this total convulsion, this metallurgical transformation of his head, but had, by an inverse phenomenon, lost all their brightness. But what was most moving was that one felt that this lost brightness was identical with his moral pride, and that somehow the physical and even the intellectual life of M. de Charlus had survived the eclipse of that aristocratic haughtiness which had in the past seemed indissolubly linked to them. To confirm this, at the moment which I am describing, there passed in a victoria, no doubt also on her way to the reception of the Prince de Guermantes, Mme de Sainte-Euverte, whom the Baron had formerly considered not smart enough for him. Jupien, who tended him like a child, whispered in his ear that it was someone with whom he was acquainted, Mme de Sainte-Euverte. And immediately, with infinite laboriousness but with all the concentration of a sick man determined to show that he is capable of all the movements which are still difficult for him, M. de Charlus lifted his hat, bowed, and greeted Mme de Sainte-Euverte as respectfully as if she had been the Queen of France or as if he had been a small child coming timidly in obedience to his mother's command to say "How do you do?" to a grown-up person. For a child, but without a child's pride, was what he had once more become. Perhaps the very difficulty that M. de Charlus had in making these gestures was in itself a reason for him to make them, in the knowledge that he would create a greater effect by an action which, painful for an invalid, became thereby doubly meritorious on the part of the man who performed it and doubly flattering to the individual to whom it was addressed, invalids, like kings, practising exaggerated civility. Perhaps, also there was in the movements of the Baron that lack of co-ordination which follows upon maladies of the spinal column and the brain, so that his gestures went beyond anything that he intended. What I myself saw in them was above all a sort of gentleness, an almost physical gentleness, and of detachment

THE BARON

from the realities of life, phenomena so strikingly apparent in those whom death has already drawn within its shadow. And the exposure of the veins of silver in his hair was less indicative of profound convulsions than this unconscious humility which turned all social relations upside down and abased before Mme de Sainte-Euverte—as it would have abased before the most vulgar of American hostesses (who at last would have been able to congratulate herself on the hitherto unattainable politeness of the Baron)—what had seemed to be the proudest snobbishness of all. For the Baron still lived, still thought; his intellect was not impaired. And more than any chorus of Sophocles on the humbled pride of Oedipus, more than death itself or any funeral oration on the subject of death, the humble greeting, full of effort to please, which the Baron addressed to Mme de Sainte-Euverte proclaimed the fragile and perishable nature of the love of earthly greatness and all human pride. M. de Charlus, who until this moment would never have consented to dine with Mme de Sainte-Euverte, now bowed to the ground in her honour. To receive the homage of M. de Charlus had been, for her, the highest ambition of snobbery, just as, for the Baron, the central principle of snobbery had been to be rude to her. And now this inaccessible and precious essence which he had succeeded in making Mme de Saint-Euverte believe to be part of his nature, had at a single stroke been annihilated by M. de Charlus, by the earnest timidity, the apprehensive zeal with which he raised a hat from beneath which, all the while that his head remained deferentially uncovered, there streamed with the eloquence of a Bossuet the torrents of his silvery hair. Jupien helped the Baron to descend and I greeted him. He spoke to me very rapidly, in a voice so inaudible that I could not distinguish what he was saying, which wrung from him, when for the third time I made him repeat his remarks, a gesture of impatience that astonished me by its contrast with the impassivity which his face had at first displayed, which was no doubt an after-effect of his stroke. But when after a while I had grown accustomed to this pianissimo of whispered words, I perceived that the sick man retained the use of his intelligence absolutely intact. There were, however, two M. de Charluses, not to mention any others. Of the two, one, the intellectual one, passed his time in complaining that he suffered from progressive aphasia, that he constantly pronounced one word, one letter by mistake for another. But as soon as he actually made such a mistake, the other M. de Charlus, the subconscious one, who was as desirous of admiration as the first was of pity and out of vanity did things that the first would have despised, immediately, like a conductor whose orchestra has blundered, checked the phrase which he had started and with infinite ingenuity made the end of his sentence follow coherently from the word which he had in fact uttered by mistake for another but which he thus appeared to have chosen. Even his memory was intact, and from it his vanity impelled him, not without the fatigue of the most laborious concentration, to drag forth this or that ancient recollection, of no importance, which concerned myself and which would demonstrate to me that he had preserved or recovered all his lucidity of mind. Without moving his head or his eyes, and without varying in the slightest degree the modulation of his voice, he said to me, for instance: "Look, there's a poster on that telegraph-pole like the one which I was standing near when I saw you for the first time at Avranches—no, I am mistaken, at Balbec." And it was in fact an advertisement for the same product.

I had found it difficult at first to understand what he was saying, just as one begins by seeing absolutely nothing in a room of which all the curtains are closed. But like one's eyes in half-darkness, my ears soon accustomed themselves to his pianissimo. The sound had in any case, I think, gradually grown in volume while the Baron was speaking, perhaps because the weakness of his voice was due in part to a nervous apprehension which was dispelled when he was distracted by the presence of another person and ceased to think about it, though possibly, on the other hand, the feeble voice corresponded to the real state of his health and the momentary strength with which he spoke in conversation was the result of an artificial, transient and even dangerous excitement, which might make strangers say: "He is much better, he must stop thinking about his illness," but in fact only aggravated the illness, which lost no time in resuming its sway. Whatever the explanation may be, the Baron at this moment (even making allowances for the improvement in my own hearing) was flinging down his words with greater force, as the tide, on days of bad weather, flings down its little contorted waves. And the traces of his recent attack caused one to hear at the back of his words a noise like that of pebbles dragged by the sea. Continuing to speak to me about the past, no doubt to prove to me that he had not lost his memory, he evoked it now—in a funereal fashion but without sadness—by reciting an endless list of all the people belonging to his family or his world who were no longer alive, less, it seemed, with any emotion of grief that they were dead than with satisfaction at having survived them. He appeared indeed, as he recalled their extinction, to enjoy a clearer perception of his own return towards health and it was with an almost triumphal sternness that he repeated, in a monotonous tone, stammering slightly and with a dull sepulchral resonance: "Hannibal de Bréauté, dead! Antoine de Mouchy, dead! Charles Swann, dead! Adalbert de Montmorency, dead! Boson de Talleyrand, dead! Sosthène de Doudeauville, dead!" And every time he uttered it, the word "dead" seemed to fall upon his departed friends like a spadeful of earth each heavier than the last, thrown by a grave-digger grimly determined to immure them yet more closely within the tomb.

The Duchesse de Létourville, who was not going to the Princesse de Guermantes's reception because she had just recovered from a long illness, passed near us at that moment on foot, and seeing the Baron, of whose recent attack she knew nothing, stopped to say good-day to him. But the effect of her own illness was to make her not more understanding but more impatient——with a nervous ill-humour that was nevertheless perhaps not without a large element of compassion——of the illnesses of others. Hearing the Baron pronounce certain words with difficulty and incorrectly and seeing the painful effort he had to make to move his arm, she cast her eyes first upon Jupien and then upon myself as though to demand an explanation of so shocking a phenomenon. As we said nothing, it was to M. de Charlus himself that she addressed a long look full of sadness but also of reproach. She seemed to think it very wrong of him to be out of doors and in her company in a condition as unusual as if he had come out without a tie or without shoes. And when yet another error in pronunciation was perpetrated by the Baron, augmenting both the distress and the indignation of the Duchess, she cried out to him: "Palamède!" in the interrogative and exasperated tone of those nervous people who cannot bear to be kept waiting for a single moment and will say to you sharply, if you let them come into your room before you are ready (with a word of apology for being still engaged upon your toilet), not so as to excuse themselves but in order to accuse you: "Oh, I'm disturbing you, am I?" as if it was your fault that you were being disturbed. Finally she left us, looking crosser and crosser and saying to the Baron: "Really, you ought to go home."

M. de Charlus said he would like to sit down on a chair to

rest while Jupien and I went for a little walk, and with some
difficulty pulled out of his pocket a book which looked to me
like a prayer-book. I was not displeased to have an opportunity
to learn from Jupien various details of the Baron's state of
health. "I am very glad to talk to you, Sir," said Jupien, "but
we won't go further than the Rond-Point. Thank heaven, the
Baron is better now, but I dare not leave him alone for long,
he is always the same, he is too kind-hearted, he would give
away everything he possesses: and then that's not the only
thing, he still tries to pick people up as if he was a young man,
and I have to keep my eyes open." "Particularly as he has
recovered the use of his own eyes," I replied; "I was very
distressed when I was told that he had lost his sight." "Yes,
it's true that his eyes were affected by his stroke. For a time he
could see nothing at all. Just imagine, during the cure, which
as a matter of fact did him a great deal of good, he was for
several months unable to see more than a man born blind."
"At least that must have made your surveillance largely unnecessary?" "Not at all, no sooner had he arrived in a hotel
than he would ask me what this or that individual on the staff
was like. I used to assure him that they were all horrors. But
he realised that that couldn't be universally true, that I must
sometimes be lying. Little rascal that he is! And then he was
extraordinarily good at guessing, from the voice perhaps, I
don't know. He used to contrive to send me on urgent errands.
One day—you will excuse my telling you this, but you came
once by chance to the Temple of Shamelessness and I have
nothing to hide from you" (in fact, it was a disagreeable
feature of his character that he seemed always to enjoy revealing secrets in his possession)—"I was returning from one
of these supposedly urgent errands, all the faster because I
guessed it to have been arranged on purpose, when as I approached the Baron's room I heard a voice saying: 'What?'

and the Baron reply: 'You don't mean that this has never happened to you before?' I went into the room without knocking, and imagine my terror! The Baron, misled by a voice which was in fact deeper than is usual at that age (remember that at this period he was completely blind and in the old days, as you know, he had always been partial to men who were not quite young), was with a little boy who could not have been ten years old."

I have been told since that at that time he suffered almost every day from severe fits of mental depression, during which, though his mind was not actually wandering, he used to proclaim aloud before people whose presence or whose strict views he forgot opinions which normally he concealed, his pro-Germanism for instance. The war had long since ended, but still he groaned over the defeat of the Germans, amongst whose number he counted himself, and would say proudly: "And yet, inevitably, we shall have our revenge. For we have proved that we are the nation with the greatest capacity for resistance, and the best organisation too." Or else his confidences would take another direction, and he would cry out angrily: "Lord X— (or the Prince de XX—) had better not dare repeat what he said yesterday, it was all I could do not to reply: 'You know you're just as much one as I am.'" Needless to say, when, at the moments when he was "not quite all there", M. de Charlus made these avowals of his pro-German or other tendencies, anybody from his immediate circle who might be with him, whether it were Jupien or the Duchesse de Guermantes, would interrupt the imprudent remarks and interpret them for the benefit of others less intimately acquainted with the Baron and less discreet in a far-fetched but honourable sense.

"But, good heavens!" cried Jupien, "I was right not to want us to go too far. Look! He's already managed to get into

conversation with a gardener's boy. I had better say good-bye
to you, Sir, I must not leave my invalid alone for a second, he
is really just a big baby now."

I got out of my cab a second time just before it reached the
house of the Princesse de Guermantes and I began once more
to reflect upon the mood of lassitude and boredom in which I
had attempted, the previous day, to note the characteristics of
that line which, in a countryside reputed one of the loveliest of
France, had separated upon the trunks of the trees the shadow
from the light. Certainly the reasoned conclusions which I had
drawn at the time did not cause me so much pain today. They
were unchanged; but at this moment, as on every occasion
when I found myself torn from my habits—in a new place, or
going out at an unaccustomed hour—I was feeling a lively
pleasure. The pleasure seemed to me today a purely frivolous
one, that of going to an afternoon party given by Mme de
Guermantes. But since I knew now that I could hope for
nothing of greater value than frivolous pleasures, what point
was there in depriving myself of them? I told myself again
that I had felt, in attempting the description, not a spark of
that enthusiasm which, if it is not the sole, is one of the first
criteria of talent. I tried next to draw from my memory other
"snapshots", those in particular which it had taken in Venice,
but the mere word "snapshot" made Venice seem to me as
boring as an exhibition of photographs, and I felt that I had
no more taste, no more talent for describing now what I had
seen in the past, than I had had yesterday for describing what
at that very moment I was, with a meticulous and melancholy
eye, actually observing. In a few minutes a host of friends
whom I had not seen for years would probably ask me to give
up being a recluse and devote my days to them. And what
reason had I to refuse their request, now that I possessed the
proof that I was useless and that literature could no longer

give me any joy whatever, whether this was my fault, through my not having enough talent, or the fault of literature itself, if it were true that literature was less charged with reality than I had once supposed?

When I thought of what Bergotte had said to me: "You are ill, but one cannot pity you for you have the joys of the mind," how mistaken he had been about me! How little joy there was in this sterile lucidity! Even if sometimes perhaps I had pleasures (not of the mind), I sacrificed them always to one woman after another; so that, had fate granted me another hundred years of life and sound health as well, it would merely have added a series of extensions to an already tedious existence, which there seemed to be no point in prolonging at all, still less for any great length of time. As for the "joys of the intelligence", could I call by that name those cold observations which my clairvoyant eye or my power of accurate ratiocination made without any pleasure and which remained always unfertile?

But it is sometimes just at the moment when we think that everything is lost that the intimation arrives which may save us; one knocks at all the doors which lead nowhere, and then one stumbles without knowing it on the only door through which one can enter—which one might have sought in vain for a hundred years—and it opens of its own accord. Revolving the gloomy thoughts which I have just recorded, I had entered the courtyard of the Guermantes mansion and in my absent-minded state I had failed to see a car which was coming towards me; the chauffeur gave a shout and I just had time to step out of the way, but as I moved sharply backwards I tripped against the uneven paving-stones in front of the coach-house. And at the moment when, recovering my balance, I put my foot on a stone which was slightly lower than its neighbour, all my discouragement vanished and in its place was that same happiness which at various epochs of my life had been given to me, by the sight of trees which I had thought that I recognised in the course of a drive near Balbec, by the sight of the twin steeples of Martinville, by the flavour of a madeleine dipped in tea, and by all those other sensations of which I have spoken and of which the last works of Vinteuil had seemed to me to combine the quintessential character. Just as, at the moment when I tasted the madeleine, all anxiety about the future, all intellectual doubts had disappeared, so now those that a few seconds ago had assailed me on the subject of the reality of my literary gifts, the reality even of literature, were removed as if by enchantment. I had followed no new train of reasoning, discovered no decisive argument, but the difficulties which had seemed insoluble a moment ago had lost all importance. The happiness which I had just felt was unquestionably the same as that which I had felt when I tasted the madeleine soaked in tea. But if on that occasion I had put off the task of searching for the profounder causes of my emotion, this time I was determined not to resign myself to a failure to understand them. The emotion was the same; the difference, purely material, lay in the images evoked: a profound azure intoxicated my eyes, impressions of coolness, of dazzling light, swirled round me and in my desire to seize them—as afraid to budge, as I had been on the earlier occasion when I had continued to savour the taste of the madeleine while I tried to draw into my consciousness whatever it was that it recalled to me—I continued, ignoring the evident amusement of the great crowd of chauffeurs, to sway as I had swayed a few seconds ago, with one foot on the higher paving-stone and the other on the lower. Every time that I merely repeated this physical movement, I achieved nothing; but if I succeeded, forgetting the Guermantes party, in recapturing what I had felt when I first placed my feet on the ground in this way, again the dazzling and indistinct vision fluttered near me, as if to say: "Seize me as I pass if you can, and try to solve the riddle of happiness which I set |you." And almost at once I recognised the vision: it was Venice, of which my efforts to describe it and the supposed snapshots taken by my memory had never told me anything, but which the sensation which I had once experienced as I stood upon two uneven stones in the baptistery of St. Mark's had, recurring a moment ago, restored to me complete with all the other sensations linked on that day to that particular sensation, all of which had been waiting in their place—from which with imperious suddenness a chance happening had caused them to emerge—in the series of forgotten days. In the same way the taste of the little madeleine had recalled Combray to me. But why had the images of Combray and of Venice, at these two different moments, given me a joy which was like a certainty and which sufficed, without any other proof, to make death a matter of indifference to me?

Still asking myself this question, and determined today to find the answer to it, I entered the Guermantes mansion, because always we give precedence over the inner task that we have to perform to the outward role which we are playing, which was, for me at this moment, that of guest. But when I had gone upstairs, a butler requested me to wait for a few minutes in a little sitting-room used as a library, next to the room where the refreshments were being served, until the end of the piece of music which was being played, the Princess having given orders for the doors to be kept shut during its performance. And at that very moment a second intimation came to reinforce the one which had been given to me by the two uneven paving-stones and to exhort me to persevere in my task. A servant, trying unsuccessfully not to make a noise, chanced to knock a spoon against a plate and again that same

species of happiness which had come to me from the uneven
paving-stones poured into me; the sensation was again of great
heat, but entirely different: heat combined with a whiff of
smoke and relieved by the cool smell of a forest background;
and I recognised that what seemed to me now so delightful
was that same row of trees which I had found tedious both to
observe and to describe but which I had just now for a
moment, in a sort of daze—I seemed to be in the railway carriage again, opening a bottle of beer—supposed to be before
my eyes, so forcibly had the identical noise of the spoon
knocking against the plate given me, until I had had time to
remember where I was, the illusion of the noise of the hammer with which a railwayman had remedied some defect
on a wheel of the train while we stopped near the little wood.
And then it seemed as though the signs which were to bring
me, on this day of all days, out of my disheartened state and
restore to me my faith in literature, were thronging eagerly
about me, for, a butler who had long been in the service of
the Prince de Guermantes having recognised me and brought
to me in the library where I was waiting, so that I might
not have to go to the buffet, a selection of *petits fours* and
a glass of orangeade, I wiped my mouth with the napkin
which he had given me; and instantly, as though I had
been the character in the *Thousand and One Nights* who
unwittingly accomplishes the very rite which can cause to
appear, visible to him alone, a docile genie ready to convey
him to a great distance, a new vision of azure passed before my
eyes, but an azure that this time was pure and saline and
swelled into blue and bosomy undulations, and so strong was
this impression that the moment to which I was transported
seemed to me to be the present moment: more bemused than
on the day when I had asked myself whether I were really
going to be received by the Princesse de Guermantes or

whether everything round me would not collapse, I thought
that the servant had just opened the window onto the beach
and that all things invited me to go down and stroll along the
promenade while the tide was high, for the napkin which I
had used to wipe my mouth had precisely the same degree of
stiffness and starchedness as the towel with which I had
found it so awkward to dry my face as I stood in front of the
window on the first day of my arrival at Balbec, and this napkin now, in the library of the Prince de Guermantes's house,
unfolded for me—concealed within its smooth surfaces and
its folds—the plumage of an ocean green and blue like the tail
of a peacock. And what I found myself enjoying was not
merely these colours but a whole instant of my life on whose
summit they rested, an instant which had been no doubt an
aspiration towards them and which some feeling of fatigue or
sadness had perhaps prevented me from enjoying at Balbec
but which now, freed from what is necessarily imperfect in
external perception, pure and disincarnate, caused me to swell
with happiness.

The piece of music which was being played might end at
any moment, and I might be obliged to enter the drawing-
room. So I forced myself to try as quickly as possible to discern
the essence of the identical pleasures which I had just experienced three times within the space of a few minutes, and
having done so to extract the lesson which they might be made
to yield. The thought that there is a vast difference between
the real impression which we have had of a thing and the
artificial impression of it which we form for ourselves when we
attempt by an act of will to imagine it did not long detain me.
Remembering with what relative indifference Swann years
ago had been able to speak of the days when he had been
loved, because what he saw beneath that phrase was not in
fact those days but something else, and on the other hand the

sudden pain which he had been caused by the little phrase of Vinteuil when it gave him back the days themselves just as they were when he had felt them in the past, I understood clearly that what the sensation of the uneven paving-stones, the stiffness of the napkin, the taste of the madeleine had reawakened in me had no connection with what I frequently tried to recall to myself of Venice, Balbec, Combray, with the help of an undifferentiated memory; and I understood that the reason why life may be judged to be trivial although at certain moments it seems to us so beautiful is that we form our judgment, ordinarily, on the evidence not of life itself but of those quite different images which preserve nothing of life —and therefore we judge it disparagingly. At most I noticed cursorily that the differences which exist between every one of our real impressions—differences which explain why a uniform depiction of life cannot bear much resemblance to the reality—derive probably from the following cause: the slightest word that we have said, the most insignificant action that we have performed at any one epoch of our life was surrounded by, and coloured by the reflection of, things which logically had no connection with it and which later have been separated from it by our intellect which could make nothing of them for its own rational purposes, things, however, in the midst of which—here the pink reflection of the evening upon the flower-covered wall of a country restaurant, a feeling of hunger, the desire for women, the pleasure of luxury; there the blue volutes of the morning sea and, enveloped in them, phrases of music half emerging like the shoulders of water-nymphs—the simplest act or gesture remains immured as within a thousand sealed vessels, each one of them filled with things of a colour, a scent, a temperature that are absolutely different one from another, vessels, moreover, which being disposed over the whole range of our years, during which we have never ceased to change if only in our dreams and our thoughts, are situated at the most various moral altitudes and give us the sensation of extraordinarily diverse atmospheres. It is true that we have accomplished these changes imperceptibly; but between the memory which brusquely returns to us and our present state, and no less between two memories of different years, places, hours, the distance is such that it alone, even without any specific originality, would make it impossible to compare one with the other. Yes: if, owing to the work of oblivion, the returning memory can throw no bridge, form no connecting link between itself and the present minute, if it remains in the context of its own place and date, if it keeps its distance, its isolation in the hollow of a valley or upon the highest peak of a mountain summit, for this very reason it causes us suddenly to breathe a new air, an air which is new precisely because we have breathed it in the past, that purer air which the poets have vainly tried to situate in paradise and which could induce so profound a sensation of renewal only if it had been breathed before, since the true paradises are the paradises that we have lost.

And I observed in passing that for the work of art which I now, though I had not yet reached a conscious resolution, felt myself ready to undertake, this distinctness of different events would entail very considerable difficulties. For I should have to execute the successive parts of my work in a succession of different materials; what would be suitable for mornings beside the sea or afternoons in Venice would be quite wrong if I wanted to depict those evenings at Rivebelle when, in the dining-room that opened on to the garden, the heat began to resolve into fragments and sink back into the ground, while a sunset glimmer still illumined the roses on the walls of the restaurant and the last water-colours of the day were still visible in the sky—this would be a new and distinct material, of a transparency and a sonority that were special, compact, cool after warmth, rose-pink.

Over all these thoughts I skimmed rapidly, for another enquiry demanded my attention more imperiously, the enquiry, which on previous occasions I had postponed, into the cause of this felicity which I had just experienced, into the character of the certitude with which it imposed itself. And this cause I began to divine as I compared these diverse happy impressions, diverse yet with this in common, that I experienced them at the present moment and at the same time in the context of a distant moment, so that the past was made to encroach upon the present and I was made to doubt whether I was in the one or the other. The truth surely was that the being within me which had enjoyed these impressions had enjoyed them because they had in them something that was common to a day long past and to now, because in some way they were extra-temporal, and this being made its appearance only when, through one of these identifications of the present with the past, it was likely to find itself in the one and only medium in which it could exist and enjoy the essence of things, that is to say: outside time. This explained why it was that my anxiety on the subject of my death had ceased at the moment when I had unconsciously recognised the taste of the little madeleine, since the being which at that moment I had been was an extra-temporal being and therefore unalarmed by the vicissitudes of the future. This being had only come to me, only manifested itself outside of activity and immediate enjoyment, on those rare occasions when the miracle of an analogy had made me escape from the present. And only this being had the power to perform that task which had always defeated the efforts of my memory and my intellect, the power to make me rediscover days that were long past, the Time that was Lost.

And perhaps, if just now I had been disposed to think Bergotte wrong when he spoke of the life of the mind and its joys, it was because what I thought of at that moment as "the life of the mind" was a species of logical reasoning which had no connection with it or with what existed in me at this moment—an error like the one which had made me find society and life itself tedious because I judged them on the evidence of untrue recollections, whereas now, now that three times in succession there had been reborn within me a veritable moment of the past, my appetite for life was immense.

A moment of the past, did I say? Was it not perhaps very much more: something that, common both to the past and to the present, is much more essential than either of them? So often, in the course of my life, reality had disappointed me because at the instant when my senses perceived it my imagination, which was the only organ that I possessed for the enjoyment of beauty, could not apply itself to it, in virtue of that ineluctable law which ordains that we can only imagine what is absent. And now, suddenly, the effect of this harsh law had been neutralised, temporarily annulled, by a marvellous expedient of nature which had caused a sensation—the noise made both by the spoon and by the hammer, for instance—to be mirrored at one and the same time in the past, so that my imagination was permitted to savour it, and in the present, where the actual shock to my senses of the noise, the touch of the linen napkin, or whatever it might be, had added to the dreams of the imagination the concept of "existence" which they usually lack, and through this subterfuge had made it possible for my being to secure, to isolate, to immobilise—for a moment brief as a flash of lightning—what normally it never apprehends: a fragment of time in the pure state. The being which had been reborn in me when with a sudden shudder of happiness I had heard the noise that was common to the spoon touching the plate and the hammer striking the wheel, or had felt, beneath my feet, the unevenness that was common to the paving-stones of the Guermantes courtyard and to those of the baptistery of St. Mark's, this being is nourished only by the essences of things, in these alone does it find its sustenance and delight. In the observation of the present, where the senses cannot feed it with this food, it languishes, as it does in the consideration of a past made arid by the intellect or in the anticipation of a future which the will constructs with frag-ments of the present and the past, fragments whose reality it still further reduces by preserving of them only what is suitable for the utilitarian, narrowly human purpose for which it intends them. But let a noise or a scent, once heard or once smelt, be heard or smelt again in the present and at the same time in the past, real without being actual, ideal without being abstract, and immediately the permanent and habitually con-cealed essence of things is liberated and our true self which seemed—had perhaps for long years seemed—to be dead but was not altogether dead, is awakened and reanimated as it receives the celestial nourishment that is brought to it. A minute freed from the order of time has re-created in us, to feel it, the man freed from the order of time. And one can understand that this man should have confidence in his joy, even if the simple taste of a madeleine does not seem logically to contain within it the reasons for this joy, one can under-stand that the word "death" should have no meaning for him; situated outside time, why should he fear the future?

But this species of optical illusion, which placed beside me a moment of the past that was incompatible with the present, could not last for long. The images presented to us by the voluntary memory can, it is true, be prolonged at will, for the voluntary memory requires no more exertion on our part than turning over the pages of a picture-book. On the day, for instance, long ago, when I was to visit the Princesse de Guermantes for the first time, I had from the sun-drenched courtyard of our house in Paris idly regarded, according to my whim, now the Place de l'Église at Combray, now the beach at Balbec, as if I had been choosing illustrations for that particular day from an album of water-colours depicting the various places where I had been; and with the egotistical pleasure of a collector, I had said to myself as I catalogued these illustrations stored in my memory: "At least I have seen some lovely things in my life." And of course my memory had affirmed that each one of these sensations was quite unlike the others, though in fact all it was doing was to make varied patterns out of elements that were homogeneous. But my recent experience of the three memories was something utterly different. These, on the contrary, instead of giving me a more flattering idea of myself, had almost caused me to doubt the reality, the existence of that self. And just as on the day when I had dipped the madeleine in the hot tea, in the setting of the place where I happened at the time to be—on that first day my room in Paris, today at this moment the library of the Prince de Guermantes, a few minutes earlier the courtyard of his house—there had been, inside me and irradiating a little area outside me, a sensation (the taste of the madeleine dipped in the tea, a metallic sound, a step of a certain kind) which was common both to my actual surroundings and also to another place (my aunt Léonie's bedroom, the railway carriage, the baptistery of St. Mark's). And now again, at the very moment when I was making these reflections, the shrill noise of water running through a pipe, a noise exactly like those long cries which sometimes on summer evenings one heard the pleasure-steamers emit as they approached Balbec from the sea, made me feel—what I had once before been made to feel in Paris, in a big restaurant, by the sight of a luxurious dining-room half-empty, summery and hot—something that was not merely a sensation analogous to the one I used to have at the end of the afternoon in Balbec when, the tables already laid and glittering with linen and silver, the vast window-bays still open from one end to the other onto the promenade without a single interruption, a single solid surface of glass or stone, while the sun slowly descended upon the sea and the steamers in the bay began to emit their cries, I had, if I wished to join Albertine and her friends who were walking on the promenade, merely to step over the low wooden frame not much higher than my ankle, into a slit in which the whole continuous range of windows had been wound down so that the air could come into the hotel. (The painful recollection of having loved Albertine was, however, absent from my present sensation. Painful recollections are always of the dead. And the dead decompose rapidly, and there remains even in the proximity of their tombs nothing but the beauty of nature, silence, the purity of the air.) It was no mere analogous sensation nor even a mere echo or replica of a past sensation that I was made to feel by the noise of the water in the pipe, it was that past sensation itself. And in this case as in all the others, the sensation common to past and present had sought to re-create the former scene around itself, while the actual scene which had taken the former one's place opposed with all the resistance of material inertia this incursion into a house in Paris of a Normandy beach or a railway embankment. The marine dining-room of Balbec, with its damask linen prepared like so many altar-cloths to receive the setting sun, had sought to shatter the solidity of the Guermantes mansion, to force open its doors, and for an instant had made the sofas around me sway and tremble as on another occasion it had done to the tables of the restaurant in Paris.

Always, when these resurrections took place, the distant scene engendered around the common sensation had for a moment grappled, like a wrestler, with the actual scene. Always the actual scene had come off victorious, and always the vanquished one had appeared to me the more beautiful of the two, so beautiful that I had remained in a state of ecstasy on the uneven paving-stones or before the cup of tea, endeavouring to prolong or to reproduce the momentary appearances of the Combray or the Balbec or the Venice which invaded only to be driven back, which rose up only at once to abandon me in the midst of the new scene which somehow, nevertheless, the past had been able to permeate. And if the actual scene had not very quickly been victorious, I believe that I should have lost consciousness; for so complete are these resurrections of the past during the second that they last, that they not only oblige our eyes to cease to see the room which is near them in order to look instead at the railway bordered with trees or the rising tide, they even force our nostrils to breathe the air of places which are in fact a great distance away, and our will to choose between the various projects which those distant places suggest to us, they force our whole self to believe that it is surrounded by these places or at least to waver doubtfully between them and the places where we now are, in a dazed uncertainty such as we feel sometimes when an indescribably beautiful vision presents itself to us at the moment of our falling asleep.

Fragments of existence withdrawn from Time: these then were perhaps what the being three times, four times brought back to life within me had just now tasted, but the contemplation, though it was of eternity, had been fugitive. And yet I was vaguely aware that the pleasure which this contemplation had, at rare intervals, given me in my life, was the only genuine and fruitful pleasure that I had known. The unreality

of the others is indicated clearly enough—is it not?—either by
their inability to satisfy us, as is the case with social pleasures,
the only consequence of which is likely to be the indigestion
that is caused by unwholesome food and drink, or with friendship, which is a simulacrum, since, for whatever moral reasons
he may do it, the artist who gives up an hour of work for an
hour of conversation with a friend knows that he is sacrificing
a reality for something that does not exist (our friends being
friends only in the light of an agreeable folly which travels
with us through life and to which we readily accommodate
ourselves, but which at the bottom of our hearts we know to
be no more reasonable than the delusion of the madman who
talks to the furniture because he believes that it is alive), or
else by the sadness which follows their satisfaction, a sadness
which I had felt, for instance, on the day when I had been
introduced to Albertine, at having taken pains (not even in
fact very great pains) in order to achieve something—getting
to know this girl, Albertine—which seemed to me trivial
simply because I had achieved it. And even a more profound
pleasure, like the pleasure which I might have hoped to feel
when I was in love with Albertine, was in fact only experienced inversely, through the anguish which I felt when she
was not there, for when I was sure that she would soon be
with me, as on the day when she had returned from the
Trocadéro, I had seemed to experience no more than a
vague dissatisfaction, whereas my exaltation and my joy grew
steadily greater as I probed more and more deeply into the
noise of the spoon on the plate or the taste of the tea which
had brought into my bedroom in Paris the bedroom of my
aunt Léonie and in its train all Combray and the two ways of
our walks.

To this contemplation of the essence of things I had decided
therefore that in future I must attach myself, so as somehow

to immobilise it. But how, by what means, was I to do this? Naturally, at the moment when the stiffness of the napkin had restored Balbec to me and for an instant caressed my imagination not only with the sight of the sea as it had been that morning but with the smell of my room, the speed of the wind, the sensation of looking forward to lunch, of wondering which of the different walks I should take (all this being attached to the feel of the linen like those thousand wings of the angels which revolve a thousand times in a minute), or at the moment when the unevenness of the two paving-stones had extended in every direction and dimension the desiccated and insubstantial images which I normally had of Venice and St. Mark's and of all the sensations which I had felt there, reuniting the piazza to the cathedral, the landing-stage to the piazza, the canal to the landing-stage, and to all that the eyes see the world of desires which is seen only by the mind—naturally at those moments I had been tempted, if not, because of the time of the year, to go and walk once more through the watery streets of Venice which for me were above all associated with the spring, at least to return to Balbec. But this thought did not for an instant detain me. I knew for one thing that countries were not such as their names painted them to my imagination, so that now it was scarcely ever except in my dreams, while I was asleep, that a place could lie spread before me wrought in that pure matter which is entirely distinct from the matter of the common things that we see and touch but of which, when I had imagined these common things without ever having seen them they too had seemed to me to be composed: and I knew also that the same was true of that other species of image which is formed by the memory, so that not only had I failed to discover the beauty of Balbec as I had imagined it when I had gone there for the first time, I had failed also when I went back the second time to rediscover the remembered beauty which that first visit had left me. Experience had taught me only too well the impossibility of attaining in the real world to what lay deep within myself; I knew that Lost Time was not to be found again on the piazza of St. Mark's any more than I had found it again on my second visit to Balbec or on my return to Tansonville to see Gilberte, and that travel, which merely dangled once more before me the illusion that these vanished impressions existed outside myself, could not be the means which I sought. And I did not want to let myself be side-tracked once more, for the task before me was to discover at long last whether or no it was possible to attain to what—disappointed as I had always been by the actuality of places and people—I had, although once the septet of Vinteuil had seemed to point to the contrary conclusion, come to think of as unrealisable. I did not intend, then, to make yet another experiment in a direction which I had long known could lead nowhere. Impressions such as those to which I wished to give permanence could not but vanish at the touch of a direct enjoyment which had been powerless to engender them. The only way to savour them more fully was to try to get to know them more completely in the medium in which they existed, that is to say within myself, to try to make them translucid even to their very depths. I had not known pleasure at Balbec any more than I had known pleasure when I lived with Albertine, for the pleasure of living with her had been perceptible to me only in retrospect. When I recapitulated the disappointments of my life as a lived life, disappointments which made me believe that its reality must reside elsewhere than in action, what I was doing was not merely to link different disappointments together in a purely fortuitous manner and in following the circumstances of my personal existence. I saw clearly that the disappointment of travel and the disappointment of love were not different disappointments at all but the varied aspects which are assumed, according to the particular circumstances which bring it into play, by our inherent powerlessness to realise ourselves in material enjoyment or in effective action. And thinking again of the extra-temporal joy which I had been made to feel by the sound of the spoon or the taste of the madeleine, I said to myself: "Was this perhaps that happiness which the little phrase of the sonata promised to Swann and which he, because he was unable to find it in artistic creation, mistakenly assimilated to the pleasures of love, was this the happiness of which long ago I was given a presentiment—as something more supraterrestrial even than the mood evoked by the little phrase of the sonata—by the appeal, the red and mysterious appeal, of that septet which Swann was never privileged to hear, having died like so many others before the truth that was made for him had been revealed? A truth that in any case he could not have used, for though the phrase perhaps symbolised an appeal, it was powerless to create strength and to make of Swann the writer that he was not."

And then, after I had dwelt for some little time upon these resurrections of the memory, the thought came to me that in another fashion certain obscure impressions, already even at Combray on the Guermantes way, had solicited my attention in a fashion somewhat similar to these reminiscences, except that they concealed within them not a sensation dating from an earlier time, but a new truth, a precious image which I had sought to uncover by efforts of the same kind as those that we make to recall something that we have forgotten, as if our finest ideas were like tunes which, as it were, come back to us although we have never heard them before and which we have to make an effort to hear and to transcribe. I remembered—with pleasure because it showed me that already in those days

I had been the same and that this type of experience sprang from a fundamental trait in my character, but with sadness also when I thought that since that time I had never progressed—that already at Combray I used to fix before my mind for its attention some image which had compelled me to look at it, a cloud, a triangle, a church spire, a flower, a stone, because I had the feeling that perhaps beneath these signs there lay something of a quite different kind which I must try to discover, some thought which they translated after the fashion of those hieroglyphic characters which at first one might suppose to represent only material objects. No doubt the process of decipherment was difficult, but only by accomplishing it could one arrive at whatever truth there was to read. For the truths which the intellect apprehends directly in the world of full and unimpeded light have something less profound, less necessary than those which life communicates to us against our will in an impression which is material because it enters us through the senses but yet has a spiritual meaning which it is possible for us to extract. In fact, both in the one case and in the other, whether I was concerned with impressions like the one which I had received from the sight of the steeples of Martinville or with reminiscences like that of the unevenness of the two steps or the taste of the madeleine, the task was to interpret the given sensations as signs of so many laws and ideas, by trying to think—that is to say, to draw forth from the shadow—what I had merely felt, by trying to convert it into its spiritual equivalent. And this method, this apparently sole method, what was it but the creation of a work of art? Already the consequences came flooding into my mind: first, whether I considered reminiscences of the kind evoked by the noise of the spoon or the taste of the madeleine, or those truths written with the aid of shapes for whose meaning I searched in my brain, where—church steeples or wild grass growing in a wall—they composed a magical scrawl, complex and elaborately flourished, their essential character was that I was not free to choose them, that such as they were they were given to me. And I realised that this must be the mark of their authenticity. I had not gone in search of the two uneven paving-stones of the courtyard upon which I had stumbled. But it was precisely the fortuitous and inevitable fashion in which this and the other sensations had been encountered that proved the trueness of the past which they brought back to life, of the images which they released, since we feel, with these sensations, the effort that they make to climb back towards the light, feel in ourselves the joy of rediscovering what is real. And here too was the proof of the trueness of the whole picture formed out of those contemporaneous impressions which the first sensation brings back in its train, with those unerring proportions of light and shade, emphasis and omission, memory and oblivion to which conscious recollection and conscious observation will never know how to attain.

As for the inner book of unknown symbols (symbols carved in relief they might have been, which my attention, as it explored my unconscious, groped for and stumbled against and followed the contours of, like a diver exploring the ocean-bed), if I tried to read them no one could help me with any rules, for to read them was an act of creation in which no one can do our work for us or even collaborate with us. How many for this reason turn aside from writing! What tasks do men not take upon themselves in order to evade this task! Every public event, be it the Dreyfus affair, be it the war, furnishes the writer with a fresh excuse for not attempting to decipher this book: he wants to ensure the triumph of justice, he wants to restore the moral unity of the nation, he has no time to think of literature. But these are mere excuses, the truth being that he has not or no longer has genius, that is to say instinct. For instinct dictates our duty and the intellect supplies us with pretexts for evading it. But excuses have no place in art and intentions count for nothing: at every moment the artist has to listen to his instinct, and it is this that makes art the most real of all things, the most austere school of life, the true last judgement. This book, more laborious to decipher than any other, is also the only one which has been dictated to us by reality, the only one of which the "impression" has been printed in us by reality itself. When an idea—an idea of any kind—is left in us by life, its material pattern, the outline of the impression that it made upon us, remains behind as the token of its necessary truth. The ideas formed by the pure intelligence have no more than a logical, a possible truth, they are arbitrarily chosen. The book whose hieroglyphs are patterns not traced by us is the only book that really belongs to us. Not that the ideas which we form for ourselves cannot be correct in logic; that they may well be, but we cannot know whether they are true. Only the impression, however trivial its material may seem to be, however faint its traces, is a criterion of truth and deserves for that reason to be apprehended by the mind, for the mind, if it succeeds in extracting this truth, can by the impression and by nothing else be brought to a state of greater perfection and given a pure joy. The impression is for the writer what experiment is for the scientist, with the difference that in the scientist the work of the intelligence precedes the experiment and in the writer it comes after the impression. What we have not had to decipher, to elucidate by our own efforts, what was clear before we looked at it, is not ours. From ourselves comes only that which we drag forth from the obscurity which lies within us, that which to others is unknown.

(A level ray of the setting sun recalls to me instantaneously an episode in my early childhood to which I had never since that time given a thought: my aunt Léonie had a fever which Doctor Percepied feared might be typhoid and for a week I was made to sleep in Eulalie's little room looking out on the Place de l'Église, which had nothing but rush mats on the floor and over the window a muslin curtain that was always buzzing with a sunshine to which I was not accustomed. And seeing how the recollection of this little old-fashioned servant's bedroom suddenly added to my past life a long stretch of time so different from the rest and so delicious, I thougth by contrast of the nothingness of the impressions which had been contributed to it by the most sumptuous entertainments in the most princely mansions. The only thing at all sad about this room of Eulalie's was that at night, because the viaduct was so near, one heard the howling of the trains. But as I knew that these were bellowings produced by machines under human control, they did not terrify me as, in a prehistoric age, I might have been terrified by the cries of a neighbouring mammoth taking a free and unpredictable stroll.)

I had arrived then at the conclusion that in fashioning a work of art we are by no means free, that we do not choose how we shall make it but that it is pre-existent to us and therefore we are obliged, since it is both necessary and hidden, to do what we should have to do if it were a law of nature, that is to say to discover it. But this discovery which art obliges us to make, is it not, I thought, really the discovery of what, though it ought to be more precious to us than anything in the world, yet remains ordinarily for ever unknown to us, the discovery of our true life, of reality as we have felt it to be, which differs so greatly from what we think it is that when a chance happening brings us an authentic memory of it we are filled with an immense happiness? In this conclusion I was confirmed by the thought of the falseness of so-called realist art, which would not be so untruthful if we had not in life acquired the habit of giving to what we feel a form of expression which differs so much from, and which we nevertheless after a little time take to be, reality itself. I began to perceive that I should not have to trouble myself with the various literary theories which had at moments perplexed me —notably those which practitioners of criticism had developed at the time of the Dreyfus affair and had taken up again during the war, according to which "the artist must be made to leave his ivory tower" and the themes chosen by the writer ought to be not frivolous or sentimental but rather such things as great working-class movements or—in default of crowds— at least no longer as in the past unimportant men of leisure ("I must confess that the depiction of these useless characters rather bores me," Bloch had been fond of saying), but noble intellectuals or men of heroic stature. In any case, quite apart from what I might think of the logical propositions which they contained, these theories seemed to me to indicate very clearly the inferiority of those who supported them—my reaction was that of the truly well-bred child who, lunching in a strange house and hearing his hosts say: "We are frank, we don't hide our light under a bushel here", feels that the remark indicates a moral quality inferior to right conduct pure and simple, which says nothing. Authentic art has no use for proclamations of this kind, it accomplishes its work in silence. Moreover, those who theorised in this way used hackneyed phrases which had a curious resemblance to those of the idiots whom they denounced. And it is perhaps as much by the quality of his language as by the species of aesthetic theory which he advances that one may judge of the level to which a writer has attained in the moral and intellectual part of his work. Quality of language, however, is something the critical theorists think that they can do without, and those who admire them are easily persuaded that it is no proof of intellectual merit, for this is a thing which they cannot infer from the beauty of an image but can recognise only when they see it directly expressed. Hence the temptation for the writer to write intellectual works, which is, however, a gross mistake. A work in which there are theories is like an object which still has the ticket that shows its price. (And as to the choice of theme, a frivolous theme will serve as well as a serious one for a study of the laws of character, in the same way that a prosector can study the laws of anatomy as well in the body of an imbecile as in that of a man of talent, since the great moral laws, like the laws of the circulation of the blood or of renal elimination, vary scarcely at all with the intellect-ual merit of individuals.) A writer reasons, that is to say he goes astray, only when he has not the strength to force himself to make an impression pass through all the successive states which will culminate in its fixation, its expression. The reality that he has to express resides, as I now began to understand, not in the superficial appearance of his subject but at a depth at which that appearance matters little; this truth had been symbolised for me by that chink of a spoon against a plate, that starched stiffness of a napkin, which had been of more value to me for my spiritual renewal than innumerable conversations of a humanitarian or patriotic or internationalist or metaphysi-cal kind. "Enough of style," had been the cry, "enough of literature, let us have life!" And one may well imagine how since the beginning of the war even the simple theories of M. de Norpois, his denunciations of the "flute-players", had enjoyed a second vogue. For plenty of people who lack the artistic sense, who lack, that is to say, the faculty of submitting to the reality within themselves, may yet possess the ability to expatiate upon the theory of art until the crack of doom. And if they happen to be diplomats or financiers to boot, involved in the "realities" of the present age, they are

likely to believe that literature is an intellectual game destined
in the future to be progressively eliminated. (Some critics now
liked to regard the novel as a sort of procession of things upon
the screen of a cinematograph. This comparison was absurd.
Nothing is further from what we have really perceived than
the vision that the cinematograph presents.)

The idea of a popular art, like that of a patriotic art, if not
actually dangerous seemed to me ridiculous. If the intention
was to make art accessible to the people by sacrificing refinements of form, on the ground that they are "all right
for the idle rich" but not for anybody else, I had seen enough
of fashionable society to know that it is there that one finds
real illiteracy and not, let us say, among electricians. In fact,
an art that was "popular" so far as form was concerned would
have been better suited to the members of the Jockey than to
those of the General Confederation of Labour—and as for
subject, the working classes are as bored by novels of popular
life as children are by the books which are written specially
for them. When one reads, one likes to be transported into a
new world, and working men have as much curiosity about
princes as princes about working men. At the beginning of
the war M. Barrès had said that the artist (he happened to be
talking about Titian) must first and foremost serve the glory
of his country. But this he can do only by being an artist,
which means only on condition that, while in his own sphere
he is studying laws, conducting experiments, making discoveries which are as delicate as those of science, he shall
think of nothing—not even his country—but the truth which
is before him. Let us not imitate the revolutionaries who out
of "civic sense" despised, if they did not destroy, the works of
Watteau and La Tour, painters who have brought more
honour upon France than all those of the Revolution.
Anatomy is not perhaps the occupation that a kind-hearted man

would choose, if he or any artist had the possibility of choice, and certainly it was not the kindness of a virtuous heart (though he was a truly kind man) that made Choderlos de Laclos write *Les Liaisons dangereuses*, nor was it any affection for the lower or upper bourgeoisie that made Flaubert choose the themes of *Madame Bovary* and *L'Éducation sentimentale* —but this is no valid criticism of the work of these writers.

Some people were also saying that the art of an age of haste would be brief, just as many people before the war had predicted that it would be short. The railway, according to this mode of thinking, was destined to kill contemplation and there was no sense in regretting the age of the diligence. But in fact the car has taken over its function and once more deposits tourists outside forgotten churches.

As I had entered the library where I had been pursuing this train of thought I had remembered what the Goncourts say about the magnificent first editions which it contains and I had promised myself that I would look at them while I was waiting. And all this while, without paying very much attention to what I was doing, I had been taking first one and then another of the precious volumes from the shelves, when suddenly, at the moment when I carelessly opened one of them— it was George Sand's *François le Champi*—I felt myself unpleasantly struck by an impression which seemed at first to be utterly out of harmony with the thoughts that were passing through my mind, until a moment later, with an emotion so strong that tears came to my eyes, I recognised how very much in harmony with them it was. Imagine a room in which a man has died, a man who has rendered great services to his country; the undertaker's men are getting ready to take the coffin downstairs and the dead man's son is holding out his hand to the last friends who are filing past it; suddenly the silence is broken by a flourish of trumpets beneath the win-

dows and he feels outraged, thinking that this must be some
plot to mock and insult his grief; but presently this man who
until this moment has mastered his emotions is dissolved in
tears, for he realises that what he hears is the band of a regiment which has come to share in his mourning and to pay
honour to his father's corpse. Like this dead man's son, I had
just recognised how completely in harmony with the thoughts
in my mind was the painful impression which I had experienced when I had seen this title on the cover of a book in the
library of the Prince de Guermantes, for it was a title which
after a moment's hesitation had given me the idea that literature did really offer us that world of mystery which I had
ceased to find in it. And yet the book was not a very extraordinary one, it was *François le Champi*. But that name, like
the name Guermantes, was for me unlike the names which I
had heard for the first time only in later life. The memory of
what had seemed to me too deep for understanding in the subject of *François le Champi* when my mother long ago had read
the book aloud to me, had been reawakened by the title, and
just as the name Guermantes, after a long period during which
I had not seen the Guermantes, contained for me the essence
of the feudal age, so *François le Champi* contained the essence
of the novel, and for a second this memory substituted itself for
the quite commonplace idea of "one of George Sand's novels
about Berry". At a dinner-party, where thought always remains superficial, I might no doubt have been able to talk
about *François le Champi* and the Guermantes without either
the novel or the family being what they had been to me at
Combray. But alone, as I was at this moment, I was plunged
by these names to a greater depth. At such moments the idea
that some woman whom I had met at parties was a cousin of
Mme de Guermantes, a cousin that is to say of a personage of
the magic lantern, seemed to me incomprehensible and equally

incomprehensible was the idea that the best books I had ever read might be—I will not say superior to, though that is in fact of course what they were—but even equal to this extraordinary *François le Champi*. This was a very deeply buried impression that I had just encountered, one in which memories of childhood and family were tenderly intermingled and which I had not immediately recognised. My first reaction had been to ask myself, angrily, who this stranger was who was coming to trouble me. The stranger was none other than myself, the child I had been at that time, brought to life within me by the book, which knowing nothing of me except this child had instantly summoned him to its presence, wanting to be seen only by his eyes, to be loved only by his heart, to speak only to him. And this book which my mother had read aloud to me at Combray until the early hours of the morning had kept for me all the charm of that night. Admittedly the "pen" of George Sand, to borrow a phrase from Brichot, who was so fond of saying that a book was written with an "alert pen", no longer seemed to me, as for so long it had seemed to my mother before she had gradually come to model her literary tastes upon mine, in the least a magic pen. But it was a pen which, unintentionally, like a schoolboy amusing himself with a real pen, I had charged with electricity, and now a thousand trifling details of Combray which for years had not entered my mind came lightly and spontaneously leaping, in follow-my-leader fashion, to suspend themselves from the magnetised nib in an interminable and trembling chain of memories.

Certain people, whose minds are prone to mystery, like to believe that objects retain something of the eyes which have looked at them, that old buildings and pictures appear to us not as they originally were but beneath a perceptible veil woven for them over the centuries by the love and contemplation of millions of admirers. This fantasy, if you transpose it into the domain of what is for each one of us the sole reality, the domain of his own sensibility, becomes the truth. In that sense and in that sense alone (but it is a far more important one than the other), a thing which we have looked at in the past brings back to us, if we see it again, not only the eyes with which we looked at it but all the images with which at the time those eyes were filled. For things—and among them a book in a red binding—as soon as we have perceived them are transformed within us into something immaterial, something of the same nature as all our preoccupations and sensations of that particular time, with which, indissolubly, they blend. A name read long ago in a book contains within its syllables the strong wind and brilliant sunshine that prevailed while we were reading it. And this is why the kind of literature which contents itself with "describing things", with giving of them merely a miserable abstract of lines and surfaces, is in fact, though it calls itself realist, the furthest removed from reality and has more than any other the effect of saddening and impoverishing us, since it abruptly severs all communication of our present self both with the past, the essence of which is preserved in things, and with the future, in which things incite us to enjoy the essence of the past a second time. Yet it is precisely this essence that an art worthy of the name must seek to express; then at least, if it fails, there is a lesson to be drawn from its impotence (whereas from the successes of realism there is nothing to be learnt), the lesson that this essence is, in part, subjective and incommunicable.

Nor is this all. A thing which we saw, a book which we read at a certain period does not merely remain for ever conjoined to what existed then around us; it remains also faithfully united to what we ourselves then were and thereafter it can be handled only by the sensibility, the personality that were then ours. If, even in thought, I pick from the bookshelf

François le Champi, immediately there rises within me a child who takes my place, who alone has the right to spell out the title *François le Champi*, and who reads it as he read it once before, with the same impression of what the weather was like then in the garden, the same dreams that were then shaping themselves in his mind about different countries and about life, the same anguish about the next day. Or if I see something which dates from another period, it is a young man who comes to life. So that my personality of today may be compared to an abandoned quarry, which supposes everything it contains to be uniform and monotonous, but from which memory, selecting here and there can, like some Greek sculptor, extract innumerable different statues. And this is true of everything that we see again after a lapse of time, books in this respect behaving just like other things: the way in which the covers of a binding open, the grain of a particular paper, may have preserved in itself as vivid a memory of the fashion in which I once imagined Venice and of the desire that I had to go there as the actual phrases of a book. An even more vivid memory perhaps, for phrases sometimes are an obstruction, just as sometimes when we look at a photograph of a person we recollect him less clearly than we do when we are merely thinking about him. Certainly, there are many books which I read in my childhood, including even, I am sorry to say, some of those of Bergotte himself, which now, if I happen to be tired one evening, I take up merely in the spirit in which I might go for a train journey, with the hope, that is, of resting myself by the sight of objects that I do not see every day and by breathing the atmosphere of an earlier time. But it can happen that this deliberate attempt at evocation so far from being assisted is actually thwarted by the prolonged reading of the book. There is, for instance, a book by Bergotte (there was a copy in the Prince's library, with a

dedication both sycophantic and platitudinous in the extreme),
which I read years ago one winter day when I was unable to
see Gilberte and which I now search in vain for the phrases
which I then thought wonderful. Certain words almost make
me believe that I have found them, but it cannot be so, for of
the beauty that I once saw in them there is no trace. But the
volume itself still glistens with the snow that covered the
Champs Elysées on the day when I first read it—I open its
pages and the scene is before my eyes.

So it is that, if I had been tempted to become a bibliophile
like the Prince de Guermantes, I should only have been one
in my own peculiar fashion, though I should not have
despised that beauty, independent of the intrinsic value of a
book, which is attached to it in the eyes of collectors by their
knowing the libraries through which it has passed, knowing
for instance that it was given by such and such a sovereign,
on the occasion of such and such an event, to such and such a
famous man, by their having followed it from sale to sale
through the course of its life—that beauty, which is in a
certain sense the historic beauty of a book, would not be lost
upon me. But it is rather in the history of my own life, and
not simply as a connoisseur of the past in general, that I
should seek this beauty; and I should attach it often not to a
particular copy but to the work itself, to *François le Champi*,
for instance, first contemplated by me in my little bedroom at
Combray, during the night perhaps the sweetest and the sad-
dest of my life, when I had alas! (at a time when the Guermantes still seemed to me mysterious and inaccessible) won
from my parents that first abdication of their authority from
which, later, I was to date the decline of my health and my
will and my renunciation, each day disastrously confirmed, of
a task that daily became more difficult—and rediscovered by
me today, in the library of these same Guermantes, on this

most wonderful of all days which had suddenly illuminated for me not only the old groping movements of my thought, but even the whole purpose of my life and perhaps of art itself. As for particular copies of books, I should have been able to take an interest in them too, but in a living sense. The first edition of a work would have been more precious in my eyes than any other, but by this term I should have understood the edition in which I read it for the first time. I should seek out original editions, those, that is to say, in which I once received an original impression of a book. For the impressions that one has later are no longer original. In the case of novels I should collect old-fashioned bindings, those of the period when I read my first novels, those that so often heard Papa say to me: "Hold yourself straight." Like the dress which a woman was wearing when we saw her for the first time, they would help me to rediscover the love that I then had, the beauty on which I have since superimposed so many less and less loved images, they would help me to find that first image again, even though I am no longer the "I" who first beheld it, even though I must make way for the "I" that I then was if that "I" summons the thing that it once knew and that the "I" of today does not know. The library which I should thus assemble would contain volumes of an even greater value; for the books which I read in the past at Combray or in Venice, enriched now by my memory with vast illuminations representing the church of Saint-Hilaire or the gondola moored at the foot of San Giorgio Maggiore and the Grand Canal incrusted with sparkling sapphires, would have become the equals of those ancient "books with images"—historiated bibles or books of hours—which the collector nowadays opens not to read their text but to savour once more the enchantment of the colours which some rival of Foucquet has added to it and which make these volumes the treasures that they are. And yet, even to open these books for the purpose merely of looking at the images with which, when I read them long ago, they were not yet adorned, would seem to me in itself so dangerous that, even in the sense which I have described, which is the only one that I can understand, I should not, I think, be tempted to become a bibliophile. I know very well how easily these images, deposited by the mind, can be effaced by the mind. For the old images it substitutes new ones which no longer have the same power of resurrection. And if I still possessed the *François le Champi* which Mama unpacked one evening from the parcel of books which my grandmother was to have given me for my birthday, I should never look at it; I should be too afraid that I might gradually insinuate into it my impressions of today and smother my original impressions beneath them, that I might see it become so far a thing of the present that, when I asked it to evoke once more the child who spelt out its title in the little bedroom at Combray, the child, not recognising its voice, would no longer reply to its summons and would remain for ever buried in oblivion.

An image presented to us by life brings with it, in a single moment, sensations which are in fact multiple and heterogeneous. The sight, for instance, of the binding of a book once read may weave into the characters of its title the moonlight of a distant summer night. The taste of our breakfast coffee brings with it that vague hope of fine weather which so often long ago, as with the day still intact and full before us we were drinking it out of a bowl of white porcelain, creamy and fluted and itself looking almost like vitrified milk, suddenly smiled upon us in the pale uncertainty of the dawn. An hour is not merely an hour, it is a vase full of scents and sounds and projects and climates, and what we call reality is a certain connection between these immediate sensations and the memories which envelop us simultaneously with them —a connection that is suppressed in a simple cinematographic vision, which just because it professes to confine itself to the truth in fact departs widely from it—a unique connection which the writer has to rediscover in order to link for ever in his phrase the two sets of phenomena which reality joins together. He can describe a scene by describing one after another the innumerable objects which at a given moment were present at a particular place, but truth will be attained by him only when he takes two different objects, states the connection between them—a connection analogous in the world of art to the unique connection which in the world of science is provided by the law of causality—and encloses them in the necessary links of a well wrought style; truth—and life too—can be attained by us only when, by comparing a quality common to two sensations, we succeed in extracting their common essence and in reuniting them to each other, liberated from the contingencies of time, within a metaphor. Had not nature herself—if one considered the matter from this point of view—placed me on the path of art, was she not herself a beginning of art, she who, often, had allowed me to become aware of the beauty of one thing only in another thing, of the beauty, for instance, of noon at Combray in the sound of its bells, of that of the mornings at Doncières in the hiccups of our central heating? The link may be uninteresting, the objects trivial, the style bad, but unless this process has taken place the description is worthless.

But my train of thought led me yet further. If reality were indeed a sort of waste product of experience, more or less identical for each one of us, since when we speak of bad weather, a war, a taxi rank, a brightly lit restaurant, a garden full of flowers, everybody knows what we mean, if reality were no more than this, no doubt a sort of cinematograph film of these things would be sufficient and the "style", the "literature" that departed from the simple data that they provide would be superfluous and artificial. But was it true that reality was no more than this? If I tried to understand what actually happens at the moment when a thing makes some particular impression upon me—on the day, for instance, when as I crossed the bridge over the Vivonne the shadow of a cloud upon the water had made me cry: "Damn!" and jump for joy; or the occasion when, hearing a phrase of Bergotte's, all that I had disengaged from my impression was the not specially relevant remark: "How splendid!"; or the words I had once heard Bloch use in exasperation at some piece of bad behaviour, words quite inappropriate to a very commonplace incident; "I must say that that sort of conduct seems to me absolutely fffantastic!"; or that evening when, flattered at the politeness which the Guermantes had shown to me as their guest and also a little intoxicated by the wines which I had drunk in their house, I could not help saying to myself half aloud as I came away alone: "They really are delightful people and I should be happy to see them every day of my life"—I realised that the words in each case were a long way removed from the impressions that I or Bloch had in fact received. So that the essential, the only true book, though in the ordinary sense of the word it does not have to be "invented" by a great writer—for it exists already in each one of us—has to be translated by him. The function and the task of a writer are those of a translator.

And if in some cases—where we are dealing, for instance, with the inaccurate language of our own vanity—the rectification of an oblique interior discourse which deviates gradually more and more widely from the first and central impression, so that it is brought back into line and made to merge with the authentic words which the impression ought to have generated, is a laborious undertaking which our idleness would prefer to shirk, there are other circumstances—for example, where love is involved—in which this same process is actually painful. Here all our feigned indifferences, all our indignation at the lies of whoever it is whom we love (lies which are so natural and so like those that we perpetrate ourselves), in a word all that we have not ceased, whenever we are unhappy or betrayed, not only to say to the loved one but, while we are waiting for a meeting with her, to repeat endlessly to ourselves, sometimes aloud in the silence of our room, which we disturb with remarks like: "No, really, this sort of behaviour is intolerable," and: "I have consented to see you once more, for the last time, and I don't deny that it hurts me", all this can only be brought back into conformity with the felt truth from which it has so widely diverged by the abolition of all that we have set most store by, all that in our solitude, in our feverish projects of letters and schemes, has been the substance of our passionate dialogue with ourselves.

Even where the joys of art are concerned, although we seek and value them for the sake of the impression that they give us, we contrive as quickly as possible to set aside, as being inexpressible, precisely that element in them which is the impression that we sought, and we concentrate instead upon that other ingredient in aesthetic emotion which allows us to savour its pleasure without penetrating its essence and lets us suppose that we are sharing it with other art-lovers, with whom we find it possible to converse just because, the personal root of our own impression having been suppressed, we are discussing with them a thing which is the same for them and for us. Even in those moments when we are the most disinterested spectators of nature, or of society or of love or of art itself, since every impression is double and the one half which is sheathed in the object is prolonged in ourselves by another half which we alone can know, we speedily find means to neglect this second half, which is the one on which we ought to concentrate, and to pay attention only to the first half which, as it is external and therefore cannot be intimately explored, will occasion us no fatigue. To try to perceive the little furrow which the sight of a hawthorn bush or of a church has traced in us is a task that we find too difficult. But we play a symphony over and over again, we go back repeatedly to see a church until—in that flight to get away from our own life (which we have not the courage to look at) which goes by the name of erudition—we know them, the the symphony and the church, as well as and in the same fashion as the most knowledgeable amateur of music or archaeology. And how many art-lovers stop there, without extracting anything from their impression, so that they grow old useless and unsatisfied, like life-long bachelors! They suffer, but their sufferings, like the sufferings of virgins and of lazy people, are of a kind that fecundity or work would cure. They get more excited about works of art than real artists, because for them their excitement is not the object of a laborious and inward-directed study but a force which bursts outwards, which heats their conversations and empurples their cheeks; at concerts they will shout "Bravo, bravo" till they are hoarse at the end of a work they admire and imagine as they do so that they are discharging a duty. But demonstrations of this kind do not oblige them to clarify the nature of their admiration and of this they remain in ignorance. Meanwhile, like a stream which can find no useful channel their love of art flows over into even their calmest conversations, so that they make wild gestures and grimace and toss their heads whenever they mention the subject. "I was at a concert the other day. They played the first piece and I must say it left me cold. Then they started on the quartet. By Jove, what a difference!" (At this moment the face of the music-lover expresses a sudden anxiety, as if he were thinking: "Don't I see sparks? And I smell burning! Something's on fire.") "It's the most exasperating thing I've ever heard, damn it! It's not exactly a good composition, but it's stunning, it's something quite out of the ordinary." And yet, ludicrous though they may be, such people are not altogether to be despised. They are the first attempts of nature in her struggle to create the artist, experiments as misshapen, as unviable as those first animals that came before the species of today and were so constituted that they could not survive for long. And, with their sterile velleities, the art-lovers are as touching to contemplate as those early machines which tried to leave the ground and could not, but which yet held within them, if not the secret, the still to be discovered means, at least the desire of flight. "You know, old boy," goes on the music-lover, as he takes you by the elbow, "this is the eighth time I've heard it, and I promise you it won't be the last." And indeed, since they fail to assimilate what is truly nourishing in art, they need artistic pleasures all the time, they are victims of a morbid hunger which is never satisfied. So they go to concert after concert to applaud the same work and think that they have a duty to put in an appearance whenever it is performed just as other people think they have a duty to attend a board meeting or a funeral. Then presently, whether it be in music or in literature or in painting, other works come along, works that may even be the very opposite of the ones which they supersede. For the ability to launch ideas and systems—and still more of course the ability to assimilate them—has always been much commoner than genuine taste, even among those who themselves produce works of art, and with the multiplication of reviews and literary journals (and with them of factitious vocations as writer or artist) has become very much more wide-spread. Not so long ago, for instance, the best part of the younger generation, the most intelligent and the most disinterested of them, through a change of fashion admired nothing but works with a lofty moral and sociological, and even religious, significance. This they imagined to be the criterion of a work's value, renewing the old error of David and Chenavard and Brunetière and all those who in the past thought like them. Bergotte, whose prettiest phrases even had in fact demanded much deeper reflection on the part of the reader, was rated lower now than writers who seemed more profound simply because they wrote less well. The intricacy of his style was all right for fashionable people but not for anybody else, said democratic critics, paying to fashionable people a tribute which they did not deserve. The truth is that as soon as the reasoning intelligence takes upon itself to judge works of art, nothing is any longer fixed or certain: you can prove anything you wish to prove. Whereas the reality of talent is something universal, whether it be a gift or an acquirement, and the first thing that a reader has to do is to find out whether this reality is present beneath a writer's superficial mannerism of thought and style, it is upon just these superficial mannerisms that criticism seizes when it sets out to classify authors. Because he has a peremptory tone, because he parades his contempt for the school that preceded him, criticism consecrates as a prophet a writer who in fact has no message that is new. And so frequent are these aberrations of criticism that a writer might almost with reason prefer to be judged by the general public, were not the public incapable even of understanding what an artist has attempted in a realm of discovery which is outside its experience. For there is a closer analogy between the instinctive life of the public and the talent of a great writer, which is simply an instinct religiously listened to in the midst of a silence imposed upon all other voices, an instinct made perfect and understood, than between this same talent and the superficial verbiage and changing criteria of the established judges of literature. From decade to decade their wordy battles are renewed, for it is not only social groups that are kaleidoscopic but ideas too about society and politics and religion; refracted through large bodies they can assume a momentary amplitude but their life-span is the brief one of ideas which owe their success to their novelty and gain the adherence only of such minds as are not particular about proofs. So it is that parties and schools follow upon one another's heels, attaching to themselves always the same minds, those men of moderate intelligence who are an easy prey to the successive enthusiasms into which others more scrupulous and less easily satisfied in the matter of proof will decline to plunge. And unfortunately, just because those in the first category are no more than half-minds, they need to complete themselves in action, with the result that, being more active than the better minds, they draw the crowd after them and create around them not only inflated reputations and victims of undeserved contempt but wars too, both civil and foreign, which a little self-examination of an old-fashioned Jansenist kind might well have prevented.

To turn to the enjoyment which is derived by a really discerning mind and a truly living heart from a thought beautifully expressed in the writings of a great writer, this is no doubt an entirely wholesome enjoyment, but, precious though the men may be who are truly capable of enjoying this pleasure—and how many of them are there in a generation? —they are nevertheless in the very process reduced to being no more than the full consciousness of another. If, for instance, a man of this type has done everything in his power to make himself loved by a woman who could only have made

him unhappy, but has not even succeeded, in spite of efforts
redoubled over the years, in persuading her to meet him in
private, instead of seeking to express his sufferings and the
danger from which he has escaped, he reads over and over
again, appending to it "a million words" and the most moving
memories of his own life, this observation of La Bruyère:
"Men often want to love where they could not hope to
succeed; they seek their own undoing without being able to
compass it, and, if I may say so, they are forced against their
will to remain free." Whether or no this is the meaning that
the aphorism had for the man who wrote it (to give it this
meaning, which would make it more beautiful, he should have
said "want to be loved" instead of "want to love"), there is
no doubt that, with this meaning, the sensitive lover of literature reanimates it and puffs it up with significance until it is
ready to burst, he cannot repeat it to himself without overflowing with joy, so true and beautiful does he find it—but
in spite of all this he has added to it nothing, it remains
merely an observation of La Bruyère.

How could the literature of description possibly have any
value, when it is only beneath the surface of the little things
which such a literature describes that reality has its hidden
existence (grandeur, for example, in the distant sound of an
aeroplane or the outline of the steeple of Saint-Hilaire, the
past in the taste of a madeleine, and so on) and when the things
in themselves are without significance until it has been extracted from them? Gradually, thanks to its preservation by
our memory, the chain of all those inaccurate expressions in
which there survives nothing of what we have really experienced comes to constitute for us our thought, our life, our
"reality", and this lie is all that can be reproduced by the art
that styles itself "true to life", an art that is as simple as life,
without beauty, a mere vain and tedious duplication of what

our eyes see and our intellect records, so vain and so tedious that one wonders where the writer who devotes himself to it can have found the joyous and impulsive spark that was capable of setting him in motion and making him advance in his task. The greatness, on the other hand, of true art, of the art which M. de Norpois would have called a dilettante's pastime, lay, I had come to see, elsewhere: we have to rediscover, to reapprehend, to make ourselves fully aware of that reality, remote from our daily preoccupations, from which we separate ourselves by an ever greater gulf as the conventional knowledge which we substitute for it grows thicker and more impermeable, that reality which it is very easy for us to die without ever having known and which is, quite simply, our life. Real life, life at last laid bare and illuminated—the only life in consequence which can be said to be really lived—is literature, and life thus defined is in a sense all the time immanent in ordinary men no less than in the artist. But most men do not see it because they do not seek to shed light upon it. And therefore their past is like a photographic dark-room encumbered with innumerable negatives which remain useless because the intellect has not developed them. But art, if it means awareness of our own life, means also awareness of the lives of other people—for style for the writer, no less than colour for the painter, is a question not of technique but of vision: it is the revelation, which by direct and conscious methods would be impossible, of the qualitative difference, the uniqueness of the fashion in which the world appears to each one of us, a difference which, if there were no art, would remain for ever the secret of every individual. Through art alone are we able to emerge from ourselves, to know what another person sees of a universe which is not the same as our own and of which, without art, the landscapes would remain as unknown to us as those that may exist in the moon. Thanks to art, instead of seeing one world only, our own, we see that world multiply itself and we have at our disposal as many worlds as there are original artists, worlds more different one from the other than those which revolve in infinite space, worlds which, centuries after the extinction of the fire from which their light first emanated, be that fire called Rembrandt or Vermeer, send us still each one its special radiance.

This work of the artist, this struggle to discern beneath matter, beneath experience, beneath words, something that is different from them, is a process exactly inverse to that which, in those everyday lives which we live with our gaze averted from ourself, is at every moment being accomplished by vanity and passion and the intellect, and habit too, when they smother our true impressions, so as entirely to conceal them from us, beneath a whole heap of verbal concepts and practical purposes which we falsely call life. In short, this art which is so complicated is in fact the only living art. It alone expresses for others and renders visible to ourselves that life of ours which cannot effectually observe itself and of which the observable manifestations need to be translated and, often, to be read backwards and laboriously deciphered. Our vanity, our passions, our spirit of imitation, our abstract intelligence, our habits have long been at work, and it is the task of art to undo this work of theirs, making us travel back in the direction from which we have come to the depths where what has really existed lies unknown within us. And surely this was a most tempting prospect, this task of re-creating one's true life, of rejuvenating one's impressions. But it required courage of many kinds, courage even of a sentimental order. For above all it meant the abrogation of one's dearest illusions, it meant giving up one's belief in the objectivity of what one had oneself elaborated, so that now, instead of soothing oneself for the hundredth time with the words: "She was very kind," one would have to transpose the phrase so that it read: "I experienced pleasure when I kissed her." Certainly, what I had felt in my hours of love is what all men feel. One feels, yes, but what one feels is like a negative which shows only blackness until one has placed it near a special lamp and which, it too, must be looked at in reverse. So with one's feelings: until one has brought them within range of the intellect one does not know what they represent. Then only, when the intellect has shed light upon them, has intellectualised them, does one distinguish, and with what difficulty, the lineaments of what one felt.

But I realised also that the suffering caused by the thought that our love does not belong to the person who inspires it, a suffering which I had first known in connection with Gilberte, is for two reasons salutary. The first and the less important is that, brief though our life may be, it is only while we are suffering that we see certain things which at other times are hidden from us—we are, as it were, posted at a window, badly placed but looking out over an expanse of sea, and only during a storm, when our thoughts are agitated by perpetually changing movements, do they elevate to a level at which we can see it the whole law-governed immensity which normally, when the calm weather of happiness leaves it smooth, lies beneath our line of vision; perhaps only for a few great geniuses does this movement of thought exist all the time, uncontingent upon the agitations of personal grief, yet can we be sure, when we contemplate the ample and regular development of their joyous creations, that we may not too readily infer from the joyousness of their work that there was joy also in their lives, which perhaps on the contrary were almost continuously unhappy? But the principal reason is that, if our love is not only the love of a Gilberte (and this fact is what we find so painful), the reason is not that it is also the love of an Albertine but that it is a portion of our mind more durable than the various selves which successively die within us and which would, in their egoism, like to keep it to themselves, a portion of our mind which must, however much it hurts us (and the pain may in fact be beneficial), detach itself from individuals so that we can comprehend and restore to it its generality and give this love, the understanding of this love, to all, to the universal spirit, and not merely first to one woman and then to another with whom first one and then another of the selves that we have successively been has desired to be forever united.

I was surrounded by symbols (Guermantes, Albertine, Gilberte, Saint-Loup, Balbec, etc.) and to the least of these I had to restore the meaning which habit had caused them to lose for me. Nor was that all. When we have arrived at reality, we must, to express it and preserve it, prevent the intrusion of all those extraneous elements which at every moment the gathered speed of habit lays at our feet. Above all I should have to be on my guard against those phrases which are chosen rather by the lips than by the mind, those humorous phrases such as we utter in conversation and continue at the end of a long conversation with other people to address, factitiously, to ourselves although they merely fill our mind with lies—those, so to speak, purely physical remarks, which, in the writer who stoops so low as to transcribe them, are accompanied always by, for instance, the little smile, the little grimace which at every turn disfigures the spoken phrase of a Sainte-Beuve, whereas real books should be the offspring not of daylight and casual talk but of darkness and silence. And as art exactly reconstitutes life, around the truths to which we have attained inside ourselves there will always float an atmosphere of poetry, the soft charm of a mystery which is merely a vestige of the shadow which we have had to traverse, the indication, as precise as the markings of an altimeter, of the depth of a work. (For the quality of depth is not inherent in certain subjects, as those novelists believe who are spiritually minded only in a materialistic way: they cannot penetrate beneath the world of appearances and all their noble intentions, like the endless virtuous tirades of certain people who are incapable of the smallest act of kindness, should not blind us to the fact that they have lacked even the strength of mind to rid themselves of those banalities of form which are acquired through imitation.)

As for the truths which the intellectual faculty—even that of the greatest minds—gathers in the open, the truths that lie in its path in full daylight, their value may be very great, but they are like drawings with a hard outline and no perspective; they have no depth because no depths have had to be traversed in order to reach them, because they have not been re-created. Yet it happens to many writers that after a certain age, when more mysterious truths no longer emerge from their innermost being, they write only with their intellect, which has grown steadily in strength, and then the books of their riper years will have, for this reason, greater force than those of their youth but not the same velvety texture.

I felt, however, that these truths which the intellect educes directly from reality were not altogether to be despised, for they might be able to enshrine within a matter less pure indeed but still imbued with mind those impressions which are conveyed to us outside time by the essences that are common to the sensations of the past and of the present, but which, just because they are more precious, are also too rare for a work of art to be constructed exclusively from them. And—capable of being used for this purpose—I felt jostling each other within me a whole host of truths concerning human passions and character and conduct. The perception of these truths caused me joy; and yet I seemed to remember that more than one of them had been discovered by me in suffering, and others in very trivial pleasures (every individual who makes us suffer can be attached by us to a divinity of which he or she is a mere fragmentary reflection, the lowest step in the ascent that leads to it, a divinity or an Idea which, if we turn to contemplate it, immediately gives us joy instead of the pain which we were feeling before—indeed the whole art of living is to make use of the individuals through whom we suffer as a step enabling us to draw nearer to the divine form which they reflect and thus joyously to people our life with divinities). And then a new light, less dazzling, no doubt, than that other illumination which had made me perceive that the work of art was the sole means of rediscovering Lost Time, shone suddenly within me. And I understood that all these materials for a work of literature were simply my past life; I understood that they had come to me, in frivolous pleasures, in idleness, in affection, in unhappiness, and that I had laid them up in store without divining the purpose for which they were destined or even their continued existence any more than a seed does when it forms within itself a reserve of all the nutritious substances from which it will feed a plant. Like the seed, I should be able to die once the plant had developed and I began to perceive that I had lived for the sake of the plant without knowing it, without ever realising that my life needed to come into contact with those books which I had wanted to write and for which, when in the past I had sat down at my table to begin, I had been unable to find a subject. And thus my whole life up to the present day might and yet might not have been summed up under the title: A Vocation. Insofar as literature had played no part in my life the title would not have been accurate. And yet it would have been accurate because this life of mine, the memories of its sadnesses and its joys, formed a reserve which fulfilled the same function as the albumen lodged in the germ-cell of a plant, from which that cell starts to draw the nourishment which will transform it into a seed long before there is any outward sign that the embryo of a plant is developing, though already within the cell there are taking place chemical and respiratory changes, secret but extremely active. In the same way my life was linked to what, eventually, would bring about its maturation, but those who would one day draw nourishment from it would remain ignorant, as most of us do when we eat those grains that are human food, that the rich substances which they contain were made for the nourishment not of mankind but of the grain itself and have had first to nourish its seed and allow it to ripen.

In this context, certain comparisons which are false if we start from them as premises may well be true if we arrive at them as conclusions. The man of letters envies the painter, he would like to take notes and make sketches, but it is disastrous for him to do so. Yet when he writes, there is not a single gesture of his characters, not a trick of behaviour, not a tone of voice which has not been supplied to his inspiration by his memory; beneath the name of every character of his invention he can put sixty names of characters that he has seen, one of whom has posed for the grimaces, another for the monocle, another for the fits of temper, another for the swaggering movement of the arm, etc. And in the end the writer realises that if his dream of being a sort of painter was not in a conscious and intentional manner capable of fulfilment, it has nevertheless been fulfilled and that he too, for his work as a writer, has unconsciously made use of a sketch-book. For, impelled by the instinct that was in him, the writer, long before he thought that he would one day become one, regularly omitted to look at a great many things which other people notice, with the result that he was accused by others of being absent-minded and by himself of not knowing how to listen or look, but all this time he was instructing his eyes and his ears to retain for ever what seemed to others puerile trivialities, the tone of voice with which a certain remark had been made, or the facial expression and the movement of the shoulders which he had seen at a certain moment, many years ago, in somebody of whom perhaps he knows nothing else whatsoever, simply because this tone of voice was one that he had heard before or felt that he might hear again, because it was something renewable, lasting. There is a feeling for generality which, in the future writer, itself picks out what is general and can for that reason one day enter into a work of art. And this has made him listen to people only when, stupid or absurd though they may have been, they have turned themselves, by repeating like parrots what other people of similar character are in the habit of saying, into birds of augury, mouthpieces of a psychological law. He remembers only things that are general. By such tones of voice, such variations in the physiognomy, seen perhaps in his earliest childhood, has the life of other people been represented for him and when, later, he becomes a writer, it is from these observations that he composes his human figures, grafting onto a movement of the shoulders common to a number of people—a movement as truthfully delineated as though it had been recorded in an anatomist's note-book, though the truth which he uses it to express is of a psychological order—a movement of the neck made by someone else, each of many individuals having posed for a moment as his model.

(It may be that, for the creation of a work of literature, imagination and sensibility are interchangeable qualities and that the latter may without any great inconvenience be substituted for the former, just as in people whose stomach is incapable of digesting this function is relegated to the intestine. A man born with sensibility but without imagination might, in spite of this deficiency, be able to write admirable novels. For the suffering inflicted upon him by other people, his own efforts to ward it off, the long conflict between his unhappiness and another person's cruelty, all this, interpreted by the intellect, might furnish the material for a book not merely as beautiful as one that was imagined, invented, but also in as great a degree exterior to the day-dreams that the author would have had if he had been left to his own devices and happy, and as astonishing to himself, therefore, and as accidental as a fortuitous caprice of the imagination.)

The stupidest people, in their gestures, their remarks, the sentiments which they involuntarily express, manifest laws which they do not themselves perceive but which the artist surprises in them, and because he makes observations of this kind the writer is popularly believed to be ill-natured. But this belief is false: in an instance of ridiculous behaviour the artist sees a beautiful generality, and he no more condemns on this account the individual in whom he observes it than a surgeon would despise a patient for suffering from some quite common disorder of the circulation; the writer, in fact, is the least inclined of all men to scoff at folly. Unhappily, it cannot also be said that he is not unhappy, for when it comes to his own passions, though he is as well acquainted as other people with the general laws which govern them, he is not so skilful at liberating himself from the personal suffering which they cause. Naturally, when some insolent fellow insults us, we would rather he had paid us a compliment, and *a fortiori*, when a woman whom we adore betrays us, what would we not give for this not to have happened! But were our wish to be granted, the stinging pain of an affront, the anguish of being abandoned would have remained for us lands which we should never have known, lands whose discovery, painful though it may be for the man, is nevertheless invaluable for the artist. And so, though it is neither his wish nor theirs, the ill-natured and the ungrateful find their place in his work. The writer who writes a pamphlet involuntarily associates with his glory the riff-raff whom he castigates in it, and in every work of art one can recognise those whom the artist has most hated and also, alas! those whom he has most loved. They indeed have quite simply been posing for the artist at the very moment when, much against his will, they made him suffer most. When I was in love with Albertine, I had realised very clearly that she did not love me and I had had to resign myself to the thought that through her I could gain nothing more than the experience of what it is to suffer and to love, and also, just at the beginning, to be happy.

And when we seek to extract from our grief the generality that lies within it, to write about it, we are perhaps to some extent consoled for yet another reason apart from those that I have mentioned, which is that to think in terms of general truths, to write, is for the writer a wholesome and necessary function the fulfilment of which makes him happy, it does for him what is done for men of a more physical nature by exercise, perspiration, baths. This conclusion, I must admit, I was a little reluctant to accept. I was ready to believe that the supreme truth of life resides in art, and I could see, too, that I was no more capable by an effort of memory of being still in love with Albertine than I was of continuing to mourn my grandmother's death, and yet I asked myself whether a work of art of which they would not be conscious could really for them, for the destiny of these two poor dead creatures, be a fulfilment. My grandmother, whom with so little feeling I had seen agonise and die beside me! I longed that in expiation, when my work should be finished, I might, incurably stricken, suffer for long hours, abandoned by all, and then die! And there were others less dear to me, or for whom I had cared nothing at all, for whom I felt an infinite pity, all those whose sufferings, or merely whose follies, my thought, in its effort to understand their destinies, had used for its own selfish purpose. All those men and women who had revealed some truth to me and who were now no more, appeared again before me, and it seemed as though they had lived a life which had profited only myself, as though they had died for me. Saddening too was the thought that my love, to which I had clung so tenaciously, would in my book be so detached from any individual that different readers would apply it, even in detail, to what they had felt for other women. But had I a right to be shocked at this posthumous infidelity, shocked that strangers should find new and alien objects for my sentiments in unknown women, when this infidelity, this division of love between a number of women, had begun in my life-time and even before I had started to write? It was true that I had suffered successively for Gilberte, for Mme de Guermantes, for Albertine. But successively I had also forgotten them, and only the love which I dedicated to different women had been lasting. The profanation of one of my memories by unknown readers was a crime that I had myself committed before them. I felt something near to horror at myself, the self-horror that some nationalist party might come to feel after a long war fought in its name, from which it alone had profited and in which many noble victims had suffered and succumbed without ever knowing (and for my grandmother at least what a recompense this would have been!) what the issue of the struggle would be. And my only consolation for the thought that she did not know that at last I was starting to work was (such is the lot of the dead) that, if she could not enjoy my progress, she had at least long ceased to be conscious of my inactivity, of my wasted life, which had been such an unhappiness to her. And certainly there were others besides my grandmother and Albertine, there were many from whom I had been able to assimilate a single phrase or look although as individual human beings I had no recollection of them; a book is a huge cemetery in which on the majority of the tombs the names are effaced and can no longer be read. Sometimes on the other hand we remember a name well enough but do not know whether anything of the individual who bore it survives in our pages. That girl with the very deep-set eyes and the drawling voice, is she here? and if she is, in what part of the ground does she lie? we no longer know, and how are we to find her beneath the flowers? But since we live at a great distance from other human beings, since even our strongest feelings—and in this class had been my love for my grandmother and for Albertine—at the end of a few years have vanished from our hearts and become for us merely a word which we do not understand, since we can talk casually of these dead people with fashionable acquaintances whose houses we still visit with pleasure though all that we loved has died, surely then, if there exists a method by which we can learn to understand these forgotten words once more, is it not our duty to make use of it, even if this means transcribing them first into a language which is universal but which for that very reason will at least be permanent, a language which may make out of those who are no more, in their truest essence, a lasting acquisition for the minds of all mankind? And as for that law of change which made these loved words unintelligible to us, if we succeed at least in explaining it, is not even our infirmity transformed into strength of a new kind?

And so I had to resign myself, since nothing has the power to survive unless it can become general and since the mind's own past is dead to its present consciousness, to the idea that even the people who were once most dear to the writer have in the long run done no more than pose for him like models for a painter.

When we turn to our own future, the work in which our unhappiness has collaborated may be interpreted both as an ominous sign of suffering and as an auspicious sign of consolation. For, when we say that the loves, the sufferings of a poet have been useful to him, have helped him to construct his work, that the unknown women who had not the least idea what they were doing, have—one through her cruelty to him, another through her mockery—brought each their stone for the building of the monument which they will never see, we do not sufficiently reflect that the life of the writer does not come to an end with this particular work, that the same nature which caused him to have certain sufferings, and which then entered into his work, will continue to live after the work has been concluded and will cause him to love other women in conditions which would be similar, were they not made slightly to differ by the modifications that time brings about in circumstances, in the subject himself, in his appetite for love and in his resistance to pain. And from this point of view this first work of his must be considered simply as an unhappy love which fatally presages others of the kind: his life will resemble his work and in future the poet will scarcely need to write, for he will be able to find in what he has already written the anticipatory outline of what will then be happening. Thus it was that my love for Albertine, however different the two might be, was already inscribed in my love for Gilberte, in the midst of the happy days of which I had for the first time heard the name of Albertine pronounced and her character described by her aunt, without suspecting that this insignificant seed would develop and would one day overshadow the whole of my life.

But from another point of view the work is a promise of

happiness, because it shows us that in every love the particular and the general lie side by side and it teaches us to pass from one to the other by a species of gymnastic which fortifies us against unhappiness by making us neglect its particular cause in order to gain a more profound understanding of its essence. Indeed—as I was to experience in the sequel—even at a time when we are in love and suffer, if our vocation has at last been realised, we feel so strongly during the hours in which we are at work that the individual whom we love is being dissolved into a vaster reality that at moments we succeed in forgetting her and we come to suffer from our love merely as we might from some purely physical disease in which the loved one played no part, some kind of malady of the heart. It is true that this only happens at a certain stage of our love and that if the work comes a little later its effect may appear to be the opposite. For when once the women whom we love, through their cruelty or their triviality have succeeded in spite of us in destroying our illusions, have reduced themselves to nothing and become detached from the amorous chimaera which we had fabricated in our imagination—if at this point we set ourselves to work, our mind will exalt them once more and identify them, for the purposes of our self-analysis, with objects of our love, and in this case literature, recommencing the ruined work of amorous illusion, will give a sort of second life to sentiments which have ceased to exist. And certainly we are obliged to re-live our individual suffering, with the courage of the doctor who over and over again practises on his own person some dangerous injection. But at the same time we have to conceptualise it in a general form which will in some measure enable us to escape from its embrace, which will turn all mankind into sharers in our pain, and which is even able to yield us a certain joy. Where life immures, the intellect cuts a way out, for if there exists no remedy for a love that is not shared, the awareness of a state of suffering is something from which we can extricate ourselves, if only by deducing the consequences which it entails. The intellect knows nothing of those closed situations of life from which there is no escape.

Sometimes, when we have made a rough sketch of a painful passage in our writing and can advance no further, a new affection and a new suffering come our way which enable us to complete it, to give it substance. And on the score of these great but useful unhappinesses we have little ground for complaint: they are plentiful and we seldom have to wait long for one. (In love, our fortunate rival, which is as much as to say our enemy, is our benefactor. To a woman who previously excited in us a mere paltry physical desire he instantly adds an immense value, foreign to her but confounded by us with her. If we had no rivals, pleasure would not transform itself into love. If we had none, or if we believed that we had none. For it is not necessary that rivals should really exist. The progress of our work requires only that they should have that illusory life which is conferred upon non-existent rivals by our suspicion, our jealousy.) Nevertheless one must make haste to take advantage of them when they come, for they do not last very long: either one consoles oneself or else, when they are too severe, if one's heart is no longer very robust one dies. For if unhappiness develops the forces of the mind, happiness alone is salutary to the body. But unhappiness, even if it did not on every occasion reveal to us some new law, would nevertheless be indispensable, since through its means alone are we brought back time after time to a perception of the truth and forced to take things seriously, tearing up each new crop of the weeds of habit and scepticism and levity and indifference. Yet it is true that truth, which is not compatible with happiness or with physical health, is not always compatible even with life.

Unhappiness ends by killing. At every new torment which is too hard to bear we feel yet another vein protrude, to unroll its sinuous and deadly length along our temples or beneath our eyes. And thus gradually are formed those terrible ravaged faces, of the old Rembrandt, the old Beethoven, at whom the whole world mocked. And the pockets under the eyes and the wrinkled forehead would not matter much were there not also the suffering of the heart. But since force of one kind can change into a force of another kind, since heat which is stored up can become light and the electricity in a flash of lightning can cause a photograph to be taken, since the dull pain in our heart can hoist above itself like a banner the visible permanence of an image for every new grief, let us accept the physical injury which is done to us for the sake of the spiritual knowledge which grief brings; let us submit to the disintegration of our body, since each new fragment which breaks away from it returns in a luminous and significant form to add itself to our work, to complete it at the price of sufferings of which others more richly endowed have no need, to make our work at least more solid as our life crumbles away beneath the corrosive action of our emotions. Ideas come to us as the successors to griefs, and griefs, at the moment when they change into ideas, lose some part of their power to injure our heart; the transformation itself, even, for an instant, releases suddenly a little joy. But successors only in the order of time, for the primary element, it seems, is the Idea, and grief is merely the mode in which certain ideas make their first entry into us. But within the tribe of ideas there are various families and some of them from the very first moment are joys.

These reflections enabled me to give a stronger and more precise meaning to the truth which I had often dimly perceived, particularly when Mme de Cambremer had expressed surprise that I could give up seeing a remarkable man like

Elstir for the sake of Albertine. Even from an intellectual point of view I had felt that she was wrong, but I did not know what it was that she had failed to understand: the nature of the lessons through which one serves one's apprenticeship as a man of letters. In this process the objective value of the arts counts for little; what we have to bring to light and make known to ourselves is our feelings, our passions, that is to say the passions and feelings of all mankind. A woman whom we need and who makes us suffer elicits from us a whole gamut of feelings far more profound and more vital than a man of genius who interests us. It is for us later to decide, according to the plane upon which we are living, whether an infidelity through which some woman has made us suffer is of little or great account beside the truths which it has revealed to us and which the woman who triumphed in our suffering would hardly have been able to understand. In any case these infidelities are not likely to be wanting. A writer need have no anxieties on that score when he embarks upon a long labour. Let his intellect begin the work and as he proceeds he will meet with griefs, enough or more than enough, which will undertake to finish it. As for happiness, that is really useful to us in one way only, by making unhappiness possible. It is necessary for us to form in happiness ties of confidence and attachment that are both sweet and strong in order that their rupture may cause us the heart-rending but so valuable agony which is called unhappiness. Had we not been happy, if only in hope, the unhappinesses that befall us would be without cruelty and therefore without fruit.

And more even than the painter the writer, in order to achieve volume and substance, in order to attain to generality and, so far as literature can, to reality, needs to have seen many churches in order to paint one church and for the portrayal of a single sentiment requires many individuals. For if art is long and life is short, we may on the other hand say that, if inspiration is short, the sentiments which it has to portray are not of much longer duration. It is our passions which draw the outline of our books, the ensuing intervals of repose which write them. And when inspiration is born again, when we are able to resume our work, the woman who was posing for us to illustrate a sentiment no longer has the power to make us feel it. We must continue to paint the sentiment from another model, and if this means infidelity towards the individual, from a literary point of view, thanks to the similarity of our feelings for the two women, which makes a work at the same time a recollection of our past loves and a prophecy of our new ones, there is no great harm in these substitutions. And this is one reason for the futility of those critical essays which try to guess who it is that an author is talking about. A work, even one that is directly autobiographical, is at the very least put together out of several intercalated episodes in the life of the author—earlier episodes which have inspired the work and later ones which resemble it just as much, the later loves being traced after the pattern of the earlier. For to the woman whom we have loved most in our life we are not so faithful as we are to ourself, and sooner or later we forget her in order—since this is one of the characteristics of that self—to be able to begin to love again. At most our faculty of loving has received from this woman whom we so loved a particular stamp, which will cause us to be faithful to her even in our infidelity. We shall need, with the woman who succeeds her, those same morning walks or the same practice of taking her home every evening or giving her a hundred times too much money. (A curious thing, this circulation of the money which we give to women who because of that make us unhappy, that is to say are the cause of our writing books: it almost seems as though a writer's works, like the water in an artesian well, mount to a height which is in proportion to the depth to which suffering has penetrated his heart.) These substitutions add then to our work something that is disinterested and more general and they convey also the austere lesson that it is not to individuals that we should attach ourselves, that it is not individuals who really exist and are, in consequence, capable of being expressed, but ideas. Nevertheless, while we have these models at our disposition we must make haste and lose no time; for those who pose to us as "happiness" can in general spare us only a few sittings, and the same may be true alas!—since grief, yes, grief too passes so quickly—of those who pose as "grief". Yet grief, even when it does not, by revealing it to us, provide the raw material of our writing, is valuable to us as an incitement to work. The imagination, the reflective faculty may be admirable machines in themselves but they may also be inert. Suffering sets them in motion. And then at least the woman who poses for us as grief favours us with an abundance of sittings, in that studio which we enter only in these periods and which lies deep within us. And they are, these periods, like an image of our life with its different griefs. For they too contain different griefs within themselves, and at the very moment when we thought that all had become calm a new one makes its appearance. New in every sense of the word: perhaps because an unforeseen situation forces us to enter more profoundly into contact with ourself, these painful dilemmas which love is constantly putting in our way teach us and reveal to us, layer after layer, the material of which we are made. So when Françoise, seeing that Albertine had the run of the flat and passed in and out of all the rooms like a dog creating disorder everywhere and that she was ruining me and causing me unhappiness of every kind, used to say (for at that time I had already written some articles and done a few translations): "Ah! if only, instead of this girl who makes him waste all his time,

Monsieur had got himself a nicely brought up young secretary who could have sorted all Monsieur's paperies for him!", I had perhaps been wrong in thinking that she spoke wisely. By making me waste my time, by causing me unhappiness, Albertine had perhaps been more useful to me, even from a literary point of view, than a secretary who would have arranged my "paperies". But all the same, when a living creature is so faultily constituted (and perhaps, if such a creature exists in nature, it is man) that he cannot love without suffering, and that he has to suffer in order to apprehend truths, the life of such a creature becomes in the end extremely wearisome. The happy years are the lost, the wasted years, one must wait for suffering before one can work. And then the idea of the preliminary suffering becomes associated with the idea of work and one is afraid of each new literary undertaking because one thinks of the pain one will first have to endure in order to imagine it. And once one understands that suffering is the best thing that one can hope to encounter in life, one thinks without terror, and almost as of a deliverance, of death.

If I had had to admit, albeit I found the idea somewhat repugnant, that the writer plays with life and exploits other people for the purpose of his books, I could not fail to observe also that this is sometimes very far from being the case. The history and the circumstances of Werther, the noble Werther had not alas! been mine. Without for a moment believing in Albertine's love I had twenty times wanted to kill myself for her, I had ruined myself, I had destroyed my health for her. For when it is a question of writing, one is scrupulous, one examines things meticulously, one rejects all that is not truth. But when it is merely a question of life, one ruins oneself, makes oneself ill, kills oneself all for lies. It is true that these lies are a lode from which, if one has passed the age for writing poetry, one can at least extract a little truth. Sufferings are

K*   281

servants, obscure and detested, against whom one struggles, beneath whose dominion one more and more completely falls, dire and dreadful servants whom it is impossible to replace and who by subterranean paths lead us towards truth and death. Happy are those who have first come face to face with truth, those for whom, near though the one may be to the other, the hour of truth has struck before the hour of death!

When I considered my past life, I understood also that its slightest episodes had contributed towards giving me the lesson in idealism from which I was going to profit today. My meetings with M. de Charlus, for instance, had they not even before his pro-German tendencies had taught me the same lesson, demonstrated to me, even better than my love for Mme de Guermantes or for Albertine, or Saint-Loup's love for Rachel, the truth of the axiom that matter is indifferent and that anything can be grafted upon it by thought; an axiom which in the phenomenon, so ill-understood and so needlessly condemned, of sexual inversion is seen to be of even greater scope than in that, in itself so instructive, of love. For love shows us Beauty fleeing from the woman whom we no longer love, and coming to take up her abode in a face which anybody else would find hideous and which to ourselves too might have seemed, as one day it will seem, unpleasing: but even more striking is the spectacle of the goddess, taking with her the reverent homage of a great nobleman who thereupon instantly abandons a beautiful princess, migrating to a new perch beneath the cap of an omnibus conductor. And my astonishment every time I had seen after an interval, in the Champs Elysées or in the street or on the beach, the face of Gilberte or of Mme. de Guermantes or of Albertine, was this not a proof that a memory is prolonged only in a direction which diverges from the impression with which originally it coincided but from which gradually it further and further departs?

The writer must not be indignant if the invert who reads his book gives to his heroines a masculine countenance. For only by the indulgence of this slightly aberrant peculiarity can the invert give to what he is reading its full general import. Racine himself was obliged, as a first step towards giving her a universal validity, for a moment to turn the antique figure of Phèdre into a Jansenist; and if M. de Charlus had not bestowed upon the "traitress" for whom Musset weeps in *La Nuit d'Octobre* or *Le Souvenir* the features of Morel, he would neither have wept nor have understood, since it was only along this path, narrow and indirect, that he had access to the verities of love. For it is only out of habit, a habit contracted from the insincere language of prefaces and dedications, that the writer speaks of "my reader". In reality every reader is, while he is reading, the reader of his own self. The writer's work is merely a kind of optical instrument which he offers to the reader to enable him to discern what, without this book, he would perhaps never have perceived in himself. And the recognition by the reader in his own self of what the book says is the proof of its veracity, the contrary also being true, at least to a certain extent, for the difference between the two texts may sometimes be imputed less to the author than to the reader. Besides, the book may be too learned, too obscure for a simple reader, and may therefore present to him a clouded glass through which he cannot read. And other peculiarities can have the same effect as inversion. In order to read with understanding many readers require to read in their own particular fashion, and the author must not be indignant at this; on the contrary, he must leave the reader all possible liberty, saying to him: "Look for yourself, and try whether you see best with this lens or that one or this other one."

If I had always taken so great an interest in dreams, was this not because, making up for lack of duration by their potency, they help us better to understand the subjective element in, for instance, love through the simple fact that —but with miraculous swiftness—they reproduce the process vulgarly known as getting a woman under one's skin, so effectively that within a sleep of a few minutes we can fall passionately in love with an ugly woman, a thing which in real life could only happen after years of habit and intimacy— as though they were intravenous injections of love discovered by some wonder-working doctor, of love and sometimes also of suffering? With the same speed the amorous suggestions which they have instilled into us are dissipated, and sometimes, when the loving nocturnal visitant has vanished from our sight and reappeared in her familiar shape of an ugly woman, there vanishes with her something more precious, a whole ravishing landscape of sentiments of tenderness, of voluptuous pleasure, of vaguely blurred regrets, a whole embarkation for the Cythera of passion, of which we should like to note, for our waking state, the subtle and deliciously lifelike gradations of tone, but which fades away like a discoloured canvas that can no longer be restored. And it was perhaps also because of the extraordinary effects which it achieves with Time that the dream had fascinated me. Have we not often seen in a single night, in a single minute of a night, remote periods, relegated to those enormous distances at which we can no longer distinguish anything of the sentiments which we felt in them, come rushing upon us with almost the speed of light as though they were giant aeroplanes instead of the pale stars which we had supposed them to be, blinding us with their brilliance and bringing back to our vision all that they had once contained for us, giving us the emotion, the shock, the brilliance of their immediate nearness, only, once we are awake, to resume their position on the far side of the gulf which they had miraculously traversed, so that we are tempted to believe—wrongly, however—

that they are one of the modes of rediscovering Lost Time?

I had realised before now that it is only a clumsy and erroneous form of perception which places everything in the object, when really everything is in the mind; I had lost my grandmother in reality many months after I had lost her in fact, and I had seen people present various aspects according to the idea that I or others possessed of them, a single individual being several different people for different observers (Swann, for instance, for my family and for his friends in society, the Princesse de Luxembourg for the chief magistrate and for those who knew her identity) or even for the same observer at different periods over the years (the name of Gilberte, the different Swanns for me). I had seen that love places in a person who is loved what exists only in the person who loves, indeed I could hardly have failed to become aware of this when I had seen stretched to its maximum the distance between objective reality and love (in Rachel, for instance, as she appeared to Saint-Loup and to me, in Albertine as she appeared to me and to Saint-Loup, in Morel or the omnibus conductor as they appeared to other people and to M. de Charlus, who in spite of this showered delicate attentions upon them, recited Musset's poems to them, etc.). Finally, to a certain extent, the germanophilia of M. de Charlus (like the expression on the face of Saint-Loup when he had looked at the photograph of Albertine) had helped me to free myself for a moment, if not from my germanophobia, at least from my belief in the pure objectivity of this sentiment, had helped to make me think that perhaps what applied to love applied also to hate and that, in the terrible judgement with which at this time France judged Germany—that she was a nation outside the pale of humanity—the most important element was an objectification of feelings as subjective as those which had caused Rachel and Albertine to appear so precious, the one to Saint-Loup and the other to me. What, in fact, made it possible that this perversity was not entirely intrinsic to Germany was that, just as I as an individual had had successive loves and at the end of each one its object had appeared to me valueless, so I had already seen in my country successive hates which had, for example, at one time condemned as traitors—a thousand times worse than the Germans into whose hands they were delivering France—those very Dreyfusards such as Reinach with whom today patriotic Frenchmen were collaborating against a race whose every member was of necessity a liar, a savage beast, a madman, excepting only those Germans who, like the King of Rumania, the King of the Belgians, or the Empress of Russia, had embraced the French cause. It is true that the anti-Dreyfusards would have replied to me: "But it is not the same thing." But then it never is the same thing, any more than it is the same person with whom after an interval we fall in love; otherwise, faced with the same phenomenon as before, someone who was a second time taken in by it would have no alternative but to blame his own subjective condition, he could not again believe that the qualities or the defects resided in the object. And so, since the phenomenon, outwardly, is not the same, the intellect has no difficulty in basing upon each set of circumstances a new theory (that it is against nature to have schools directed by the religious orders, as the radicals believe, or that it is impossible for the Jewish race to be assimilated into a nation, or that there exists an undying hatred between the Teutonic and the Latin races, the yellow race having been temporarily rehabilitated). This subjective element in the situation struck one forcibly if one had any conversation with neutrals, since the pro-Germans among them had, for instance, the faculty of

ceasing for a moment to understand and even to listen when
one spoke to them about the German atrocities in Belgium.
(And yet they were real, these atrocities: the subjective
element that I had observed to exist in hatred as in vision
itself did not imply that an object could not possess real
qualities or defects and in no way tended to make reality
vanish into pure relativism.) And if, after so many years
had slipped away and so much time had been lost, I felt this
influence to be dominant even in the sphere of international
relations, had I not already had some notion of its existence
right at the beginning of my life, when I was reading in the
garden at Combray one of those novels by Bergotte which,
even today, if I chance to turn over a few of its forgotten
pages where I see the wiles of some villain described, I
cannot put down until I have assured myself, by skipping a
hundred pages, that towards the end this same villain is
humiliated as he deserves to be and lives long enough to learn
that his sinister schemes have failed? For I no longer have any
clear recollection of what happened to these characters,
though in this respect they are scarcely to be distinguished
from the men and women who were present this afternoon at
Mme de Guermantes's party and whose past life, in many
cases at least, was as vague in my mind as if I had read it in a
half-forgotten novel. The Prince d'Agrigente, for instance,
had he ended by marrying Mlle X—? Or was it rather the
brother of Mlle X— who might have married the sister
of the Prince d'Agrigente? Or was I making a confusion out
of something that I had read long ago or recently dreamed?

The dream was another of the facts of my life which had
always most profoundly impressed me and had done most to
convince me of the purely mental character of reality, and in
the composition of my work I should not disdain its aid. At
a time when I was still living, in a rather less disinterested

fashion, for love of one kind or another, a dream would come to me, bringing with it in a sudden strange return to proximity which annihilated vast distances of lost time, perhaps my grandmother, perhaps Albertine, whom briefly I began to love again because in my sleep she had given me a version, much attenuated, of the episode with the laundress girl in Touraine. And I thought that in the same way dreams would bring sometimes within my grasp truths or impressions which my efforts alone and even the contingencies of nature failed to present to me; that they would re-awaken in me something of the desire, the regret for certain non-existent things which is the necessary condition for working, for freeing oneself from the dominion of habit, for detaching oneself from the concrete. And therefore I should not disdain this second muse, this nocturnal muse who might sometimes do duty for the other one.

I had seen aristocrats turn into ordinary people when their intelligence was ordinary. ("Make yourself at home," for instance the Duc de Guermantes would say, using the same vulgar expression that Cottard might have used.) I had seen everybody believe, during the Dreyfus affair or during the war, and in medicine too, that truth is a particular piece of knowledge which cabinet ministers and doctors possess, a Yes or No which requires no interpretation, thanks to the possession of which the men in power *knew* whether Dreyfus was guilty or not and *knew*, without having to send Roques to make an enquiry on the spot, whether Sarrail in Salonika had or had not the resources to launch an offensive at the same time as the Russians, in the same way that an X-ray photograph is supposed to indicate without any need for interpretation the exact nature of a patient's disease.

It occurred to me, as I thought about it, that the raw material of my experience, which would also be the raw

material of my book, came to me from Swann, not merely
because so much of it concerned Swann himself and Gilberte, but because it was Swann who from the days of Combray had inspired in me the wish to go to Balbec, where
otherwise my parents would never have had the idea of sending me, and but for this I should never have known Albertine.
Certainly, it was to her face, as I had seen it for the first time
beside the sea, that I traced back certain things which I should
no doubt include in my book. And in a sense I was right to
trace them back to her, for if I had not walked on the front
that day, if I had not got to know her, all these ideas would
never have been developed (unless they had been developed by
some other woman). But I was wrong too, for this pleasure
which generates something within us and which, retrospectively, we seek to place in a beautiful feminine face, comes
from our senses: but the pages I would write were something
that Albertine, particularly the Albertine of those days, would
quite certainly never have understood. It was, however, for
this very reason (and this shows that we ought not to live in
too intellectual an atmosphere), for the reason that she was so
different from me, that she had fertilised me through unhappiness and even, at the beginning, through the simple effort
which I had had to make to imagine something different from
myself. Had she been capable of understanding my pages, she
would, just for that reason, not have inspired them. But
Swann had been of primary importance, for had I not gone to
Balbec I should never have known the Guermantes e ither, or
my grandmother would not have renewed her friendship with
Mme de Villeparisis nor should I have made the acquaintance
of Saint-Loup and M. de Charlus, and it was through this that
I had got to know the Duchesse de Guermantes and through
her her cousin, so that even my presence at this very moment
in the house of the Prince de Guermantes, where out of the

blue the idea for my work had just come to me (and this meant that I owed to Swann not only the material but also the decision), came to me from Swann. A rather slender stalk, perhaps, to support thus the whole development of my life, for the "Guermantes way" too, on this interpretation, had emanated from "Swann's way". But often this begetter of all the various aspects of a man's life is someone very much inferior to Swann, someone utterly insignificant. Suppose some schoolfriend who meant nothing to me had described an attractive girl who was to be enjoyed there (whom probably I should not in fact have met), would not that have been enough to send me to Balbec? Often, meeting years later some friend of our youth whom we never particularly liked, we scarcely trouble to shake hands with him, and yet, did we but think of it, it is from a casual remark which he made to us, "You ought to come to Balbec" or something of the kind, that our whole life and our work have originated. But if it does not occur to us to thank him, this is no proof of ingratitude. For when he uttered those words he had no thought of the huge consequences which they would have for us. It is our sensibility and our intelligence which have exploited the circumstances, which, once he has given them their first impulsion, have engendered one another as cause and effect without his having been able to foresee either—to return to my own story—my living with Albertine or the masked ball given by the Guermantes or anything else that had happened. No doubt the impulsion that he gave was necessary, and on that account the external form of our life and even the material which we shall use in our work derive from him. Without Swann, as I have said, my parents would never have had the idea of sending me to Balbec. (Yet Swann was not for this reason responsible for the sufferings which he himself had indirectly caused me: they sprang from my weakness, just as his own weakness had made him suffer through Odette.) But whoever it is who has thus determined the course of our life has, in so doing, excluded all the lives which we might have led instead of our actual life. If Swann had not talked to me about Balbec, I should not have known Albertine, the dining-room of the hotel, the Guermantes. I should have gone to some other town, I should have known other people, my memory and my books would be filled with quite different scenes, which I cannot even imagine and the novelty of which, their unknownness I find so seductive that I almost regret that I was not directed instead towards them and that Albertine and the beach of Balbec and Rivebelle and the Guermantes did not for ever remain unknown to me.

Jealousy is a good recruiting-sergeant who, when there is a gap in our picture, goes out into the street and brings us in the desirable woman who was needed to fill it. Perhaps in our eyes she had ceased to be a beauty? She has become one again, for we are jealous of her and therefore she will fill the gap. Once we are dead, we shall have no joy that our picture was completed in this fashion. But this consideration does not in the least discourage us. We feel merely that life is a little more complicated than it is said to be, and circumstances too. And it is absolutely necessary that we should portray this complexity. The jealousy that is so useful is not necessarily born of a look, or a description, or a backward turn of the head. It may be found, ready to sting us, between the leaves of a directory—what for Paris is called *Tout-Paris* and for the country the *Annuaire des Châteaux*. We had heard, for instance, but without paying any attention, some beauty to whom we have become indifferent say that she would have to go and see her sister for a few days in the Pas de Calais, near Dunkirk; we had also, in the past, but again without paying any attention, thought that perhaps the beauty had formerly been pursued by Monsieur E——, whom she had ceased to see, since she had ceased to go to the bar where she used to meet him. What could her sister be? A housemaid perhaps? Out of tact, we had never asked. And now suddenly, opening the *Annuaire des Châteaux* at random we find that Monsieur E—— has his country-house in the Pas de Calais, near Dunkirk. At once all is clear: to oblige the beauty he has taken her sister into his employment as a housemaid, and if the beauty no longer sees him in the bar, the reason is that he gets her to come and see him at home, either in Paris, where he lives most of the year, or in the Pas de Calais, since he cannot do without her even for the few weeks that he is there. Drunk with rage and love, we paint furiously away at the picture. And yet, suppose we are wrong? May not the truth be that Monsieur E—— no longer sees the beauty but, wanting to help her, has recommended her sister to a brother of his who lives all the year round in the Pas de Calais? And in that case she is going, perhaps quite by chance, to see her sister at a time when Monsieur E—— is not there, for they are no longer interested in each other. And then there is another possibility, that the sister is not a housemaid in the house near Dunkirk or anywhere else, but has relations in the Pas de Calais. Our anguish of the first moment gives way before these last hypotheses, which calm our jealousy. But it makes no difference. Jealousy, concealed between the leaves of the *Annuaire des Châteaux*, came at the right moment, and now the space that stood empty in our canvas is filled to abundance. And the whole composition takes shape, thanks to the presence, evoked by jealousy, of the beauty of whom already we are no longer jealous and whom we no longer love.

At this moment the butler came in to tell me that the first piece of music was finished, so that I could leave the library and go into the rooms where the party was taking place. And thereupon I remembered where I was. But I was not in the least disturbed in the train of thought upon which I had embarked by the fact that a fashionable gathering, my return to society, had provided me with that point of departure for a new life which I had been unable to find in solitude. There was nothing extraordinary about this fact, there was no reason why an impression with the power to resuscitate the timeless man within me should be linked to solitude rather than to society (as I had once supposed and as had perhaps once been the case for me, and perhaps ought still to have been the case, had I developed harmoniously instead of going through this long period of arrest which seemed only now to be coming to an end). For, as this impression of beauty came to me only when an immediate sensation—no matter how insignificant—having been thrust upon my consciousness by chance, a similar sensation, spontaneously born again within me, somehow in a single moment diffused the first sensation over different periods of my life and succeeded in filling with a general essence the empty space which particular sensations never failed to leave in my mind, as this was how I came to experience beauty I might just as well receive sensations of the appropriate kind in a social as in a natural environment, since they are supplied by chance, aided no doubt by that special kind of excitement which, on the days when we happen to be jolted out of the normal routine of our lives, causes even the simplest things to begin once again to give us those sensations which Habit, in its economical way, ordinarily begrudges our nervous system. Why it was that precisely and uniquely this kind of sensation should lead to the production of a work of art was a question to which I proposed to try and find an objective answer, by following up the thoughts which had come to me, linked in a continuous chain, in the library, and I felt that the impulse given to the intellectual life within me was so vigorous now that I should be able to pursue these thoughts just as well in the drawing-room, in the midst of the guests, as alone in the library; it seemed to me that, from this point of view, even in the midst of a numerous gathering I should be able to maintain my solitude. For just as great events that impinge upon us from without fail to influence the powers of our mind, so that a mediocre writer who lives in a heroic age does not cease to be a mediocre writer, for the same reason, I realised, what is dangerous in social life is merely the social and worldly inclinations with which one approaches it. In itself it can no more turn one into a mediocre writer than an epic war can turn a bad poet into a sublime one. In any case, whether or no it was a good plan, theoretically, for a work of art to be constructed in this fashion, and whatever might be the result of the examination of this point which I intended to make, I could not deny that, so far as I was concerned, whenever genuinely aesthetic impressions had come to me, they had always followed upon sensations of this kind. It is true that such impressions had been rather rare in my life, nevertheless they dominated it, they were summits of thought, and some of those which in the past I had unwisely lost sight of I could still rediscover and I could be careful not to make the same mistake again. And already I could say that this characteristic, though it might, in the exclusive importance that it assumed in my thinking, be personal to me, was nevertheless, as I was reassured to find, akin to characteristics, less marked but still perceptible and at bottom not at all dissimilar, of certain well-known writers. Is it not from a sensation of the same species as that of the madeleine that Chateaubriand suspends the loveliest episode in the *Mémoires d'Outre-tombe*: "Yesterday evening I was walking alone . . . I was roused from my reflections by the

twittering of a thrush perched upon the highest branch
of a birch-tree. In a moment the magic sound caused my
father's estate to re-appear before my eyes; I forgot the catastrophes of which I had recently been the witness and, transported suddenly into the past, I saw again those country
scenes in which I had so often heard the fluting notes of the
thrush." And of all the lovely sentences in those memoirs are
not these some of the loveliest: "A sweet and subtle scent of
heliotrope was exhaled by a little patch of beans that were in
flower; it was brought to us not by a breeze from our own
country but by a wild Newfoundland wind, unrelated to the
exiled plant, without sympathy of shared memory or pleasure.
In this perfume, not breathed by beauty, not cleansed in her
bosom, not scattered where she had walked, in this perfume
of a changed sky and tillage and world there was all the diverse
melancholy of regret and absence and youth." And in one of
the masterpieces of French literature, Gérard de Nerval's
Sylvie, just as in the book of the *Mémoires d'Outre-tombe*
which describes Combourg, there figures a sensation of the
same species as the taste of the madeleine and the twittering
of the thrush. Above all in Baudelaire, where they are more
numerous still, reminiscences of this kind are clearly less
fortuitous and therefore, to my mind, unmistakable in their
significance. Here the poet himself, with something of a
slow and indolent choice, deliberately seeks, in the perfume
of a woman, for instance, of her hair and her breast, the
analogies which will inspire him and evoke for him

> *l'azur du ciel immense et rond*

and

> *un port rempli de flammes et de mâts.*

I was about to search in my memory for the passages in
Baudelaire at the heart of which one may find this kind of

transposed sensation, in order once and for all to establish my place in so noble a line of descent and thus to give myself the assurance that the work which I no longer had any hesitation in undertaking was worthy of the pains which I should have to bestow upon it, when, having arrived at the foot of the flight of stairs which led down from the library, I found myself suddenly in the main drawing-room, in the middle of a party which, as I soon discovered, was to seem to me very different from those that I had attended in the past, and was to assume a special character in my eyes and take on a novel significance. In fact, as soon as I entered the crowded room, although I did not weaken in the project which I had gone so far towards formulating within me, I was witness of a spectacular and dramatic effect which threatened to raise against my enterprise the gravest of all objections. An objection which I should manage no doubt to surmount, but which, while I continued silently to reflect upon the conditions that are necessary to a work of art, could not fail, by presenting to my gaze in a hundred different forms a consideration more likely than any other to make me hesitate, at every moment to interrupt my train of thought.

For a few seconds I did not understand why it was that I had difficulty in recognising the master of the house and the guests and why everyone in the room appeared to have put on a disguise—in most cases a powdered wig—which changed him completely. The Prince himself, as he stood receiving his guests, still had that slightly unreal look of a king in a fairy-story which I had remarked in him the first time I had been to his house, but today, as though he too felt bound to comply with the rules for fancy dress which he had sent out with the invitations, he had got himself up with a white beard and dragged his feet along the ground as though they were weighted with soles of lead, so that he gave the impression of trying to impersonate one of the "Ages of Man". (His moustaches were white too, as though the hoar-frost of Hop o' My Thumb's forest still lay thick upon them. They seemed to get in the way of his mouth, which he had difficulty in moving, and one felt that having made his effect he ought to have taken them off.) So successful was this disguise that I recognised him only by a process of logical deduction, by inferring from the mere resemblance of certain features the identity of the figure before me. I do not know what young Fezensac had put on his face, but, while others had whitened either half their beard or merely their moustache, he had not bothered to use a dye like the rest but had found some means of covering his features with wrinkles and making his eyebrows sprout with bristles; and all this did not suit him in the least, it had the effect of making his face look hardened, bronzed, rigid and solemn, and aged him to such an extent that one would no longer have said he was a young man at all. Still greater was my surprise when a moment later I heard the name of Duc de Châtellerault applied to a little elderly man with the silvery moustaches of an ambassador, in whom, thanks to a tiny fragment which still survived of the look that I remembered, I was just able to recognise the youth whom I had once met at Mme de Villeparisis's tea-party. The first time that I thus succeeded in identifying somebody, by trying to dismiss from my mind the effects of his disguise and building up, through an effort of memory, a whole familiar face round those features which had remained unaltered, my first thought ought to have been—and perhaps for a fraction of a second was—to congratulate him on having made himself up with such wonderful skill that one had initially, before recognising him, that hesitation which a great actor, appearing in a role in which he is unlike himself, can cause an audience to feel when he first comes onto the stage, so that knowing from the programme what to expect, it yet, for a moment, remains silent and puzzled before bursting into applause.

From the point of view of disguise, the most extraordinary of all the guests, the real star turn of the afternoon, was my personal enemy, M. d'Argencourt. Not only had he concealed his real beard, which was hardly even pepper-and-salt in colour, beneath a fantastic bushy growth of a quite improbable whiteness, but altogether (such is the power of small material changes to shrink or enlarge a human figure and, even more, to alter the apparent character, the personality of an individual) he had turned into a contemptible old beggarman, and the diplomat whose solemn demeanour and starched rigidity were still present to my memory acted his part of old dotard with such verisimilitude that his limbs were all of a tremble and the features of what had once been a haughty countenance were permanently relaxed in an expression of smiling idiocy. Disguise, carried to this extent, ceases to be a mere art, it becomes a total transformation of the personality. And indeed, although certain details assured me that it was really Argencourt who presented this ludicrous and picturesque spectacle, I had to traverse an almost infinite number of successive states of a single face if I wished to rediscover that of the Argencourt whom I had known and who was now, though he had had no other materials than his own body with which to effect the change, so different from himself. Clearly this was the last extremity to which that body could be brought without suffering utter disintegration; already the immobile face and the proudly arched chest were no more than a bundle of rags, twitching and convulsed. With difficulty, by recalling certain smiles with which in the past Argencourt had sometimes for a moment tempered his disdain, was I able to see in the man before me the Argencourt whom I had once known, to understand that this smile of a doddering old-clothes-man existed potentially in the correct gentleman of an earlier day. But even supposing that the same intention lay behind Argencourt's smile now as in the past, because of the prodigious transformation of his face the actual physical matter of the eye through which he had to express this intention was so different that the smile which resulted was entirely new and even appeared to belong to a new person. I was tempted to laugh aloud at the sight of this sublime old gaffer, as senile in his amiable caricature of himself as was, in a more tragic vein, M. de Charlus thunderstruck into humble politeness. M. d'Argencourt, in his impersonation of an aged man in a farce by Regnard rewritten in an exaggerated fashion by Labiche, was as easy of access, as affable as M. de Charlus in the role of King Lear, punctiliously doffing his hat to the most unimportant passer-by. Yet it did not occur to me to tell him how impressed I was by the extraordinary vision which he offered to my eyes. And this was not because of any survival of my old feeling of antipathy, for indeed he had so far become unlike himself that I had the illusion of being in the presence of a different person, as gentle, as kindly, as inoffensive as the other Argencourt had been hostile, overbearing, and dangerous. So far a different person that the sight of this hoary clown with his ludicrous grin, this snow-man looking like General Dourakine in his second childhood, made me think that it must be possible for human personality to undergo metamorphoses as total as those of certain insects. I had the impression that I was looking into a glass-case in a museum of natural history at an instructive example of a later phase in the life-cycle of what had once been the swiftest and surest of predatory insects, and before this flabby chrysalis, more subject to vibration than capable of movement, I could not feel the sentiments which in the past M. d'Argencourt had always inspired in me.

However, I was silent, I refrained from congratulating him on presenting a spectacle which seemed to extend the boundaries within which the transformations of the human body can take place.

For whereas at a fancy-dress ball or behind the scenes at a theatre civility leads one, if anything, to exaggerate the difficulty—to talk even of the impossibility—of recognising the person beneath the disguise, here on the contrary an instinct had warned me to do just the contrary; I felt that the success of the disguise was no longer in any way flattering because the transformation was not intentional. And I realised something that I had not suspected when I entered the room a few minutes earlier: that every party, grand or simple, which takes place after a long interval in which one has ceased to go into society, provided that it brings together some of the people whom one knew in the past gives one the impression of a masquerade, a masquerade which is more successful than any that one has ever been to and at which one is most genuinely "intrigued" by the identity of the other guests, but with the novel feature that the disguises, which were assumed long ago against their wearers' will, cannot, when the party is over, be wiped off with the make-up. Intrigued, did I say, by the identity of the other guests? No more, alas, than they are intrigued by one's own. For the difficulty which I experienced in putting a name to the faces before me was shared evidently by all those who, when their eyes rested for a moment upon mine, paid no more attention to it than if they had never seen it before or else laboriously sought to extract from my present appearance a very different recollection.

In performing this extraordinary "number", this brilliant study in caricature which offered certainly the most striking vision which I was likely to retain of him, M. d'Argencourt might be likened to an actor who at the end of a play makes a final appearance on the stage before the curtain falls for the last time in the midst of a storm of laughter. And if I no longer felt any ill will towards him, it was because in this man who had rediscovered the innocence of the golden age there was no longer any recollection of the contemptuous notions which he might once have had of me, no longer any memory of having seen M. de Charlus suddenly drop my arm, either because these sentiments had ceased to exist in him or because in order to arrive at me they were obliged to pass through physical refractors which so deformed them that in the course of their journey they completely changed their meaning, so that M. d'Argencourt appeared to be kind for want of the physical means of expressing that he was still unkind, from inability to repress his unfailingly friendly mirth. I have compared him to an actor, but in fact, unencumbered as he was by any conscious soul, it was rather as a puppet, a trembling puppet with a beard of white wool, that I saw him being shakily put through his paces up and down this drawing-room, in a puppet-show which was both scientific and philosophical and in which he served—as though it had been at the same time a funeral oration and a lecture at the Sorbonne—both as a text for a sermon on the vanity of all things and as an object lesson in natural history.

A puppet-show, yes, but one in which, in order to identify the puppets with the people whom one had known in the past, it was necessary to read what was written on several planes at once, planes that lay behind the visible aspect of the puppets and gave them depth and forced one, as one looked at these aged marionettes, to make a strenuous intellectual effort; one was obliged to study them at the same time with one's eyes and with one's memory. These were puppets bathed in the immaterial colours of the years, puppets which exteriorised Time, Time which by Habit is made invisible and to become visible seeks bodies, which wherever it finds it seizes, to display its magic lantern upon them. As immaterial now as Golo long ago on the door-handle of my room at Combray, the new, the unrecognisable Argencourt was there before me as the revelation of Time, which by his agency was rendered partially visible, for in the new elements which went to compose his face and his personality one could decipher a number which told one the years of his age, one could recognise the hieroglyph of life—of life not as it appears to us, that is to say permanent, but as it really is: an atmosphere so swiftly changing that at the end of the day the proud nobleman is portrayed, in caricature, as a dealer in old clothes.

There were other people in the room in whom these changes, these veritable alienations seemed to belong rather to the realm of human psychology than of natural history, so that one was astonished, when one heard certain names, to learn that the same individual could present, not like M. d'Argencourt the characteristics of a new and different species but the external features of a different personality. From this young girl, for instance, as from M. d'Argencourt, time had extracted possibilities that one could never have suspected, but these possibilities, though it was through her physiognomy or her body that they had expressed themselves, seemed to be of a moral order. The features of the face, if they change, if they group themselves differently, if their oscillations take on a slower rhythm, assume with a different aspect a different significance. In a woman, for instance, whom one had known as stiff and prim an enlargement out of all recognition of the cheeks, an unpredictable arching of the nose, caused one the same surprise—and often it was an agreeable surprise—as one would have felt at some sensitive and profound remark, some noble and courageous action that one would never have expected of her. On either side of this nose, this new nose, one saw opening out horizons which one would not have dared to hope for. With these cheeks kindness and delicate affection, once out of the question, had become possible. And in the presence of this chin one could utter sentiments that one would never have dreamed of voicing when confronted with its predecessor. All these new features of the face implied new features also of the character; the thin, severe girl had turned into a vast and indulgent dowager. And no longer in a zoological sense, as with M. d'Argencourt, but in a social and moral sense one could say of her that she was a different person.

For all these reasons a party like this at which I found myself was something much more valuable than an image of the past: it offered me as it were all the successive images—which I had never seen—which separated the past from the present, better still it showed me the relationship that existed between the present and the past; it was like an old-fashioned peepshow, but a peepshow of the years, the vision not of a moment but of a person situated in the distorting perspective of Time.

As for the woman whose lover M. d'Argencourt had been, considering the length of time that had elapsed she had not changed very much, that is to say her face was not too utterly demolished for the face of a human being subject, as we all are, to deformation at every moment of her trajectory into the abyss towards which she had been launched, that abyss whose direction we can express only by means of comparisons that are all equally invalid, since we can borrow them only from the world of space and their sole merit, whether we give them the orientation of height, length or depth, is to make us feel that this inconceivable yet apprehensible dimension exists. To find a name for the faces before me I had been obliged, in effect, to follow the course of the years back towards their source, and this forced me, by a necessary consequence, to re-establish, to give their real place to those years whose passage I had hardly noticed. And from this point of view, freeing me from the illusions produced in us by the apparent identity of space, the totally changed aspect of, for instance, M. d'Argencourt was a striking revelation to me of that chronological reality which under normal conditions is no more than an abstract conception to us, just as only the first sight of some strange dwarf tree or giant baobab apprises us that we have arrived in a new latitude.

Life at such moments seems to us like a fairy-tale at the theatre, in which from one act to another we see the baby turn into a youth and the youth into a mature man, who in the next act totters towards the grave. And as it is through endless small changes that we feel that these beings, who enter our field of vision only at long intervals, can have become so different, we feel that we ourselves must have followed the same law in virtue of which they have been so totally transformed that, without having ceased to exist, indeed just because they have never ceased to exist, they no longer in any way resemble what we observed them to be in the past.

A young woman whom I had known long ago, white-haired now and compressed into a little old witch, seemed to suggest that it is necessary, in the final scene of a theatrical entertainment, for the characters to be disguised beyond all recognition. But her brother was still so straight-backed, so like himself, that one was surprised on his youthful face to see a bristling moustache dyed white. Indeed everywhere the patches of white in beards and moustaches hitherto entirely black lent a note of melancholy to the human landscape of the party, as do the first yellow leaves of the trees when one is still looking forward to a long summer, when before one has scarcely begun to enjoy the hot weather one sees that the autumn has arrived. So that at last I, who from childhood had lived from day to day and had received, of myself and of others, impressions which I regarded as definitive, became aware as I had never been before——by an inevitable inference from the metamorphoses which had taken place in all the people around me——of the time which had passed for them, a notion which brought with it the overwhelming revelation that it had passed also for me. And their old age, in itself a matter of indifference to me, froze my blood by announcing to me the approach of my own. At this point, as though to proclaim the lesson aloud and drive it home, there came to my ears at brief intervals a series of remarks which struck them like the trump of the Last Judgement. The first of these was made by the Duchesse de Guermantes; I had just caught sight of her, passing between a double hedge of curious on-lookers, who, not fully aware of the marvellous artifices of toilet and aesthetic which evoked these responses within them, yet feeling themselves moved by the sight of this fair, reddish head, this salmon-pink body almost concealed by its fins of black lace and throttled by jewels, gazed at it, with its heredi-tary sinuosity of line, as they might have gazed at some archaic sacred fish, loaded with precious stones, in which was incarn-ate the protective genius of the Guermantes family. "Ah! how wonderful to see you," she said to me, "you, my oldest friend!" And though the vanity of the sometime young man from Combray who had never for a moment thought that he might become one of her friends, really participating in the real mysterious life that went on in the houses of the Guer-mantes, with the same title to her friendship as M. de Bréauté or M. de Forestelle or Swann or all those others who were now dead, might well have been flattered by these words, more than anything I was saddened by them. "Her oldest friend!" I said to myself. "Surely she exaggerates. One of the oldest perhaps, but can I really be . . ." At that moment a nephew of the Prince came up to me: "You, as a veteran Parisian . . ." he said to me, and while he was still speaking I was handed a note. Outside the house I had made the acquaintance of a young Létourville, who was related in some way which I had forgotten to the Duchess but who knew at least who I was. He had just left Saint-Cyr, and, telling myself that he would be a nice friend for me, like Saint-Loup, who could initiate me into military matters and explain the changes which had taken place in the army, I had told him that I would see him again at the party and that we might arrange to have dinner together one evening, and for this he had thanked me very civilly. But I had stayed too long lost in thought in the library and the note which he had left for me was to tell me that he had not been able to wait, and to leave me his address. The letter of this imagined equal companion ended thus: "With all respect, your young friend, Létourville." "Young friend!" That was how in the past I had written to men thirty years older than myself, to Legrandin, for example. And now this second lieutenant whom in my mind's eye I saw as my comrade after the fashion of Saint-Loup, called himself my "young friend"! Since the days of Doncières, it seemed, it was not only military methods that had changed; from this M. de Létourville, with whom I imagined myself sharing the pleasures of a youthful comradeship—and why not, since I appeared to myself to be youthful? —I was separated, it seemed, by an arc traced by an invisible compass whose existence I had not suspected, which removed me so far from the boyish second lieutenant that in the eyes of this "young friend" I was an old gentleman.

Almost immediately afterwards, hearing someone mention the name of Bloch, I asked whether he meant young Bloch or his father (who, though I was not aware of this, had died during the war, from grief, it was said, at seeing France in-

MADAME VERDURIN,
THE NEW PRINCESSE DE GUERMANTES

vaded). "I didn't know he had any children," said the Prince, "I didn't even know he was married. But clearly it is the father we are talking about. He is not in the least like a young Bloch," he added with a laugh. "He is quite old enough to have grown-up sons." And I realised that it was my former school-friend who was being discussed. A moment later he came into the room. And indeed superimposed upon the features of Bloch I saw the mild but didactic countenance, the frail movements of the head quickly coming to rest like a piece of clockwork, in which I should have recognised the well-informed weariness of some amiable old man if at the same time I had not recognised my friend standing before me, so that at once my memories animated him with an uninterrupted flow of youthful enthusiasm which he now no longer seemed to possess. For me, who had known him on the threshold of life and had never ceased to see him thus, he was the friend of my boyhood, an adolescent whose youth I measured by the youth which unconsciously, not believing that I had lived since that time, I attributed to myself. I heard someone say that he quite looked his age, and I was astonished to observe on his face some of those signs which are indeed characteristic of men who are old. Then I understood that this was because he was in fact old and that adolescents who survive for a sufficient number of years are the material out of which life makes old men.

Someone, hearing that I had not been well, asked me whether I was not afraid of catching the influenza of which there was an epidemic at that moment, whereupon another well-wisher reassured me by saying: "Oh! no, it's usually only the young who get it. A man of your age has very little to fear." I was assured also that some of the servants had recognised me. They had whispered my name, and had even, as a lady related to me ("You know the expressions they use"), been heard by her to say: "Look, there's Father. . . ." (and then my surname), and as I had no children this could only be an allusion to my age.

"What? Did I know the Marshal?" said the Duchess to me. "But I knew figures far more typical of the period: the Duchesse de Galliera, Pauline de Périgord, Monsignor Dupanloup." Hearing her, I naïvely regretted that I had not known what she described as relics of an earlier time. I ought to have reflected that what one calls an earlier time is the period of which one has oneself known only the end: things that we see on the horizon assume a mysterious grandeur and seem to us to be closing over a world which we shall not behold again; but meanwhile we are advancing, and very soon it is we ourselves who are on the horizon for the generations that come after us; all the while the horizon retreats into the distance, and the world, which seemed to be finished, begins again. "I even, when I was a girl," Mme de Guermantes went on, "once saw the Duchesse de Dino. But then, you know I'm no longer a chicken." These last words upset me. "She shouldn't have said that," I thought, "that's the way for an old woman to talk." And immediately I reflected that in fact she was an old woman. "As for you," she continued, "you are always the same, you never seem to change." And this remark I found almost more painful than if she had told me that I had changed, for it proved—if it was so extraordinary that there was so little sign of change in me—that a long time had elapsed. "Yes," she said, "you are astonishing, you look as young as ever", another melancholy remark, which can only mean that in fact, if not in appearance, we have grown old. There was worse to come, for she added: "I have always regretted that you never married. But, who knows, perhaps after all it is fortunate. You would have been old enough to have sons in the war, and if they had been killed, like poor Robert (I still often think of him), sensitive as you are, how would you ever have survived their loss?" And I was able to see myself, as though in the first truthful mirror which I had ever encountered, reflected in the eyes of old people, still young in their own opinion as I in mine, who, when I spoke of "an old man like myself" in the hope of being contradicted, showed in their answering looks, which saw me not as they saw themselves but as I saw them, not a glimmer of protest. For we failed to see our own appearance, our own age, but each one of us, as though it were a mirror that faced him, saw those of the others. And no doubt the discovery that they have grown old causes less sadness to many people than it did to me. But in the first place old age, in this respect, is like death. Some men confront them both with indifference, not because they have more courage than others but because they have less imagination. And then, a man who from his childhood on has aimed at one single idea and who, from idleness and perhaps also because of poor health, has perpetually put off its realisation, every evening striking out as though it had never existed the day that has slipped away and is lost, so that the illness which hastens the ageing of his body retards that of his mind, such a man is more surprised and more appalled to see that all the while he has been living in Time than one who lives little inside himself and, regulating his activities by the calendar, does not in a single horrifying moment discover the total of the years whose mounting sum he has followed day by day. But there was a more serious reason for my distress: I had made the discovery of this destructive action of Time at the very moment when I had conceived the ambition to make visible, to intellectualise in a work of art, realities that were outside Time.

In some of the guests at the party the successive replacement, accomplished in my absence, of each cell by other cells, had brought about a change so complete, a metamorphosis so entire that I could have dined opposite them in a restaurant a hundred times without suspecting that I had known them in the past any more than I would have guessed the royal identity of a sovereign travelling incognito or the vicious nature of a stranger. And even this comparison is hardly adequate to the cases in which I had heard the name of the person before me, for it is perhaps not so extraordinary that a stranger sitting opposite one should be a criminal or a king, but these were people whom I had once known, or rather I had known people who bore the same name and yet were so different that I could not believe that they were the same. Nevertheless, just as I would have tried to introduce into the stranger the idea of royalty or of vice, which in a very short time can give a new face to the unknown person towards whom one might so easily, when one's eyes were still blindfolded, have committed the gaffe of behaving with inappropriate insolence or civility, and in whose unchanged features, once one knows who he is, one discerns traces of distinction or of guilt, so now I set to work to introduce into the face of the unknown, utterly unknown, woman before me the idea that she was, let us say, Mme Sazerat, and I succeeded eventually in restoring the meaning that I had once known to reside in her face, which would, however, have remained for me utterly alienated from its owner—as much the face of another person, wanting in all the human attributes which I had once known it to possess, as that of a man turned back into a monkey—if the name and the affirmation of identity had not, in spite of the arduous nature of the problem, set me on the path of its solution. Sometimes, however, the old image came to light again in my mind with such precision that I was able to essay a confrontation; and then, like a witness brought face to face with a suspect, I was obliged, so great was the difference, to say: "No, I do not recognise this person."

But was I right to tell myself that these special character-istics of individuals would die? I had always considered each one of us to be a sort of multiple organism or polyp, not only at a given moment of time—so that when a speck of dust passes it the eye, an associated but independent organ, blinks without having received an order from the mind, and the intestine, like an embedded parasite, can fall victim to an infection without the mind knowing anything about it—but also, similarly, where the personality is concerned and its dur-ation through life, I had thought of this as a sequence of juxta-posed but distinct "I's" which would die one after the other or even come to life alternately, like those which at Combray took one another's place within me when the evening ap-proached. But I had seen also that these moral cells of which an individual is composed are more durable than the individual himself. I had seen the vices and the courage of the Guer-mantes recur in Saint-Loup, as also at different times in his single life his own strange and ephemeral defects of character, and as in Swann his Semitism. And now I could observe the same phenomenon in Bloch. He had lost his father some years previously, and when I had written to him at the time, he had at first been unable to answer my letter, for, quite apart from the strong family sentiments which often exist in Jewish families, the idea that his father was an altogether exceptional man had imparted to his affection the character of a cult. He had found his loss unbearable and had had to take refuge in a sanatorium, where he stayed for nearly a year. To my con-dolences he replied in a tone of profound grief which was at the same time almost haughty, so enviable in his eyes was the privilege which he had enjoyed of approaching this excep-tional man whose very ordinary two-horse carriage he would have liked to present to some historical museum. And now, as he sat at table in the midst of his family, he was animated by the same wrath against his father-in-law as had animated his own father against M. Nissim Bernard and even interrupted his meals to deliver the same tirades against him. So that just as, in listening to the conversation of Cottard and Brichot and so many others, I had felt that, through the influence of culture and fashion, a single undulation propagates identical mannerisms of speech and thought through a whole vast extent of space, it seemed to me now that throughout the whole duration of time great cataclysmic waves lift up from the depths of the ages the same wraths, the same sadnesses, the same heroisms, the same manias, through one superimposed generation after another, and that each geological section cut through several individuals of the same series offers the repetition, as of shadows thrown upon a succession of screens, of a picture as unchanged—though often not so insignificant—as that of Bloch exchanging angry words with his father-in-law, M. Bloch the elder doing the same in the same fashion with M. Nissim Bernard, and many other pairs of disputants whom I had myself never known.

Gilberte de Saint-Loup said to me: "Shall we go and dine together by ourselves in a restaurant?" and I replied: "Yes, if you don't find it compromising to dine alone with a young man." As I said this, I heard everybody round me laugh, and I hastily added: "or rather, with an old man". I felt that the phrase which had made people laugh was one of those which my mother might have used in speaking of me, my mother for whom I was still a child. And I realised that I judged myself from the same point of view as she did. If in the end I had registered, as she had, certain changes which had taken place since my early childhood, these were, nevertheless, changes which were now very remote. I had not advanced beyond the particular one which, long ago, almost before the remark corresponded with the facts, had made people say: "He's almost a grown-up man now." I still thought that that was what I was, but by now the description was absurdly out of date. I did not realise how much I had changed. And indeed, though these people just now had burst out laughing, what was it that made them so sure of the change? I had not a single grey hair, my moustache was black. I should have liked to ask them what the evidence was which revealed the terrible fact.

And now I began to understand what old age was—old age, which perhaps of all the realities is the one of which we preserve for longest in our life a purely abstract conception, looking at calendars, dating our letters, seeing our friends marry and then in their turn the children of our friends, and yet, either from fear or from sloth, not understanding what all this means, until the day when we behold an unknown silhouette, like that of M. d'Argencourt, which teaches us that we are living in a new world; until the day when a grandson of a woman we once knew, a young man whom instinctively we try to treat as an equal companion, smiles as though we were making fun of him because to him it seems that we are old enough to be his grandfather—and I began to understand too what death meant and love and the joys of the spiritual life, the usefulness of suffering, a vocation, etc. For if names had lost most of their individuality for me, words on the other hand now began to reveal their full significance. The beauty of images is situated in front of things, that of ideas behind them. So that the first sort of beauty ceases to astonish us as soon as we have reached the things themselves, the second is something that we understand only when we have passed beyond them.

The cruel discovery which I had just made could not fail

to be of service to me so far as the actual material of my book
was concerned. For I had decided that this could not consist
uniquely of the full and plenary impressions that were outside
time, and amongst those other truths in which I intended to
set, like jewels, those of the first order, the ones relating to
Time, to Time in which, as in some transforming fluid, men
and societies and nations are immersed, would play an important part. I should pay particular attention to those changes
which the aspect of living things undergoes, of which every
minute I had fresh examples before me, for, whilst all the
while thinking of my work, which I now felt to be launched
with such momentum that no passing distractions could check
its advance, I continued to greet old acquaintances and to
enter into conversation with them. The process of ageing, I
found, was not marked in them all by signs of the same sort. I
saw someone who was enquiring my name, and I was told that
it was M. de Cambremer. He came up to me and to show that
he had recognised me, "Do you still have your attacks of
asthma?" he asked, and, upon my replying in the affirmative,
went on: "Well, at least you see that it is no bar to long life,"
as if I were already a centenarian. While speaking to him, I
fixed my eyes on two or three features which I was able, by
an effort of thought, to reintegrate into that complex of my
recollections—totally different though it was—which I called
his personality. But for a brief moment he turned his head
aside. And then I saw that he had been made unrecognisable
by the attachment of enormous red pockets to his cheeks,
which prevented him from opening his mouth or his eyes
completely, and the sight of these startled me into silence,
since I did not dare to look at what I took to be some form
of anthrax which it seemed more polite not to refer to unless
he mentioned it first. However, like a courageous invalid, he
made no allusion to his malady but talked and laughed, and I

feared to appear lacking in sympathy if I did not ask, no less
than in tact if I did ask, what was its nature. "But surely they
have become less frequent with age?" he continued, still on
the subject of my attacks of asthma. I replied that they had
not. "Oh! but my sister has them much less than she used to,"
he said, in a tone of contradiction, as though what was true
of his sister must also be true of me, and as though age were
one of a number of remedies which had helped Mme de
Gaucourt and which, therefore, he was quite certain must be
beneficial to me. Mme de Cambremer-Legrandin joined us
and I became more and more afraid that they must think me
callous for failing to deplore the symptoms which I observed
on her husband's face, yet still I could not pluck up courage
to broach the subject myself. "I expect you're glad to see him
again," she said. "Yes, but how is he?" I replied, as though
doubtful what answer I should receive. "Good heavens, pretty
well, as you can see for yourself." She had not noticed the
disfigurement which offended my eyes and which was merely
one of the masks in the collection of Time, a mask which
Time had fastened to the face of the Marquis, but gradually,
adding layer to layer so slowly that his wife had perceived
nothing. When M. de Cambremer had finished his questions
about my asthma, it was my turn to enquire in a low voice
of someone standing near whether the Marquis's mother was
still alive. And now I was beginning to discover that, in the
appreciation of the passage of time, it is only the first step that
is painful. At first one finds it extremely difficult to imagine
that so much time has elapsed, later the difficulty is to understand how the lapse can have been so slight. Similarly, when
one first suddenly becomes aware of the distance separating
the thirteenth century from the present, it is difficult to believe that churches built in that age can still exist—but in fact
they are to be found all over France. Within a few minutes

I had developed, though very much more rapidly, in the same fashion as those who, after finding it hard to believe that somebody they knew in their youth has reached the age of sixty, are very much more surprised fifteen years later to learn that the same person is still alive and is only seventy-five. Having been assured that M. de Cambremer's mother had not died, I asked him how she was. "She is wonderful still," he said, using to describe her an adjective which in certain families —by contrast with those tribes where aged parents are treated without pity—is applied to old people in whom the continued exercise of the most rudimentary and unspiritual faculties, such as hearing, going to mass on foot, sustaining the demise of their relatives with insensibility, is endowed in the eyes of their children with an extraordinary moral beauty.

If some of the women in the room had acknowledged the arrival of old age by starting to paint their faces, it was also manifested in a contrary fashion by the absence of make-up on the features of certain men, where I had never consciously observed it in the past and who yet seemed to me greatly changed since they had given up the hopeless attempt to please and ceased to use it. One of these was Legrandin. The suppression of the pink, which I had never suspected of being artificial, upon his lips and his cheeks gave to his countenance the greyish tinge and also the sculptural precision of stone, so that with his long-drawn and gloomy features he was like some Egyptian god. Or perhaps less like a god than a ghost. He had lost the courage not only to paint himself but to smile, to make his eyes sparkle, to elaborate his ingenious speeches. One was astonished to see him so pale and so dejected, opening his mouth only at rare intervals to make remarks as trivial as those uttered by the spirits of the dead when we summon them to our presence. One asked oneself what could be the cause that prevented him from being lively, eloquent, charming, as one does when a medium, putting questions that call for long and fascinating answers to the "double" of a man who in his lifetime was brilliant, elicits from him only the most uninteresting replies. And one told oneself that this cause, which had substituted for a Legrandin of rapid movements and rich colour a pale and melancholy phantom Legrandin, was old age.

There were some people whose hair had not turned white. I recognised for instance, when he came up to say a word to his master, the old valet of the Prince de Guermantes. The coarse hairs which bristled all over his cheeks as well as on his skull were still of a red that verged upon pink, yet one could hardly suspect him of using dye like the Duchesse de Guermantes. Nevertheless, he appeared old. One felt merely that in the human race there exist species, like the mosses and the lichens and a great many others in the vegetable kingdom, which do not change at the approach of winter.

Others again had preserved their faces intact and seemed merely to walk with difficulty; at first one supposed that they had something wrong with their legs, only later did one realise that age had fastened its soles of lead to their feet. A few, of whom the Prince d'Agrigente was one, seemed actually to have been embellished by age. His tall, thin figure, with its lack-lustre eye and hair that seemed destined to remain a carroty red for all eternity, had turned, through a metamorphosis more appropriate to an insect, into an entirely different old man, whose red hair, too long exposed to view, had been taken out of service like a table-cloth too long in use and replaced by white. His chest had acquired a novel corpulence, robust and almost military, which must have necessitated a positive explosion of the fragile chrysalis that I had known; a conscious gravity flooded his eyes, which were tinged also with a new kindliness which made him bow to right and left. And as, in spite of his altered appearance, a certain resemblance could be detected between the puissant prince before me and the portrait preserved in my memory, I had to admire the power to renew in fresh forms that is possessed by Time, which can thus, while respecting the unity of the individual and the laws of life, effect a change of scene and introduce bold contrasts into two successive aspects of a single person; for many of these people could be identified immediately, but only as rather bad portraits of themselves hanging side by side in an exhibition in which an inaccurate and spiteful artist has hardened the features of one sitter, robbed another of her fresh complexion and her slender figure, spread a gloom over the countenance of a third. Comparing these effigies with those that the eyes of my memory could show me, I preferred the latter. Just as often, when asked by a friend to choose a photograph, one finds the one he offers less good than some other and would like to refuse it, so to each of these people, presented with the new image which they showed me of themselves, I should have liked to say: "No, not this one, it is not so good of you, it's not really like you." I would not have dared to add: "Instead of your own straight and handsome nose, it has given you your father's crooked nose, which I have never seen in you." And yet this was what had happened: the nose was new, but it was a family nose. If this was a portrait-gallery, Time, the artist, had made of all the sitters portraits that were recognisable; yet they were not likenesses, and this was not because he had flattered them but because he had aged them. He was an artist, moreover, who worked very slowly. That replica of Odette's face, for instance, which I had seen as the merest outline of a sketch in Gilberte's face on the day on which I first met Bergotte, Time had at long last now wrought into the most perfect likeness; he was one of those painters who keep a work by them for half a lifetime, adding to it year after year until it is completed.

In some of the guests I recognised after a while not merely themselves but themselves as they had been in the past. Ski, for instance, was no more altered than a flower or a fruit which has been dried. Aged but still immature, one of those first attempts which nature abandons in the rough, he was a living confirmation of the theory which I had been formulating about the bachelor devotees of art. "Marvellous!" he said, taking me by the arm. "I have heard it eight times. . . ." There were others, too, who had not ripened with age, not only art-lovers like Ski but men who had spent their lives in society. Their faces might be surrounded with a first circle of wrinkles and a sweep of white hair but they were still the same babyish faces, with the naïve enthusiasm of an eighteen-year-old. They were not old men, they were very young men in an advanced stage of withering. The marks of life were not deeply scored here, and death, when it came, would find it as easy to restore to these features their youthfulness as it is to clean a portrait which only a little surface dirt prevents from shining with its original brilliance. These men made me think that we are victims of an illusion when, hearing talk of a celebrated old man, we instantly make up our minds that he is kind and just and gentle; for I felt that, forty years earlier, these elderly men had been ruthless young men and that there was no reason to suppose that they had not preserved their youthful arrogance and their vanity, their duplicity and their guile.

And yet, in complete contrast with these, I had the surprise of talking to men and women whom I remembered as unendurable and who had now, I found, lost almost every one of their defects, possibly because life, by disappointing or by gratifying their desires, had got rid of most of their conceit or their bitterness. A rich marriage, with the consequence that struggle and ostentation had ceased to be necessary, the influence perhaps of the wife herself, the slowly acquired knowledge of values beyond those that had formed the whole creed of a frivolous youth, had allowed them to relax the tensions in their character and to display their good qualities. Growing old, they seemed to have acquired a different personality, like those trees whose essential nature appears to be changed by the autumn which alters their colours; the essential marks of old age were manifested in them, but old age, here, was a moral phenomenon. In others, it was almost entirely physical, and so strange were its effects that a person (Mme d'Arpajon, for instance) seemed to me at the same time unknown and familiar. Unknown, for it was impossible to suspect that it was she and in spite of every effort I could not help showing signs, as I responded to her salutation, of the mental activity which made me hesitate between three or four individuals, not one of whom was Mme d'Arpajon and any one of whom I thought that I might be greeting, and greeting with a fervour which must have astonished her, for, fearing in my uncertainty to appear too chilly should she turn out to be an old and close friend, I had made up for the doubtful expression of my eyes by the warmth of my hand-shake and my smile. And yet, in a way, her novel appearance was not unfamiliar to me. It was the appearance, often seen by me in the course of my life, of certain vigorous elderly women, of whom at the time I had never suspected that many years earlier, they could have looked like Mme d'Arpajon. So different was she to look at from the woman I had known that one was tempted to think of her as a creature condemned, like a character in a pantomime, to appear first as a young girl, then as a stout matron, with no doubt a final appearance still to come as a quavering, bent old crone. Like a swimmer in difficulties almost out of sight of the shore, she seemed with infinite effort scarcely to move through the waves of time which beat upon her and threatened to submerge her. Yet gradually, as I studied her face, hesitant and uncertain like a failing memory which has begun to lose the images of the past, I succeeded in rediscovering something of the face which I had known, by playing a little game of eliminating the squares and the hexagons which age had added to her cheeks. For in her case the material which the years had superimposed consisted of geometrical shapes, though on the cheeks of other women it might be of quite a different character. On those, for instance, of Mme de Guermantes, in many respects so little changed and yet composite now like a bar of nougat, I could distinguish traces here and there of verdigris, a small pink patch of fragmentary shell-work, and a little growth of an indefinable character, smaller than a mistletoe berry and less transparent than a glass bead.

Some men walked with a limp, and one was aware that this was the result not of a motor accident but of a first stroke: they had already, as the saying is, one foot in the grave. There were women too whose graves were waiting open to receive them: half paralysed, they could not quite disentangle their dress from the tomb-stone in which it had got stuck, so that they were unable to stand up straight but remained bent towards the ground, with their head lowered, in a curve which seemed an apt symbol of their own position on the trajectory from life to death, with the final vertical plunge not far away. Nothing now could check the momentum of this parabola upon which they were launched; they trembled all over if they attempted to straighten themselves, and their fingers let fall whatever they tried to grasp.

Certain faces, beneath their hood of white hair, had already the rigidity, the sealed eyelids of those who are about to die, and their lips, shaken by an incessant tremor, seemed to be muttering a last prayer. A countenance of which every line was unchanged needed only the substitution of white hair for black or fair to look totally different, for, as theatrical costumiers know, a powdered wig is in itself an adequate disguise which will make its wearer unrecognisable. The Comte de X——, whom I had seen, as a young lieutenant, in Mme de Cambremer's box on the day on which Mme de Guermantes had been with her cousin in hers, still had the same perfectly regular features, indeed they had become even more regular, since the pathological rigidity brought about by arterio-sclerosis had even further exaggerated the impassive rectitude of his dandy's physiognomy and given to his features the intense hardness of outline, almost grimacing in its immobility, that they might have had in a study by Mantegna or Michelangelo. His complexion, once almost ribaldly red, was now solemnly pale; silvery hair, a slight portliness, the dignity of a Doge, an air of fatigue, even of somnolence, all combined to give him a new and premonitory impression of doomed majesty. The square light brown beard had gone and in its place was a square white beard, of the same trim proportions, which so totally transformed his appearance that, noticing that the second lieutenant whom I remembered now had five bands of braid on his sleeve, my first thought was to congratulate him, not on having been promoted colonel but on looking so well in the part of colonel, a disguise for which he seemed to have borrowed, together with the uniform, the lugubrious gravity of the senior officer that his father had been. But there was another guest whose face, in spite of the substitution of a white for a fair beard, had remained lively, smiling and boyish, so that the change of beard merely made him appear more rubicund and more pugnacious and enhanced the sparkle in his eye, giving to the still youthful man about town the inspired air of a prophet.

The transformations effected, in the women particularly, by white hair and by other new features, would not have held my attention so forcibly had they been merely changes of colour, which can be charming to behold; too often they were changes of personality, registered not by the eye but, disturbingly, by the mind. For to "recognise" someone, and, *a fortiori*, having failed to recognise someone to learn his identity, is to predicate two contradictory things of a single subject, it is to admit that what was here, the person whom one remembers, no longer exists, and also that what is now here is a person whom one did not know to exist; and to do this we have to apprehend a mystery almost as disturbing as that of death, of which it is, indeed, as it were the preface and the harbinger. I knew what these changes meant, I knew what they were the prelude to, and that is why the white hair of these women, along with all the other changes, profoundly disquieted me. I was told a name and I was dumbfounded to think that it could be used to describe both the fair-haired girl, the marvellous waltzer, whom I had known in the past, and the massive white-haired lady making her way through the room with elephantine tread. Along with a certain rosiness of complexion, the name was perhaps the only thing common to these two women, the girl in my memory and the lady at the Guermantes party, who were more unlike one another than an *ingénue* and a dowager in a play. To have succeeded in giving to the waltzer this huge body, in encumbering and retarding her movements by the adjustment of an invisible metronome, in substituting—with perhaps as sole common factor the cheeks, larger certainly now than in youth but already in those days blotched with red—for the feather-light fair girl this ventripotent old campaigner, it must have been necessary for life to accomplish a vaster work of dismantlement and reconstruction than is involved in the replacement of a steeple by a dome, and when one considered that this work had been effected not with tractable inorganic matter but with living flesh which can only change imperceptibly, the overwhelming contrast between the apparition before me and the creature that I remembered pushed back the existence of the latter into a past that was more than remote, that was almost unimaginable. One was terrified, because it made one think of the vast periods which must have elapsed before such a revolution could be accomplished in the geology of a face, to see what erosions had taken place all the way along the nose, what huge alluvial deposits at the edge of the cheeks surrounded the whole face with their opaque and refractory masses. It was difficult to find a link between the two figures, past and present, to think of the two individuals as possessing the same name; for just as one has difficulty in thinking that a dead person was once alive or that a person who was alive is now dead, so one has difficulty, almost as great and of the same kind (for the extinction of youth, the destruction of a person full of energy and high spirits is already a kind of annihilation), in conceiving that she who was once a girl is now an old woman when the juxtaposition of the two appearances, the old and the young, seems so totally to exclude the possibility of their belonging to the same person that alternately it is the old woman and then the girl and then again the old woman who seems to one to be a dream, so that one might well refuse to believe that *this* can ever have been *that*, that the material of *that* has not taken refuge elsewhere but has itself, thanks to the subtle manipulations of Time, turned into *this*, that it is the same matter incorporated in the same body, were it not for the evidence of the similar name and the corroborative testimony of friends, to which an appearance of verisimilitude is given only by the pink upon the cheeks, once a small patch surrounded by the golden corn of fair hair, now a broad expanse beneath the snow.

And often these fair-haired dancers had acquired, along with a wig of white hair, the friendship of duchesses whom in the past they had not known. Nor was this all: having in their youth done nothing but dance, they had been "touched" by art as once a noble lady might have been touched by grace. And as the seventeenth-century lady, when this happened, withdrew into a life of religion, so now her descendant lived in an apartment filled with cubist paintings, a cubist painter worked for her alone and she lived only for him.

As in a snowy landscape, the degree of whiteness attained by a person's hair seemed in general to be an indication of the depth of time through which he or she had lived, just as in a range of mountains the higher peaks, even though they appear to the eye to be on the same level as the rest, nevertheless reveal their greater altitude by the intensity of their snowy whiteness. But there were exceptions to this rule, particularly among the women. Thus the tresses of the Princesse de Guermantes, which, when they were grey and had the lustre of silk, seemed to surround her bulging temples with silver, having in the process of turning white acquired the matness of wool or tow, seemed now on the contrary, for that reason, to be grey, like snow which has become dirty and lost its brilliance.

Some of the old men whose features had changed tried nevertheless to preserve, fixed upon them in a state of permanency, one of those fugitive expressions which one assumes for a second when posing for a photograph, either in order to show off some good point in one's appearance to the best effect or to conceal a deformity; they seemed to have become, once and for all, snapshots of themselves insusceptible of change.

All these people had taken so much time putting on their disguises that generally these passed unobserved by the men and women who saw them every day. Often they had even been granted a reprieve, thanks to which up to a very late hour they were able to remain themselves. But in these cases the disguise, when it finally came, was assumed more rapidly; for disguise, one way or another, was unavoidable. Mme X——, for instance, had never seemed to me to bear any resemblance to her mother, whom I had known only as an old woman, looking like a little hunched Turk. The daughter, on the other hand, I had always known as a charming woman with an upright carriage, and this for many years she had continued to be, for too many years, in fact, for like someone who must not forget, before night falls, to put on his Turkish disguise, she had left things late and had then been obliged precipitately, almost instantaneously, to hunch herself up so as faithfully to reproduce the appearance of an old Turkish woman that had once been presented by her mother.

At the party was a friend of my youth, whom for ten years I had seen almost every day. We were re-introduced to each other and, as I went up to him, he said, in a voice which I recognised very well: "How delightful to see you again after all these years!" But if he was delighted, I was astonished. The familiar voice seemed to be emitted by a gramophone more perfect than any I had ever heard, for, though it was the voice of my friend, it issued from the mouth of a corpulent gentleman with greying hair whom I did not know, and I could only suppose that somehow artificially, by a mechanical device, the voice of my old comrade had been lodged in the frame of this stout elderly man who might have been anybody. And yet I knew that this was my friend; the man who had re-introduced us after all these years was not someone one could suspect of playing a practical joke. My friend himself declared that I had not changed, and I realised that in his own eyes he had not changed. I looked at him more closely. And in fact, except that he had grown so much stouter, he had preserved many features of his former self. And yet I could not take it in that it was he. Then I made an effort to remember. In his youth he had had blue eyes, always laughing and perpetually mobile, in search evidently of something the nature of which I had not asked myself, but something no doubt entirely disinterested, Truth perhaps, pursued in perpetual uncertainty, with a sort of boyish irresponsibility and yet with a wavering respect for all the friends of his family. And now that he had become an important politician, able and masterful, his blue eyes, which in any case had not found what they were seeking, had lost their mobility, and this gave them a look of narrow concentration, as though the brow above them were constantly frowning. His expression was no longer one of gaiety, innocence and spontaneity but of guile and dissimulation. Decidedly, I thought, this must be somebody else, but then suddenly I heard, evoked by something that I had said, his laugh, his old loud, unforced laugh, the one that went with the perpetual gay mobility of his glance. Experienced concert-goers find that orchestrated by X— the music of Z— becomes absolutely different, a somewhat subtle distinction which the ignorant public does not comprehend—but to hear the wild, choking laugh of a boy emerge from beneath a look which was as pointed as a well sharpened blue pencil though set slightly crooked in the face, was more than a mere difference of orchestration. He stopped laughing; I should have liked to recognise my friend, but, like Ulysses in the Odyssey when he rushes forward to embrace his dead mother, like the spiritualist who tries in vain to elicit from a ghost an answer which will reveal its identity, like the visitor at an exhibition of electricity who cannot believe that the voice which the gramophone restores unaltered to life is not a voice spontaneously emitted by a human being, I was obliged to give up the attempt.

Nobody was exempt from change, but I had to qualify this statement with the observation that for certain people the *tempo* of Time itself may be accelerated or retarded. By chance I had met in the street, some four or five years earlier, the Vicomtesse de Saint-Fiacre (the daughter-in-law of the one who had been a friend of the Guermantes). Her sculptural features seemed to assure her of eternal youth, and indeed she was still young. But I was quite unable to recognise her now, in spite of her smiles and her greetings, in the lady before me whose features were so eroded that the original lines of her face could no longer be restored. For three years she had been taking cocaine and other drugs. Her eyes, deeply ringed with black, were almost haggard, and her mouth opened in a ghastly grin. She spent months on end now, I was told, without leaving her bed or her *chaise longue*, and had got up just for this party. Time has, it seems, special express trains which bring their passengers swiftly to a premature old age. But on the parallel track trains almost as rapid may be moving in the opposite direction. I took M. de Courgivaux for his son, for he looked the younger of the two—though he must have been more than fifty, he seemed younger than he had when he was thirty. He had found an intelligent doctor and given up alcohol and salt, and the result was that he had returned to his early thirties and on this particular day looked even younger still, for the reason that, that very morning, he had had his hair cut.

A curious thing was that the phenomenon of old age seemed, in its different modes, to take into account certain social habits. Thus certain great noblemen, who had always worn the plainest alpaca cloth and on their heads old straw hats which a man of the lower middle class would have refused to put on, had aged in the same fashion as the gardeners and the peasants in whose society they had spent their lives. Patches of brown had begun to spread over their cheeks and their faces had turned yellower and darker like the pages of an old book.

I thought also of all those who were not at the party because they were too weak or too ill to be there, those whom their secretary, seeking to give the illusion of their survival, had excused by one of those telegrams which from time to time were handed to the Princess, those invalids, moribund for years, who no longer leave their beds, no longer move, and even in the midst of the frivolous attentions of visitors, drawn to them by the curiosity of a tourist or the pious hopes of a pilgrim, with their eyes closed and their rosaries clutched in hands which feebly push back the sheet that is already a mortuary shroud, are like monumental figures, carved by illness until the skeleton is barely covered by a flesh which is white and rigid as marble, lying stretched upon a tomb.

There were men in the room whom I knew to be related to each other without it ever having crossed my mind that they had a feature in common. In admiring, for instance, the old hermit with white hair who was Legrandin in a new guise, I suddenly observed, with the satisfaction almost of a zoologist when he makes a scientific discovery, in the transitions between the planes of his cheeks the same construction as in the cheeks of his young nephew, Léonor de Cambremer, who appeared nevertheless to bear no resemblance to him; and to this first common feature I added another which I had never yet noticed in Léonor de Cambremer, and then again others, none of which was included in the youthful synthesis of the nephew which habitually presented itself to me, until soon I had of him a caricature which was truer and more profound for not being a literal representation: his uncle now seemed to me simply a young Cambremer who to amuse himself had assumed the countenance of the old man that he would in fact one day be, so that now it was not merely what had become of the young men of my own youth but what would one day become of those of today that impressed upon me with such force the sensation of Time.

The women sought to remain in contact with whatever had been most individual in their charm, but often the new matter of their face no longer lent itself to this purpose. Those features upon which had been engraved, if not their youth, at least their beauty, had disappeared, and they had endeavoured, with the face that remained to them, to construct a new beauty for themselves. Displacing, if not the centre of gravity, at least the central point of the perspective of their face, and grouping their features around it in a new pattern, they began at the age of fifty to display a beauty of a new type, in the same way that late in life a man may embark on a new profession or a piece of ground which has become useless as a vineyard may be turned over to the production of sugar beet. And in the midst of these new features a second youth was made to bloom. The only women who failed to adjust themselves to this kind of transformation were the ones who were either too beautiful or too ugly. The former were like some block of marble, the lines in which, once it had been carved, are final and admit of no change; ageing, they merely crumbled away like a statue. The others, those who had some deformity of face, actually had certain advantages over the beautiful women. In the first place they were the only women whom one instantly recognised. One knew, for example, that in the whole of Paris there could only be one mouth like *that*, so that at this party, where I failed to recognise almost everybody, I could at least put a name to the possessor of the mouth.

And then they did not even appear to have aged. Old age is something human; these were monsters, and they no more seemed to have "changed" than whales.

Others too, both men and women, seemed not to have aged; their figures were just as slim, their faces as young. But if, to speak to them, one approached rather near to the face with the smooth skin and the delicate contours it then appeared quite different, like the surface of a plant or a drop of water or blood when you look at it under a microscope. At close quarters I could distinguish numerous greasy marks upon the skin which I had supposed to be smooth and which now, because of these marks, I found repulsive. Nor could the lines of the face stand up to this magnification. That of the nose was seen now to be broken and rounded, its regularity marred by the same oily patches as the rest of the face; and the eyes at short range retreated behind pockets of flesh which destroyed the resemblance of the person before me to the one whom I had known in the past and thought that I had met again. So that these particular guests were young when seen at a distance but their age increased with the enlargement of their face and the possibility of studying its different planes; it was dependent upon the spectator, who to see them as young had to place himself correctly and to view them only with that distant inspection which diminishes its object like the lens selected by an oculist for a long-sighted elderly person; old age here, like the presence of infusoria in a drop of water, was made apparent not so much by the advance of the years as by a greater degree of accuracy in the scale of the observer's vision.

Some women no doubt were still easily recognisable: their faces had remained almost the same and they had merely, out of propriety and in harmony with the season, put on the grey hair which was their autumn attire. But there were others, and there were men too, whose metamorphosis was so complete, their identity so impossible to establish—that old monk, for instance, in a corner of the room and the notorious rake whom one remembered, were they the same person?—that it was of the art not so much of the actor as of certain prodigiously gifted mimes, of whom the supreme example is Fregoli, that these fabulous transformations made one think. The old woman whose charm had resided in her indefinable and melancholy smile would have liked to weep, at first, when she realised that this smile could no longer break through with its radiance to the surface of the plaster mask with which age had covered her face. Then suddenly, weary of trying to please and finding it more intelligent, more amusing to resign herself to the inevitable, she had started to use it like a mask in the theatre, as a way of making people laugh. But with few exceptions the women strained every nerve in a ceaseless struggle against old age and held out the mirror of their features towards beauty, as it receded, as to a setting sun whose last rays they longed passionately to preserve. To achieve this end some of them tried to plane away all the irregularities of their face, to enlarge its smooth, white surface, renouncing the piquancy of dimples that had not long to live, the archness of a smile condemned and already half disarmed, while others, seeing that beauty had vanished beyond recall and taking refuge perforce in expression, like an actress whose skill in the art of diction makes up for the loss of her voice, clung desperately to a pout, to a pretty crow's foot, to a dreamy glance, to a smile sometimes which, because of the incoordination of muscles that no longer obeyed the brain, made them look as though they were in tears.

Even in the case of the men who had changed but little—those, for instance, whose moustaches had merely turned white—one felt that the changes were not strictly speaking material. One might have been looking at these men through

a vapour which imparted its own colour to them, or through a
tinted optical glass which altered the appearance of their faces
and above all, by making them slightly blurred, showed one
that what it enabled us to see "life-size" was in reality a long
way away, separated from us, it is true, by a distance other
than spatial but from the depths of which, nevertheless, as
from a further shore, we felt that they had as much difficulty
in recognising us as we them. Only perhaps Mme de Forcheville, as though she had been injected with some liquid, some
sort of paraffin with the property of inflating the skin but pro-
tecting it from change, might have been an old-fashioned
cocotte "stuffed" for the benefit of posterity. Setting out from
the idea that people have remained unchanged, one finds them
old. But once one starts with the idea that they are old, meeting them again one does not think that they look too bad. In
the case of Odette one could say much more than this; her
appearance, once one knew her age and expected to see an old
woman, seemed a defiance of the laws of chronology, more
miraculous even than the defiance of the laws of nature by the
conservation of radium. If I failed at first to recognise her, this
was, uniquely, not because she had but because she had not
changed. I had learnt in the last hour to take into account the
new items that are added to people by Time and that had to be
subtracted by me if I wanted to find my friends again as I had
known them in the past, and I now rapidly made this calculation, adding to the old Odette the number of years which had
passed over her; but the result at which I arrived was a person
who could not, it seemed, be the one before me, precisely
because she, the woman at the party, was so like the Odette of
old days. In part, of course, this effect was achieved by rouge
and dye. Beneath her flat golden hair—a little like the ruffled
chignon of a big mechanical doll, above a face with a fixed
expression of surprise which might also have belonged to a

doll—on top of which rested a straw hat that was also flat, she might well have been "The Exhibition of 1878" (of which she would without a doubt, above all had she then been as old as she was today, have been the most fantastic marvel) coming forward onto the stage to speak her two lines in a New Year revue, but the Exhibition of 1878 played by an actress who was still young.

Another figure from the same period, who had been a minister before the era of Boulangism and was now in the government again, passed beside us, wafting to the ladies a tremulous and remote smile, but with the air of being imprisoned in a thousand chains of the past, like a little phantom paraded up and down by an invisible hand or—diminished in stature and altered in substance—a reduced version of himself in pumice stone. This former Prime Minister, now so well received in the Faubourg Saint-Germain, had at one time been the object of criminal proceedings, and had been execrated both by society and by the people. But thanks to the renewal of the individuals who compose these two bodies and to the renewal, within the individuals who survive, of passions and even of memories, nobody now knew this and he was held in high honour. For the fact is that there is no humiliation so great that one should not accept it with unconcern, knowing that at the end of a few years our misdeeds will be no more than an invisible dust buried beneath the smiling and blooming peace of nature. The man whose reputation is momentarily under a cloud will soon find himself, thanks to the balancing mechanism of Time, caught and held between two new social levels which will have for him nothing but deference and admiration. But Time alone will achieve this result and at the moment of his downfall nothing can console him for the fact that the young dairy-maid across the street heard the crowd shout "Bribery and corruption!" at him and saw them shake their fists as he climbed into the Black Maria—for the dairy-maid does not see things in the perspective of Time and does not know that the men who receive the incense of praise from this morning's newspapers were yesterday in disgrace and that the fallen politician, who at this moment feels the shadow of prison bars upon him and yet perhaps, as he thinks of the dairy-maid, cannot find within himself the humble words which might win her sympathy, will one day be extolled by the press and sought after by duchesses. And Time in the same way makes family quarrels recede into the distance. At the Princesse de Guermantes's party, for instance, there was a couple, husband and wife, who were respectively nephew and niece of two men, now dead, who had once come to blows and—worse still—one of them, still further to humiliate the other, had sent him as witnesses his porter and his butler, indicating that in his judgement gentlemen would have been too good for him. But these stories slumbered in the pages of the newspapers of thirty years ago and nobody now remembered them. And thus the drawing-room of the Princesse de Guermantes—illuminated, oblivious, flowery—was like a peaceful cemetery. Time in this room had done more than decompose the living creatures of a former age, it had rendered possible, had created new associations.

To return to the politician, in spite of his change of physical substance, just as profound as the transformation of the moral ideas which his name now connoted to the public, in spite (to say the same thing more simply) of the lapse of so many years since he had been Prime Minister, he was once again a member of the cabinet, whose leader had given him a portfolio in the recent re-shuffle rather in the way that a theatrical producer gives a part to an old actress friend long since retired, whom he judges nevertheless to be, even now, better able to interpret a part with subtlety than any of her younger successors and whom he knows, also, to be in financial straits, and who in the event, at the age of nearly eighty, exhibits once more to the public almost the fulness of her talent, with that continued vitality which one is later astonished to have observed up to the very threshold of death.

But if the politician was extraordinary, Mme de Forcheville was so miraculous that one could not even say that she had grown young again—it was more as though, with all her carmines and her russets, she had bloomed for a second time. Even more than the embodiment of the Universal Exhibition of 1878, she might have been the principal rarity and attraction of a flower show of today. And indeed, for me she seemed to say, not so much: "I am the Exhibition of 1878" as: "I am the Allée des Acacias of 1892". That was where, it seemed, she still might have been. And just because she had not changed she seemed scarcely to be alive. She looked like a rose that has been sterilised. I greeted her and her eyes travelled for a while over my face, searching for my name as a schoolboy searches on the face of his examiner for the answer that he might more easily have found in his own head. Then I told her who I was and at once, as though the sound of my name had broken a spell and I had lost the look of an arbutus tree or a kangaroo which age no doubt had given me, she recognised me and started to talk to me in that strangely individual voice which people who had admired her acting in some little theatre were astonished, when they were invited to meet her at a luncheon party, to find again, throughout the whole conversation, for as long as they cared to listen, in each one of her remarks. It was a voice that had not changed, unnecessarily warm, caressing, with a trace of an English accent. And yet, just as her eyes appeared to be looking at me from a distant shore, her voice was sad, almost suppliant, like the voice of the shades in the Odyssey. Odette would still have been able to

act. I complimented her on her youthfulness. "How nice of
you, my dear boy," she said, "thank you," and, as it was
difficult for her to express a sentiment, even the most sincere,
in a manner that was not rendered artificial by her anxiety to
be what she supposed was smart, she repeated several times:
"Thank you *so* much, thank you *so* much." I meanwhile, who
had once walked miles to see her pass in the Bois, who the
first time that I had visited her house had listened to the sound
of her voice as it fell from her mouth as though it were some
priceless treasure, now found the minutes that I was obliged to
pass in her company interminable simply because I did not
know what on earth to say to her, and I withdrew, thinking
to myself that not only had Gilberte's remark "You take me
for my mother" been true, but that the likeness could only be
flattering to the daughter.

Gilberte, for that matter, was by no means the only guest at
the party in whom family features had become apparent which
hitherto had remained as invisible in their faces as the coiled
and hidden parts of a seed which one day will burst out into
growth in a manner that it is impossible to foresee. Thus, in
this woman or that man, at about the age of fifty an enormous
maternal hook had arrived to transform a nose which until
then had been straight and pure. And the complexion of
another woman, a banker's daughter, from being as fresh as
that of a milkmaid grew first russet and then coppery and
finally assumed as it were a reflection of the gold which her
father had so lovingly handled. Some people had even in the
end come to resemble the district in which they lived, bearing
on their faces a sort of replica of the Rue de l'Arcade or the
Avenue du Bois or the Rue de l'Élysée. But most commonly
they reproduced the features of their parents.

Alas, Mme de Forcheville's second flowering was not to
last for ever. Less than three years later I was to see her at an

evening party given by Gilberte, not quite in her dotage but showing signs of senility and grown incapable of concealing beneath a mask of immobility what she was thinking, or rather (for thinking is too elevated a term) what she was passively experiencing, nodding her head, compressing her lips, shaking her shoulders in response to every impression that she felt, like a drunkard or a small child or those poets who, unaware of their surroundings and seized by inspiration, compose verses in the midst of a social occasion and frown and pout as they proceed to the dinner-table with an astonished lady on their arm. The impressions of Mme de Forcheville—save that single sentiment which was the cause of her presence at the party: her tender affection for her beloved daughter and her pride that she should be giving so brilliant a party, a pride which, in the mother, could not disguise the melancholy of being herself now nothing—these impressions were not joyful, their message was merely that she must not relax her defence against the snubs which were showered upon her, a defence, however, as timorous as that of a child. On all sides one heard people say: "I don't know whether Mme de Forcheville recognises me, perhaps I ought to get someone to introduce me to her again." "You may as well spare yourself the trouble," a booming voice would reply, its owner not suspecting that Gilberte's mother could hear every word—or perhaps not caring if she could. "It's quite unnecessary. You wouldn't find her at all amusing! She's best left alone in her corner. She's a bit gaga, you know." Furtively Mme de Forcheville shot a glance from her eyes which had remained so beautiful at the authors of these offensive remarks, then swiftly withdrew it for fear of having been rude, but was distressed nevertheless by the insult, and though she smothered her feeble indignation one saw her head shake and her breast heave until presently another glance was shot at another guest

who had expressed himself just as discourteously—yet nothing
of all this seemed to surprise her very much, for having felt
extremely unwell for several days, she had covertly suggested
to her daughter that she should put off her party, but her
daughter had refused. Mme de Forcheville loved her none the
less for this: the sight of all the duchesses entering the room,
the admiration of all the guests for the large new house,
flooded her heart with joy, and when finally the Marquise de
Sabran was announced, who was at that moment the lady at
whom one arrived after laboriously ascending the topmost
rungs of the social ladder, Mme de Forcheville felt that she
had been a good and far-sighted mother and that her maternal
task was accomplished. New guests arrived to titter at her and
again she shot her glances and spoke to herself, if a mute
language expressed only in gesture can be described as speech.
Beautiful still, she had become—what she had never been in
the past—infinitely pathetic; she who had been unfaithful to
Swann and to everybody found now that the entire universe
was unfaithful to her, and so weak had she become that, the
roles being reversed, she no longer dared to defend herself
even against men. And soon she would not defend herself even
against death. But we have anticipated, and let us now go
back three years, to the afternoon party which is being given
by the Princesse de Guermantes.

I had difficulty in recognising my friend Bloch, who was
now in fact no longer Bloch since he had adopted, not merely
as a pseudonym but as a name, the style of Jacques du Rozier,
beneath which it would have needed my grandfather's flair to
detect the "sweet vale of Hebron" and those "chains of Israel"
which my old comrade appeared definitively to have broken.
Indeed an English *chic* had completely transformed his appearance and smoothed away, as with a plane, everything in
it that was susceptible of such treatment. The once curly hair,

now brushed flat, with a parting in the middle, glistened with brilliantine. His nose remained large and red, but seemed now to owe its tumescence to a sort of permanent cold which served also to explain the nasal intonation with which he languidly delivered his studied sentences, for just as he had found a way of doing his hair which suited his complexion, so he had found a voice which suited his pronunciation and which gave to his old nasal twang the air of a disdainful refusal to articulate that was in keeping with his inflamed nostrils. And thanks to the way in which he brushed his hair, to the suppression of his moustache, to the elegance of his whole figure—thanks, that is to say, to his determination—his Jewish nose was now scarcely more visible than is the deformity of a hunch-backed woman who skilfully arranges her appearance. But above all—and one saw this the moment one set eyes on him—the significance of his physiognomy had been altered by a formidable monocle. By introducing an element of machinery into Bloch's face this monocle absolved it of all those difficult duties which a human face is normally called upon to discharge, such as being beautiful or expressing intelligence or kindliness or effort. The monocle's mere presence even absolved an interlocutor, in the first place, from asking himself whether the face was pleasant to look at or not, just as, when a shop-assistant has told you that some object imported from England is "the last word in *chic*", you no longer dare to ask yourself whether you really like it. In any case, behind the lens of this monocle Bloch was now installed in a position as lofty, as remote and as comfortable as if it had been the glass partition of a limousine and, so that his face should match the smooth hair and the monocle, his features never now expressed anything at all.

Bloch asked me to introduce him to the Prince de Guermantes, and this operation raised for me not a shadow of those difficulties which I had come up against on the day when I went to an evening party at his house for the first time, difficulties which had then seemed to me a part of the natural order whereas now I found it the simplest thing in the world to introduce to the Prince a guest whom he had invited himself and I should even have ventured, without warning, to bring to his party and introduce to him someone whom he had not invited. Was this because, since that distant era, I had become an intimate member though for a long time now a forgotten one, of that fashionable world in which I had then been so new? Was it, on the contrary, because I did not really belong to that world, so that all the imaginary difficulties which beset people in society no longer existed for me once my shyness had vanished? Was it because, having gradually come to see what lay behind the first (and often the second and even the third) artificial appearance of others, I sensed behind the haughty disdain of the Prince a great human avidity to know people, to make the acquaintance even of those whom he affected to despise? Was it also because the Prince himself had changed, like so many men in whom the arrogance of their youth and of their middle years is tempered by the gentleness of old age—particularly as the new men and the unknown ideas whose progress they had once resisted are now familiar to them, at least by sight, and they see that they are accepted all round them in society—a change which takes place more effectually if old age is assisted in its task by some good quality or some vice in the individual which enlarges the circle of his acquaintance, or by the revolution wrought by a political conversion such as that of the Prince to Dreyfusism?

Bloch started to question me, as years ago, when I first began to go to parties, I had questioned others—a habit which I had not quite lost—about the people whom I had known in society in the old days and who were as remote, as unlike anybody else, as those inhabitants of the world of Combray whom I had often sought to "place" exactly. But Combray for me had a shape so distinctive, so impossible to confuse with anything else, that it might have been a piece of a jig-saw puzzle which I could never succeed in fitting into the map of France. "So the Prince de Guermantes can give me no idea either of Swann or of M. de Charlus?" asked Bloch, whose manner of speaking I had borrowed long ago and who now frequently imitated mine. "None at all." "But what was so different about them?" "To know that, you would have had to hear them talk yourself. But that is impossible. Swann is dead and M. de Charlus is as good as dead. But the differences were enormous." And seeing Bloch's eyes shine at the thought of what these marvellous personages must have been, I wondered whether I was not exaggerating the pleasure which I had got from their company, since pleasure was something that I had never felt except when I was alone and the real differentiation of impressions takes place only in our imagination. Bloch seemed to guess what I was thinking. "Perhaps you make it out to be more wonderful than it really was," he said; "our hostess today, for instance, the Princesse de Guermantes, I know she is no longer young, still it is not so many years since you were telling me about her incomparable charm, her marvellous beauty. Well, I grant you she has a certain splendour, and she certainly has those extraordinary eyes you used to talk about, but I can't say I find her so fantastically beautiful. Of course, one sees that she is a real aristocrat, but still. . . ." I was obliged to tell Bloch that the woman I had described to him was not the one he was talking about. The Princesse de Guermantes had died and the present wife of the Prince, who had been ruined by the collapse of Germany, was the former Mme Verdurin. "That can't be right, I looked in this year's Gotha," Bloch naïvely confessed

to me, "and I found the Prince de Guermantes, living at this
address where we are now and married to someone of the
utmost grandeur, let me try to remember, yes, married to
Sidonie, Duchesse de Duras, *née* des Baux." This was correct.
Mme Verdurin, shortly after the death of her husband, had
married the aged and impoverished Duc de Duras, who had
made her a cousin of the Prince de Guermantes and had died
after two years of marriage. He had served as a useful transition for Mme Verdurin, who now, by a third marriage, had
become Princesse de Guermantes and occupied in the Faubourg Saint-Germain a lofty position which would have
caused much astonishment at Combray, where the ladies of
the Rue de l'Oiseau, Mme Goupil's daughter and Mme
Sazerat's step-daughter, had during these last years, before
she married for the third time, spoken with a sneer of "the
Duchesse de Duras" as though this were a role which had
been allotted to Mme Verdurin in a play. In fact, the Combray principle of caste requiring that she should die, as she
had lived, as Mme Verdurin, her title, which was not
deemed to confer upon her any new power in society, did not
so much enhance as damage her reputation. For "to make
tongues wag", that phrase which in every sphere of life is
applied to a woman who has a lover, could be used also in the
Faubourg Saint-Germain of women who write books and in
the respectable society of Combray of those who make marriages which, for better or for worse, are "unsuitable". After
the twice-widowed lady had married the Prince de Guermantes, the only possible comment was that he was a false
Guermantes, an impostor. For me, in this purely nominal
identity, in the fact that there was once again a Princesse de
Guermantes and that she had absolutely nothing in common
with the one who had cast her spell upon me, who now no
longer existed and had been robbed of name and title like a

defenceless woman of her jewels, there was something as profoundly sad as in seeing the material objects which the Princess Hedwige had once possessed—her country house and everything that had been hers—pass into the possession and enjoyment of another woman. The succession of a new individual to a name is melancholy, as is all succession, all usurpation of property; and yet for ever and ever, without interruption, there would come, sweeping on, a flood of new Princesses de Guermantes—or rather, centuries old, replaced from age to age by a series of different women, of different actresses playing the same part and then each in her turn sinking from sight beneath the unvarying and immemorial placidity of the name, one single Princesse de Guermantes, ignorant of death and indifferent to all that changes and wounds our mortal hearts.

Of course, even these external changes in the figures whom I had known were no more than symbols of an internal change which had been effected day by day. Perhaps these people had continued to perform the same actions, but gradually the idea which they entertained both of their own activities and of their acquaintances had slightly altered its shape, so that at the end of a few years, though the names were unchanged, the activities that they enjoyed and the people whom they loved had become different and, as they themselves had become different individuals, it was hardly surprising that they should have new faces.

But there were also guests whom I failed to recognise for the reason that I had never known them, for in this drawing-room, as well as upon individuals the chemistry of Time had been at work upon society. This coterie, within the specific nature of which, delimited as it was by certain affinities that attracted to it all the great princely names of Europe and by forces of an opposite kind which repelled from it anything

that was not aristocratic, I had found, I thought, a sort of
corporeal refuge for the name of Guermantes, this coterie,
which had seemed to confer upon that name its ultimate
reality, had itself, in its innermost and as I had thought stable
constitution, undergone a profound transformation. The
presence of people whom I had seen in quite different social
settings and whom I would never have expected to penetrate
into this one, astonished me less than the intimate familiarity
with which they were now received in it, on Christian name
terms; a certain complex of aristocratic prejudices, of snobbery, which in the past automatically maintained a barrier
between the name of Guermantes and all that did not har-
monise with it, had ceased to function. Enfeebled or broken,
the springs of the machine could no longer perform their task
of keeping out the crowd; a thousand alien elements made
their way in and all homogeneity, all consistency of form and
colour was lost. The Faubourg Saint-Germain was like some
senile dowager now, who replies only with timid smiles
to the insolent servants who invade her drawing-rooms,
drink her orangeade, present their mistresses to her. However, the sensation of time having slipped away, and of
the annihilation of a small part of my own past, was conveyed to me less vividly by the destruction of that coherent
whole which the Guermantes drawing-room had once been
than by the annihilation of even the knowledge of the
thousand reasons, the thousand subtle distinctions thanks to
which one man who was still to be found in that drawing-
room today was clearly in his natural and proper place there
while another, who rubbed shoulders with him, wore in these
surroundings an aspect of dubious novelty. And this ignorance
was not merely ignorance of society, but of politics, of everything. For memory was of shorter duration in individuals
than life, and besides, the very young, who had never possessed

the recollections which had vanished from the minds of their elders, now formed part of society (and with perfect legitimacy, even in the genealogical sense of the word), and the origins of the people whom they saw there being forgotten or unknown, they accepted them at the particular point of their elevation or their fall at which they found them, supposing that things had always been as they were today, that the social position of Mme Swann and the Princesse de Guermantes and Bloch had always been very great, that Clemenceau and Viviani had always been conservatives. And as certain facts have a greater power of survival than others, the detested memory of the Dreyfus affair persisting vaguely in these young people thanks to what they had heard their fathers say, if one told them that Clemenceau had been a Dreyfusard, they replied: "Impossible, you are making a confusion, he is absolutely on the other side of the fence." Ministers with a tarnished reputation and women who had started life as prostitutes were now held to be paragons of virtue. (Among the guests was a distinguished man who had recently, in a famous lawsuit, made a deposition of which the sole value resided in the lofty moral character of the witness, in the face of which both judge and counsel had bowed their heads, with the result that two people had been convicted. Consequently, when he entered the room there was a stir of curiosity and of deference. This man was Morel. I was perhaps the only person present who knew that he had once been kept by Saint-Loup and at the same time by a friend of Saint-Loup. In spite of these recollections he greeted me with pleasure, though with a certain reserve. He remembered the time when we had seen each other at Balbec, and these recollections had for him the poetry and the melancholy of youth.) Someone having enquired of a young man of the best possible family whether Gilberte's mother had not formerly been the subject of scandal, the young nobleman replied that it

was true that in the earlier part of her life she had been married
to an adventurer of the name of Swann, but that subsequently
she had married one of the most prominent men in society,
the Comte de Forcheville. No doubt there were still a few
people in the room—the Duchesse de Guermantes was one—
who would have smiled at this assertion (which, in its denial of
Swann's position as a man of fashion, seemed to me monstrous,
although I myself, long ago at Combray, had shared my
great-aunt's belief that Swann could not be acquainted with
"princesses"), and others also not in the room, women who
might have been there had they not almost ceased to leave
their homes, the Duchesses of Montmorency and Mouchy
and Sagan, who had been close friends of Swann and had
never set eyes on this man Forcheville, who was not received
in society at the time when they went to parties. But it could
not be denied that the society of those days, like the faces now
drastically altered and the fair hair replaced by white, existed
now only in the memories of individuals whose number was
diminishing day by day. During the war Bloch had given up
going out socially, had ceased to visit the houses which he had
once frequented and where he had cut anything but a brilliant
figure. On the other hand, he had published a whole series of
works full of those absurd sophistical arguments which, so as
not to be inhibited by them myself, I was struggling to
demolish today, works without originality but which gave to
young men and to many society women the impression of a
rare and lofty intellect, a sort of genius. And so it was after a
complete break between his earlier social existence and this
later one that he had, in a society itself reconstituted, embarked upon a new phase of his life, honoured and glorious, in
which he played the role of a great man. Young people naturally did not know that at his somewhat advanced age he was in
fact making his first appearance on the social scene, particularly

as, by sprinkling his conversation with the few names which he had retained from his acquaintance with Saint-Loup, he was able to impart to his prestige of the moment a sort of indefinite recession in depth. In any case he was regarded as one of those men of talent who in every epoch have flourished in the highest society, and nobody thought that he had ever frequented any other.

Survivors of the older generation assured me that society had completely changed and now opened its doors to people who in their day would never have been received, and this comment was both true and untrue. On the one hand it was untrue, because those who made it failed to take into account the curve of time which caused the society of the present to see these newly received people at their point of arrival, whilst they, the older generation, remembered them at their point of departure. And this was nothing new, for in the same way, when they themselves had first entered society, there were people in it who had just arrived and whose lowly origins others remembered. In society as it exists today a single generation suffices for the change which formerly over a period of centuries transformed a middle-class name like Colbert into an aristocratic one. And yet, from another point of view there was a certain truth in the comment; for, if the social position of individuals is liable to change (like the fortunes and the alliances and the hatreds of nations), so too are the most deeply rooted ideas and customs and among them even the idea that you cannot receive anybody who is not *chic*. Not only does snobbishness change in form, it might one day altogether disappear—like war itself—and radicals and Jews might become members of the Jockey. Some people, who in my own early days in society, giving grand dinner-parties with only such guests as the Princesse de Guermantes, the Duchesse de Guermantes and the Princesse de Parme, and themselves being entertained by these ladies with every show of respect, had been regarded, perhaps correctly, as among the most unimpeachable social figures of the time, had passed away without leaving any trace behind them. Possibly they were foreign diplomats, formerly *en poste* in Paris and now returned to their own countries. Perhaps a scandal, a suicide, an elopement had made it impossible for them to reappear in society; perhaps they were merely Germans. But their name owed its lustre only to their own vanished social position and was no longer borne by anyone in the fashionable world; if I mentioned them nobody knew whom I was talking about, if I spelt out the name the general assumption was that they were some sort of adventurers. People, on the other hand, who according to the social code with which I had been familiar ought not to have been at this party, were now to my great astonishment on terms of close friendship with women of the very best families and the latter had only submitted to the boredom of appearing at the Princesse de Guermantes's party for the sake of these new friends. For the most characteristic feature of this new society was the prodigious ease with which individuals moved up or down the social scale.

If in the eyes of the younger generations the Duchesse de Guermantes seemed to be of little account because she was acquainted with actresses and such people, the elder, the now old ladies of her family still considered her to be an extraordinary personage, partly because they knew and appreciated her birth, her heraldic pre-eminence, her intimate friendships with what Mme de Forcheville would have called "royalties", but even more because she despised the parties given by the family and was bored at them and her cousins knew that they could never count upon her attendance. Her connections with the theatrical and political worlds, in any case only vaguely known in the family, merely had the effect of enhancing her rarity and therefore her prestige. So that while in political and artistic society she was regarded as a creature whom it was hard to define, a sort of unfrocked priestess of the Faubourg Saint-Germain who consorted with Under-Secretaries of State and stars of the theatre, in the Faubourg Saint-Germain itself if one was giving an important evening party one would say: "Is it worth while even asking Oriane? She won't come. Perhaps one should, just for form's sake, but one knows what to expect." And if, at about half-past ten, in a dazzling costume and with a hard glint in her eyes which bore witness to her contempt for all her female cousins, Oriane made her entrance, pausing first on the threshold with a sort of majestic disdain, and remained for a whole hour, this was even more of a treat for the old and noble lady who was giving the party than it would have been in the past for a theatrical manager who had obtained a vague promise from Sarah Bernhardt that she would contribute something to a programme, had the great actress, contrary to all expectation, turned up and recited, in the most unaffected and obliging way, not the piece which she had promised but twenty others. For although all the women there were among the smartest in Paris, the presence of this Oriane who was addressed in a condescending manner by Under-Secretaries and continued none the less ("intelligence governs the world") to try to make the acquaintance of more and more of them, had had the effect which nothing could have achieved without her, of placing the dowager's evening party in a class apart from and above all the other dowagers' evening parties of the same "season" (to use another of those English expressions of which Mme de Forcheville was so fond) which she, Oriane, had not taken the trouble to attend.

As soon as I had finished talking to the Prince de Guermantes, Bloch seized hold of me and introduced me to a young woman who had heard a lot about me from the Duchesse de

Guermantes and who was one of the most fashionable women of the day. Not only was her name entirely unknown to me, but it appeared that those of the various branches of the Guermantes family could not be very familiar to her, for she enquired of an American woman how it was that Mme de Saint-Loup seemed to be on such intimate terms with all the most aristocratic people in the room. Now the American was married to the Comte de Farcy, an obscure cousin of the Forchevilles, for whom Forcheville was the grandest name in the world. So she replied ingenuously: "Well, isn't she a Forcheville by birth? And what could be grander than that?" But at least Mme de Farcy, though she naïvely believed the name of Forcheville to be superior to that of Saint-Loup, knew something about the latter. But to the charming lady who was a friend of Bloch and the Duchesse de Guermantes it was utterly unknown, and, being somewhat muddleheaded, she replied in all good faith to a young girl who asked her how Mme de Saint-Loup was related to their host, the Prince de Guermantes: "Through the Forchevilles," a piece of information which the girl passed on as if she had known it all her life to one of her friends, a bad-tempered and nervous girl, who turned as red as a turkey cock the first time a gentleman said to her that it was not through the Forchevilles that Gilberte was connected with the Guermantes, with the result that the gentleman supposed that he had made a mistake, adopted the erroneous explanation himself and lost no time in propagating it. For the American woman dinner parties and fashionable entertainments were a sort of Berlitz School. She heard the names and she repeated them, without having first learnt their precise value and significance. To someone who asked whether Tansonville had come to Gilberte from her father M. de Forcheville I heard the explanation given that, on the contrary, it was a property in her husband's family, that Tansonville

was a neighbouring estate to Guermantes and had belonged to Mme de Marsantes, that it had been heavily
mortgaged and the mortgage paid off with Gilberte's dowry.
And finally, a veteran of the old guard having exchanged
memories with me of Swann, friend of the Sagans and the
Mouchys, and Bloch's American friend having asked me how
I had known Swann, the old man declared that this must have
been in the house of Mme de Guermantes, not suspecting that
what Swann represented for me was a country neighbour and
a young friend of my grandfather. Mistakes of this kind have
been made by the most distinguished men and are regarded as
particularly serious in any society of a conservative temper.
Saint-Simon, wishing to show that Louis XIV was of an
ignorance which "sometimes made him fall, in public, into
the most gross absurdities", gives of this ignorance only two
examples, which are that the King, not knowing either that
Renel belonged to the family of Clermont-Gallerande or that
Saint-Herem belonged to that of Montmorin, treated these
two men as though they were of low extraction. But at least,
in so far as concerns Saint-Herem, we have the consolation of
knowing that the King did not die in error, for "very late in
life" he was disabused by M. de La Rochefoucauld. "Even
then," adds Saint-Simon with a touch of pity, "it was necessary
to explain to him what these houses were, for their names conveyed nothing to him."

This oblivion, which with its vigorous growth covers so
rapidly even the most recent past, this encroaching ignorance,
creates as its own counter-agent a minor species of erudition,
all the more precious for being rare, which is concerned with
genealogies, the true social position of people, the reasons of
love or money or some other kind for which they have allied
or misallied themselves in marriage with this family or that,
an erudition which is highly prized in all societies where a

conservative spirit rules, which my grandfather possessed in
the highest degree with regard to the upper middle classes of
Combray and of Paris and which Saint-Simon valued so highly
that when he comes to celebrate the marvellous intelligence
of the Prince de Conti, before speaking of the recognised
branches of knowledge, or rather as though this were the first
of them all, he praises him as "a man of a very fine mind,
luminous, just, exact, wide-ranging; vastly well read and of a
retentive memory; skilled in genealogies, their chimaeras and
their realities; of a politeness variously accommodated to rank
and merit, rendering all those courtesies that the princes of the
blood owe but no longer render and even explaining why he
acted as he did and how the other princes exceeded their rights.
The knowledge which he had gained from books and from
conversation afforded him material for the most obliging
comments possible upon the birth, the offices, etc." In a less
exalted sphere, in all that pertained to the bourgeois society of
Combray and Paris, my grandfather possessed this same knowledge with no less exactitude and savoured it with no less
relish. The epicures, the connoisseurs who knew that Gilberte
was not a Forcheville, that Mme de Cambremer had not been
born a Méséglise nor her nephew's young wife a Valentinois,
were already reduced in number. Reduced in number and perhaps not even recruited from among the highest aristocracy
(it is not necessarily among devout believers, or even among
Catholics of any kind, that you will find those who are most
learned on the subject of the *Golden Legend* or the stained
glass of the thirteenth century), but often from a minor aristocracy, whose scions have a keener appetite for the great
world which they themselves can but seldom approach and
which the little time that they spend in it leaves them all the
more leisure to study. Still, they meet together from time to
time and enjoy making each other's acquaintance and giving

succulent corporate dinners, like those of the Society of Biblio-
philes or the Friends of Rheims, at which the items on the
menu are genealogies. To these feasts wives are not admitted,
but the husbands, when they get home, remark: "A most interesting dinner. There was a M. de la Raspelière there who
kept us spell-bound with his explanation of how that Mme de
Saint-Loup with the pretty daughter is not really a Forcheville at all. It was as good as a novel."

The friend of Bloch and of the Duchesse de Guermantes
was not only beautifully dressed and charming, she was also
intelligent and conversation with her was agreeable, but for
me rendered difficult by the novelty to my ears of the names
not only of my interlocutress herself but also of most of the
people she talked about, although they were the very people
who formed the core of society today. The converse also was
true: at her request I related various anecdotes of the past, and
many of the names which I pronounced meant absolutely
nothing to her, they had all sunk into oblivion (all those at least
which had shone only with the individual brilliance of a single
person and were not the surname, permanent and generic, of
some famous aristocratic family, whose exact title even so the
young woman seldom knew, having perhaps recently mis-
heard a name at a dinner-party and proceeded to form quite
wrong ideas about its pedigree) and she had for the most part
never heard them mentioned, having, not merely because she
was young but because she had not lived in France for long
and when she first arrived had known nobody, only started to
go into society some years after I myself had withdrawn from
it. So that though for ordinary speech she and I used the same
language, when it came to names our vocabularies had nothing
in common. The name of Mme Leroi happened to fall from
my lips, and by chance, thanks to some elderly admirer, himself an old friend of Mme de Guermantes, my interlocutress

had heard of her. But only vaguely and inaccurately, as I saw from the contemptuous tone in which this snobbish young woman replied to me: "Yes, I know whom you mean by Mme Leroi, an old friend of Bergotte's, I believe," a tone which barely concealed the comment: "a woman whom I should never have wished to have in my house." I realised at once that the old friend of Mme de Guermantes, as a perfect man of the world imbued with the Guermantes spirit, one of the essential elements of which was not to appear to attach too much importance to aristocratic friendships, had thought it too stupid, too anti-Guermantes to say: "Mme Leroi, who was a friend of every Royalty and Duchess in Paris," and had preferred to say: "She could be quite amusing. Let me tell you the retort she made to Bergotte one day." But for people who are not already in the know information gleaned in this way from conversation is equivalent only to that which is doled out to the masses by the press and which makes them believe alternatively, depending upon the views of their newspaper, either that M. Loubet and M. Reinach are brigands or that they are great patriots. In the eyes of my interlocutress Mme Leroi had been something like Mme Verdurin as she was before her social transformation, but with less brilliance and with a little clan consisting of one member only, Bergotte. But at least this young woman, by pure chance, had heard the name of Mme Leroi, and she is one of the last of whom so much can be said. Today that name is utterly forgotten, nor is there any good reason why it should be remembered. It does not figure even in the index to the post-humous memoirs of Mme de Villeparisis, whose mind was so much occupied with the lady who bore it. And if the Marquise has omitted to mention Mme Leroi, this is less because in her life-time that lady had been scarcely friendly towards her than because, once she was dead, no one was likely to take any interest in her, it is a silence dictated less by the social resentment of a woman than by the literary tact of an author. My conversation with Bloch's fashionable friend was delightful, for she was an intelligent young woman; but this difference which I have described between our two vocabularies made it at the same time both awkward and instructive. For although we know that the years pass, that youth gives way to old age, that fortunes and thrones crumble (even the most solid among them) and that fame is transitory, the manner in which—by means of a sort of instantaneous photograph—we take cognisance of this moving universe whirled along by Time, has the contrary effect of immobilising it. And the result is that we see as always young the men and women whom we have known young, that those whom we have known old we retrospectively endow in the past with the virtues of old age, that we trust unreservedly in the credit of a millionaire and the influence of a reigning monarch, knowing with our reason, though we do not effectively believe, that tomorrow both the one and the other may be fugitives stripped of all power. In a more restricted field, one that is purely social—as in a simpler problem which initiates a student into difficulties that are more complex but of the same order—the unintelligibility which, in my conversation with the young woman, resulted from the fact that the two of us had lived in the same world but with an interval of twenty-five years between us, gave me the impression, and might have strengthened within me the sense, of History.

And indeed this ignorance of people's true social position which every ten years causes the new fashionable elect to arise in all the glory of the moment as though the past had never existed, which makes it impossible for an American woman just landed in Europe to see that in an age when Bloch was nobody M. de Charlus was socially supreme in Paris and that Swann, who laid himself out to please M. Bontemps, had him-

self been treated with every mark of friendship by the Prince
of Wales, this ignorance, which exists not only in new arrivals
but also in those who have always frequented adjacent but
distinct regions of society, is itself also invariably an effect—
but an effect operative not so much upon a whole social
stratum as within individuals—of Time. No doubt we ourselves may change our social habitat and our manner of life
and yet our memory, clinging still to the thread of our personal
identity, will continue to attach to itself at successive epochs
the recollection of the various societies in which, even if it be
forty-five years earlier, we have lived. Bloch the guest of the
Prince de Guermantes remembered perfectly well the humble
Jewish environment in which he had lived at the age of
eighteen, and Swann, when he was no longer in love with
Mme Swann but with a waitress at that same Colombin's
where at one time Mme Swann had thought it smart to go and
drink tea (as she did also at the tea-room in the Rue Royale),
Swann was very well aware of his own social value—he remembered Twickenham and had no doubt in his mind about the
reasons for which he chose to go to Colombin's rather than to
call on the Duchesse de Broglie, and he knew also that, had he
been a thousand times less "smart" than he was, he would not
have become the slightest bit smarter by frequenting Colombin's or the Ritz, since anybody can go to these places who
pays. And no doubt the friends, too, of Bloch or of Swann
remembered the little Jewish coterie or the invitations to
Twickenham and thus, as though they, the friends, were other
not very clearly defined "I's" of the two men, made no division in their memories between the fashionable Bloch of today
and the sordid Bloch of the past, between the Swann who in
his latter days could be seen at Colombin's and the Swann of
Buckingham Palace. But these friends were to some extent
Swann's neighbours in life, their own lives had developed

along lines near enough to his own for their memories to be fairly full of him, whereas other men who were more remote from Swann—at a greater distance measured not perhaps socially but in terms of intimacy, which caused their knowledge of him to be vaguer and their meetings with him rarer —possessed of him recollections that were less numerous and in consequence conceptions that were less fixed. And after thirty years a comparative stranger of this kind no longer has any precise recollection with the power to change the value of the person whom he has before his eyes by prolonging him into the past. In the last years of Swann's life I had heard people, even people in society, say when his name was mentioned, as though this had been his title to fame: "You mean the Swann who goes to Colombin's?" And now, with reference to Bloch, even those who ought to have known better might be heard to enquire: "The Guermantes Bloch? The Bloch who is such a friend of the Guermantes?" These errors which split a life in two and, by isolating his present from his past, turn some man whom one is talking about into another, a different man, a creation of yesterday, a man who is no more than the condensation of his current habits (whereas the real man bears within himself an awareness, linking him to the past, of the continuity of his life), these errors, though they too, as I have said, are a result of the passage of Time, are not a social phenomenon but one of memory. And at that very moment I was presented with an example, of a different variety, it is true, but all the more impressive for that, of this forgetfulness which modifies for us our image of a human being. Long ago a young nephew of Mme de Guermantes, the Marquis de Villemandois, had behaved towards me with a persistent insolence which had obliged me to retaliate by adopting an equally insulting attitude towards him, so that tacitly we had become as it were two enemies. This man, while I was engaged in my reflections upon Time at the Princesse de Guermantes's party, asked someone to introduce him to me, saying that he thought that I had known some of his family, that he had read articles of mine and wanted to make, or re-make, my acquaintance. Now it is true to say that with age he had become, like many others, serious instead of rude and frivolous and that he had lost much of his former arrogance, and it is also true that I was a good deal talked about now, though on the strength of some very slight articles, in the circles which he frequented. But these motives for his cordial-ity, for his making advances to me, were no more than acces-sory. The principal motive, or at least the one which permitted the others to come into play, was that—either because he had a worse memory than I or because in the past, since I was then for him a much less important personage than he for me, he had paid less attention to my ripostes than I to his attacks—he had completely forgotten our feud. At most my name re-called to him that he must have seen me, or some member of my family, in the house of one of his aunts. And being uncer-tain whether he was being introduced to me for the first time or whether we were old acquaintances, he made haste to talk to me about the aunt in whose house he was sure that we had met, remembering that my name had often been mentioned there and not remembering our quarrels. A name: that very often is all that remains for us of a human being, not only when he is dead, but sometimes even in his life-time. And our notions about him are so vague or so bizarre and correspond so little to those that he has of us that we have entirely for-gotten that we once nearly fought a duel with him but remem-ber that, when he was a child, he used to wear curious yellow gaiters in the Champs Elysées, where he, on the contrary, in spite of our assurances, has no recollection of ever having played with us.

Bloch had come bounding into the room like a hyena. "He is at home now," I thought, "in drawing-rooms into which twenty years ago he would never have been able to penetrate." But he was also twenty years older. He was nearer to death. What did this profit him? At close quarters, in the translucency of a face in which, at a greater distance or in a bad light, I saw only youthful gaiety (whether because it survived there or because I with my recollections evoked it), I could detect another face, almost frightening, racked with anxiety, the face of an old Shylock, waiting in the wings, with his make-up prepared, for the moment when he would make his entry onto the stage and already reciting his first line under his breath. In ten years, in drawing-rooms like this which their own feebleness of spirit would allow him to dominate, he would enter on crutches to be greeted as "the Master" for whom a visit to the La Trémoïlles was merely a tedious obligation. And what would this profit him?

From changes accomplished in society I was all the better able to extract important truths, worthy of being used as the cement which would hold part of my work together, for the reason that such changes were by no means, as at the first moment I might have been tempted to suppose, peculiar to the epoch in which we lived. At the time when I, myself only just "arrived"—newer even than Bloch at the present day— had made my first entry into the world of the Guermantes, I must have contemplated in the belief that they formed an integral part of that world elements that were in fact utterly foreign to it, recently incorporated and appearing strangely new to older elements from which I failed to distinguish them and which themselves, though regarded by the dukes of the day as members of the Faubourg from time immemorial, had in fact —if not themselves, then their fathers or their grandfathers— been the upstarts of an earlier age. So much so that it was not any inherent quality of "men of the best society" which made this world so brilliant, but rather the fact of being more or less completely assimilated to this world which out of people who fifty years later, in spite of their diverse origins, would all look very much the same, formed "men of the best society". Even in the past into which I pushed back the name of Guermantes in order to give it its full grandeur—and with good reason, for under Louis XIV the Guermantes had been almost royal and had cut a more splendid figure than they did today—the phenomenon which I was observing at this moment had not been unknown. The Guermantes of that time had allied themselves, for instance, with the family of Colbert, which today, it is true, appears to us in the highest degree aristocratic, since a Colbert bride is thought an excellent marriage even for a La Rochefoucauld. But it is not because the Colberts, then a purely bourgeois family, were aristocratic that the Guermantes had sought them in a matrimonial alliance, it was because of this alliance with the Guermantes that the Colberts became aristocratic. If the name of Haussonville should be extinguished with the present representative of that house, it will perhaps owe its future renown to the fact that the family today is descended from Mme de Staël, regardless of the fact that before the Revolution M. d'Haussonville, one of the first noblemen of the kingdom, found it gratifying to his vanity to be able to tell M. de Broglie that he was not acquainted with the father of that lady and was therefore no more in a position to present him at court than was M. de Broglie himself, neither of the two men for one moment suspecting that their own grandsons would later marry one the daughter and the other the grand-daughter of the authoress of *Corinne*. From the remarks of the Duchesse de Guermantes I realised that it would have been in my power to play the role of the fashionable commoner in grand society, the man whom everybody supposes to have been from his earliest days affiliated to the aristocracy, a role once played by Swann and before him by M. Lebrun and M. Ampère and all those friends of the Duchesse de Broglie who herself at the beginning of her career had by no means belonged to the best society. The first few times I had dined with Mme de Guermantes how I must have shocked men like M. de Beauserfeuil, less by my actual presence than by remarks indicating how entirely ignorant I was of the memories which constituted his past and which gave its form to the image that he had of society! Yet the day would come when Bloch, as a very old man, with recollections from a now distant past of the Guermantes drawing-room as it presented itself to his eyes at this moment, would feel the same astonishment, the same ill-humour in the presence of certain intrusions and certain displays of ignorance. And at the same time he would no doubt have developed and would radiate around him those qualities of tact and discretion which I had thought were the privilege of men like M. de Norpois but which, when their original avatars have vanished from the scene, form themselves again for a new incarnation in those of our acquaintance who seem of all people the least likely to possess them. It was true that my own particular case, the experience that I had had of being admitted to the society of the Guermantes, had appeared to me to be something exceptional. But as soon as I got outside myself and the circle of people by whom I was immediately surrounded, I could see that this was a social phenomenon less rare than I had at first supposed and that from the single fountain-basin of Combray in which I had been born there were in fact quite a number of jets of water which had risen, in symmetry with myself, above the liquid mass which had fed them. No doubt, since circumstances have always about them something of the particular and characters something of the individual, it was in an entirely different fashion that Legrandin (through his nephew's strange marriage) had in his turn penetrated into this exalted world, a fashion quite different to that in which Odette's daughter had married into it or those in which Swann long ago and I myself had reached it. Indeed to me, passing by shut up inside my own life so that I saw it only from within, Legrandin's life seemed to bear absolutely no resemblance to my own, the two seemed to have followed widely divergent paths, and in this respect I was like a stream which from the bottom of its own deep valley does not see another stream which proceeds in a different direction and yet, in spite of the great loops in its course, ends up as a tributary of the same river. But taking a bird's eye view, as the statistician does who, ignoring the reasons of sentiment or the avoidable imprudences which may have led some particular person to his death, counts merely the total number of those who have died in a year, I could see that quite a few individuals, starting from the same social *milieu*, the portrayal of which was attempted in the first pages of this work, had arrived finally in another *milieu* of an entirely different kind, and the probability is that, just as every year in Paris there take place an average number of marriages, so any other rich and cultivated middle-class *milieu* might have been able to show a roughly equal proportion of men who, like Swann and Legrandin and myself and Bloch, could be found at a later stage in their lives flowing into the ocean of "high society". Moreover, in their new surroundings they recognised each other, for if the young Comte de Cambremer won the admiration of society for his distinction, his refinement, his sober elegance, I myself was able to recognise in these qualities—and at the same time in his fine eyes and his ardent craving for social success—characteristics that were already present in his uncle Legrandin, who in spite of his aristocratic elegance of figure had been no more than a typical middle-class friend of my parents.

Kindness, a simple process of maturation which in the end sweetens characters originally more acid even than that of Bloch, is as widely disseminated as that belief in justice thanks to which, if our cause is good, we feel that we have no more to fear from a hostile judge than from one friendly towards us. And the grandchildren of Bloch would be kind and modest almost from birth. Bloch himself had perhaps not yet reached this stage of development. But I noticed that, whereas once he had pretended to think himself obliged to make a two hours' railway journey in order to visit someone who had scarcely even asked him to come, now that he was flooded with invitations not only to lunch and to dine but to stay for a fortnight here and a fortnight there, he refused many of them and did this without telling people, without bragging that he had received and refused them. Discretion, both in action and in speech, had come to him with social position and with longevity, with, if one may use the expression, a sort of social longevity. No doubt in the past Bloch had lacked discretion, just as he had been incapable of kindness and devoid of good sense. But certain defects, certain qualities are attached less to this or that individual than to this or that moment of existence considered from the social point of view. One may almost say that they are external to individuals, who merely pass beneath the radiance that they shed as beneath so many solstices, varying in their nature but all pre-existent, general and unavoidable. In the same way a doctor who is trying to find out whether some medicine diminishes or augments the acidity of the stomach, whether it activates or inhibits its secretions, will obtain results which differ not according to the stomach from whose secretions he has removed a small quantity of gastric juice, but according to the more or less advanced stage in the process of ingestion of the drug at which he conducts the experiment.

To return to the name of Guermantes, considered as an agglomeration of all the names which it admitted into itself and into its immediate neighbourhood, at every moment of its duration it suffered losses and recruited fresh ingredients, like a garden in which from week to week flowers scarcely in bud and preparing to take the places of those that have already begun to wither are confounded with the latter in a mass which presents always the same appearance, except to the people who have not seen the newest blooms before and still preserve in their memories a precise image of the ones that are no longer there.

More than one of the men and women who had been brought together by this party, or of whose existence it had reminded me by evoking for me the aspects which he or she had in turn presented as from the midst of different, perhaps opposite circumstances one after another they had risen before me, brought vividly before my mind the varied aspects of my own life and its different perspectives, just as a feature in a landscape, a hill or a large country house, by appearing now on the right hand and now on the left and seeming first to dominate a forest and then to emerge from a valley, reveals to a traveller the changes in direction and the differences in altitude of the road along which he is passing. As I followed the stream of memory back towards its source, I arrived eventually at images of a single person separated from one another by an interval of time so long, preserved within me by "I's" that were so distinct and themselves (the images) fraught with meanings that were so different, that ordinarily when I surveyed (as I supposed) the whole past course of my relations with that particular person I omitted these earliest images and had even ceased to think that the person to whom they referred was the same as the one whom I had later got to know, so that I needed a fortuitous lightning-flash of attention before I could re-attach this latter-day acquaintance, like a word to its etymology, to the primitive significance which he or she had once possessed for me. Mlle Swann, on the other side of the hedge of pink hawthorn, throwing me a look, a look of which, as a matter of fact, I had been obliged retrospectively to re-touch the significance, having learnt that it was a look of desire; Mme Swann's lover—or the man who according to Combray gossip occupied that position—studying me from behind that same hedge with an air of disapproval which, in this case too, had not the meaning which I had ascribed to it at the time, and then later so changed that I had quite failed to recognise him as the gentleman at Balbec examining a poster outside the Casino, the man of whom, when once every ten years I happened to remember that first image, I would say to myself: "How strange! That, though I did not know it, was M. de Charlus!"; Mme de Guermantes at the marriage of Dr. Percepied's daughter; Mme Swann in a pink dress in my great-uncle's study; Mme de Cambremer, Legrandin's sister, so fashionable that he was terrified that we might ask him to give us an introduction to her—all these images and many others associated with Swann, Saint-Loup and others of my friends were like illustrations which sometimes, when I chanced to come across them, I amused myself by placing as frontispieces on the threshold of my relations with these various people, but always with the feeling that they were no more than images, not something deposited within me by this particular person, not something still in any way linked to him. Not only do some people have good memories and others bad (without going so far as that perpetual oblivion which is the native element of such creatures as the Turkish Ambas-sadress, thanks to which—one piece of news having evaporated by the end of the week or the next piece having the power to exorcise its predecessor—they are always able to find room in

their minds for the news that contradicts what they have previously been told), we find also that two people with an equal
endowment of memory do not remember the same things.
One of two men, for instance, will have paid little attention to
an action for which the other will long continue to feel great
remorse, but will have seized on the other hand upon some
random remark which his friend let fall almost without thinking and taken it to be the key to a sympathetic character.
Again, the fact that we prefer not to be proved wrong when
we have uttered a false prophecy cuts short the duration of our
memory of such prophecies and permits us very soon to affirm
that we never uttered them. Finally, preferences of a more
profound and more disinterested kind diversify the memories
of different people, so that a poet, for example, who has almost
entirely forgotten certain facts which someone else is able to
recall will, nevertheless, have retained—what for him is more
important—a fleeting impression. The effect of all these
causes is that after twenty years of absence where one expected
to find rancour one finds often involuntary and unconscious
pardon, but sometimes also we stumble upon a bitterness for
which (because we have ourselves forgotten some bad impression that we once made) we can provide no reasonable explanation. Even where the people whom we have known best
are concerned, we soon forget the dates of the various episodes
in their lives. And because it was at least twenty years since
she had first set eyes on Bloch, Mme de Guermantes would
have sworn that he had been born in the world to which
she herself belonged and had been dandled on the knees
of the Duchesse de Chartres when he was two years
old.

How often had all these people re-appeared before me in
the course of their lives, the diverse circumstances of which
seemed to present the same individuals always, but in forms and

for purposes that were shifting and varied! And the diversity of the points in my life through which, like so many interwoven threads, those of each of these personages had passed had in the end brought into conjunction even those that seemed the furthest apart from one another, as though for the execution of infinitely varied patterns life possessed only a limited number of threads. What, for instance, in my various pasts, could be more widely separated than my visits to my great-uncle Adolphe, the nephew of Mme de Villeparisis who was herself a cousin of the Marshal, Legrandin and his sister, and the former tailor who lived in our courtyard and was a friend of Françoise? And yet today all these different threads had been woven together to form the fabric, there of the married lives of Robert and Gilberte Saint-Loup, here of the young Cambremer couple, not to mention Morel and all the others whose conjunction had played a part in forming a set of circumstances of such a nature that the circumstances seemed to me to be the complete unity and each individual actor in them merely a constituent part of the whole. And by now my life had lasted so long that not infrequently, when it brought a person to my notice, I was able, by rummaging in quite different regions of my memory, to find another person, unlike though with the same identity, to add to and complete the first. Even to the Elstirs which I saw hanging here in a position which was itself an indication of his glory I was able to add very ancient memories of the Verdurins, the Cottards, my first conversation with the painter in the restaurant at Rivebelle, the tea-party in his studio at which I had been introduced to Albertine, and a host of other memories as well. Thus a connoisseur of painting who is shown one wing of an altarpiece remembers in what church or which museums or whose private collection the other fragments of the same work are dispersed and, in the same way as by studying the catalogues of sales and haunting the shops of the antique-dealers he finds, in the end, some object which is a twin to one he already possesses and makes a pair with it, he is able to reconstruct in his mind the predella and the whole altar as they once were. And just as a bucket being hauled up by a winch swings first against one side of the descending rope and then against the other until it has touched it at every point, so there was scarcely a character, scarcely even a thing which had found a place in my life and had not turn and turn about played in it a whole series of different roles. If after an interval of several years I rediscovered in my memory a mere social acquaintance or even a physical object, I perceived that life all this while had been weaving round person or thing a tissue of diverse threads which ended by covering them with the beautiful and inimitable velvety patina of the years, just as in an old park a simple runnel of water comes with the passage of time to be enveloped in a sheath of emerald.

It was not merely the outward appearance of these people that made one think of them as people in a dream. In their inward experience too life, which already when they were young, when they were in love, had been not far from sleep, had now more and more become a dream. They had forgotten even their resentments, their hatreds, and in order to be certain that the person before them was the one with whom ten years earlier they had not been on speaking terms they would have had to consult some mnemonic register, but one which, unfortunately, was as vague as a dream in which one has been insulted one does not quite know by whom. All these dreams together formed the substance of the apparent contradictions of political life, where one saw as colleagues in a government men who had once accused each other of murder or treason. And this dreamlike existence became as torpid as death in certain old men on the days that followed any day on which they had chanced to make love. During those days it was useless to make any demands on the President of the Republic, he had forgotten everything. Then, if he was left in peace for a day or two, the memory of public affairs slowly returned to him, as haphazard as the memory of a dream.

Sometimes it was not merely in a single vivid image that the stranger so unlike the man or woman whom I had later come to know had first appeared before me. For years I had thought of Bergotte as the sweet singer with the snowy locks, for years my limbs had been paralysed, as though I had seen a ghost, by the apparition of Swann's grey top-hat or his wife's violet cloak, or by the mystery with which, even in a drawing-room, the name of her race enveloped the Duchesse de Guermantes; with all these, and with others too, my relations, which in the sequel were to become so commonplace, had had their origin almost in legend, in a delightful mythology which still at a later date prolonged them into the past as into some Olympian heaven where they shone with the luminous brilliance of a comet's tail. And even those of my acquaintanceships which had not begun in mystery, that for instance with Mme de Souvré, so arid today, so purely social in its nature, had preserved among their earliest moments the memory of a first smile calmer and sweeter than anything that was to follow, a smile mellifluously traced in the fullness of an afternoon beside the sea or the close of a spring day in Paris, a day of clattering carriages, of dust rising from the streets and sunny air gently stirring like water. And perhaps Mme de Souvré, had she been removed from this frame, would have been of little significance, like those famous buildings—the Salute, for example—which, without any great beauty of their own, are so well suited to a particular setting that they compel our admiration, but she formed part of a bundle of memories which I valued "all in", as the auctioneers say, at a certain price, without stopping to ask exactly how much of this value appertained to the lady herself.

One thing struck me even more forcibly in all these people than the physical or social changes which they had undergone, and this was the modification in the ideas which they possessed of one another. Legrandin in the past had despised Bloch and never addressed a word to him. Now he went out of his way to be civil. And this was not because of the improvement which had taken place in Bloch's social position—were this the case the fact would scarcely be worthy of mention, for social changes inevitably bring in their train a new pattern of relationships among those who have been affected by them. No: the reason was that people—and in saying "people" I mean "what people are for us"—do not in our memory possess the unvariability of a figure in a painting. Oblivion is at work within us, and according to its arbitrary operation they evolve. Sometimes it even happens that after a time we confuse one person with another. "Bloch? Oh yes, he was someone who used to come to Combray," and when he says Bloch, the speaker is in fact referring to me. Conversely, Mme Sazerat was firmly persuaded that it was I who was the author of a certain historical study of Philip II which was in fact by Bloch. More commonly, you forget after a while how odiously someone has behaved towards you, you forget his faults of character and your last meeting with him when you parted without shaking hands, and you remember on the other hand an earlier occasion when you got on excellently together. And it was to an earlier occasion of this kind that the manners of Legrandin adverted in his new civility towards Bloch, whether because he had lost the recollection of a particular past or because he thought it was to be deliberately eschewed, from a mixture of forgiveness and oblivion and that indifference which is another effect of Time. And then, as we have seen, the memories which two people preserve of each other, even in love, are not the same. I had seen Albertine reproduce with perfect accuracy some remark which I had made to her at one of our first meetings and which I had entirely forgotten. Of some other incident, lodged for ever in my head like a pebble flung with force, she had no recollection. Our life together was like one of those garden walks where, at intervals on either side of the path, vases of flowers are placed symmetrically but not opposite to one another. And if this discrepancy of memories may be observed even in the relation of love, even more understandable is it that when your acquaintance with someone has been slight you should scarcely remember who he is or should remember not what you used to think of him but something different, perhaps something that dates from an earlier epoch or that is suggested by the people in whose midst you have met him again, who may only recently have got to know him and see him therefore endowed with good qualities and a social prestige which in the past he did not possess but which you, having forgotten the past, instantly accept.

No doubt life, by placing each of these people on my path a number of times, had presented them to me in particular circumstances which, enclosing them finally on every side, had restricted the view which I had of them and so prevented me from discovering their essence. For between us and other people there exists a barrier of contingencies, just as in my hours of reading in the garden at Combray I had realised that in all perception there exists a barrier as a result of which there is never absolute contact between reality and our intelligence. Even those Guermantes around whom I had built such a vast fabric of dream had appeared to me, when at last I had first approached two of them, one in the guise of an old friend of my grandmother and the other in that of a gentleman who had looked at me in a most disagreeable

372

manner one morning in the gardens of the Casino. So that it was in each case only in retrospect, by reuniting the individual to the name, that my encounter with them had been an encounter with the Guermantes. And yet perhaps this in itself made life more poetic for me, the thought that the mysterious race with the piercing eyes and the beak of a bird, the unapproachable rose-coloured, golden race, had so often and so naturally, through the effect of blind and varied circumstances, chanced to offer itself to my contemplation, to admit me to the circle of its casual and even of its intimate friends, to such a point that when I had wanted to get to know Mlle de Stermaria or to have dresses made for Albertine, it was to one or another of the Guermantes, as being the most obliging of my friends, that I had appealed for help. Admittedly I was bored when I went to their houses, no less bored than I was in the houses of the other society people whom I had later come to know. And in the case of the Duchesse de Guermantes, as in that of certain pages of Bergotte, even her personal charm was visible to me only at a distance and vanished as soon as I was near her, for the reason that it resided in my memory and my imagination. But still, in spite of everything, the Guermantes—and in this respect Gilberte resembled them—differed from other society people in that they plunged their roots more deeply into my past life, down to a level at which I had dreamed more and had had more belief in individuals. Bored I may have been as I stood talking this afternoon to Gilberte or Mme de Guermantes, but at least as I did so I held within my grasp those of the imaginations of my childhood which I had found most beautiful and thought most inaccessible and, like a shopkeeper who cannot balance his books, I could console myself by forgetting the value of their actual possession and remembering the price which had once been attached to them by my desire. But with other people I had not even this consolation, people however with whom my relations had at one time been swollen to an immense importance by dreams that were even more ardent and formed without hope, dreams into which my life of those days, dedicated entirely to them, had so richly poured itself that I could scarcely understand how their fulfilment could be merely this thin, narrow, colourless ribbon of an indifferent and despised intimacy, in which I could rediscover nothing of what had once been their mystery, their fever and their sweetness.

"What has become of the Marquise d'Arpajon?" enquired Mme de Cambremer. "She died," replied Bloch. "Aren't you confusing her with the Comtesse d'Arpajon, who died last year?" The Princesse d'Agrigente joined in the discussion; as the young widow of an old husband who had been very rich and the bearer of a great name she was much sought in marriage, and this had given her great self-assurance. "The Marquise d'Arpajon is dead too," she said, "she died nearly a year ago." "A year ago!" exclaimed Mme de Cambremer, "that can't be right, I was at a musical party in her house less than a year ago." Bloch was as incapable as any young man about town of making a useful contribution to the subject under discussion, for all these deaths of elderly people were at too great a distance, from the young men because of the enormous difference in age and from a man like Bloch, because of his recent arrival in an unfamiliar society, by way of an oblique approach, at a moment when it was already declining into a twilight which was for him illumined by no memories of its past. And even for people of the same age and the same social background death had lost its significance of strangeness. Hardly a day passed without their having to send to enquire for news of friends and relations *in articulo mortis*, some of whom, they would be told, had recovered

374

while others had "succumbed", until a point was reached where they no longer very clearly remembered whether this or that person who was no longer seen anywhere had "pulled through" his pneumonia or had expired. In these regions of advanced age death was everywhere at work and had at the same time become more indefinite. And in this drawing-room where two generations and two societies met and intersected, all of them for different reasons so ill placed for distinguishing death that they almost confused it with life, the former of these two conditions had been turned into a social incident, an attribute to be predicated of somebody to a greater or less degree, without the tone of voice in which it was mentioned in any way indicating that for the person in question this "incident" was the end of everything. I heard people say: "But you forget that so and so is dead," exactly as they might have said "he has had a decoration" or "he has been elected to the Academy" or—and these last two happenings had much the same effect as death, since they too prevented a man from going to parties—"he is spending the winter on the Riviera" or "his doctor has sent him to the mountains." Perhaps, where a man was well known, what he left behind him at his death helped others to remember that his existence had come to an end. But in the case of ordinary society people of an advanced age it was easy to make a mistake as to whether or no they were dead, not only because one knew little about their past or had forgotten it but because they were in no way whatever linked to the future. And the difficulty that was universally experienced in these cases in choosing from among the alternatives of illness, absence, retirement to the country and death the one that happened to be correct, sanctioned and confirmed not merely the indifference of the survivors but the insignificance of the departed.

"But if she is still alive, why is it that one never sees her anywhere now, nor her husband either?" asked an unmarried woman, who liked to make what she supposed was witty conversation. "For the obvious reason," replied her mother, who in spite of her years never missed a party herself, "that they are old; when you get to that age you stay at home." Before you got to the cemetery, it seemed, there was a whole closed city of the old, where the lamps always glimmered in the fog. Mme de Sainte-Euverte cut short the debate by saying that the Comtesse d'Arpajon had died in the previous year after a long illness and that more recently the Marquise d'Arpajon had also died, very rapidly, "in some quite unremarkable way," a death which, in virtue of this latter characteristic, resembled the lives of all these people (its unremarkableness explained too why it had passed unnoticed and excused those who had been in doubt). When she heard that Mme d'Arpajon really had died, the unmarried woman cast an anxious glance at her mother, for she feared that the news of the death of one of her "contemporaries" might "be a blow" to her—indeed she already imagined people talking about her mother's death and explaining it in this way: "Madame d'Arpajon's death had been a *great blow* to her." But the old lady on the contrary, far from justifying her daughter's fears, felt every time someone of her own age "disappeared" that she had gained a victory in a contest against formidable competitors. Their deaths were the only fashion in which she still for a moment became agreeably conscious of her own life. The unmarried woman noticed that her mother, who had seemed not displeased to remark that Mme d'Arpajon was one of those tired old people whose days are spent in homes from which they seldom emerge, had been even less displeased to learn that the Marquise had entered the city of hereafter, the home from which none of us ever emerges at all. This observation of her mother's want of feeling amused the daughter's sarcastic mind. And to make her own "contemporaries" laugh she gave them afterwards a comical account of the gleeful fashion in which her mother had said, rubbing her hands: "Gracious me, it appears to be true that poor Madame d'Arpajon is dead." Even the people who did not need this death to make them feel any joy in being alive, were rendered happy by it. For every death is for others a simplification of life, it spares them the necessity of showing gratitude, the obligation of paying calls. And yet this was not the manner in which Elstir had received the news of the death of M. Verdurin.

A lady left the room, for she had other afternoon parties to attend, and had also received the commands of two queens to take tea with them. It was the Princesse de Nassau, that great courtesan of the aristocratic world whom I had known in the past. Were it not that she had shrunk in height (which gave her, her head being now situated at a much lower elevation than formerly, an air of having "one foot in the grave"), one could scarcely have said that she had aged. She had remained a Marie Antoinette with an Austrian nose and an enchanting glance, preserved, one might almost say embalmed, by a thousand cosmetics adorably blended so as to compose for her a face that was the colour of lilac. Over this face there floated that confused and tender expression which I remembered, which was at once an allusion to all the fashionable gatherings where she was expected and an intimation that she was obliged to leave, that she promised sweetly to return, that she would slip away without any fuss. Born almost on the steps of a throne, three times married, richly kept for years at a time by great bankers, not to mention the thousand caprices in which she had permitted herself to indulge, she bore lightly beneath her gown, mauve like her wonderful round eyes and her painted face, the slightly tangled memories of the innumerable incidents of her life. As she passed near me, making her discreet exit, I bowed to her. She recognised me, took my hand and pressed it, and fixed upon me the round mauve pupils which seemed to say: "How long it is since we have seen each other! We must talk about all that another time." Her pressure of my hand became a squeeze, for she had a vague idea that one evening in her carriage, when she had offered to drop me at my door after a party at the Duchesse de Guermantes's, there might have been an embrace between us. Just to be on the safe side, she seemed to allude to something that had in fact never happened, but this was hardly difficult for her since a strawberry tart could send her into an ecstasy and whenever she had to leave a party before the end of a piece of music she put on a despairing air of tender, yet not final, farewell. But she was uncertain what had passed between us in the carriage, so she did not linger long over the furtive pressure of my hand and said not a word. She merely looked at me in the manner which I have described, the manner which signified: "How long it is!" and in which one caught a momentary glimpse of her husbands and the men who had kept her and two wars, while her stellar eyes, like an astronomical clock cut in a block of opal, marked successively all those solemn hours of a so distant past which she rediscovered every time she wanted to bid you a casual good-bye which was always also an apology. And then having left me, she started to trot towards the door, partly so that her departure should not inconvenience people, partly to show me that if she had not stopped to talk it was because she was in a hurry, partly also to recapture the seconds which she had lost in pressing my hand and so arrive on time at the Queen of Spain's, where she was to have tea alone with the Queen. I even thought, when she got near the door, that she was going to break into a gallop. And indeed she was galloping towards her grave.

A stout lady came up to me and greeted me, and during the few moments that she was speaking the most diverse thoughts jostled each other in my mind. I hesitated an instant to reply to her, for I was afraid that possibly, recognising people no better than I did, she might have mistaken my identity, but then the assurance of her manner caused me on the contrary, for fear that she might be someone whom I had known extremely well, to exaggerate the amiability of my smile, while my eyes continued to scan her features for some trace of the name which eluded me. As a candidate for a degree fixes his eyes upon the examiner's face in the vain hope of finding there the answer that he would do better to seek in his own memory, so, still smiling, I fixed my eyes upon the features of the stout lady. They seemed to be those of Mme Swann, and there crept into my smile the appropriate shade of respect, while my indecision began to subside. But a moment later I heard the stout lady say: "You took me for Mama, and it's quite true that I'm beginning to look very like her." And I recognised Gilberte.

We had a long talk about Robert, Gilberte speaking of him in an almost reverent tone, as though he had been a superior being whom she was anxious to show me that she had admired and understood. We recalled to one another the ideas which he had expounded in the past upon the art of war (for he had often repeated to her at Tansonville the arguments that I had heard him develop at Doncières and elsewhere) and we marvelled how often, and on how many different points, his views had been proved correct by the events of the late war.

"I cannot tell you," I said, "how struck I am now by even the least of the things that I heard him say at Doncières and also during the war. Almost the last remark that he ever made to me, just before we said good-bye for the last time, was that he expected to see Hindenburg, a Napoleonic general, fight one of the types of the Napoleonic battle, the one which aims at driving a wedge between two hostile armies—perhaps, he had added, the English and ourselves. Now scarcely a year after Robert was killed, a critic for whom he had a profound admiration and who manifestly exercised a great influence upon his military ideas, M. Henry Bidou, was saying that the Hindenburg offensive of March 1918 was 'the battle of separation fought by a single concentrated army against two armies in extended formation, a manœuvre which the Emperor executed successfully in the Apennines in 1796 but in which he failed in Belgium in 1815.' In the course of the same conversation Robert had compared battles to plays in which it is not always easy to know what the author has intended, in which perhaps the author himself has changed his plan in mid-campaign. Now admittedly, to take this same German offensive of 1918, had Robert interpreted it in this fashion he would not have been in agreement with M. Bidou. But other critics believe that it was Hindenburg's success in the direction of Amiens, followed by his check there, then his success in Flanders and then another check, which, by virtue really of a series of accidents, made first of Amiens and then of Boulogne objectives which he had not fixed upon before the engagement began. And as every critic can refashion a play or a campaign in his own way, there are some who see in this offensive the prelude to a lightning attack upon Paris and others a succession of uncoordinated hammer-blows intended to destroy the English army. And even if the orders actually given by the commander do not fit in with this or that conception of his plan, the critics will always be at liberty to say, as the actor Mounet-Sully said to Coquelin when the latter assured him that *Le Misanthrope* was not the gloomy melodrama that he wanted to make it (for Molière himself, according to the evidence of contemporaries, gave a comical interpretation of the part and played it for laughs): 'Well, Molière was wrong.' "

"And when aeroplanes first started"—it was Gilbert's turn now—"you remember what he used to say (he had such charming expressions): 'Every army will have to be a hundred-eyed Argus'? Alas, he never lived to see his prediction fulfilled!" "Oh! yes, he did," I replied, "he saw the battle of the Somme and he knew that it began with blinding the enemy by gouging out his eyes, by destroying his aeroplanes and his captive balloons." "Yes, that is true. And then," she went on, for now that she "lived only for the mind" she had become a little pedantic, "he maintained that we return always to the methods of the ancients. Well, do you realise that the Mesopotamian campaigns of this war" (she must have read this comparison at the time in Brichot's articles) "recall at every moment, almost without alteration, Xenophon's *Anabasis*? And that to get from the Tigris to the Euphrates the English command made use of the *bellam*, the long narrow boat—the gondola of the country—which was already being used by the Chaldeans at the very dawn of history." These words did indeed give me a sense of that stagnation of the past through which in certain parts of the world, by virtue of a sort of specific gravity, it is indefinitely immobilised, so that it can be found after centuries exactly as it was. But I must admit that, because of the books which I had read at Balbec at no great distance from Robert himself, I myself had been more impressed first in the fighting in France to come again upon those "trenches" that were familiar to me from the pages of Mme de Sevigné and then in the Middle East, apropos of the siege of Kut-el-Amara (Kut-of-the-Emir, "just as we say Vaux-le-Vicomte or Bailleau-l'Evêque", as the curé of Combray would have said had he extended his thirst for etymologies to the languages of the

East), to see the name of Baghdad once more attended closely by that of Basra, which is the Bassorah so many times mentioned in the *Thousand and One Nights*, the town which, whenever he had left the capital or was returning thither, was used as his port of embarkation or disembarkation, long before the days of General Townshend and General Gorringe, when the Caliphs still reigned, by no less a personage than Sindbad the Sailor.

"There is one aspect of war," I continued, "which I think Robert was beginning to comprehend: war is human, it is something that is lived like a love or a hatred and could be told like the story of a novel, and consequently, if anyone goes about repeating that strategy is a science, it won't help him in the least to understand war, since war is not a matter of strategy. The enemy has no more knowledge of our plans than we have of the objective pursued by the woman whom we love, and perhaps we do not even know what these plans are ourselves. Did the Germans in their offensive of March 1918 aim at capturing Amiens? We simply do not know. Perhaps they did not know themselves, perhaps it was what happened—their advance in the west towards Amiens—that determined the nature of their project. And even if war were scientific, it would still be right to paint it as Elstir painted the sea, by reversing the real and the apparent, starting from illusions and beliefs which one then slowly brings into line with the truth, which is the manner in which Dostoievsky tells the story of a life. Quite certainly, however, war is not strategic, it might better be described as a pathological condition, because it admits of accidents which even a skilled physician could not have foreseen, such as the Russian Revolution."

Throughout this conversation Gilberte had spoken of Robert with a deference which seemed to be addressed more to my sometime friend than to her late husband. It was as though she were saying to me: "I know how much you admired him. Please believe that I too understand what a wonderful person he was." And yet the love which she assuredly no longer had for his memory was perhaps the remote cause of certain features of her present life. Thus Gilberte now had an inseparable friend in Andrée. And although the latter was beginning, thanks largely to her husband's talent and her own intelligence, to penetrate, if not into the society of the Guermantes, at least into circles infinitely more fashionable than those in which she had formerly moved, people were astonished that the Marquise de Saint-Loup should condescend to be her closest friend. The friendship was taken to be a sign in Gilberte of her penchant for what she supposed was an artistic existence and for what was, unequivocally, a social decline. This explanation may be the true one. But another occurred to me, convinced as I had always been that the images which we see anywhere assembled are generally the reflection, or in some indirect fashion an effect, of a first group of different images—quite unlike the second and at a great distance from it, though the two groups are symmetrical. If night after night one saw Andrée and her husband and Gilberte in each other's company, I wondered whether this was not because, so many years earlier, one might have seen Andrée's future husband first living with Rachel and then leaving her for Andrée. Very likely Gilberte at the time, in the too remote, too exalted world in which she lived, had known nothing of this. But she must have learned of it later, when Andrée had climbed and she herself had descended enough to be aware of each other's existence. And when this happened she must have felt very strongly the prestige of the woman for whom Rachel had been abandoned by the man— the no doubt fascinating man—whom she, Rachel, had preferred to Robert. So perhaps the sight of Andrée recalled to Gilberte the youthful romance that her love for Robert had been, and inspired in her a great respect for Andrée, who even now retained the affections of a man so loved by that Rachel whom Gilberte felt to have been more deeply loved by Saint-Loup than she had been herself. But perhaps on the contrary these recollections played no part in Gilberte's fondness for the artistic couple, and one would have been right to see in her conduct, as many people did, an instance merely of those twin tastes, so often inseparable in society women, for culture and loss of caste. Perhaps Gilberte had forgotten Robert as completely as I had forgotten Albertine, and even, if she knew that Rachel was the woman whom the man of many talents had left for Andrée, never when she saw them thought about this fact which had in no way influenced her liking for them. Whether my alternative explanation was not merely possible but true was a question that could be determined only by appeal to the testimony of the parties themselves, the sole recourse which is open in such a case—or would be if they were able to bring to their confidences both insight and sincerity. But the first of these is rare in the circumstances and the second unknown. Whatever the true explanation of this friendship might be, the sight of Rachel, now a celebrated actress, could not be very agreeable to Gilberte. So I was sorry to hear that she was going to recite some poetry at this party, the programme announced being Musset's *Le Souvenir* and some fables of La Fontaine.

In the background one could hear the Princesse de Guermantes repeating excitedly, in a voice which because of her false teeth was like the rattle of old iron: "Yes, that's it, we will forgather! We will summon the clan! I love this younger generation, so intelligent, so ready to join in! Ah!" (to a young woman) "what a mujishun you are!" And she fixed her great monocle in her round eye, with an expression half of amusement, half of apology for her inability to sustain gaiety for any length of time, though to the very end she was determined to "join in" and "forgather".

"But how do you come to be at a party of this size?" Gilberte asked me. "To find you at a great slaughter of the innocents like this doesn't at all fit in with my picture of you. In fact, I should have expected to see you anywhere rather than at one of my aunt's kettle-drums, because of course she is my aunt," she added meaningly, for having become Mme de Saint-Loup at a slightly earlier date than that of Mme Verdurin's entry into the family she thought of herself as a Guermantes from the beginning of time and therefore attainted by the misalliance which her uncle had contracted when he married Mme Verdurin, a subject, it is true, on which she had heard a thousand sarcastic remarks made in her presence by members of the family, while naturally it was only behind her back that they discussed the misalliance which Saint-Loup had contracted when he married her. The disdain that she affected for this pinchbeck aunt was not diminished by the fact that the new Princesse de Guermantes, from the sort of perversity which drives intelligent people to behave unconventionally, from the need also to reminisce which is common in old people, and in the hope lastly of conferring a past on her new fashionable status, was fond of saying when the name of Gilberte arose in conversation: "Of course I have known her for donkey's years, I used to see a lot of the child's mother; why, she was a great friend of my cousin Marsantes. And it was in my house that she got to know Gilberte's father. And poor Saint-Loup too, I knew all his family long before he married her, indeed his uncle was one of my dearest friends in the La Raspelière days." "You see," people would say to me, hearing the Princesse de Guermantes talk in this vein, "the Verdurins were not at all bohemian, they had always been friends of Mme de Saint-Loup's family." I was perhaps alone in knowing, through my grandfather, how true it was that the Verdurins were not bohemian. But this was hardly because they had known Odette. However, you can easily dress up stories about a past with which no one is any longer familiar, just as you can about travels in a country where no one has ever been. "But really," Gilberte concluded, "since you sometimes emerge from your ivory tower, wouldn't you prefer little intimate gatherings which I could arrange, with just a few intelligent and sympathetic people? These great formal affairs are not made for you at all. I saw you a moment ago talking to my aunt Oriane, who has all the good qualities in the world, but I don't think one is doing her an injustice, do you, if one says that she scarcely belongs to the aristocracy of the mind."

I was unable to acquaint Gilberte with the thoughts which had been passing through my mind for the last hour, but it occurred to me that, simply on the level of distraction, she might be able to minister to my pleasures, which, as I now foresaw them, would no more be to talk literature with the Duchesse de Guermantes than with Mme de Saint-Loup. Certainly it was my intention to resume next day, but this time with a purpose, a solitary life. So far from going into society, I would not even permit people to come and see me at home during my hours of work, for the duty of writing my book took precedence now over that of being polite or even kind. They would insist no doubt, these friends who had not seen me for years and had now met me again and supposed that I was restored to health, they would want to come when the labour of their day or of their life was finished or interrupted, or at such times as they had the same need of me that I in the past had had of Saint-Loup; for (as I had already observed at Combray when my parents chose to reproach me at those very moments when, though they did not know it, I had just formed the most praiseworthy resolutions) the internal time-pieces which are allotted to different human beings are by no means synchronised: one strikes the hour of rest while another is striking that of work, one, for the judge, that of punishment when already for the criminal that of repentance and self-perfection has long since struck. But I should have the courage to reply to those who came to see me or tried to get me to visit them that I had, for necessary business which required my immediate attention, an urgent, a supremely important appointment with myself. And yet I was aware that, though there exists but little connection between our veritable self and the other one, nevertheless, because they both go under the same name and share the same body, the abnegation which involves making a sacrifice of easier duties and even of pleasures appears to other people to be egotism.

Was it not, surely, in order to concern myself with them that I was going to live apart from these people who would complain that they did not see me, to concern myself with them in a more fundamental fashion than would have been possible in their presence, to seek to reveal them to themselves, to realise their potentialities? What use would it have been that, for a few more years, I should waste hour after hour at evening parties pursuing the scarce expired echo of other people's remarks with the no less vain and fleeting sound of my own, for the sterile pleasure of a social contact which precluded all penetration beneath the surface? Was it not more worthwhile that I should attempt to describe the curves, to educe the laws which governed these gestures that they made, these remarks that they uttered, their very lives and natures? Unfortunately, I should have to struggle against that habit of putting oneself in another person's place which, if it favours the conception of a work of art, is an obstacle to its execution. A habit this is which leads people, through a superior form of politeness, to sacrifice to others not only their pleasure but their duty, since from the standpoint of other people our duty, whatever it may be—and duty for a man who can render no good service at the front may be to remain behind the lines where he is useful—appears illusorily to be our pleasure.

And far from thinking myself wretched—a belief which some of the greatest men have held—because of this life without friends or familiar talk that I should live, I realised that our powers of exaltation are being given a false direction when we spend them in friendship, because they are then diverted from those truths towards which they might have guided us to aim at a particular friendship which can lead to nothing. Still, intervals of rest and society would at times be necessary to me and then, I felt, rather than those intellectual conversations which fashionable people suppose must be useful to writers, a little amorous dalliance with young girls in bloom would be the choice nutriment with which, if with anything, I might indulge my imagination, like the famous horse that was fed on nothing but roses. What suddenly I yearned for once more was what I had dreamed of at Balbec, when, still strangers to me, I had seen Albertine and Andrée and their friends pass across the background of the sea. But alas! I could no longer hope to find again those particular girls for whom at this moment my desire was so strong. The action of the years which had transformed all the individuals whom I had seen today, and among them Gilberte herself, had assuredly transformed those of the girls of Balbec who survived, as it would have transformed Albertine had she not been killed, into women too sadly different from what I remembered. And it hurt me to think that I was obliged to look for them within myself, since Time which changes human beings does not alter the image which we have preserved of them. Indeed nothing is more painful than this contrast between the mutability of people and the fixity of memory, when it is borne in upon us that what has preserved so much freshness in our memory can no longer possess any trace of that quality in life, that we cannot now, outside ourselves, approach and behold again what inside our mind seems so beautiful, what excites in us a desire (a desire apparently so individual) to see it again, save by seeking it in a person of the same age, by seeking it, that is to say, in a different person. Often had I had occasion to suspect that what seems to be unique in a person whom we desire does not in fact belong to her. And of this truth the passage of time was now giving me a more complete proof, since after twenty years, spontaneously, my impulse was to seek, not the girls whom I had known in the past, but those who now possessed the youthfulness which the others had then had. (Nor is it only the re-awakening of our old sensual desires which fails to correspond to any reality because it fails to take into account the Time that has been Lost. Sometimes I found myself wishing that, by a miracle, the door might open and through it might enter—not dead, as I had supposed, but still alive—not just Albertine but my grandmother too. I imagined that I saw them, my heart leapt forward to greet them. But I had forgotten one thing, that, if in fact they had not died, Albertine would now have more or less the appearance that Mme Cottard had presented in the Balbec days and my grandmother, being more than ninety-five years old, would show me nothing of that beautiful calm, smiling face with which I still imagined her, but only by an exercise of the fancy no less arbitrary than that which confers a beard upon God the Father or, in the eighteenth century, regardless of their antiquity, represented the heroes of Homer in all the accoutrements of a gentleman of that age.)

I looked at Gilberte, and I did not think: "I should like to see her again," I said merely, in answer to her offer, that I should always enjoy being invited to meet young girls, poor girls if possible, to whom I could give pleasure by quite small gifts, without expecting anything of them in return save that they should serve to renew within me the dreams and the sadnesses of my youth and perhaps, one improbable day, a single chaste kiss. Gilberte smiled and then looked as though she were seriously giving her mind to the problem.

Just as Elstir loved to see incarnate before him, in his wife, that Venetian beauty which he had often painted in his works, so I excused myself by saying that there was an aesthetic element in the egotism which attracted me to the beautiful women who had the power to make me suffer, and I had a sentiment almost of idolatry for the future Gilbertes, the future Duchesses de Guermantes, the future Albertines whom I might meet and who might, I thought, inspire me as a sculptor is inspired when he walks through a gallery of noble antique marbles. I ought to have reflected, however, that prior to each of the women whom I had loved there had existed in me a sentiment of the mystery by which she was surrounded and that therefore, rather than ask Gilberte to introduce me to young girls, I should have done better to go to places where there were girls with whom I had not the slightest connection, those places where between oneself and them one feels an insurmountable barrier, where at a distance of three feet, on the beach, for instance, as they pass one on their way to bathe, one feels separated from them by the impossible. It was in this fashion that a sentiment of mystery had attached itself for me first to Gilberte, then to the Duchesse de Guermantes, then to Albertine and to so many others. (Later no doubt the unknown, the almost unknowable, had become the known, the familiar, perhaps painful, perhaps indifferent, but retaining still from an earlier time a certain charm.) And to tell the truth, as in those calendars which the postman brings us in the hope of a New Year's gift, there was not one of the years of my life that did not have, as a frontispiece, or intercalated between its days, the image of a woman whom I had desired during that year; an image sometimes entirely arbitrary, for the reason that, often, I had never seen the woman in question, whether she were Mme Putbus's maid or Mlle d'Orgeville or some young woman or other whose name had caught my eye on the society page of a newspaper, amongst "the swarm of charming waltzers". I guessed her to be beautiful, I fell in love with her and I constructed for her an ideal body which towered above some landscape in the region of France where I had read in the *Annuaire des Châteaux* that the estates of her family were situated. In cases, however, where I had met and known the woman, the landscape against which I saw her was, at the very least, double. First she rose, each one of these women, at a different point in my life, with the imposing stature of a tutelar local deity, in the midst of one of those landscapes of my dreams which lay side by side like some chequered network over my past, the landscape to which my imagination had sought to attach her; then later I saw her from the side of memory, surrounded by the places in which I had known her and which she recalled to me and unable to detach herself from them, for if our life is vagabond our memory is sedentary and though we ourselves rush ceaselessly forward our recollections, indissolubly bound to the sites which we have left behind us, continue to lead a placid and sequestered existence among them, like those friends whom a traveller makes for a brief while in some town where he is staying and whom, leaving the town, he is obliged to leave behind him, because it is there that they, who stand on the steps of their house to bid him good-bye, will end their day and their life, regardless of whether he is still with them or not, there beside the church, looking out over the harbour, beneath the trees of the promenade. So that the shadow of, for instance, Gilberte lay not merely outside a church in the Ile de France where I had imagined her, but also upon a gravelled path in a park on the Méséglise way, and the shadow of Mme de Guermantes not only on a road in a watery landscape beside which rose pyramid-shaped clusters of red and purple flowers but also upon the matutinal gold of a pavement in Paris. And this second image, the one born not of desire but of memory, was, for each of these women, not unique. For my friendship with each one had been multiple, I had known her at different times when she had been different women for me and I myself had been a different person, steeped in dreams of a different colour. And the law which had governed the dreams of each year polarised around those dreams my recollections of any woman whom I had known during that year: all that related, for instance, to the Duchesse de Guermantes in the time of my childhood was concentrated, by a magnetic force, around Combray, while all that concerned the Duchesse de Guermantes who would presently invite me to luncheon was disposed around a quite different centre of sensibility; there existed several Duchesses de Guermantes, just as, beginning with the lady in pink, there had existed several Mme Swanns, separated by the colourless ether of the years, from one to another of whom it was as impossible for me to leap as it would have been to leave one planet and travel across the ether to another. And not merely separated but different, bedecked each one with the dreams which I had had at very different periods as with a characteristic and unique flora which will be found on no other planet;

so much so that, having decided that I would not accept an invitation to luncheon either from Mme de Forcheville or from Mme de Guermantes, I was only able to say to myself—for in saying this I was transported into another world—that one of these ladies was identical with the Duchesse de Guermantes who was descended from Geneviève de Brabant and the other with the lady in pink because a well-informed man within me assured me that this was so, in the same authoritative manner as a scientist might have told me that a milky way of nebulae owed its origin to the fragmentation of a single star. Gilberte, too, whom nevertheless a moment ago I had asked, without perceiving the analogy, to introduce me to girls who might be friends for me of the kind that she had been in the past, existed for me now only as Mme de Saint-Loup. No longer was I reminded when I saw her of the role which had been played long ago in my love for her by Bergotte, Bergotte whom she had forgotten as she had forgotten my love and who for me had become once more merely the author of his books, without my ever recalling now (save in rare and entirely unconnected flashes of memory) the emotion which I had felt when I was presented to the man, the disillusion, the astonishment wrought in me by his conversation, in that drawing-room with the white fur rugs and everywhere bunches of violets, where the footmen so early in the afternoon placed upon so many different consoles such an array of lamps. In fact all the memories that went to make up the first Mlle Swann were withdrawn from the Gilberte of the present day and held at a distance from her by the forces of attraction of another universe, where, grouped around a phrase of Bergotte with which they formed a single whole, they were for ever drenched with the scent of hawthorn.

The fragmentary Gilberte of today listened to my request with a smile and then assumed a serious air as she gave it her consideration. I was pleased to see this, for it prevented her from paying attention to a group which it could hardly have been agreeable for her to observe. In this group was the Duchesse de Guermantes, deep in conversation with a hideous old woman whom I studied without being able to guess in the least who she was—she seemed to be a complete stranger to me. It was in fact to Rachel, that is to say to the actress, the famous actress now, who was going to recite some poems by Victor Hugo and La Fontaine in the course of this party, that Gilberte's aunt was talking. For the Duchess, too long conscious that she occupied the foremost social position in Paris and failing to realise that a position of this kind exists only in the minds of those who believe in it and that many newcomers to the social scene, if they never saw her anywhere and never read her name in the account of any fashionable entertainment, would suppose that she occupied no position at all, now scarcely saw—save when, as seldom as possible, and then with a yawn, she paid a few calls—the Faubourg Saint-Germain which, she said, bored her to death, and instead did what amused her, which was to lunch with this or that actress whom she declared to be enchanting. In the new circles which she frequented, having remained much more like her old self than she supposed, she continued to think that to be easily bored was a mark of intellectual superiority, but she expressed this sentiment now with a positive violence which turned her voice into a hoarse bellow. When, for instance, I mentioned Brichot, "Tedious man!" she broke in, "how he has bored us all for the last twenty years!", and when Mme de Cambremer was heard to say: "You must re-read what Schopenhauer says about music," the Duchess drew our attention to this phrase by exclaiming: "Re-read! It's a masterpiece! No, really, she shouldn't inflict that on us." Old M. d'Albon smiled, recognising in this outburst a sample of the Guermantes wit. In Gilberte, who was more modern, it evoked no response. Daughter of Swann though she was, like a duckling hatched by a hen she was more romantically minded than her father. "I find that most touching," she would say, or: "He has a charming sensibility."

I told Mme de Guermantes that I had met M. de Charlus. She found him much more "altered" for the worse than in fact he was, for people in society make distinctions, in the matter of intelligence, not only between different members of their set between whom there is really nothing to choose in this respect, but also, in a single individual, between different phases of his life. Then she went on: "He has always been the image of my mother-in-law, but now the likeness is even more striking." There was nothing very extraordinary in this resemblance: it is well known that women sometimes so to speak project themselves into another human being with the most perfect accuracy, with the sole error of a transposition of sex. This, however, is an error of which one can scarcely say: "*Felix culpa*," for the sex has repercussions upon the personality, so that in a man femininity becomes affectation, reserve touchiness and so on. Nevertheless, in the face, though it may be bearded, in the cheeks, florid as they are beneath their side-whiskers, there are certain lines which might have been traced from some maternal portrait. Almost every aged Charlus is a ruin in which one may recognise with astonishment, beneath all the layers of paint and powder, some fragments of a beautiful woman preserved in eternal youth. While we were talking, Morel came in. The Duchess treated him with a civility which disconcerted me a little. "I never take sides in family quarrels," she said. "Don't you find them boring, family quarrels?"

If in a period of twenty years, like this that had elapsed since my first entry into society, the conglomerations of social groups had disintegrated and re-formed under the magnetic influence of new stars destined themselves also to fade away and then to reappear, the same sequence of crystallisation followed by dissolution and again by a fresh crystallisation might have been observed to take place within the consciousness of individuals. If for me Mme de Guermantes had been many people, for Mme de Guermantes or for Mme Swann there were many individuals who had been a favoured friend in an era that preceded the Dreyfus affair, only to be branded as a fanatic or an imbecile when the supervention of the Affair modified the accepted values of people and brought about a new configuration of parties, itself of brief duration, since later they had again disintegrated and re-formed. And what serves most powerfully to promote this renewal of old friendships, adding its influence to any purely intellectual affinities, is simply the passage of Time, which causes us to forget our antipathies and our disdains and even the reasons which once explained their existence. Had one analysed the fashionableness of the young Mme de Cambremer, one would have found that she was the niece of Jupien, a tradesman who lived in our house, and that the additional circumstance which had launched her on her social ascent was that her uncle had been a procurer of men to M. de Charlus. But all this combined had produced effects that were dazzling, while the causes were already remote and not merely unknown to many people but also forgotten by those who had once known them and whose minds now dwelt much more upon her present brilliance than upon the ignominy of her past, since people always accept a name at its current valuation. So that these drawing-room transformations possessed a double interest: they were both a phenomenon of the memory and an effect of Lost Time.

The Duchess still hesitated, for fear of a scene with M. de

Guermantes, to make overtures to Balthy and Mistinguett, whom she found adorable, but with Rachel she was definitely on terms of friendship. From this the younger generation concluded that the Duchesse de Guermantes, despite her name, must be some sort of demi-rep who had never quite belonged to the best society. There were, it was true, a few reigning princes (the honour of whose familiar friendship two other great ladies disputed with her) whom Mme de Guermantes still took the trouble to invite to luncheon. But on the one hand kings and queens do not often come to see you and their acquaintances are sometimes people of no social position, and then the Duchess, with the superstitious respect of the Guermantes for old-fashioned protocol (for while well-bred people bored her to tears, she was at the same time horrified by any departure from good manners), would put on her invitation cards: "Her Majesty has commanded the Duchesse de Guermantes", or "has deigned", etc. And new-comers to society, in their ignorance of these formulae, inferred that their use was simply a sign of the Duchess's lowly situation. From the point of view of Mme de Guermantes herself, this intimacy with Rachel signified perhaps that we had been mistaken when we supposed her to be hypocritical and untruthful in her condemnations of a purely fashionable life, when we imagined that in refusing to go and see Mme de Sainte-Euverte she acted in the name not of intelligence but of snobbery, finding the Marquise stupid only because, not having yet attained her goal, she allowed her snobbery to appear on the surface. But the intimacy with Rachel might also signify that the intelligence of the Duchess was no more than commonplace, but had remained unsatisfied and at a late hour, when she was tired of society, had driven her, totally ignorant as she was of the veritable realities of the intellectual life, to seek for intellectual fulfilment with a touch of that spirit of

397

fantasy which can cause perfectly respectable ladies, thinking to themselves: "How amusing it will be!" to end an evening with a prank which is in fact deadly dull: you go off and wake up some acquaintance and then, when you are in his room, you don't know what to say, so, after standing awkwardly by his bed for a few moments in your evening clothes and realising how late it is, there is nothing left to do but go home to bed yourself.

One must add that the antipathy which the changeable Duchess had recently come to feel for Gilberte may have caused her to take a certain pleasure in receiving Rachel, a course of conduct which enabled her also to proclaim aloud one of the favourite Guermantes maxims, to wit, that the family was too numerous for its members to have to espouse one another's quarrels (or even, some might have said, to take notice of one another's bereavements), an independence, a spirit of "I can't see that I am obliged" which had been reinforced by the policy that it had been necessary to adopt with regard to M. de Charlus, who, had you followed him, would have involved you in hostilities with all your acquaintances.

As for Rachel, if the truth was that she had taken very great pains to form this friendship with the Duchesse de Guermantes (pains which the Duchess had failed to detect beneath a mask of simulated disdain and deliberate incivility, which had put her on her mettle and given her an exalted idea of an actress so little susceptible to snobbery), this was no doubt in a general fashion an effect of the fascination which after a certain time the world of high society exercises upon even the most hardened bohemians, a fascination paralleled by that which the same bohemians themselves exercise upon people in society, flux and reflux which correspond to—in the political order—the reciprocal curiosity, the desire to form a mutual alliance, of two nations which have recently been at war with each other. But Rachel's desire had possibly a more particular cause. It was in Mme de Guermantes's house, it was at the hands of Mme de Guermantes herself, that she had in the past suffered the most terrible humiliation of her life. This snub Rachel had with the slow passage of time if not forgotten forgiven, but the extraordinary prestige which the event had conferred upon the Duchess in her eyes could never be effaced.

The conversation from which I was anxious to divert Gilberte's attention was, in any case, presently interrupted, for the mistress of the house came in search of the actress to tell her that the moment for her recital had arrived. She left the Duchess and a little later appeared upon the platform.

Meanwhile at the other end of Paris there was taking place a spectacle of a very different kind. Mme Berma, as I have said, had invited a number of people to a tea-party in honour of her daughter and her son-in-law. But the guests were in no hurry to arrive. Having learnt that Rachel was to recite poetry at the Princesse de Guermantes's (which utterly scandalised Berma, who from her own lofty position as a great artist looked down upon Rachel as still no more than a kept woman who, because Saint-Loup paid for the dresses which she wore on the stage, was allowed to appear in the plays in which she herself, Berma, took the leading roles—and scandalised her all the more because a rumour had run round Paris that, though the invitations were in the name of the Princesse de Guermantes, it was in effect Rachel who was acting as hostess in the Princess's house), Berma had written a second time to certain faithful friends to insist that they should not miss her tea-party, for she was aware that they were also friends of the Princesse de Guermantes, whom they had known when she was Mme Verdurin. And now the hours were passing, and still nobody arrived to visit Berma. Bloch, having been asked whether he meant to come, had ingenuously replied: "No, I would rather go to the Princesse de Guermantes's", and this, alas! was what everyone in his heart of hearts had decided. Berma, who suffered from a deadly disease which had obliged her to cut down her social activities to a minimum, had seen her condition deteriorate when, in order to pay for the luxurious existence which her daughter demanded and her son-in-law, ailing and idle, was unable to provide, she had returned to the stage. She knew that she was shortening her days, but she wanted to give pleasure to her daughter, to whom she handed over the large sums that she earned, and to a son-in-law whom she detested but flattered— for she feared, knowing that his wife adored him, that if she, Berma, did not do what he wanted, he might, out of spite, deprive her of the happiness of seeing her child. This child, with whom secretly the doctor who looked after her husband was in love, had allowed herself to be persuaded that these performances in *Phèdre* were not really dangerous for her mother. She had more or less forced the doctor to tell her this, or rather of all that he had said to her about her mother's health she had retained only this in her memory, the truth being that, in the midst of various objections of which she had taken no notice, he had remarked that he saw no grave harm in Berma's appearing on the stage. He had said this because he had sensed that in so doing he would give pleasure to the young woman whom he loved, perhaps also from ignorance and also because he knew that the disease was in any case incurable, since a man readily consents to cut short the martyrdom of an invalid when the action that will have this effect will be advantageous to himself—and perhaps also from the stupid idea that acting made Berma happy and was therefore likely to do her good, a stupid idea which had appeared to him to be corroborated when, having been given a box by Berma's daughter and son-in-law and having deserted all his patients for the occasion, he had found her as extraordinarily charged with life on the stage as she seemed to be moribund if you met her off it. And indeed our habits enable us to a large degree, enable even the organs of our bodies, to adapt themselves to an existence which at first sight would appear to be utterly impossible. Have we not all seen an elderly riding-master with a weak heart go through a whole series of acrobatics which one would not have supposed his heart could stand for a single minute? Berma in the same way was an old campaigner of the stage, to the requirements of which her organs had so perfectly adapted themselves that she was able, by deploying her energies with a prudence invisible to the public, to give an illusion of good health troubled only by a purely nervous and imaginary complaint. After the scene in which Phèdre makes her declaration of love to Hippolyte Berma herself might be conscious only of the appalling night which awaited her as a result of her exertions, but her admirers burst into tumultuous applause and said that she was more wonderful than ever. She would go home in terrible pain, happy nevertheless because she brought back to her daughter the blue banknotes which, with the playfulness of a true child of the footlights, she had the habit of squeezing into her stockings, whence she would draw them out with pride, hoping for a smile, a kiss. Unfortunately these banknotes merely made it possible for her son-in-law and her daughter to make new embellishments to their house, which was next door to Berma's own: hence constant hammering, which interrupted the sleep of which the great actress was so desperately in need. According to the latest change in fashion, or to conform to the taste of M. de X— or M. de Y— whom they hoped to attract to their house, they altered every room in it. And Berma, realising that sleep, which alone would have deadened her pain, had gone for good, would resign herself to lying awake, not without a secret contempt for this determination to be smart which was hastening her death and making her last days an agony. That these were its consequences was no doubt in part the reason why she despised this social ambition, contempt being a natural form of revenge upon something that does us harm and that we are powerless to prevent. But there was another reason, which was that, conscious of her own genius and having learnt at a very early age the meaninglessness of all these decrees of Fashion, she for her part had remained faithful to Tradition, which she had always respected and of which she was herself an embodiment, and which caused her to judge things and people as she would have judged them thirty years earlier, to judge Rachel, for example, not as the well-known actress that she was today, but as the little tart that she had once been. Berma was, one must add, no better natured than her daughter, for it was from her mother that the young woman had derived, through heredity and through the contagion of an example which an only too natural admiration had rendered more than usually potent, her egotism, her pitiless mockery, her unconscious cruelty. But all this Berma had sacrificed to her daughter and in this way she had liberated herself from it. However, even if Berma's daughter had not incessantly had workmen in her house, she would have tired her mother out just the same, since inevitably youth with its powers of attraction, its ruthless and inconsiderate strength, tires out old age and ill health, which overtax themselves in the effort to keep up with it. Every day there was yet another luncheon party, and Berma would have been condemned as selfish had she deprived her daughter of this pleasure, or even had she refused to be present herself at entertainments where the prestige of the famous mother was counted upon as a means of drawing to the house, not without difficulty, certain recent acquaintances who needed to be coaxed. And even away from home her attendance at a social function might be "promised" to these same acquaintances as a way of doing them a civility. So that the poor mother, seriously engaged in her intimate dialogue with the death that was already installed within her, was compelled to get up early in the morning and drag herself out of the house. Nor was this enough. At about this time Réjane, in the full blaze of her talent, made some appearances on the stage in foreign countries which had an enormous success, and the son-in-law decided that Berma must not allow herself to be put in the shade; determined that his own family should pick up some of the same easily acquired glory, he forced his mother-in-law to set out on tours on which she was obliged to have injections of morphia, which might at any moment have killed her owing to the condition of her kidneys.

This same ambition to be smart, this longing for social prestige, for life, had on the day of the Princesse de Guermantes's reception acted in the manner of a suction-pump, drawing to her house with the irresistible force of some such machine even Berma's loyalest friends, so that at the actress's party there was, in contrast and in consequence, an absolute and deathlike void. One solitary young man had come, thinking that possibly Berma's party might be just as fashionable as the other. When Berma saw the hour pass for which she had issued the invitations and realised that everybody had deserted her, she ordered tea to be served and the four people in the room sat down at the table as though it had been spread for a funeral feast. Nothing now in her face recalled the countenance of which the photograph, one distant New Year's Day, had so disturbed me. Death, as the saying goes, was written all over her face, and she resembled nothing so much as one of the marble figures from the Erechtheum. Her hardened arteries were already almost petrified, so that what appeared to be long sculptural ribbons ran across her cheeks, with the rigidity of a mineral substance. The dying eyes were still relatively alive, by contrast at least with the terrible ossified mask, and glowed feebly like a snake asleep in the midst of a pile of stones. But already the young man, who had sat down only because it would have been rude to do anything else, was incessantly looking at his watch, for he too felt the attraction of the brilliant party in the Guermantes mansion. Berma uttered not a word in reproach of the friends who had deserted her and who were foolish enough to hope that she would not discover that they had been to the Guermantes's. She murmured only: "A Rachel giving a party in the Princesse de Guermantes's house—that is something that could only happen in Paris." And silently and with a solemn slowness she continued to eat the cakes which the doctor had forbidden her, still with the air of playing her part in a funerary rite. The gloom of the tea-party was made more intense by the vile temper of the son-in-law, who was furious that Rachel, whom he and his wife knew very well, had not invited them. To crown his indignation the young man who had come told him that he knew Rachel so well that, if he went off to the Guermantes party straight away, he could even at this eleventh hour ask her to invite the frivolous couple. But Berma's daughter was too well aware of the ignominy which in her mother's eyes attached to Rachel, she knew that she would die of despair at the thought of her daughter begging for an invitation from the former prostitute. So she told the young man and her husband that what he suggested was impossible. But she took her revenge as she sat at the tea-table by a series of little grimaces expressive of the desire for pleasure and the annoyance of being deprived of it by her kill-joy mother. The latter pretended not to see her daughter's cross looks and from time to time, in a dying voice, addressed an amiable remark to the solitary guest. But soon the rush of air which was sweeping everything towards the Guermantes mansion, and had swept me thither myself, was too much for him; he got up and said good-bye, leaving Phèdre or death—one scarcely knew which of the two it was—to finish, with her daughter and her son-in-law, devouring the funeral cakes.

My conversation with Gilberte was interrupted by the voice of the actress which now made itself heard. Her style of recitation was intelligent, for it presupposed the existence of the poem whose words she was speaking as a whole which had been in being before she opened her mouth, a whole of which we were hearing merely a fragment, as though for a few moments, as the actress passed along a road, she had happened to be within earshot of us.

The announcement that she was to recite poems with which nearly everybody was familiar had been well received. But when the actress, before beginning to speak, was seen to shoot searching and bewildered glances in every direction, to lift her hands with an air of supplication and then to utter each word as though it were a groan, the general reaction was to feel embarrassed, almost shocked by this display of sentiment. Nobody had said to himself that a recital of poetry could be anything like this. Gradually, however, each member of an audience grows accustomed to what is taking place before him, he forgets his first sensation of discomfort, he picks out what is good in a performance, he mentally compares different ways of reciting and passes judgement: "this is excellent, this is not so good." But for the first few moments, just as when, in a trivial case in a law-court, we see a barrister advance, raise a toga'd arm in the air and start to speak in a threatening tone, we hardly dare look at our neighbours. For our immediate reaction is that this is grotesque—but we cannot be sure that it is not in fact magnificent, so for the present we suspend judgement.

A ripple of astonishment ran through the room when it was seen that this woman, before she had emitted a single sound, bent her knees, became suddenly bandy-legged, stretched out her arms to cradle an invisible body and then, to recite some very well known lines of poetry, started to speak in a voice of entreaty. People looked at one another, not knowing what expression to put on their faces; a few bright young things without any manners almost burst into hysterics; everyone glanced at his neighbour with that stealthy glance which at a smart dinner party, when you find beside your plate an un-familiar implement, a lobster-fork or sugar-sifter perhaps, of which you know neither what it is for nor how to use it, you cast at some more authoritative guest in the hope that he will pick it up before you and so give you a chance to imitate him —or with which, when someone quotes a line of poetry which you do not know but of which you do not wish to appear ignorant, you turn towards a man better read than yourself and relinquish to him, as though it were a favour, as though you were courteously letting him pass through a door before you, the pleasure of naming the author. With just this same glance, as they listened to the actress, each member of the audience waited, his head lowered but his eyes furtively pry-ing, for others to take the initiative and decide whether to laugh or to criticise, to weep or to applaud. Mme de Forche-ville, who had come back specially for the occasion from Guermantes, whence, as we shall see, the Duchess had been almost expelled, had assumed an expression that was attentive, concentrated, almost bad-tempered, either in order to show that she was a connoisseur of the drama and had not come merely for social reasons, or to present a hostile front to people who were less versed in literature and might have talked to her about other things, or from the intensity with which with all her faculties she strove to discover whether she "liked" or "did not like" the performance, or perhaps because, while she found it "interesting", she nevertheless "did not like" the manner in which certain lines were recited. This attitude might, one would have thought, have been more appropriate to the Princesse de Guermantes. But as the recitation was taking place in her house and as, having become as avaricious as she was rich, she had decided that her payment to Rachel would consist of five roses, she chose rather to act as claque and gave the signal for a forced display of enthusiasm by a series of exclamations of delight. And here alone could her Verdurin past be recognised, for she had the air of listening to the poems for her own private enjoyment, of having felt a desire for someone to come and recite them to her alone, so that it seemed to be mere chance that there were in the room five hundred people, her friends, whom she had permitted to come unobtrusively and share in her pleasure.

Meanwhile I observed—without any satisfaction to my vanity, for she was old and ugly—that the actress, in a somewhat restrained fashion, was giving me the glad eye. All the time that she was reciting she allowed to flutter in and out of her eyes a smile that was both repressed and penetrating and that seemed to be the first hint of an acquiescence which she would have liked to see come from me. Certain elderly ladies meanwhile, little accustomed to the recitation of poetry, were saying to their neighbours: "Did you see?", a question which had reference to the solemn, tragic miming of the actress, which they had no words to describe. The Duchesse de Guermantes sensed the slight wavering of opinion and turned the scale of victory with a cry of "Admirable!", ejaculated at a pause in the middle of the poem which perhaps she mistook for the end. More than one guest thought it incumbent upon him to underline this exclamation with a look of approval and an inclination of the head, less perhaps to display his comprehension of the reciter's art than his friendly relations with the Duchess. When the poem was finished, I heard the actress thank Mme de Guermantes, who was standing near her, as I was myself, and at the same time, taking advantage of my presence beside the Duchess, she turned to me and greeted me with charming civility. At this point I realised that she was somebody whom I ought to have known and that, whereas long ago I had mistaken the passionate glances of M. de Vaugoubert for the salutation of someone who was confused as to my identity, today on the contrary what I had taken in the actress to be a look of desire was no more than a decorous attempt to make me recognise and greet her. I responded with a smile and a gesture. "I am sure he does not recognise me," said the reciter to the Duchess. "Of course I do," I said confidently, "I recognise you perfectly." "Well then, who am I?" I had not the slightest idea and my position was becoming awkward. But fortunately, if throughout one of La Fontaine's finest poems this woman who was reciting it with such conviction had, whether from good nature or stupidity or embarrassment, thought of nothing but the difficulty of saying good-afternoon to me, throughout this same beautiful poem Bloch had been wondering only how to manœuvre himself so as to be ready, the moment the poem ended, to leap from his seat like a beleaguered army making a sally and, trampling if not upon the bodies at least upon the feet of his neighbours, arrive and congratulate the reciter, perhaps from an erroneous conception of duty, perhaps merely from a desire to make people look at him. "How curious it is to see Rachel here!" he whispered in my ear. At once the magic name broke the enchantment which had given to the mistress of Saint-Loup the unknown form of this horrible old woman. And once I knew who she was, I did indeed recognise her perfectly. "You were wonderful," Bloch said to Rachel, and having said these simple words, having satisfied his desire, he started on his return journey—but encountered so many obstacles and made so much noise in reaching his place that Rachel had to wait more than five minutes before beginning her second poem. This was *Les Deux Pigeons*, and at the end of it Mme de Morienval came up to Mme de Saint-Loup, whom she knew to be very well read without remembering that she had inherited the oblique and sarcastic wit of her father. "That *is* La Fontaine's fable, isn't it?" she asked, thinking that she had recognised it but not being absolutely certain, since she did not know the fables of La Fontaine at all well and in any case supposed them to be childish things which no one would recite at a fashionable gathering. To have such a success the entertainer had no doubt produced a pastiche of La Fontaine, thought the good lady. Unintentionally Gilberte confirmed her in this idea, for, disliking Rachel and wanting to say that with her style of diction there was nothing left of the fables, she said it in that over-subtle manner which had been her father's and which left simple people in doubt as to the speaker's meaning: "One quarter is the invention of the actress, a second is lunacy, a third is meaningless and the rest is La Fontaine," a remark which encouraged Mme de Morienval to maintain that the poem which had just been recited was not La Fontaine's *Les Deux Pigeons*, but an arrangement of which at most a quarter was by La Fontaine himself. Given the extraordinary ignorance of all these people, this assertion caused no surprise whatever.

Meanwhile, one of his friends having arrived after the recital was over, Bloch had the satisfaction of asking him whether he had ever heard Rachel and of painting for his benefit an extraordinary picture of her art, exaggerating, indeed suddenly discovering, as he described and revealed this modernistic diction to another person, a strange pleasure of which he had felt nothing as he listened to it. Then, with exaggerated emotion, he again congratulated Rachel in a high-pitched voice which proclaimed his sense of her genius and introduced his friend, who declared that his admiration for her was unbounded. To this Rachel, who was now acquainted with ladies of the best society and unwittingly copied them, replied: "Oh! I am most flattered, most honoured by your appreciation." Bloch's friend asked her what she thought of Berma. "Poor woman, it seems that she is living in the most abject poverty. She was once I will not say not without talent, for what she possessed was not true talent—her taste was appalling—still, one must admit she had merit of a kind: she was more alive on the stage than most actresses, and then she had nice qualities, she was generous, she ruined herself for others. And as it is years now since she has earned a penny, because the public these days loathes the sort of thing she does ... But of course," she added with a laugh, "I must admit that someone of my generation, naturally, only heard her right at the end of her career, and even then I was really too young to form an opinion." "She didn't recite poetry very well, did she?" hazarded Bloch's friend, to flatter Rachel. "Poetry!" she replied, "she had no idea how to recite a single line. It might have been prose, or Chinese, or Volapük—anything, rather than poetry."

In spite of Rachel's words I was thinking myself that time, as it passes, does not necessarily bring progress in the arts. And just as some author of the seventeenth century, who knew nothing of the French Revolution or the discoveries of science or the war, may be superior to some writer of today, just as perhaps Fagon was as great a doctor as du Boulbon (a superiority in genius compensating in this case an inferiority in knowledge), so Berma was, as the phrase goes, head and shoulders above Rachel, and Time, when simultaneously it turned Rachel into a star and Elstir into a famous painter, had inflated the reputation of a mediocrity as well as consecrated a genius.

It was scarcely surprising that Saint-Loup's former mistress should speak maliciously about Berma. She would have done this when she was young, and even if she would not have done it then, she was bound to now. When a society woman becomes an actress, a woman even of the highest intelligence and the greatest goodness of heart, and in this unfamiliar occupation displays great talent and encounters nothing but success, one will be surprised, meeting her years later, to hear on her lips not her own individual language but that which is common to the theatrical profession, the special brand of obloquy that actresses have for their colleagues, those special qualities which are added to a member of the human race by the passage over him of "thirty years on the stage". These qualities Rachel inevitably had and her origin, as we know, was not in good society.

"You can say what you like, it was a wonderful performance, it had line, it had character, it was intelligent, one has never heard anyone recite poetry like that before," said the Duchess, for fear that Gilberte should make disparaging remarks. Gilberte wandered off towards another group, to avoid an argument with her aunt, whose comments upon Rachel were indeed of the most commonplace kind. But then, since even the best writers cease often, at the approach of old age or after producing too much, to have any talent, society women may well be excused if sooner or later they cease to have any wit. Swann already in the sharp-edged wit of the Duchesse de Guermantes found it difficult to recognise the gentle raillery of the young Princesse des Laumes. And now late in life, wearied by the least effort, Mme de Guermantes said a prodigious number of stupid things. It was true that at any moment, as happened more than once in the course of this party, she could re-become the woman whom I had known in the past and talk wittily on social topics. But alongside these moments there were others, and they were no less frequent, when beneath her beautiful eyes the sparkling conversation which for so many years, from its throne of wit, had held sway over the most distinguished men in Paris, shone, in so far as it still shone at all, in a meaningless way. When the moment came to make a joke, she would check herself for the same number of seconds as in the past, she would appear to hesitate, to have something within her that was struggling to emerge, but the joke, when at last it arrived, was pitifully feeble. But how few of her listeners noticed this! Because the procedure was the same they believed that the wit too had survived intact, like those people who, superstitiously attached to some particular make of confectionery, continue to order their *petits fours* from a certain shop without noticing that they have become almost uneatable. Already during the war the Duchess had shown signs of this decay. If someone pronounced the word "culture", she would stop him, smile, kindle a light in her beautiful eyes and ejaculate: "KKKKultur," which raised a laugh among her friends, who saw in this remark the latest manifestation of the Guermantes wit. And certainly the mould was the same, and the intonation and the smile, the same that had once enchanted Bergotte, who for his part too had preserved the individual rhythm of his phrases, his interjections, his aposiopeses, his epithets, but with all this rhetorical apparatus no longer had anything to say. But newcomers, who did not know her, were surprised and said sometimes, unless they had chanced to encounter her on a day when she was amusing and "at her best": "What a stupid woman this is!"

As her life drew to its close, Mme de Guermantes had felt the quickening within her of new curiosities. Society no longer had anything to teach her. The idea that she occupied the first place in it was as evident to her as the altitude of the blue sky above the earth, and she saw no need to strengthen a position which she deemed to be unshakable. On the other hand she read and she went to the theatre, and enjoying these activities she would have been glad to prolong them; just as in the past, in the little narrow garden where she sipped orangeade with her friends, all that was most choice in the world of grand society would come familiarly, among the scented breezes of the evening and the gusts of pollen, to sustain in her the pleasure that this grand world gave her and her appetite for it, so now a different appetite caused her to want to know the reasons behind this or that literary controversy, to want to meet the authors whose books she had read, to make friends with the actresses whom she had seen on the stage. Her tired mind required a new form of food, and in order to get to know theatrical and literary people she now made herself pleasant to women with whom formerly she would have refused to exhange cards but who, in the hope of getting the Duchess to come to their parties, could boast to her of their great friendship with the editor of some review. The first actress to be invited to her house thought that she was the only one of her kind in an exotic *milieu*, which however appeared more commonplace to the second when she saw that she had a predecessor. The Duchess, because on certain evenings she received reigning monarchs, thought that there was no change in her social position. But the truth was that she who alone could boast of a blood that was absolutely without taint, she who had been born a Guermantes and who when she did not sign herself "La Duchesse de Guermantes" had the right to put "Guermantes-Guermantes", she who even to her husband's sisters seemed to be something more precious than they were themselves, like a Moses saved from the waters or Christ escaped into Egypt or Louis XVII rescued from his prison in the Temple, she the pure of the pure had now, sacrificing no doubt to that hereditary need for spiritual nourishment which had brought about the social decline of Mme de Villeparisis, herself become a Mme de Villeparisis, in whose house snobbish women were afraid of meeting this or that undesirable and of whom the younger generation, observing the *fait accompli* and not knowing what had gone before it, supposed that she was a Guermantes from an inferior cask or of a less good vintage, a Guermantes *déclassé*.

If, however, the Duchess indulged a taste for the society of her inferiors, she was careful to confine this activity within strict limits and not allow it to contaminate those members of her family from whom she derived the gratification of an aristocratic pride. If at the theatre, for instance, in order to fill her role of protectress of the arts, she had invited a minister or a painter and her guest had been so ingenuous as to ask whether her sister-in-law or her husband were not in the audience, the Duchess, with a superb assumption of lofty indifference which concealed her alarm, would haughtily reply: "I have not the slightest idea. As soon as I leave my house, I know nothing of what my family is doing. For politicians, for artists, whoever they may be, I am a widow." In this way she sought to prevent the too eager social climber from drawing upon himself a snub and upon her a reprimand from Mme de Marsantes or from Basin.

"I can't tell you how pleased I am to see you," said the Duchess. "Good heavens, when was it that I saw you last?" "I believe it was at Mme d'Agrigente's—I was paying a call and I found you there, as I often did." "But of course, I was constantly going there, my dear boy, since Basin was in love with her in those days. And calling on Basin's sweetheart of the moment was always where my friends were most likely to find me, because he used to say: 'I shall expect you to visit her without fail.' I must admit that there seemed to me to be a slight impropriety in these 'digestive visits' on which he used to send me to thank the lady for her entertainment of him. But I quite soon grew accustomed to them. The tiresome thing was, however, that I was obliged to continue my relations with his mistress after he had broken off his own. I was always reminded of the line in Victor Hugo:

Emporte le bonheur et laisse-moi l'ennui.

Naturally—you remember how the poem goes on—'I entered smiling none the less,' but it really was not fair, he ought to have left me the right to be inconstant, for in the end I accumulated so many of his discards that I had not a single afternoon to myself. Still, compared with the present that epoch now seems to me relatively agreeable. That he has started to be unfaithful again is, of course, something that I can only find flattering, it almost makes me feel younger. But I preferred his old way of doing it. Unfortunately, he was so out of practice that he had forgotten how to set about it. However, in spite of it all we are on excellent terms, we talk to each other, we are even quite fond of each other,"— this the Duchess added because she was afraid that I might think that she and her husband were completely separated, rather as one says apropos of someone who is desperately ill: "But he is still able to speak, I read to him this morning for an hour." "I will tell him you are here," she continued, "he will be delighted to see you." And she went towards the Duke, who was sitting on a sofa in conversation with a lady. I observed with admiration that, except that his hair was whiter, he had scarcely changed, being still as majestic and as handsome as ever. But seeing his wife approach to speak to him he assumed an air of such fury that she had no alternative but to retreat. "I can't interrupt him just now, I don't know what he is doing, we shall see presently," said Mme de Guermantes, preferring to leave me to form my own conclusions.

Bloch now came up to us and on behalf of his American enquired the identity of a young Duchess who was at the party. I replied that she was a niece of M. de Bréauté, which caused Bloch, as this name meant nothing to him, to ask for further explanations. "Bréauté!" the Duchess exclaimed, turning to me. "You remember all that, of course. How ancient it seems now, how far away! Well,"—this to Bloch— "Bréauté was a snob. They were people who lived near my mother-in-law in the country. This couldn't possibly interest you, Monsieur Bloch—though it may amuse this young man, who knew all that world long ago when I was in the midst of it myself." This last remark referred to me, and by it Mme de Guermantes brought home to me in a number of different ways how long was the time that had elapsed. First, her own friendships and opinions had so greatly changed since that period that now, in retrospect, she looked upon her charming Babal as a snob. And then, not only was he now seen at the other end of a great vista of time, but—and of this I had been quite unaware when at my first entry into society I had supposed him to be one of the quintessential notabilities of Paris, who would for ever remain associated with its social history as Colbert with the history of the reign of Louis XIV—he too bore the stamp of a provincial origin, he was a country neighbour of the old Duchess and it was as such that the Princesse des Laumes had made his acquaintance.

Moreover this Bréauté, stripped of his wit and relegated to a distant past for which he himself provided a date (which proved that between then and now he had been entirely forgotten by the Duchess) and to the countryside near Guermantes, was—and this too I would never have thought possible that first evening at the Opéra, when he had appeared to me in the guise of a marine deity dwelling in his glaucous cavern—a link between the Duchess and myself, because she remembered that I had known him and therefore had been a friend of hers, if not of the same social origin as herself at any rate an inhabitant of the same social world for very much longer than a great many people who were at the party today, she remembered this and yet remembered it so hazily that she had forgotten certain details which to me on the contrary had then seemed to be of prime importance, such as that I never went to Guermantes and at the time when she came to the mass in honour of Mlle Percepied's marriage was merely a boy of a middle-class Combray family, and that, in spite of all the prayers of Saint-Loup, throughout the year which followed her apparition at the Opéra she had never invited me to her house. To me this seemed to be of supreme importance, for it was precisely during this brief period that the life of the Duchesse de Guermantes had appeared to me to be a paradise into which I should never enter. But for her, her life then was merely a part like any other of her normal, commonplace life, and as from a certain moment onwards I had dined often at her house and had also, even before that date, been a friend of her aunt and of her nephew, she no longer knew exactly at what period our friendship had begun and was unaware of the grave anachronism that she was perpetrating in supposing that we had become friends a few years earlier than in fact we had. For this would have meant that I had known the Mme de Guermantes of the name of

Guermantes, whose essence it was to be unknowable, that I had been permitted to enter the name of the golden syllables, had been received into the Faubourg Saint-Germain, whereas in fact I had merely been to dine at the house of a lady who was already nothing more in my eyes than a very ordinary woman and who had occasionally invited me, not to descend into the submarine kingdom of the Nereids but to spend an evening with her in her cousin's box. "If you want to know anything more about Bréauté," Mme de Guermantes continued, still speaking to Bloch, "though there is no earthly reason why you should, ask our friend here, who is a hundred times more interesting than Bréauté ever was. He must have dined at my house with him fifty times. It was at my house, was it not, that you got to know Bréauté? In any case, it was there that you met Swann." And I was just as surprised that she should imagine that I might have met M. de Bréauté elsewhere than at her house (which could only have happened had I moved in that society before I became acquainted with her) as I was to see that she believed that it was through her that I had met Swann. Less untruthfully than Gilberte, who had been in the habit of saying of Bréauté: "He is an old country neighbour, I so enjoy talking to him about Tansonville," whereas in fact in the past he had never visited the Swanns at Tansonville, I might have said of Swann: "He was a country neighbour who often used to come round and see us in the evening," for indeed the memories which he recalled to my mind had nothing to do with the Guermantes. "I don't know how to describe him," she went on. "He was a man whose only subject of conversation was people with grand titles. He had a whole collection of curious anecdotes about my Guermantes relations and about my mother-in-law and about Mme de Varambon before she became a lady-in-waiting to the Princesse de Parme. But does anybody today know who Mme de Varambon was? Our friend here, yes, he knew all those people. But it is all ancient history, they are not even names today, and in any case they don't deserve to be remembered." And again it struck me that, in spite of the apparent unity of that thing which we call "society", in which, it is true, social relations reach their maximum of concentration (for all paths meet at the top) and in which there are no barriers to communication, there exist nevertheless within it, or at least there are created within it by Time, separate provinces which after a while change their names and are no longer comprehensible to those who arrive in society only when its pattern has been altered. "Mme de Varambon was a good lady who said things of an incredible stupidity," continued the Duchess, who failed to appreciate that poetry of the incomprehensible which is an effect of Time and chose rather to extract from every situation its element of ironic humour, the element that could be transformed into literature of the type of Meilhac or into the Guermantes brand of wit. "At one moment she had a mania for swallowing a certain kind of lozenge which people used to take in those days for coughs and which was called" (and she laughed as she pronounced a name that was so special, so well known formerly and so unknown today to everyone around her) "a Géraudel lozenge. 'Madame de Varambon,' my mother-in-law used to say to her, 'if you don't stop swallowing a Géraudel lozenge every five minutes, you will injure your stomach.' 'But Madame la Duchesse,' replied Mme de Varambon, 'how can they possibly injure the stomach when they go into the bronchial tubes?' And then it was she who made the remark: 'The Duchess has a most beautiful cow, so beautiful that it is always taken for a bull!'" And Mme de Guermantes would gladly have gone on relating anecdotes of Mme de Varambon, of which she and I knew hundreds, but we realised that in the ignorant memory of Bloch this name evoked none of those images which rose up for us as soon as there was mention of her or of M. de Bréauté or of the Prince d'Agrigente, though perhaps for this very reason all these names were endowed in his eyes with a prestige which I knew to be exaggerated but which I found comprehensible —though not because I myself had at one time felt its influence, for it is rarely that our own errors and absurdities, even when we have penetrated to the truth behind them, make us more indulgent to those of others.

The past had been so transformed in the mind of the Duchess (or else the distinctions which existed in my mind had been always so absent from hers that what had been an event for me had gone unnoticed by her) that she was able to suppose that I had first met Swann in her house and M. de Bréauté elsewhere, thus conferring upon me a past as man about town of which she exaggerated the remoteness from the present. For the notion of Time elapsed which I had just acquired was something that the Duchess had too, and, whereas my illusion had been to believe the gap between past and present shorter than in fact it was, she on the contrary actually overestimated it, she placed events further back than they really were, a notable consequence of this being her disregard of that supremely important line of demarcation between the epoch when she had been for me first a name and then the object of my love and the utterly different epoch when she had been for me merely a society woman like any other. It was of course only during this second period, when she had become for me a different person, that I had been to her house. But to her own eyes these differences were invisible and she would have seen nothing in the least odd in my going to her house two years earlier, for how was she to know that she had then been a different woman and even her door-mat a different door-mat, since her personality did not present to her that break in continuity which it presented to me?

"All this reminds me", I said to her, "of that first evening when I went to the Princesse de Guermantes's, when I wasn't sure that I had been invited to her party and half expected to be shown the door, and when you wore a red dress and red shoes." "Good heavens, how long ago all that was!" said the Duchesse de Guermantes, accentuating by her words my own impression of Time elapsed. She seemed to be gazing into this remote past in a melancholy mood, and yet she laid a particular emphasis upon the red dress. I asked her to describe it to me, which she did most willingly. "One couldn't possibly wear a thing like that now. It was the sort of dress that was worn in those days." "But it was pretty, wasn't it?" I said. She was always afraid of giving away a point in conversation, of saying something that might depreciate her in the eyes of others. "Personally, I found it a charming fashion. If nobody wears those dresses today, it is simply because it isn't done. But they will come back, as fashions always do—in clothes, in music, in painting," she added with vigour, for she supposed there to be a certain originality in this philosophic reflection. Then the sad thought that she was growing old caused her to resume her languid manner, which a smile, however, momentarily contradicted: "Are you sure that they were red shoes that I wore? I thought they were gold." I assured her that I had the most vivid recollection of the colour of her shoes, though I preferred not to describe the incident which made me so certain on this point. "How kind of you to remember that!" she said to me sweetly, for women call it kindness when you remember their beauty, just as painters do when you admire their work. And then, since the past, however remote it may be for a woman

like the Duchess who has more head than heart, may nevertheless chance to have escaped oblivion, "Do you recall," she
said, as though to thank me for remembering her dress and
her shoes, "that Basin and I brought you home in our
carriage? You couldn't come in with us because of some girl
who was coming to see you after midnight. Basin thought it
the funniest thing in the world that you should receive visits
at such an hour." Indeed that was the evening when Albertine had come to see me after the Princesse de Guermantes's
party and I recalled the fact just as clearly as the Duchess, I
to whom Albertine was now as unimportant as she would have
been to Mme de Guermantes had Mme de Guermantes
known that the girl because of whom I had had to refuse their
invitation was Albertine. (In fact, she was quite in the dark
as to the identity of this girl, had never known it and only
referred to the incident because of the circumstances and the
singular lateness of the hour.) Yes, I recalled the fact, for,
long after our poor dead friends have lost their place in our
hearts, their unvalued dust continues to be mingled, like some
base alloy, with the circumstances of the past. And though
we no longer love them, it may happen that in speaking of a
room, or a walk in a public park, or a country road where
they were present with us on a certain occasion, we are obliged, so that the place which they occupied may not be left
empty, to make allusion to them, without, however, regretting them, without even naming them or permitting others
to identify them. Such are the last, the scarcely desirable
vestiges of survival after death.

If the opinions which the Duchess expressed about Rachel
were in themselves commonplace, they interested me for the
reason that they too marked a new hour upon the dial. For
Mme de Guermantes had no more completely forgotten than
Rachel the terrible evening which the latter had endured in

her house, but in the Duchess's mind too this memory had been transformed. "Of course," she said to me, "it interests me all the more to hear her, and to hear her acclaimed, because it was I who discovered her, who saw her worth and praised her and got people to listen when she was quite unknown and everybody thought her ridiculous. Yes, my dear boy, this will surprise you, but the first house in which she recited in public was mine! Yes, while all the so-called *avant garde*, like my new cousin," she said, with an ironic smile in the direction of Mme de Guermantes, who for Oriane had remained Mme Verdurin, "would have allowed her to die of hunger rather than condescend to listen to her, I had made up my mind that she was interesting and I offered her a fee to come and act in my house in front of the most distinguished audience that I could muster. I may say, though the word is rather stupid and pretentious—for the truth is that talent needs nobody to help it—that I launched her. But I am not suggesting that she needed me." I made a vague gesture of protest, and I saw that Mme de Guermantes was quite prepared to accept the contrary thesis. "You don't agree? You think that talent needs a support, needs someone to bring it into the light of day? Well, perhaps you are right. Curiously enough, that is exactly what Dumas used to say to me. In this case I am extremely flattered if I have done anything, however little, to promote not of course the talent but the reputation of so fine an artist." Mme de Guermantes preferred to abandon her idea that talent, like an abscess, forces its way to the surface unaided, partly because the alternative hypothesis was more flattering for her, but also because for some time now, mixing with newcomers to the social scene and being herself fatigued, she had become almost humble, questioning others and asking them their opinion before she formed her own. "I don't need to tell you," she went on, "that that intelligent public which calls itself society understood absolutely nothing of her art. They boo'd and they tittered. It was no use my saying: 'This is strange, interesting, something that has never been done before," nobody believed me, just as nobody has ever believed anything I have said. And it was exactly the same with the piece that she recited, which was a scene from Maeterlinck. Now, of course, it is very well known but in those days people merely thought it ridiculous—not I, however, I admired it. I must say I am surprised, when I think of it, that a mere peasant like myself, with no more education than all the other provincial girls around her, should from the very first moment have felt drawn to these things. Naturally I couldn't have said why, but I liked them, I was moved—indeed, even Basin, who can hardly be called hypersensitive, was struck by the effect that they had on me. 'I won't have you listening to these absurdities,' he said, 'it makes you ill.' And he was right, because although I'm supposed to be a woman without any feeling I'm really a bundle of nerves."

At this moment an unexpected incident occurred. A footman came up to Rachel and told her that the daughter and son-in-law of Berma were asking to speak to her. As we have seen, Berma's daughter had resisted the desire, to which her husband would have yielded, to ask Rachel for an invitation. But after the departure of the solitary guest the irritation of the young pair as they sat with their mother had increased. The thought that other people were enjoying themselves had become a torment to them and presently, profiting from a momentary absence of Berma, who had retired to her room spitting a little blood, they had thrown on some smarter clothes, called for a cab and come, without an invitation, to the Princesse de Guermantes's house. Rachel, guessing what had happened and secretly flattered, put on an arrogant air

and told the footman that she could not be disturbed, the
visitors must write a line to explain the object of their curious
procedure. Soon the footman came back with a card on which
Berma's daughter had scribbled a few words to the effect that
she and her husband had not been able to resist the desire to
hear Rachel—might they have her permission to come in?
Rachel smiled at the naïvety of the pretext and at her own
triumph. She sent back a reply that she was terribly sorry
but she had finished her recital. In the ante-room, where the
couple had now been waiting for an embarrassingly long time,
the footmen were beginning to jeer at the two rejected
petitioners. But the ignominy of a rebuff, and the thought too
of the worthlessness of Rachel in comparison with her mother,
drove Berma's daughter to pursue to final victory an enterprise on which she had first embarked merely from an appetite for pleasure. She sent a message to Rachel, asking as a
favour that, even if she had missed the privilege of hearing her,
she should be allowed to shake her by the hand. Rachel was
talking to an Italian prince, said to be not insensible to the
attractions of her large fortune, the origin of which was now
to some extent disguised by her partial acceptance in the world
of society. And here at her feet were the daughter and the
son-in-law of the illustrious Berma, a reversal of positions
which she was able to savour to the full. After giving a ludicrous account of what had happened to everybody within earshot, she ordered the young couple to be admitted and in they
came without waiting to be asked twice, thus at a single
stroke ruining Berma's social position just as they had destroyed her health. Rachel had foreseen this; she knew that
an amiable condescension on her part would do more than a
refusal to win for herself a reputation in society for goodness
of heart and for the young couple one for grovelling servility.
So she welcomed them with a theatrical gesture of open arms

and a few words spoken in the role of an exalted patroness momentarily laying aside her dignity: "Ah! here you are, it is so lovely to see you. The Princess will be delighted." Not knowing that in the world of the theatre it was generally believed that she had sent out the invitations herself, she had feared perhaps that, if she refused to let Berma's daughter and son-in-law come in, they might have doubts as to the extent, not so much of her good nature, which would scarcely have worried her, as of her influence. Instinctively the Duchesse de Guermantes drifted away, for in proportion as anyone betrayed a desire to seek out fashionable society, he or she sank in her esteem. At the moment she was uniquely impressed with Rachel's goodness, and had the daughter and son-in-law been presented to her she would have turned her back on them. Rachel meanwhile was already composing in her head the gracious phrase with which she would annihilate Berma when she saw her the following day back stage: "I was distressed and appalled that your poor daughter should be made to dance attendance on me. If I had only realised! She kept sending me card after card." Her spirits rose as she thought of this blow that she would deal to Berma. Yet perhaps she would have flinched had she known that it would be mortal. We like to have victims and we like them to suffer, but we do not exactly want to incriminate ourselves, we want them to remain alive. Not that she would really feel herself to be guilty. A few days later she was heard to say, with a laugh: "It's a bit much. I try to be kinder to her children than she ever was to me, and now I'm practically accused of murdering her. The Duchess will be my witness." So died Berma. It seems that the children of actors inherit from their parents all their ugly emotions and all the artificiality of theatrical life, but not, as a by-product of these, the stubborn will to work that their father or mother possessed, and Berma is not the only great tragic actress who has died as the victim of a domestic plot woven around her, repeating in her own person the fate that she so many times suffered in the final act of a play.

In spite of her new interests the life of the Duchess was now very unhappy, for the reason to which she had briefly alluded in her conversation with me, a reason which had, as a further consequence, a parallel degradation of the society which M. de Guermantes frequented. The Duke was still robust, but with the advance of age his desires had grown less imperious and he had long ceased to be unfaithful to Mme de Guermantes, when suddenly, without anyone knowing quite how the liaison had begun, he had fallen in love with Mme de Forcheville. When one considered what her age must now be, this seemed extraordinary. But perhaps she had been very young when she started on her career of gallantry. And then there are women who, decade after decade, are found in a new incarnation, having new love affairs (sometimes long after one had thought they were dead) and causing the despair of young wives who are abandoned for them by their husbands. In any case, the Duke's liaison with Mme de Forcheville had assumed such proportions that the old man, imitating in this final love the pattern of those that he had had in the past, watched jealously over his mistress in a manner which, if my love for Albertine had, with important variations, repeated the love of Swann for Odette, made that of M. de Guermantes for this same Odette recall my own for Albertine. He insisted that she should lunch with him and dine with him and he was always in her house, so that she was able to show him off to friends who without her would never have made the acquaintance of a Duc de Guermantes and who came there to meet him rather as one might go to the house of a courtesan to meet a king, her lover. It was true that Mme de Forcheville

had long ago become a society lady. But starting again
late in life to be kept, and to be kept by an old man of such
enormous pride who, in spite of the situation, was the important person in her house, she was herself not too proud
to wear only those wraps which pleased him, to serve only
the dishes that he liked, and to flatter her friends by telling
them that she had spoken of them to her new lover just as in
the old days she would tell my great-uncle that she had spoken
of him to the Grand Duke who sent her cigarettes; in a word,
in spite of all that she had accomplished in building up a social
position, she was tending under pressure of new circumstances
to become once more, as she had first appeared to me in my
earliest childhood, the lady in pink. (It was, of course, many
years since my uncle Adolphe had died, but the replacement
of the old figures around us by new ones does not necessarily
prevent us from beginning our old life again.) If Odette had
yielded to the pressure of her new circumstances, this was
no doubt partly from greed, but also because, having been
much sought after in society as the mother of an eligible
daughter and then ignored once Gilberte had married Saint-
Loup, she foresaw that the Duc de Guermantes, who would
have done anything for her, would rally to her side a number
of duchesses who would perhaps be delighted to do an ill
turn to their friend Oriane; and perhaps too she warmed to
the game when she saw how it distressed the Duchess, in
whose discomfiture a feminine sentiment of rivalry caused her
to rejoice. Even among the Duke's relations she now had her
partisans. Saint-Loup up to his death had continued loyally
to visit her with his wife. Were not he and Gilberte heirs
both to M. de Guermantes and to Odette, who would herself
no doubt be the principal beneficiary of the Duke's will?
And even Courvoisier nephews with the most exacting standards, even the Princesse de Trania and Mme de Marsantes,

came to her house in the hope of a legacy, without worrying about the pain that this might cause the Duchess, of whom Odette, stung by past affronts, spoke in the most scurrilous fashion. As for the Duke's own social position, his liaison with Mme de Forcheville—this liaison which was merely a pale copy of earlier affairs of the same kind—had recently caused him for the second time in his life to lose his chance of the presidency of the Jockey and a vacant seat in the Académie des Beaux-Arts, just as the way of life of M. de Charlus and his public association with Jupien had cost him the presidency of the Union and that also of the Société des Amis du Vieux Paris when these were within his grasp. Thus the two brothers, so different in their tastes, had lost their reputations from a common indolence and a common lack of will, qualities already perceptible, but in a more agreeable fashion, in the Duc de Guermantes their grandfather, member of the Académie Française, but which, re-appearing in his two grandsons, had permitted a natural taste in the one and what passes for an unnatural taste in the other to alienate their possessors from their proper social sphere.

The old Duke no longer went anywhere, for he spent his days and his evenings with Mme de Forcheville. But today, as he would find her here, he had come for a moment, in spite of the vexation of having to meet his wife. I had not seen him and I would certainly have failed to recognise him, had he not been clearly pointed out to me. He was no more than a ruin now, a magnificent ruin—or perhaps not even a ruin but a beautiful and romantic natural object, a rock in a tempest. Lashed on all sides by the surrounding waves—waves of suffering, of wrath at being made to suffer, of the rising tide of death—his face, like a crumbling block of marble, preserved the style and the poise which I had always admired; it might have been one of those fine antique heads, eaten

away and hopelessly damaged, which you are proud nevertheless to have as an ornament for your study. In one respect
only was it changed: it seemed to belong to a more ancient
epoch than formerly, not simply because of the now rough
and rugged surfaces of what had once been a more brilliant
material, but also because to an expression of keen and
humorous enjoyment had succeeded one, involuntary and unconscious, built up by illness, by the struggle against death, by
passive resistance, by the difficulty of remaining alive. The
arteries had lost all suppleness and gave to the once expan-
sive countenance a hard and sculptural quality. And though
the Duke had no suspicion of this, there were aspects of his
appearance, of his neck and cheeks and forehead, which suggested to the observer that the vital spirit within, compelled
to clutch desperately at every passing minute, was buffeted by
a great tragic gale, while the white wisps of his still magnificent but now sparse hair lashed with their foam the half
submerged promontory of his face. And just as there are
strange and unique reflections which only the approach of a
supreme all-foundering storm can impart to rocks that
hitherto have been of a different colour, so I realised that the
leaden grey of the stiff, worn cheeks, the almost white, fleecy
grey of the drifting wisps of hair, the feeble light that still
shone from the eyes that scarcely saw, were not unreal hues
and glimmers—they were only too real but they were fantastic, they were borrowed from the palette and the illumination, inimitable in their terrifying and prophetic sombreness,
of old age and the imminence of death.

The Duke stayed only for a few moments, long enough,
however, for me to perceive that Odette, reserving her
favours for younger wooers, treated him with contempt. But
curiously, whereas in the past he had been almost ridiculous
when he used to behave like a king in a play, he had now

assumed an appearance of true grandeur, rather like his brother, whom old age, stripping him of all unessential qualities, caused him to resemble. And—in this too resembling his brother— he who had once been proud, though not in his brother's fashion, seemed now almost respectful, though again in a different fashion. He had not suffered quite the degradation of M. de Charlus, he was not obliged by the unreliable memory of a sick man to greet with civility people whom he would once have disdained. But he was very old and when, wanting to leave, laboriously he passed through the door-way and down the stairs, one saw that old age, which is after all the most miserable of human conditions, which more than anything else precipitates us from the summit of our fortunes like a king in a Greek tragedy, old age, forcing him to halt in the *via dolorosa* which life must become for us when we are impotent and surrounded by menace, to wipe his perspiring brow, to grope his way forward as his eyes sought the step which eluded them, because for his unsteady feet no less than for his clouded eyes he needed support, old age, giving him, though he did not know it, the air of gently and timidly beseeching those near him, if it had made him august, had, even more, made him humbly suppliant.

Thus in the Faubourg Saint-Germain three apparently impregnable positions, of the Duc and the Duchesse de Guermantes and of the Baron de Charlus, had lost their inviolability, changing, as all things change in this world, under the action of an inherent principle which had at first attracted nobody's attention: in M. de Charlus his love for Charlie, which had enslaved him to the Verdurins, and then later the advent of senility; in Mme de Guermantes a taste for novelty and for art; in the Duke an exclusive amorous passion, of a kind of which he had had several in the course of his life, but one which now, through the feebleness of age, was more tyrannical than those that had gone before and of which the ignominy was no longer compensated by the opposing, the socially redeeming respectability of the Duchess's *salon*, where the Duke himself no longer appeared and which altogether had almost ceased to function. Thus it is that the pattern of the things of this world changes, that centres of empire, assessments of wealth, letters patent of social prestige, all that seemed to be forever fixed is constantly being re-fashioned, so that the eyes of a man who has lived can contemplate the most total transformation exactly where change would have seemed to him to be most impossible.

Unable to do without Odette, always installed by her fireside in the same armchair, whence age and gout made it difficult for him to rise, M. de Guermantes permitted her to receive friends who were only too pleased to be presented to the Duke, to defer to him in conversation, to listen while he talked about the society of an earlier era, about the Marquise de Villeparisis and the Duc de Chartres. At moments, beneath the gaze of the old masters assembled by Swann in a typical "collector's" arrangement which enhanced the unfashionable and "period" character of the scene, with this Restoration Duke and this Second Empire courtesan swathed in one of the wraps which he liked, the lady in pink would interrupt him with a sprightly sally: he would stop dead and fix her with a ferocious glance. Perhaps he had come to see that she too, like the Duchess, sometimes made stupid remarks; perhaps, suffering from an old man's delusion, he imagined that it was an ill-timed witticism of Mme de Guermantes that had checked his flow of reminiscence, imagined that he was still in his own house, like a wild beast in chains who for a brief second thinks that he is still free in the deserts of Africa. And brusquely raising his head, with his little round, yellow eyes which themselves had the glitter of the eyes of a wild animal, he fastened upon her one of those looks which sometimes in Mme de Guermantes's drawing-room, when the Duchess talked too much, had made me tremble. So for a moment the Duke glared at the audacious lady in pink. But she, unflinching, held him in her gaze, and after a few seconds which seemed interminable to the spectators, the old tame lion recollecting that he was not free, with the Duchess beside him, in that Sahara which one entered by stepping over a door-mat on a landing, but in Mme de Forcheville's domain, in his cage in the Zoological Gardens, he allowed his head, with its still thick and flowing mane of which it would have been hard to say whether it was yellow or white, to slump back between his shoulders and continued his story. He seemed not to have understood what Mme de Forcheville was trying to say, and indeed there was seldom any very profound meaning in her remarks. He did not forbid her to have friends to dinner with him, but, by a mania copied from his former love-affairs which was hardly likely to surprise Odette, who had been used to the same thing with Swann, and which to me seemed touching because it recalled to me my life with Albertine, he insisted that these guests should take their leave early so that he might be the last to say good-night to her. Needless to say, the moment he was out of the house she went off to meet other people. But of this the Duke had no suspicion or perhaps preferred her to think that he had no suspicion. The sight of old men grows dim as their hearing grows less acute, their insight too becomes clouded and even their vigilance is relaxed by fatigue, and at a certain age, inevitably, Jupiter himself is transformed into a character in one of Molière's plays, and not even into the Olympian lover of Alcmène but into a ludicrous Géronte. It must be added that Odette was unfaithful to M. de Guermantes in the same fashion that she looked after him, that is to say without charm and without dignity. She was common-place in this role as she had been in all her others. Not that life had not frequently given her good parts; it had, but she had not known how to play them.

On several occasions after the Guermantes party I attempted to see her again, but each time I was unsuccessful, for M. de Guermantes, in order to satisfy the requirements not only of his jealous nature but also of his medical regime, allowed her to attend social functions only in the day-time and even then placed an embargo upon dances. This seclusion in which she was kept she frankly avowed to me when at last we met, for several reasons. The principal one was that, although I had only written a few articles and published some essays, she imagined me to be a well-known author, an idea which even caused her naïvely to exclaim, recalling the days when I used to go to the Avenue des Acacias to see her pass by and later visited her in her home: "Ah! if I had only guessed that he would be a great writer one day!" And having heard that writers seek the society of women as a means of collecting material for their work and like to get them to describe their love-affairs, she now, in order to interest me, reassumed the character of an out-and-out tart. She would tell me stories of this sort: "And then once there was a man who was mad about me, and I was desperately in love with him too. We were having a heavenly life together. He had to go to America for some reason, and I was to go with him. The day before we were to leave I decided that, as our love could not always remain at such a pitch of intensity, it was more beautiful not to let it slowly fade to nothing. We had a last evening together —he of course believed that I was coming with him—and then a night of absolute madness, in which I was ecstatically happy in his arms and at the same time in despair because I knew that I should never see him again. A few hours earlier

I had gone up to some traveller whom I did not know and given him my ticket. He wanted at least to buy it from me, but I replied: 'No, you are doing me a service by taking it, I don't want any money.' " Here was another: "One day I was in the Champs Elysées and M. de Bréauté, whom I had only met once, began to stare at me so insistently that I stopped and asked him why he took the liberty of staring at me like that. He replied: 'I am looking at you because you are wearing a ridiculous hat.' This was quite true. It was a little hat with pansies, the fashions were dreadful in those days. But I was furious and said to him: 'I cannot allow you to talk to me like that.' At that moment it started to rain. I said to him: 'I would only forgive you if you had a carriage.' 'But I have one,' he replied, 'and I will accompany you.' 'No, I want your carriage but I don't want you.' I got into the carriage and he walked off in the rain. But the same evening he arrived on my door-step. For two years we were madly in love with each other. Come and have tea with me one day, and I will tell you how I made the acquaintance of M. de Forcheville. The truth is," she went on with a melancholy air, "that I have spent my life in cloistered seclusion because my great loves have all been for men who were horribly jealous. I am not speaking of M. de Forcheville, who was at bottom a common-place man—and I have never really been able to love anyone who was not intelligent. But M. Swann for one was as jealous as the poor Duke here, for whose sake I renounce all enjoyment, because I know that he is so unhappy in his own home. With M. Swann it was different, I was desperately in love with him and it seems to me only reasonable to sacrifice dancing and society and all the rest of it for a life which will give pleasure to a man who loves you, or will merely prevent him from suffering. Poor Charles, how intelligent he was, how fascinating, just the type of man I liked." And perhaps this

was true. There had been a time when she had found Swann
attractive, which had coincided with the time when she to him
had been "not his type". The truth was that "his type" was
something that, even later, she had never been. And yet how
he had loved her and with what anguish of mind! Ceasing to
love her, he had been puzzled by this contradiction, which
really is no contradiction at all, if we consider how large a
proportion of the sufferings endured by men in their lives is
caused to them by women who are "not their type". Perhaps
there are many reasons why this should be so: first, because a
woman is "not your type" you let yourself, at the beginning,
be loved by her without loving in return, and by doing this
you allow your life to be gripped by a habit which would not
have taken root in the same way with a woman who was
"your type", who, conscious of your desire, would have
offered more resistance, would only rarely have consented to
see you, would not have installed herself in every hour of
your days with that familiarity which means that later, if
you come to love her and then suddenly she is not there,
because of a quarrel or because of a journey during which you
are left without news of her, you are hurt by the severance
not of one but of a thousand links. And then this habit, not
resting upon the foundation of strong physical desire, is a
sentimental one, and once love is born the brain gets much
more busily to work: you are plunged into a romance, not
plagued by a mere need. We are not wary of women who are
"not our type", we let them love us, and if, subsequently, we
come to love them we love them a hundred times more than
we love other women, without even enjoying in their arms
the satisfaction of assuaged desire. For these reasons and for
many others the fact that our greatest unhappinesses come to
us from women who are "not our type" is not simply an instance of that mockery of fate which never grants us our

wishes except in the form which pleases us least. A woman who is "our type" is seldom dangerous, she is not interested in us, she gives us a limited contentment and then quickly leaves us without establishing herself in our life, and what on the contrary, in love, is dangerous and prolific of suffering is not a woman herself but her presence beside us every day and our curiosity about what she is doing every minute: not the beloved woman, but habit.

I was cowardly enough to say that it was kind and generous of her to talk to me in this way, but I knew how little truth there was in my remark, I knew that with her frankness there were mixed up all sorts of lies. And as she continued to regale me with adventures from her past life, I thought with terror how much there was that Swann had not known—though some of it he had guessed almost to the point of certainty, merely from the look in her eyes when she saw a man or a woman whom she did not know and whom she found attractive—and how much the knowledge of it would have made him suffer, because he had fastened his sensibility to this one individual. And why was she now so outspoken? Simply in order to give me what she believed were subjects for novels. In this belief she was mistaken. It was true that from my earliest years she had supplied my imagination with abundance of material to work on, but in a much more involuntary fashion, through an act which originated with myself when I sought, unbeknown to her, to deduce from my observation of her the laws which governed her life.

M. de Guermantes now reserved his thunderbolts solely for the Duchess, to whose somewhat indiscriminate associations Mme de Forcheville did not fail to draw his wrathful attention. And so Mme de Guermantes was very unhappy. It is true that M. de Charlus, with whom I had once discussed the subject, maintained that the original transgressions had not been on his brother's side and that beneath the legendary purity of the Duchess there in fact lay skilfully concealed an incalculable number of love-affairs. But I had never heard any gossip to this effect. In the eyes of almost all the world Mme de Guermantes was a woman of a very different kind, and the idea that she had always been irreproachable went unchallenged. Which of these two ideas accorded with the truth I was unable to determine, the truth being almost always something that to three people out of four is unknown. I well recalled certain glances, blue and vagabond, which I had intercepted as they shot from the eyes of the Duchesse de Guermantes down the nave at Combray, but I could not really say that either of the two ideas was disproved by these glances, since both the one and the other could give them meanings which, though different, were equally acceptable. In my foolishness, child as I then was, I had for a moment taken them to be glances of love directed at myself. Later I had realised that they were merely the gracious looks that a sovereign lady, like the one in the stained-glass windows of the church, bestows upon her vassals. Was I now to suppose that my first idea had been correct and that, if in the sequel the Duchess had never spoken to me of love, this was because she had been more afraid to compromise herself with a friend of her nephew and her aunt than with an unknown boy encountered by chance in the church of Saint-Hilaire at Combray?

Perhaps the Duchess had been pleased for a moment to feel that her past had more substance because it had been shared by me, but certain questions which I put to her on the provincialism of M. de Bréauté, whom at the time I had scarcely distinguished from M. de Sagan or M. de Guermantes, caused her to resume the normal point of view of a society woman, the point of view, that is to say, of a woman who affects to despise society. While we were talking, she

438

took me on a tour of the house. In one or two smaller sitting-rooms we came upon special friends of our hostess who had preferred to get away from the crowd in order to listen to the music. One of these was a little room with Empire furniture, where a few men in black evening clothes were sitting about on sofas, listening, while beside a tall mirror supported by a figure of Minerva a *chaise longue*, set at right angles to the wall but with a curved and cradle-like interior which contrasted with the straight lines all round it, disclosed the figure of a young woman lying at full length. The relaxation of her pose, from which she did not even stir when the Duchess entered the room, was set off by the marvellous brilliance of her Empire dress, of a flame-red silk before which even the reddest of fuchsias would have paled and upon whose nacreous texture emblems and flowers seemed to have been imprinted in some distant past, for their patterns were sunk beneath its surface. To acknowledge the presence of the Duchess she made a slight bow with her beautiful, dark head. Although it was broad daylight, she had asked for the curtains to be drawn as an aid to the silence and concentration which the music required and, to prevent people from stumbling over the furniture, an urn had been lit upon a tripod and from it came a faint, iridescent glimmer. I enquired of the Duchess who the young woman was, and she told me that her name was Mme de Saint-Euverte. This led me to enquire further how she was related to the Mme de Saint-Euverte whom I had known. Mme de Guermantes said that she was the wife of one of old Mme de Saint-Euverte's great-nephews and appeared to think it possible that her maiden name had been La Rochefoucauld, but denied that she had ever herself known any Saint-Euvertes. I recalled to her the evening party (known to me, it is true, only from hearsay) at which, when she was still Princesse des Laumes, she had unexpectedly

REMEMBRANCE OF THINGS PAST

met Swann. Mme de Guermantes assured me that she had
never been at this party. The Duchess had never been very
truthful and now told lies more readily than ever. For her
Mme de Saint-Euverte was a hostess—and one whose reputation, with the passage of time, had sunk very low indeed—
whom she chose to disown. I did not insist. "No, someone
you may perhaps have seen in my house—because at least he
was amusing—is the husband of the woman you are talking
about, but I never had anything to do with his wife." "But
she didn't have a husband." "That is what you imagined,
because they were separated. In fact he was much nicer than
she was." At length it dawned upon me that an enormous
man, of vast height and strength, with snow-white hair,
whom I used to meet in various houses and whose name I
had never known, was the husband of Mme de Saint-Euverte.
He had died in the previous year. As for the great-niece, I do
not know whether it was owing to some malady of the
stomach or the nerves or the veins, or because she was about to
have or had just had a child or perhaps a miscarriage, that she
lay flat on her back to listen to the music and did not budge for
anyone. Very probably she was simply proud of her magnificent red silks and hoped on her *chaise longue* to look
like Mme Récamier. She could not know that for me she
was giving birth to a new efflorescence of the name of
Saint-Euverte, which recurring thus after so long an interval
marked both the distance travelled by Time and its continuity.
Time was the infant that she cradled in her cockle-shell,
where the red fuchsias of her silk dress gave an autumnal
flowering to the name of Saint-Euverte and to the Empire
style. The latter Mme de Guermantes declared that she had
always detested, a remark which meant merely that she detested it now, which was true, for she followed the fashion,
even if she did not succeed in keeping up with it. To say

nothing of David, whose work she hardly knew, when she was quite young she had thought M. Ingres the most boring and academic of painters, then, by a brusque reversal—which caused her also to loathe Delacroix—the most delectable of the masters revered by *art nouveau*. By what gradations she had subsequently passed from this cult to a renewal of her early contempt matters little, since these are shades of taste which the writings of an art critic reflect ten years before the conversation of clever women. After having delivered herself of some strictures upon the Empire style, she apologised for having talked to me about people of as little interest as the Saint-Euvertes and subjects as trivial as the provincial side of Bréauté's character, for she was as far from guessing why these things could interest me as was Mme de Saint-Euverte *née* La Rochefoucauld, seeking in her supine pose the well-being of her stomach or an Ingresque effect, from suspecting that her name—her married name, not the infinitely more distinguished one of her own family—had enchanted me and that I saw her, in this room full of symbolic attributes, as a Nymph cradling the Infant Time.

"But how can I talk to you about this nonsense, how can it possibly interest you?" exclaimed the Duchess. She had uttered these words in an undertone and nobody had been able to hear what she was saying. But a young man (who interested me later when I discovered his name, which had been much more familiar to me at one time than that of Saint-Euverte) got up with an air of exasperation and moved away from us in order to listen undisturbed. For the Kreutzer Sonata was now being played, but having lost his place in the programme the young man thought that it was a piece by Ravel, which he had been told was as beautiful as Palestrina but difficult to understand. In his haste to move to another seat, he bumped violently against an escritoire which he had not seen in the half-dark, and the noise had the effect of slewing round the heads of several people, for whom the trifling physical exertion of looking over their shoulder was a welcome interruption to the torture of listening "religiously" to the Kreutzer Sonata. Mme de Guermantes and I, who had caused this unfortunate little incident, hurriedly left the room. "Yes," she went on, "how can these inanities interest a man of your talent? That is what I asked myself just now, when I saw you talking to Gilberte de Saint-Loup. You should not waste your time on her. For me that woman is quite literally nothing—she is not even a woman, merely the most artificial and *bourgeois* phenomenon that I have ever encountered" (for even when she was defending intellectualism the Duchess did not divest herself of her aristocratic prejudices). "What, in any case, are you doing in a house like this? I can just see that you might want to be here today, because there was this recitation by Rachel and naturally that interests you. But wonderful though she was, she does not give of her best before a public like this. You must come and have luncheon alone with her in my house. Then you will see what an extraordinary being she is. She is worth a hundred times more than all this riff-raff. And after luncheon she will recite Verlaine for you. You will be amazed! But otherwise your coming to a great omnium gatherum like this is something I simply cannot understand. Unless perhaps your interest is professional . . ." she added with a doubtful and mistrustful air and without venturing to follow this speculation too far, for she had no very precise ideas as to the nature of the improbable operations to which she alluded. She went on to tempt me with the glittering prospect of her "afternoons": every day after luncheon there was X— and there was Y—, and I found that her views on these matters were now those of all women who preside over a *salon*, those women whom in the past (though she denied it today) she had despised and whose great superiority, whose sign of election lay, according to her present mode of thinking, in getting "all the men" to come to them. If I happened to say that some great lady with a *salon* had spoken with malice of Mme Howland when she was alive, the Duchess burst out laughing at my simplicity: "But of course, she had all the men and Mme Howland was trying to get them away from her."

"Don't you think," I said to the Duchess, "that it must be painful for Mme de Saint-Loup to have to listen, as she has just been doing, to a woman who was once her husband's mistress?" I saw form in Mme de Guermantes's face one of those oblique bars which indicate that a train of thought is linking something a person has just heard to some disagreeable subject of reflection. A train of thought, it is true, which usually remains unexpressed, for seldom if ever do we receive any answer to the unpleasant things that we say or write. Only a fool begs vainly ten times in succession for a reply to a letter which was a blunder and which he ought never to have written, for the only reply ever vouchsafed to this sort of letter is in the form of action: the lady whom you suppose to be merely an unpunctual correspondent addresses you as "Monsieur" when she next meets you instead of calling you by your Christian name. My reference to Saint-Loup's liaison with Rachel was, however, not seriously unpleasant and could only cause Mme de Guermantes a moment's annoyance by reminding her that I had been Robert's closest friend and that he had perhaps confided in me on the subject of the snubs which Rachel had suffered when she gave her performance at the Duchess's party. But Mme de Guermantes did not persist in these reflections, the stormy bar faded from her face and she replied to my question concerning Mme de Saint-Loup: "Frankly, it is my belief that it can matter very little

443

to Gilberte, since she never loved her husband. She is a quite dreadful young woman. She loved the social position and the name and being my niece and getting away from the slime where she belonged, but then having done this her one idea was to return to it. I don't mind telling you that I suffered a great deal for poor Robert, because, though he may not have been an eagle, still he had eyes and he must have seen a thousand things. Perhaps I shouldn't say it, because after all she is my niece and I have no absolute proof that she was unfaithful to him, but there were any number of stories. Oh! yes, there were, and I know for a fact there was something between her and an officer at Méséglise. Robert wanted to challenge him. It was because of all this that Robert joined up—the war came to him as a deliverance from the misery of his family life: if you want my opinion, he wasn't killed, he got himself killed. Do you think she felt any grief? Not a scrap, she even astonished me by the extraordinary cynicism with which she displayed her indifference, and this distressed me very much, because I was really extremely fond of poor Robert. Perhaps this will surprise you, because people have a wrong idea of my character, but even now I still think of him sometimes—I never forget anybody. He never said a word to me, but he saw very clearly that I guessed everything. Do you suppose, if she had loved her husband the least little bit, that she could stoically endure like this to be in the same drawing-room as the woman with whom he was desperately in love for so many years—indeed one may say 'always', for I am quite certain that he never gave her up, even during the war. Why, she would fly at her throat!" exclaimed the Duchess, forgetting that she herself, in arranging for Rachel to be invited and so setting the stage for the drama which she judged to be inevitable if it were true that Gilberte had loved Robert, had perhaps acted cruelly. "No, in my opinion", the Duchess concluded, "she is a bitch." Such an expression on the lips of the Duchesse de Guermantes was rendered possible by the downward path which she was following, from the polished society of the Guermantes to that of her new actress friends, and came to her all the more easily because she grafted it onto an eighteenth-century mode of speech which she thought of as broad and racy—and then had she not always believed that to her all things were permitted? But the actual choice of the word was dictated by the hatred which she felt for Gilberte, by an irresistible wish to strike her at least in effigy if she could not attack her with physical blows. And at the same time the Duchess thought that somehow the word justified the whole manner in which she conducted herself towards Gilberte, or rather conducted hostilities against Gilberte, in society and in the family and even where pecuniary interests were concerned such as the succession to Robert's estate.

This savage attack on Gilberte struck me as quite unwarranted, but sometimes we pronounce a judgement which receives later from facts of which we were ignorant and which we could not have guessed an apparent justification, and Mme de Guermantes's tirade perhaps belonged to this category. For Gilberte, who had no doubt inherited certain family characteristics from her mother (and I had perhaps unconsciously anticipated some such laxness of principle in her when I had asked her to introduce me to young girls), had now had time to reflect upon my request and, anxious no doubt that the profit should stay in the family, had reached a decision bolder than any that I would have thought possible. "Let me fetch my daughter for you," she said, "I should so like to introduce her to you. She is over there, talking to young Mortemart and other babes in arms who can be of no possible interest. I am sure that she will be a charming little friend for you." I asked whether Robert had been pleased to

Q

have a daughter. "Oh! yes," she replied, "he was very proud of her. But naturally," she went on, with a certain naïvety, "I think that nevertheless, his tastes being what they were, he would have preferred a son." Years later, this daughter, whose name and fortune gave her mother the right to hope that she would crown the whole work of social ascent of Swann and his wife by marrying a royal prince, happening to be entirely without snobbery chose for her husband an obscure man of letters. Thus it came about that the family sank once more, below even the level from which it had started its ascent, and a new generation could only with the greatest difficulty be persuaded that the parents of the obscure couple had enjoyed a splendid social position. The names of Swann and Odette de Crécy came miraculously to life whenever anyone wanted to explain to you that you were wrong, that there had been nothing so very wonderful about the family, and it was generally supposed that Mme de Saint-Loup had really made as good a match for her daughter as could be expected and that the marriage of this daughter's grandfather to Mme de Crécy had been no more than an unsuccessful attempt to rise to a higher sphere—a view of Swann's marriage which would have astonished his fashionable friends, in whose eyes it had been rather the product of an idealistic theory like those which in the eighteenth century drove aristocratic disciples of Rousseau and other precursors of the Revolution to abandon their privileges and live according to nature.

My surprise at Gilberte's words and the pleasure that they caused me were soon replaced, while Mme de Saint-Loup left me and made her way into another drawing-room, by that idea of Time past which was brought home to me once again, in yet another fashion and without my even having seen her, by Mlle de Saint-Loup. Was she not—are not, indeed, the

majority of human beings?—like one of those star-shaped
cross-roads in a forest where roads converge that have come,
in the forest as in our lives, from the most diverse quarters?
Numerous for me were the roads which led to Mlle de Saint-
Loup and which radiated around her. Firstly the two great
"ways" themselves, where on my many walks I had dreamed
so many dreams, both led to her: through her father Robert
de Saint-Loup the Guermantes way; through Gilberte,
her mother, the Méséglise way which was also "Swann's
way". One of them took me, by way of this girl's mother and
the Champs Elysées, to Swann, to my evenings at Combray,
to Méséglise itself; the other, by way of her father, to those
afternoons at Balbec where even now I saw him again near
the sun-bright sea. And then between these two high roads
a network of transversals was set up. Balbec, for example, the
real Balbec where I had met Saint-Loup, was a place that I
had longed to go to very largely because of what Swann had
told me about the churches in its neighbourhood, and especially about its own church in the Persian style, and yet Robert
de Saint-Loup was the nephew of the Duchesse de Guermantes, and through him I arrived at Combray again, at the
Guermantes way. And there were many other points in my
life to which I was led by starting from Mlle de Saint-Loup,
to the lady in pink, for instance, who was her grandmother
and whom I had seen in the house of my great-uncle. And
here there was a new transversal, for this great-uncle's man-
servant, who had opened the door to me that day and who
later, by the gift of a photograph, had enabled me to identify
the lady in pink, was the father of the young man with whom
not only M. de Charlus but also Mlle de Saint-Loup's father
had been in love, the young man on whose account he had
made her mother unhappy. And was it not Swann, the grandfather of Mlle de Saint-Loup, who had first spoken to me of

447

the music of Vinteuil, just as it was Gilberte who had first spoken to me of Albertine? Yet it was in speaking of this same music of Vinteuil to Albertine that I had discovered the identity of her great friend and it was with this discovery that that part of our lives had commenced which had led her to her death and caused me such terrible sufferings. And it was also Mlle de Saint-Loup's father who had gone off to try and bring Albertine back. And indeed my whole social life, both in the drawing-rooms of the Swanns and the Guermantes in Paris and also that very different life which I had led with the Verdurins in the country, was in some sense a prolongation of the two ways of Combray, a prolongation which brought into line with one way or the other places as far apart as the Champs Elysées and the beautiful terrace of La Raspelière. Are there in fact among all our acquaintances any who, if we are to tell the story of our friendship with them, do not constrain us to place them successively in all the most different settings of our own life? A life of Saint-Loup painted by me would have as its background the various scenes of my own life, would be related to every part of that life, even those to which it was apparently most foreign, such as my grandmother and Albertine. And the Verdurins, though they might be diametrically opposed to these other characters, were yet linked to Odette through her past and to Robert de Saint-Loup through Charlie—and in the Verdurins' house too what a role, what an all-important role had the music of Vinteuil not played! And then Swann had been in love with Legrandin's sister, and Legrandin had known M. de Charlus, whose ward Legrandin's nephew, young Cambremer, had married. Certainly, if he was thinking purely of the human heart, the poet was right when he spoke of the "mysterious threads" which are broken by life. But the truth, even more, is that life is perpetually weaving fresh threads which link one individual and one event to another, and that these threads are crossed and recrossed, doubled and redoubled to thicken the web, so that between any slightest point of our past and all the others a rich network of memories gives us an almost infinite variety of communicating paths to choose from.

At every moment of our lives we are surrounded by things and people which once were endowed with a rich emotional significance that they no longer possess. But let us cease to make use of them in an unconscious way, let us try to recall what they once were in our eyes, and how often do we not find that a thing later transformed into, as it were, mere raw material for our industrial use was once alive, and alive for us with a personal life of its own. All round me on the walls were paintings by Elstir, that Elstir who had first introduced me to Albertine. And it was in the house of Mme Verdurin that I was about to be presented to Mlle de Saint-Loup whom I was going to ask to be Albertine's successor in my life, in the house of that very Mme Verdurin whom I had so often visited with Albertine—and how enchanting they seemed in my memory, all those journeys that we had made together in the little train on the way to Douville and La Raspelière—and who had also schemed first to promote and then to break not only my own love for Albertine but, long before it, that of the grandfather and the grandmother of this same Mlle de Saint-Loup. And to complete the process by which all my various pasts were fused into a single mass Mme Verdurin, like Gilberte, had married a Guermantes.

I have said that it would be impossible to depict our relationship with anyone whom we have even slightly known without passing in review, one after another, the most different settings of our life. Each individual therefore—and I was myself one of these individuals—was a measure of duration for me, in virtue of the revolutions which like some heavenly body he had accomplished not only on his own axis but also around other bodies, in virtue, above all, of the successive positions which he had occupied in relation to myself. And surely the awareness of all these different planes within which, since in this last hour, at this party, I had recaptured it, Time seemed to dispose the different elements of my life, had, by making me reflect that in a book which tried to tell the story of a life it would be necessary to use not the two-dimensional psychology which we normally use but a quite different sort of three-dimensional psychology, added a new beauty to those resurrections of the past which my memory had effected while I was following my thoughts alone in the library, since memory by itself, when it introduces the past, unmodified, into the present—the past just as it was at the moment when it was itself the present—suppresses the mighty dimension of Time which is the dimension in which life is lived.

I saw Gilberte coming across the room towards me. For me the marriage of Saint-Loup and the thoughts which filled my mind at that date—and which were still there, unchanged, this very morning—might have belonged to yesterday, so that I was astonished to see at her side a girl of about sixteen, whose tall figure was a measure of that distance which I had been reluctant to see. Time, colourless and inapprehensible Time, so that I was almost able to see it and touch it, had materialised itself in this girl, slowly moulding her into a masterpiece, whilest on me too parallelly, it had done its work, but without, alas! a master's touch. And now Mlle de Saint-Loup was standing in front of me. She had eyes that were deeply drilled and piercing, and a charming nose thrust slightly forward in the form of a beak and curved, perhaps not in the least like that of Swann but like Saint-Loup's. The soul of that particular Guermantes had fluttered away, but his charming head, as of a bird in flight, with its piercing eyes, had settled momentarily upon the shoulders of Mlle de Saint-Loup and the sight of it there aroused a train of memories and dreams in those who had known her father. I was struck too by the way in which her nose, imitating in this the model of her mother's nose and her grandmother's, was cut off by just that absolutely horizontal line at its base, that same brilliant if slightly tardy stroke of design—a feature so individual that with its help, even without seeing anything else of a head one could have recognised it out of thousands— and it seemed to me wonderful that at the critical moment nature should have returned, like a great and original sculptor, to give to the granddaughter, as she had given to her mother and her grandmother, that significant and decisive touch of the chisel. I thought her very beautiful: still rich in hopes, full of laughter, formed from those very years which I myself had lost, she was like my own youth.

The idea of Time was of value to me for yet another reason: it was a spur, it told me that it was time to begin if I wished to attain to what I had sometimes perceived in the course of my life, in brief lightning-flashes, on the Guermantes way and in my drives in the carriage of Mme de Villeparisis, at those moments of perception which had made me think that life was worth living. How much more worth living did it appear to me now, now that I seemed to see that this life that we live in half-darkness can be illumined, this life that at every moment we distort can be restored to its true pristine shape, that a life, in short, can be realised within the confines of a book! How happy would he be, I thought, the man who had the power to write such a book! What a task awaited him! To give some idea of this task one would have to borrow comparisons from the loftiest and the most varied arts; for this writer—who, moreover, to indicate the mass, the solidity of each one of his characters must find means to display that character's most opposite facets—would have to prepare his book with meticulous care, perpetually regrouping his forces like a general conducting an offensive, and he would have also to endure his book like a form of fatigue, to accept it like a discipline, build it up like a church, follow it like a medical regime, vanquish it like an obstacle, win it like a friendship, cosset it like a little child, create it like a new world without neglecting those mysteries whose explanation is to be found probably only in worlds other than our own and the presentiment of which is the thing that moves us most deeply in life and in art. In long books of this kind there are parts which there has been time only to sketch, parts which, because of the very amplitude of the architect's plan, will no doubt never be completed. How many great cathedrals remain unfinished! The writer feeds his book, he strengthens the parts of it which are weak, he protects it, but as a result it is the book that grows great, that designs its own author's tomb and defends it against rumour and for a while against oblivion. But to return to my own case, I thought more modestly of my book and it would be inaccurate even to say that I thought of those who would read it as "my" readers. For it seemed to me that they would not be "my" readers but the readers of their own selves, my book being merely a sort of magnifying glass like those which the optician at Combray used to offer his customers—it would be my book, but with its help I would furnish them with the means of reading what lay inside themselves. So that I should not ask them to praise me or to censure me, but simply to tell me whether "it really is like that", I should ask them whether the words that they read within themselves are the same as those which I have written (though a discrepancy in this respect need not always be the consequence of an error on my part, since the explanation could also be that the reader had

eyes for which my book was not a suitable instrument). And
—for at every moment the metaphor uppermost in my mind
changed as I began to represent to myself more clearly and in
a more material shape the task upon which I was about to
embark—I thought that at my big deal table, under the eyes
of Françoise, who like all unpretentious people who live at
close quarters with us would have a certain insight into the
nature of my labours (and I had sufficiently forgotten Albertine to have forgiven Françoise anything that she might have
done to injure her), I should work beside her and in a way
almost as she worked herself (or at least as she had worked
in the past, for now, with the onset of old age, she had almost
lost her sight) and, pinning here and there an extra page, I
should construct my book, I dare not say ambitiously like a
cathedral, but quite simply like a dress. Whenever I had not
all my "paperies" near me, as Françoise called them, and just
the one that I needed was missing, Françoise would understand how this upset me, she who always said that she could
not sew if she had not the right size of thread and the proper
buttons. And then through sharing my life with me had she
not acquired a sort of instinctive comprehension of literary
work, more accurate than that possessed by many intelligent
people, not to mention fools? Already years ago, when I had
written my article for *Le Figaro*, while our old butler, with
that sort of commiseration which always slightly exaggerates
the laboriousness of an occupation which the sympathiser
does not practise himself and does not even clearly visualise—
or even of a habit which he does not have himself, like the
people who say to you: "How tiring you must find it to sneeze
like that!"—expressed his quite sincere pity for writers in
the words: "That's a head-splitting job you've got there",
Françoise on the contrary both divined my happiness and
respected my toil. The only thing that annoyed her was my

speaking about the article to Bloch before it appeared, for she was afraid that he might forestall me. "You're too trustful," she would say, "all those people are nothing but copiators." And it was true that, whenever I had outlined to Bloch something that I had written and that he admired, he would provide a retrospective alibi for himself by saying: "Why, isn't that curious, I have written something very similar myself, I must read it to you one day," from which I inferred that he intended to sit down and write it that very evening.

These "paperies", as Françoise called the pages of my writing, it was my habit to stick together with paste, and sometimes in this process they became torn. But Françoise then would be able to come to my help, by consolidating them just as she stitched patches onto the worn parts of her dresses or as, on the kitchen window, while waiting for the glazier as I was waiting for the printer, she used to paste a piece of newspaper where a pane of glass had been broken. And she would say to me, pointing to my note-books as though they were worm-eaten wood or a piece of stuff which the moth had got into: "Look, it's all eaten away, isn't that dreadful! There's nothing left of this bit of page, it's been torn to ribbons," and examining it with a tailor's eye she would go on: "I don't think I shall be able to mend this one, it's finished and done for. A pity, perhaps it has your best ideas. You know what they say at Combray: there isn't a furrier who knows as much about furs as the moth, they always get into the best ones."

And in yet another way my work would resemble that of Françoise: in a book individual characters, whether human or of some other kind, are made up of numerous impressions derived from many girls, many churches, many sonatas and combined to form a single sonata, a single church, a single girl, so that I should be making my book in the same way that

Françoise made that *bœuf à la mode* which M. de Norpois had found so delicious, just because she had enriched its jelly with so many carefully chosen pieces of meat.

Thus it was that I envisaged the task before me, a task which would not end until I had achieved what I had so ardently desired in my walks on the Guermantes way and thought to be impossible, just as I had thought it impossible, as I came home at the end of those walks, that I should ever get used to going to bed without kissing my mother or, later, to the idea that Albertine loved women, though in the end I had grown to live with this idea without even being aware of its presence; for neither our greatest fears nor our greatest hopes are beyond the limits of our strength—we are able in the end both to dominate the first and to achieve the second.

Yes, upon this task the idea of Time which I had formed today told me that it was time to set to work. It was high time. But—and this was the reason for the anxiety which had gripped me as soon as I entered the drawing-room, when the theatrical disguises of the faces around me had first given me the notion of Lost Time—was there still time and was I still in a fit condition to undertake the task? For one thing, a necessary condition of my work as I had conceived it just now in the library was a profound study of impressions which had first to be re-created through the memory. But my memory was old and tired. The mind has landscapes which it is allowed to contemplate only for a certain space of time. In my life I had been like a painter climbing a road high above a lake, a view of which is denied to him by a curtain of rocks and trees. Suddenly through a gap in the curtain he sees the lake, its whole expanse is before him, he takes up his brushes. But already the night is at hand, the night which will put an end to his painting and which no dawn will follow. How could I not be anxious, seeing that nothing was yet begun and that though on the ground of age I could still hope that I had some years to live, my hour might on the other hand strike almost at once? For the fundamental fact was that I had a body, and this meant that I was perpetually threatened by a double danger, internal and external, though to speak thus was merely a matter of linguistic convenience, the truth being that the internal danger—the risk, for instance, of a cerebral haemorrhage—is also external, since it is the body that it threatens. Indeed it is the possession of a body that is the great danger to the mind, to our human and thinking life, which it is surely less correct to describe as a miraculous entelechy of animal and physical life than as an imperfect essay—as rudimentary in this sphere as the communal existence of protozoa attached to their polyparies or as the body of the whale—in the organisation of the spiritual life. The body immures the mind within a fortress; presently on all sides the fortress is besieged and in the end, inevitably, the mind has to surrender.

But—to accept provisionally the distinction which I have just made between the two sorts of danger that threaten the mind, and to begin with that which is in the fullest sense external—I recalled that it had often happened to me in the course of my life, in moments of intellectual excitement which coincided with a complete suspension of physical activity, as for example on those evenings when, half drunk, I had left the restaurant at Rivebelle in a carriage to go to some neighbouring casino, to feel very clearly within me the present object of my thought and at the same time to realise how much at the mercy of chance this intellectual activity was: how fortuitous it was that this particular thought had not entered my mind before, and how easily, through an accident to the carriage which was hurtling through the darkness, it might, along with my body, be annihilated. At the time this did not worry me. My high spirits knew neither forethought nor anxiety. The possibility that this joy might end in a second and turn into nothingness mattered to me scarcely at all. How different was my attitude now! The happiness which I was feeling was the product not of a purely subjective tension of the nerves which isolated me from the past, but on the contrary of an enlargement of my mind, within which the past was re-forming and actualising itself, giving me—but alas! only momentarily—something whose value was eternal. This I should have liked to bequeath to those who might have been enriched by my treasure. Admittedly what I had experienced in the library and what I was seeking to protect was pleasure still, but no longer pleasure of an egotistical kind, or if there were egotism in it (for all the fruitful altruisms of nature develop in an egotistical manner and any human altruism which is without egotism is sterile, like that of the writer who interrupts his work to receive a friend in distress or to accept some public function or to write articles of propaganda) it was an egotism which could be put to work for the benefit of other people. No longer was I indifferent to my fate as I had been on those drives back from Rivebelle; I felt myself enhanced by this work which I bore within me as by something fragile and precious which had been entrusted to me and which I should have liked to deliver intact into the hands of those for whom it was intended, hands which were not my own. And this feeling that I was the bearer of a work made me think in a changed way of an accident in which I might meet with death, as of something much more greatly to be feared and at the same time, to the extent to which this work of mine seemed to me necessary and durable, absurd because in contradiction with my desire, with the flight of my thought, yet none the less possible for that, since accidents, being produced by material causes, can perfectly well take place at the very moment when wishes of a quite different order which they destroy without being aware of their existence, render them most bitterly regrettable (at a trivial level of existence such accidents happen every day: at the very moment, for instance, when you are trying your hardest not to make a noise because of a friend who is asleep, a carafe placed too near the edge of his table falls to the ground and awakens him). I knew that my brain was like a mountain landscape rich in minerals, wherein lay vast and varied ores of great price. But should I have time to exploit them? For two reasons I was the only person who could do this: with my death would disappear the one and only engineer who possessed the skill to extract these minerals and—more than that—the geological formation itself. Yet presently, when I left this party to go home, it only needed a chance collision between the taxi which I should take and another car for my body to be destroyed, thus forcing my mind, from which life instantly would ebb away, for ever to abandon the new ideas which at this moment, not yet having had time to place them within the safety of a book, it anxiously embraced with the fragile protection of its own pulpy and quivering substance.

But by a strange coincidence, this rational fear of danger was taking shape in my mind just when the idea of death itself had finally become indifferent to me. In the past the fear of being no longer myself was something that had terrified me, and this had made me dread the end of each new love that I had experienced (for Gilberte, for Albertine), because I could not bear the idea that the "I" who loved them would one day cease to exist, since this in itself would be a kind of death. But by dint of repetition this fear had gradually been transformed into a calm confidence. So that if in those early days, as we have seen, the idea of death had cast a shadow over my loves, for a long time now the remembrance of love had helped me not to fear death. For I realised that dying was

not something new, but that on the contrary since my childhood I had already died many times. To take a comparatively
recent period, had I not clung to Albertine more tenaciously
than to my own life? Could I at the time when I loved her
conceive my personality without the continued existence
within it of my love for her? Yet now I no longer loved her,
I was no longer the person who loved her but a different
person who did not love her, and it was when I had become
a new person that I had ceased to love her. And yet I did
not suffer from having become this new person, from no
longer loving Albertine, and surely the prospect of one day
no longer having a body could not from any point of view seem
to me as sad as had then seemed to me that of one day no
longer loving Albertine, that prospect which now was a fact
and one which left me quite unmoved. These successive
deaths, so feared by the self which they were destined to
annihilate, so painless, so indifferent once they were accomplished and the self that feared them was no longer there to
feel them, had taught me by now that it would be the merest
folly to be frightened of death. Yet it was precisely when the
thought of death had become indifferent to me that I was
beginning once more to fear death, under another form, it is
true, as a threat not to myself but to my book, since for my
book's incubation this life that so many dangers threatened
was for a while at least indispensable. Victor Hugo says:

Il faut que l'herbe pousse et que les enfants meurent.

To me it seems more correct to say that the cruel law of art
is that people die and we ourselves die after exhausting every
form of suffering, so that over our heads may grow the grass
not of oblivion but of eternal life, the vigorous and luxuriant
growth of a true work of art, and so that thither, gaily and
without a thought for those who are sleeping beneath them,

future generations may come to enjoy their *déjeuner sur l'herbe*.

So much for the dangers from without; there were others, as I have said, that threatened me from within. Supposing that I were preserved from all accidents of an external kind, might I not nevertheless be robbed of the fruits of this good fortune by some accident occurring within myself, some internal catastrophe assailing me before the necessary months had passed and I had had time to write my book? When presently I made my way home through the Champs Elysées, who was to say that I might not be struck down by that malady which had struck my grandmother one afternoon when she had gone there with me for a walk which, though of this she had no suspicion, was destined to be her last—so ignorant are we, as ignorant as the hand of a clock when it arrives at the point upon its dial where a spring will be released within the mechanism which will cause the hour to strike. And indeed perhaps the fear that I might already have traversed almost the whole of that last minute which precedes the first stroke of the hour, that minute during which the stroke is already preparing itself, perhaps the fear of the stroke that might already be moving into action within my brain was itself a sort of obscure awareness of something that was soon to happen, a sort of reflection in the conscious mind of the precarious state of the brain whose arteries are about to give way, a phenomenon no more impossible than that sudden acceptance of death that comes to wounded men who, though the doctor and their own desire to live try to deceive them, say, realising the truth: "I am going to die, I am ready," and write their farewell lines to their wife.

Nor was anything so grave as a cerebral haemorrhage needed to hinder me in the execution of my task. Already the premonitory symptoms of the same malady, perceptible to

me in a certain emptiness in the head and a tendency to forgetfulness thanks to which I now merely stumbled upon things
in my memory by chance in the way in which, when you are
tidying your belongings, you find objects which you had forgotten even that you had to look for, were making me
resemble a miser whose strong-box has burst open and whose
treasures little by little are disappearing. For a while there
existed within me a self which deplored the loss of these
treasures, then I perceived that memory, as it withdrew from
me, carried away with it this self too.

And something not unlike my grandmother's illness itself
happened to me shortly afterwards, when I still had not started
to work on my book, in a strange fashion which I should never
have anticipated. I went out to see some friends one evening
and was told that I had never looked so well, and how wonderful it was that I had not a single grey hair. But at the end of
the visit, coming downstairs, three times I nearly fell. I had
left my home only two hours earlier; but when I got back, I
felt that I no longer possessed either memory or the power of
thought or strength or existence of any kind. People could
have come to call on me or to proclaim me king, to lay violent
hands on me or arrest me, and I should passively have submitted, neither opening my eyes nor uttering a word, like
those travellers of whom we read who, crossing the Caspian
Sea in a small boat, are so utterly prostrated by seasickness that
they offer not even a show of resistance when they are told
that they are going to be thrown into the sea. I had, properly
speaking, no illness, but I felt myself no longer capable of
anything, I was in the condition of those old men who one
day are in full possession of their faculties and the next,
having broken a thigh or had an attack of indigestion, can
only drag on for a while in their bed an existence which has
become nothing more than a preparation, longer or shorter,

for a now ineluctable death. One of my selves, the one which in the past had been in the habit of going to those barbarian festivals that we call dinner parties, at which, for the men in white shirt-fronts and the half-naked women beneath feathered plumes, values have been so reversed that a man who does not turn up after having accepted the invitation—or merely arrives after the roast has been served—is deemed to have committed an act more culpable than any of those immoral actions which, along with the latest deaths, are so lightly discussed at this feast which nothing but death or a serious illness is an acceptable excuse for failing to attend—and then only provided that one has given notice in good time of one's intention to die, so that there may be no danger for the other guests of sitting down thirteen to table—this one of my selves had retained its scruples and lost its memory. The other self, the one which had had a glimpse of the task that lay before it, on the contrary still remembered. I had received an invitation from Mme Molé and I had learnt that Mme Sazerat's son had died. I determined therefore to employ one of those few hours after which I could not hope even to pronounce another word or to swallow a mouthful of milk, since my tongue would be tied as my grandmother's had been during her agony, in addressing my excuses to the one lady and my condolences to the other. But a moment or two later I had forgotten that I had these things to do—most happily forgotten, for the memory of my real work did not slumber but proposed to employ the hour of survival which was granted me in laying my first foundations. Unfortunately, as I took up a note-book to write, Mme Molé's invitation card slipped out in front of my eyes. Immediately the forgetful self, which nevertheless was able to dominate the other—is this not always the case with those scrupulous barbarians who have learnt the lore of the dinner party?—pushed away the note-book and wrote to Mme Molé (whose esteem for me would no doubt have been great had she known that I had allowed my reply to her invitation to take precedence over my labours as an architect). Then suddenly a word in my letter reminded me that Mme Sazerat had lost her son and I wrote to her as well, after which, having sacrificed a real duty to the factitious obligation to appear polite and sympathetic, I fell back exhausted and closed my eyes, not to emerge from a purely vegetal existence before a week had elapsed. During this time, however, if all my unnecessary duties, to which I was willing to sacrifice my true duty, vanished after a few moments from my head, the idea of the edifice that I had to construct did not leave me for an instant. Whether it would be a church where little by little a group of faithful would succeed in apprehending verities and discovering harmonies or perhaps even a grand general plan, or whether it would remain, like a druidic monument on a rocky isle, something for ever unfrequented, I could not tell. But I was resolved to devote to it all my strength, which ebbed, as it seemed, reluctantly and as though to leave me time to complete the periphery of my walls and close "the funereal gate". Before very long I was able to show a few sketches. No one understood anything of them. Even those who commended my perception of the truths which I wanted eventually to engrave within the temple, congratulated me on having discovered them "with a microscope", when on the contrary it was a telescope that I had used to observe things which were indeed very small to the naked eye, but only because they were situated at a great distance, and which were each one of them in itself a world. Those passages in which I was trying to arrive at general laws were described as so much pedantic investigation of detail. What, in any case, was I hoping to achieve? In my youth I had had a certain facility, and Bergotte had praised as "admirable" the pages which I wrote while still at school. But instead of working I had lived a life of idleness, of pleasures and distractions, of ill-health and cosseting and eccentricities, and I was embarking upon my labour of construction almost at the point of death, without knowing anything of my trade. I felt that I no longer possessed the strength to carry out my obligations to people or my duties to my thoughts and my work, still less to satisfy both of these claims. As for the first, my forgetfulness of the letters I had to write and of the other things I had to do, to some extent simplified my task. But suddenly, at the end of a month, the association of ideas brought back the painful recollection of these duties and I was momentarily overwhelmed by the thought of my impotence. To my astonishment I found that I did not mind, the truth being that, since the day when my legs had trembled so violently as I was going downstairs, I had become indifferent to everything, I longed only for rest, while waiting for the great rest which would come in the end. Amongst other things I was indifferent to the verdict which might be passed on my work by the best minds of my age, and this not because I relegated to some future after my death the admiration which it seemed to me that work ought to receive. The best minds of posterity might think what they chose, their opinions mattered to me no more than those of my contemporaries. The truth was that, if I thought of my work and not of the letters which I ought to answer, this was not because I attached to these two things, as I had during my years of idleness and later, in that brief interval between the conception of my book and the day when I had had to cling to the banister, very different degrees of importance. The organisation of my memory, of the preoccupations that filled my mind, was indeed linked to my work, but perhaps simply because, while the letters which I received were forgotten a moment later, the idea of my work was inside my head, always the same, perpetually in process of becoming. But even my work had become for me a tiresome obligation, like a son for a dying mother who still, between her injections and her blood-lettings, has to make the exhausting effort of constantly bothering about him. Perhaps she still loves him, but it is only in the form of a duty too great for her strength that she is aware of her affection. In me, in the same way, the powers of the writer were no longer equal to the egotistical demands of the work. Since the day of the staircase, nothing in the world, no happiness, whether it came from friendship or the progress of my book or the hope of fame, reached me save as a sunshine unclouded but so pale that it no longer had the virtue to warm me, to make me live, to instil in me any desire; and yet, faint though it was, it was still too dazzling for my eyes, I closed them and turned my face to the wall. When a lady wrote to me: "I have been *very surprised* not to receive an answer to my letter," I must, it seemed, to judge from the sensation of movement in my lips, have twisted an infinitesimal corner of my mouth into a little smile. Nevertheless, I was reminded of her unanswered letter and I wrote her a reply. Not wishing to be thought ungrateful, I tried hard to raise my tardy civilities to the level of those which I supposed that other people, though I had forgotten it, had shown to me. And I was crushed by the effort to impose upon my moribund existence the superhuman fatigues of life. The loss of my memory helped me a little by making cuts in my obligations; they were more than made good by the claims of my work.

The idea of death took up permanent residence within me in the way that love sometimes does. Not that I loved death, I abhorred it. But after a preliminary stage in which, no doubt, I thought about it from time to time as one does about a woman with whom one is not yet in love, its image adhered now to the most profound layer of my mind, so completely that I could not give my attention to anything without that thing first traversing the idea of death, and even if no object occupied my attention and I remained in a state of complete repose, the idea of death still kept me company as faithfully as the idea of my self. And, on that day on which I had become a half-dead man, I do not think that it was the accidents characterising this condition—my inability to walk downstairs, to remember a name, get up from a chair—that had, even by an unconscious train of thought, given rise to this idea of death, this conviction that I was already almost dead, it seems to me rather that the idea had come simultaneously with the symptoms, that inevitably the mind, great mirror that it is, reflected a new reality. Yet still I did not see how from my present ailments one could pass, without warning of what was to come, to total death. Then, however, I thought of other people, of the countless people who die every day without the gap between their illness and their death seeming to us extraordinary. I thought also that it was only because I saw them from within—rather than because I saw them in the deceitful colours of hope—that certain of my ailments, taken singly, did not seem to me to be fatal although I believed that I would soon die, just as those who are most convinced that their hour has come are, nevertheless, easily persuaded that if they are unable to pronounce certain words, this is nothing so serious as aphasia or a stroke, but a symptom merely of a local fatigue of the tongue, or a nervous condition analogous to a stutter, or the lassitude which follows indigestion.

No doubt my books too, like my fleshly being, would in the end one day die. But death is a thing that we must resign ourselves to. We accept the thought that in ten years we ourselves, in a hundred years our books, will have ceased to exist.

Eternal duration is promised no more to men's works than to men.

In my awareness of the approach of death I resembled a dying soldier, and like him too, before I died, I had something to write. But my task was longer than his, my words had to reach more than a single person. My task was long. By day, the most I could hope for was to try to sleep. If I worked, it would be only at night. But I should need many nights, a hundred perhaps, or even a thousand. And I should live in the anxiety of not knowing whether the master of my destiny might not prove less indulgent than the Sultan Sheriar, whether in the morning, when I broke off my story, he would consent to a further reprieve and permit me to resume my narrative the following evening. Not that I had the slightest pretension to be writing a new version, in any way, of the *Arabian Nights*, or of that other book written by night, Saint-Simon's *Mémoires*, or of any of those books which I had loved with a child's simplicity and to which I had been as superstitiously attached as later to my loves, so that I could not imagine without horror any work which should be unlike them. But—as Elstir had found with Chardin—you can make a new version of what you love only by first renouncing it. So my book, though it might be as long as the *Arabian Nights*, would be entirely different. True, when you are in love with some particular book, you would like yourself to write something that closely resembles it, but this love of the moment must be sacrificed, you must think not of your own taste but of a truth which far from asking you what your preferences are forbids you to pay attention to them. And only if you faithfully follow this truth will you sometimes find that you have stumbled again upon what you renounced, find that, by forgetting these works themselves, you have written the *Arabian Nights* or the *Mémoires* of Saint-Simon of another age. But for me was there still time? Was it not too late?

And I had to ask myself not only: "Is there still time?" but also: "Am I well enough?" Ill health, which by compelling me, like a severe director of conscience, to die to the world, had rendered me good service ("for unless the grain of wheat dies after it has been sown, it will abide alone; but if it dies, it will bring forth much fruit"), and which, after idleness had preserved me from the dangers of facility, was perhaps going to protect me from idleness, that same ill health had consumed my strength and as I had first noticed long ago, particularly when I had ceased to love Albertine, the strength of my memory. But was not the re-creation by the memory of impressions which had then to be deepened, illumined, transformed into equivalents of understanding, was not this process one of the conditions, almost the very essence of the work of art as I had just now in the library conceived it? Ah! if I now possessed the strength which on that evening brought back to my mind by the sight of *François le Champi* today had still been intact! Was not that the evening when my mother had abdicated her authority, the evening from which dated, together with the slow death of my grandmother, the decline of my health and my will? All these things had been decided in that moment when, no longer able to bear the prospect of waiting till morning to place my lips upon my mother's face, I had made up my mind, jumped out of bed and gone in my night-shirt to post myself at the window through which the moonlight entered my room until I should hear the sounds of M. Swann's departure. My parents had gone with him to the door, I had heard the garden gate open, give a peal of its bell, and close. . . .

While I was asking myself these questions, it occurred to me suddenly that, if I had indeed the strength to accomplish my work, this afternoon—like certain days long ago at Combray which had influenced me—which in its brief compass had given me both the idea of my work and the fear of being unable to bring it to fruition, would certainly impress upon it that form of which as a child I had had a presentiment in the church at Combray but which ordinarily, throughout our lives, is invisible to us: the form of Time. Many errors, it is true, there were, as the reader will have seen that various episodes in this story had proved to me, by which our senses falsify for us the real nature of the world. Some of these, however, it would be possible for me to avoid by the efforts which I should make to give a more exact transcription of things. In the case of sounds, for instance, I should be able to refrain from altering their place of origin, from detaching them from their cause, beside which our intellect only succeeds in locating them after they have reached our ears—though to make the rain sing softly in the middle of our room or, contrarily, to make the quiet boiling of our *tisane* sound like a deluge in the courtyard outside should not really be more misleading than what is so often done by painters when they paint a sail or the peak of a mountain in such a way that, according to the laws of perspective, the intensity of the colours and the illusion of our first glance, they appear to us either very near or very far away, through an error which logical thinking subsequently corrects by, sometimes, a very large displacement. Other errors, though of a more serious kind, I might continue to commit, placing features, for instance, as we all do, upon the face of a woman seen in the street, when instead of nose, cheeks and chin there ought to be merely an empty space with nothing more upon it than a flickering reflection of our desires. But at least, after seeing what I had seen at the Guermantes party today, even if I had not the leisure to prepare—and here was a correction of a much more important kind—the hundred different masks which ought properly to be attached to a single face, if only because of the different eyes which look at it and the different meanings which they read into its features, not to mention, for the same eyes, the different emotions of hope and fear or on the contrary love and habit which for thirty years can conceal the changes brought about by age, and even if I did not attempt—though my love-affair with Albertine was sufficient proof to me that any other kind of representation must be artificial and untruthful—to represent some of my characters as existing not outside but within ourselves, where their slightest action can bring fatal disturbances in its train, and to vary also the light of the moral sky which illumines them in accordance with the variations in pressure in our own sensibility (for an object which was so small beneath the clear sky of our certainty can be suddenly magnified many times over on the appearance of a tiny cloud of danger)—if, in my attempt to transcribe a universe which had to be totally redrawn, I could not convey these changes and many others, the needfulness of which, if one is to depict reality, has been made manifest in the course of my narrative, at least I should not fail to portray man, in this universe, as endowed with the length not of his body but of his years and as obliged—task more and more heavy and in the end too great for his strength—to drag them with him wherever he goes.

Not that there was anything new in the idea that we occupy a place in Time which is perpetually being augmented. Everyone feels this, and the universality of the idea could not but rejoice me, since it was the truth, the truth dimly apprehended by each one of us, that I was to attempt to elucidate. And not only does everyone have this feeling that we occupy a place in Time, but this "place" is something that the simplest among us habitually measures in an approximative fashion, as he might measure with his eye the place which we occupy in space. People with no special perspicacity, seeing two men whom they do not know, both perhaps with black moustaches or both clean shaven, will say that of the two one is about twenty and the other about forty years old, for the face of a young man cannot possibly be confused with that of a man of middle age, which in the eyes even of the most ignorant beholder is veiled by a sort of mist of serious-ness. Of course, this evaluation of age that we make is often inaccurate, but the mere fact that we think ourselves able to make it indicates that we conceive of age as an entity which is measurable. And the second of the two men with black moustaches has, in effect, had twenty years added to his stature.

This notion of Time evaporated, of years past but not separated from us, it was now my intention to embody as clearly as possible in my work. And at this very moment, in the house of the Prince de Guermantes, as though to strengthen me in my resolve, the noise of my parents' foot-steps as they accompanied M. Swann to the door and the peal —resilient, ferruginous, interminable, fresh and shrill—of the bell on the garden gate which informed me that at last he had gone and that Mama would presently come upstairs, these sounds rang again in my ears, yes, unmistakably I heard these very sounds, situated though they were in a remote past. And as I cast my mind over all the events which were ranged in an unbroken series between the moment of my childhood when I had first heard its sound and the Guer-mantes party, I was terrified to think that it was indeed this same bell which rang within me and that nothing that I could do would alter its jangling notes. On the contrary, having forgotten the exact manner in which they faded away and wanting to re-learn this, to hear them properly again, I was obliged to block my ears to the conversations which were proceeding between the masked figures all round me, for in order to get nearer to the sound of the bell and to hear it better it was into my own depths that I had to re-descend. And this could only be because its peal had always been there, inside me, and not this sound only but also, between that distant moment and the present one, unrolled in all its vast length, the whole of that past which I was not aware that I carried about within me. When the bell of the garden gate had pealed, I already existed and from that moment onwards, for me still to be able to hear that peal, there must have been no break in continuity, no single second at which I had ceased or rested from existing, from thinking, from being conscious of myself, since that moment from long ago still adhered to me and I could still find it again, could retrace my steps to it merely by descending to a greater depth within myself. And it is because they contain thus within themselves the hours of the past that human bodies have the power to hurt so terribly those who love them, because they contain the memories of so many joys and desires already for them, who are loved, half effaced but still cruel for the lover who contemplates and prolongs in the dimension of Time the beloved body of which he is jealous, so jealous that he may even wish for its destruction. For after death Time withdraws from the body and these memories, in the loved woman herself already while she was still alive emotionless and faded, are in her instantly obliterated as they soon will be in the lover whom for a while they continue to torment but in whom before long they will perish, once the desire that owed its inspiration to a living body is no longer there to sustain them.

In this vast dimension which I had not known myself to possess, the date on which I had heard the noise of the garden bell at Combray—that far-distant noise which nevertheless was within me—was a point from which I might start to make measurements. And I felt, as I say, a sensation of weariness and almost of terror at the thought that all this length of Time had not only, without interruption, been lived, experienced, secreted by me, that it was my life, was in fact me, but also that I was compelled so long as I was alive to keep it attached to me, that it supported me and that perched on its giddy summit I could not myself make a movement without displacing it. A feeling of vertigo seized me as I looked down beneath me, yet within me, as though from a height, which was my own height, of many leagues, at the long series of the years.

I understood now why it was that the Duc de Guermantes, who to my surprise, when I had seen him sitting on a chair, had seemed to me so little aged although he had so many more years beneath him than I had, had presently, when he rose to his feet and tried to stand firm upon them, swayed backwards and forwards upon legs as tottery as those of some old arch-bishop with nothing solid about his person but his metal cruci-fix, to whose support there rushes a mob of sturdy young sem-inarists, and had advanced with difficulty, trembling like a leaf, upon the almost unmanageable summit of his eighty-three years, as though men spend their lives perched upon living stilts which never cease to grow until sometimes they become taller than church steeples, making it in the end both difficult and perilous for them to walk and raising them to an eminence from which suddenly they fall. And I was terrified by the thought that the stilts beneath my own feet might already have reached that height; it seemed to me that quite soon now I might be too weak to maintain my hold upon a past which already went down so far. But at least, if strength were granted me for long enough to accomplish my work, I should not fail, even if the result were to make them resemble monsters, to describe men first and foremost as occupying a place, a very considerable place compared with the restricted one which is allotted to them in space, a place on the contrary immoderately prolonged—for simultaneously, like giants plunged into the years, they touch epochs that are immensely far apart, separated by the slow accretion of many, many days—in the dimension of Time.